CW01336006

KISSED BY A DEMON

Kissed by a Demon
The Wild Shadows, #1

To everyone who'd fuck the villain because he'd burn down the world for you.

Trigger Warnings

This novel contains mature elements and themes, including (but not limited to) explicit sexual scenes, questionable consent, sexual assault, violence, and torture. Reader discretion is advised.

Chapter One

ARABELLA

Wild shadows stretched out long fingers from the forest that never slept toward the remote village of Shadowbank, promising death to all those who drew near.

Arabella eyed the line of trees, fingers tightening around the bow in her fist, as she waited for whatever creatures of the dark might emerge. But as the forest's edge remained motionless except for a flicker of shadows, she resumed her pace atop the three-story stone wall—a poor barrier between the villagers and the demons that paid too many house calls.

Far above, the ward rippled around the village, the translucent dome a far paler purple-blue hue than it was a few years ago. Unlike the hardy villagers, the ward was worn down and near to collapse, and she feared one targeted strike would bring it down.

Turning on a heel, she weaved behind a line of archers, eyes swiveling between the line of trees on one side of the wall and the rows of houses with thatched roofs on the other side. The path atop the wall was barely wide enough for three people to walk abreast without weapons.

While Shadowbank was no true city, the large village surrounded by a mountainous forest on three sides and a bay on

1

the other boasted several districts along with a port that sustained a small trading business. If it wasn't for the demons and monsters lurking in the shadows, perhaps the village would have grown far larger. As it was, too few people dared to venture this far from civilization. The risk for a swift and violent end was too great.

"Enchantress," the archers said softly, chins dipping over shoulders in deference.

She nodded to them as she pushed back her thick braid of dark brown hair over a shoulder.

Dressed head to toe in black leather with her hood pulled back to reveal overlapping silver chains and a teardrop that hung to the center of her forehead, none would mistake her for anything but what she was—an enchantress, a protector of mankind.

The enchantresses had started joining the human soldiers atop the stone walls encircling Shadowbank since the ward's decline had become more rapid. It would only be a matter of time until the demons and beasts of the forest discovered the weak spots and came through.

There was a flash of movement near the line of trees.

Arabella spun, her bow directed toward the forest alongside the human archers. She didn't dare release her magic through the ward and risk punching a hole through it that wouldn't repair itself. But arrows were small and didn't have magic, so the ward should be minimally impacted.

"No way," said one archer. "I thought she wasn't coming for another week."

Relief flooded Arabella's chest as brilliant as a sunrise, and tears welled in her eyes.

"Finally!" she exclaimed, pushing her bow and quiver into a guard's hands.

Then she was running.

Bolting across the wall, she bounded down the stairs, running into several soldiers as she turned around a corner. She shouted an apology over her shoulder as she pushed toward the gates. At the base of the wall, dirt roads stretched out toward the city proper, which would eventually turn into the cobblestone streets of the main thoroughfare. But even at this hour, the dirt streets filled with soldiers and squires, carrying weapons and other supplies.

"Approacher!" guards atop the wall called, which was followed by echoing shouts until the air above the main gates filled with the calls of soldiers preparing for the worst.

They didn't dare say who it was. Not when demons so often wore the faces of men.

But this wasn't just anyone, and Arabella wasn't about to wait to find out if it was a trick or some kind of trap. Giddy excitement filled her.

As she turned the corner and the gate rose before her, she spotted the forms of several dozen enchantresses striding through the streets in black leather, blades in their fists and magic billowing off them. Visible only to her eye—and the eyes of every other magic wielder—were countless golden weaves of earthen magic arching toward the sky like long tentacles, prepared to strike at a moment's notice.

"Not another step," Iris, the Head Enchantress, called toward Arabella as she pushed toward the rising gate.

Arabella pulled her twin swords free from the sheaths at her back, spinning them in her grip. Offering an apologetic smile to the Head Enchantress, she nodded to the soldiers cranking the gears and pulling the gate up.

"Don't you—" Iris began, but Arabella didn't wait to hear the rest.

Her friend had returned.

One of her family.

And there was nothing she wouldn't do for one of the Circle, the Order of Enchantresses.

Then Arabella was running again before she slid beneath the rising gate. She didn't stop. Pushing back to her feet in a smooth roll, still holding on to her blades, she hurried toward the edge of the ward's barrier. The wall far behind her, she crossed an open plain of grass, which lay before the forest and its wild shadows.

Sparing a glance back, she spotted Iris and the other enchantresses atop the wall, their weaves extending far into the air above the wall itself—ready in case a demon broke through the ward. Arabella reached for her enchantress magic, pulling it from deep within her and from deep within the earth itself. She wove the two together in tight plaits until she had several golden weaves stretching around her. Then she turned her attention forward.

A woman stood just beyond the line of trees. She wore identical black leathers to Arabella's, though her sheaths were empty of weapons.

Arabella spared a moment to question her recklessness—to wonder if this was, in fact, a wise decision. But excitement at the sight of her friend won out. After years, she was finally back. Then she threw caution to the wind and pushed through the ward. It rippled around her like disturbed water. There was a popping sensation, and then she was through.

She skidded to a stop just out of reach of the thing that wore her friend's face. Extending a weave out, she tried to sense any strange magic around her, but all she could feel was the familiar sense of earth and air that all enchantresses emitted.

Lowering her weaves somewhat, Arabella looked the female over.

To her surprise, her friend didn't seem undernourished or ill as she'd suspected after being in the clutches of a demon for so long. Instead, her dark skin was vibrant with life, and her hair looked full and as healthy as her youthful pallor. But her eyes were vacant, and she ran her fingers over her black leathers as though surprised to find herself in them.

"Where am I?" Scarlett's brows drew together as she looked around. As though seeing Arabella for the first time, Scarlett's gaze fell on her. "Arabella? You look... older."

Tears welled in Arabella's eyes as she strode forward, offering Scarlett a sympathetic smile. "Ten years will do that to you."

Scarlett frowned before realization dawned. "You don't mean... I wasn't... Was I?"

Arabella wasn't one to lie or mix honey with a bitter truth. So, she nodded. "You don't remember anything?"

Scarlett shook her head, eyes growing round and distant.

What a shock it must be to have gone through what she had and not remember a thing.

But just like the other offerings, she'd returned without even a wisp of memories from the past decade.

Reaching out, Arabella wrapped her arms around Scarlett, and slowly, the female melted into her. For a moment, Arabella thought to wonder whether this was a demon and if it would strike out and run her through while her guard was down. But nothing happened. Instead, Scarlett's shoulders shook as Arabella held her.

"You're home now," Arabella said. "You're safe."

But were any of them truly safe?

There was a rustling in the trees, and Arabella pulled back, gripping her swords and lowering into a crouch. Scarlett turned toward the sound as well, her teary eyes wide.

A dark figure hovered in the line of trees, no more than a deepening shadow.

Arabella sensed its presence at once with her dark ability—the one she could never speak of. At that moment, like called to like. Power bloomed from the other presence like a storm cloud surging over the horizon, promising an unrelenting torrent.

The Devourer.

The founders of Shadowbank had made a deal more than a century ago with this forest demon. Every ten years, it took a new offering. In exchange, it wouldn't attack Shadowbank.

None remembered just what this demon was or what it did with its offerings. Rumors said it was powerful, one of the most powerful demons in the forest, which had scared the founding humans and enchantresses of Shadowbank to make this deal.

Whatever it was, it wanted something from the mortals. But *what?*

What it wanted wouldn't matter—not if it was dead.

You'll never touch my family again, Arabella thought, glaring at the creature that had taken her friend ten years ago.

The agreement be damned.

"Run," Arabella whispered to Scarlett, not taking her eyes from the line of trees.

Scarlett remained at her side, and Arabella could sense her hesitation.

Fear laced her veins, and she knew it filled Scarlett as well. But she pushed it down, holding desperately on to the anger filling her chest, letting it fuel her.

Pulling the living magic of the air into her and weaving it into her magic, Arabella formed two more bands of golden magic. She released one at Scarlett's chest and the other beneath her feet. There were dual blasts of wind. Scarlett flew backward toward the safety of the ward and the town beyond it. But Arabella soared over the remaining distance of open grass—and into the forest that she'd been taught to fear.

Swords in her fists, she arced them up, preparing to bring them down on the dark figure. All the while, she held on to her weaves of earthen magic. But when her feet connected with the forest floor and she swung her blades down, the figure in the shadow disappeared, and she rolled to a stop where it had just been.

"Show yourself, coward," Arabella said into the trees' thick, leafy canopies that snuffed out the autumn sunlight. "Or are you only interested in stealing away defenseless females?"

The forest consumed her words in its eerie silence as though absorbing all hope and defiance and replacing it with thorny desolation.

Arabella stepped forward, her booted feet crunching on underbrush. Swords held high, she glanced between massive trunks of trees, over weaving roots, and beyond protruding boulders. The gemstone on her forehead bumped gently as she moved.

The earthen weaves she held soured as the dark magic of the forest surrounded her. It was as though the weaves of sunlight and growing things had turned thick and greasy. It felt like the land itself was sick, and it sought to corrupt her weaves. But she held fast. She couldn't detect the Devourer's presence with her magic as she stretched out long, shimmering tentacles into the trees that now surrounded her.

Taking a breath, she allowed herself to reach for the darkness beneath her feet and in the trees all around. The shadows whispered and shivered as though awakening from a deep slumber. Now that she was out of sight of the other enchantresses, she didn't risk death or exile by reaching for the rippling dark. The forbidden magic. But at that moment, it was the only thing that would give her a chance at destroying the thing that threatened her family, her order of sisters.

In the shadows, she sensed no small forest creatures or birds. There was no life at all except for one lurking presence as oily and dark as the forest itself.

"A coward, you say?" came a deep voice from somewhere beyond her line of sight. "And this coming from one who has sworn a truce. Do you seek to kill me, little enchantress?"

Through her shadows, she sensed pressure on the ground from her left. She didn't turn toward it, not wanting it to know she could locate it.

"I never made a bargain with you," she said, twisting one boot in the dirt, leaning on the balls of her feet.

The creature chuckled, and the sound wasn't entirely human.

"I was promised generations," it rumbled before she sensed it moving through the deeper shadows of the forest again.

This time, the creature was on her far right, stirring the shadows in the corner of her mind. How did it move so fast?

Patience, she thought. *Not yet.*

"I spoke no such words," Arabella replied, her voice cold. "You won't take anyone else from my family."

Although the bargain didn't demand an enchantress as an offering, most of the offerings to this demon in the last few decades had been enchantresses. Besides being the protectors of mankind, the lives of enchantresses were longer than that of humans—about one hundred fifty years. As such, ten years was a lesser sacrifice in their lifespan.

But every year with her family was precious, and she wasn't about to let this demon take even a moment more.

Suddenly, the presence was behind her, and she felt the caress of a warm breath on the back of her neck. Bands of blue magic wrapped around her, pinning her arms to her sides. She thrashed against it, managing to hold on to her swords, but it was too strong. Her grip on her weaves snapped, and the magic retreated into the earth.

"Does that mean you intend to offer yourself?"

The voice held a deep, melodic tone, and she found her eyes fluttering closed. Her breaths came in ragged gasps, and it had nothing to do with fear.

For a moment, all she wanted to do was lean her head back into the looming presence over her shoulder. Something deep within her stirred, and she licked suddenly dry lips as her thoughts muddied.

A distant part of her mind screamed at her to lash out with her magic, but she found her head turning back toward the figure that had pinned her with magic that far exceeded her own. She was like a dewdrop in a bucket compared to whatever power this demon had.

At that moment, she knew she had no hope of overpowering it.

Something gripped her chin, keeping her facing forward, and she could have sworn the touch felt like fingers. But that wasn't possible. This was a demon she faced.

"Ah-ah," the voice chided, tsking. "If you wish to lay your eyes upon me, it will be in three days' time."

"That won't happen," Arabella managed, but even to her ears, her voice sounded breathy.

What was happening to her?

Her heart pounded like the drums at the autumn festival, and her nipples hardened beneath her leather corset. Something like desire swirled in her stomach, and a need so overwhelming grew between her legs that it nearly had her gasping.

What she thought was an arm wrapped around her waist, but she couldn't move with the bands of magic tying her arms to her sides.

"I suppose we shall see," the demon said, "when I return."

The bands holding her released, and the shadows behind her rippled. As they did, she turned, slashing with her swords. She pulled bands from the earth, tying them hastily with her magic before unleashing herself. Weaves of earth lashed where the demon had just been, but they plunged into the soil, digging deep grooves into the earth.

Shadows at the edge of her vision stirred, reminding her of skipping stones across still water as the Devourer moved fluidly deeper into the forest. Then the presence of the demon was gone.

Arabella growled, glancing around the trees.

What just came over me? Why couldn't I fight?

None of it made sense. Just what had that thing been?

As she thought, she felt the rumblings of other creatures in the forest. It was a shifting in the trees as though something awakened, full of fury and a deep, unrelenting hunger. Turning, she ran through the trees back toward Shadowbank and its failing ward. Her presence there was awakening creatures of the deep, and she didn't dare lurk a moment longer in case the scent of her blood attracted demons even in the daylight hours.

While she hadn't been able to kill the Devourer, she now had clues that could help her find out just what it was—and its weakness. She had three days to learn how to defeat this demon. It was that or lose someone else for ten years—if the ward hadn't fallen before then.

As she moved, desire swirled through her.

Desire for a demon.

Chapter Two

ARABELLA

Hours later, Arabella returned to her place atop the wall, resuming guard duty alongside the human archers and guards. The healers had taken Scarlett to examine her, but Arabella knew what they would find—a mind void of memories for the last ten years with no way of accessing what had been.

As she strode, a figure appeared down the straight of this section of the wall, emerging from nearby stairs.

"It's about time," Arabella said, smiling. "My shift's been over for an hour."

The figure returned the smile, closing the distance between them.

Like Arabella, Jessamine wore an enchantress' garb—head to toe in black leather, which was thick and reinforced with magic. Unlike Arabella's dark hair, long blonde locks came to Jessamine's mid-back, curling at the ends despite the humidity and framing a face with olive skin that always looked sun-kissed even in the darkest months of winter.

"I got held up," Jessamine said, clapping a hand on Arabella's shoulder.

"Iris?" Arabella asked.

The Head Enchantress had been up to her neck in responsibilities since holes started appearing in the ward around the village.

Jessamine nodded, her head coming to Arabella's shoulders. "Another hole. Biggest one yet on the eastern wall."

Heart racing, Arabella was careful to keep her face neutral and her voice low for the sake of the jittery archers they strode past. "Did you close it?"

"Barely," Jessamine said, her voice equally low. "The Head Enchantress would have called for you. But... you were here."

Arabella sighed. "You should've sent word. I would have come."

Jessamine shrugged. "I'm just following orders."

"For once."

The corner of Jessamine's lips quirked up. "For once," she agreed. Then she nodded toward the ward beyond the wall. "The Head Enchantress wants you to look at a weak spot in the ward beyond the front gates."

Arabella raised a brow. "She's willing to let me outside the village gates after earlier? I'm surprised."

Snorting, Jessamine said, "One of the few perks of there being so few of us."

With a wave of farewell, Arabella turned toward the stairs and headed for the gates. Once again, guards raised the gate for her. Only this time, she strode through. A few moments later, she heard the gates close behind her with a *thud*.

The weak spot in question was a few hundred feet outside of the walls. When she got closer, she noted what she feared—the ward had thinned in a patch two stories up. Instead of its usual purple-blue hue, it was nearly transparent.

After months of research, the only thing she'd been able to discover about wards was that a magic wielder who possessed the same magic as those who created the ward could create patches that allowed a ward to repair itself. There had been nothing on reinforcing or strengthening a failing ward or even how to create a ward at all. It was an old magic—one that had fallen out of time thanks to the greed of mortals, leaving the following generations vulnerable. Leaving Shadowbank vulnerable.

The weak spot hadn't yet torn, so there was little she could do for it now—not until there was a hole to repair.

With a sigh, she started to turn back toward Shadowbank when movement in the corner of her vision caught her attention.

Not again, she thought as she turned to face the line of trees. Had the Devourer returned?

But nothing prepared her for the sight before her as shapes emerged from the forest.

Arabella's stomach plummeted to her boots.

Several hundred feet away were a dozen fengrine—wolf-like creatures the size of two carriages with canines as long as Arabella's forearm and fur of varying colors of gray, brown, and black. Lips peeled back to reveal two rows of sharp teeth as the head of the pack, a fengrine with gray fur, growled, its eyes fixing on her.

Arabella freed her swords from their sheaths and quickly wove bands of magic back together. This time, instead of tendrils that snaked out from her and could lash at nearby opponents, she fixed her weaves into thin pinpricks as sharp and unforgiving as crossbow bolts.

Then the beasts charged at the ward.

For a moment, time slowed, and she watched in horror as the fengrine barreled toward the ward, clawed paws pushing off the ground, and dirt and grass flying in every direction.

They had all feared this day. The day that monsters attacked and the ward failed to meet the threat. The day the ward would fall. She could only hope that today wasn't that day.

Turning, she ran for all she was worth. Behind her, she heard gnashing teeth.

The archers had arrows nocked in bows, aimed at the fengrine, though none loosed them. Enchantresses quickly filled in the gaps behind them with golden bolts like Arabella's hovering above their shoulders.

Arabella's eyes darted from the gates to the wall.

There was no way for her to use her weaves to launch herself into the air and on top of the stone walls. There was as good a chance of them landing atop the soldiers' swords or arrows as it was for them to go flying past the walls and land in a pile of bones and sinew on the cobblestone street behind it.

Beads of sweat ran in rivulets down the sides of her face, and her heart raced.

Behind her, the sounds of the fengrine thrashing against the wards filled the air. Their massive talons at the end of their paws were larger than her head and scraped against the magical barrier that was as thin as ice above a frozen lake when the weather turned toward spring.

At that moment, Arabella knew the ward wouldn't hold. There were mere moments until the fengrine broke through.

"Open the gates!" Arabella shouted to the archers and her sisters, who lined every inch of the wall. But no one moved. Some heads turned to the figure standing at the head of the archers and enchantresses.

The Head Enchantress.

Iris' eyes filled with fear. Even from where she stood, Arabella could see the woman who'd been like a mother to her—the woman who'd taken her in when she'd appeared from the forest twenty years ago without a family or home to call her own— weighing whether to prioritize the love between them or her duty to the people of Shadowbank.

Iris shook her head, brows drawn together as she studied the rippling ward, and then shifted her gaze down to Arabella.

"I can't," Iris said, seeming far older than her eighty years in an enchantress' long life. Though to a human, she'd appear no older than her forties. "There isn't enough time to open it and lower it again before—"

Before the fengrine were through.

Arabella nodded.

It was a call she'd have made, too.

It was the job of every enchantress to protect the humans under their charge. And opening the gates could jeopardize everyone inside.

Arabella turned back toward where the monsters climbed on top of each other, clawing at the ward, which bent and bubbled. The weak spot was a mere ten feet above where they were.

Then the alpha pushed off one of the other beasts, a massive claw scraping down the weak spot of the ward.

And then, at last, it happened.

It was like the tearing of old parchment. The split in the ward started at the weak spot and spread downward as the creature fell back toward the ground, its claw creating a rift as large as the wall itself. Then the beasts were through.

Swinging her swords in her grip, she took a deep breath and aimed the bolts of her magic.

There was a heavy thump and rush of wind somewhere behind her, and Arabella didn't need to glance over her shoulder to know who now stood beside her.

"Damsel in distress isn't a good look on you," Jessamine said, countless knives in sheaths at her waist, a quiver strapped to her back, and a bow with a nocked arrow aimed at the approaching fengrine.

"Rugged hero doesn't look flattering on you," Arabella said, not taking her eyes off the monsters as she tied more weaves together and loosed bolts of magic at the fengrine that were spreading out.

As she did, bolts of magic flew over them and rained down upon the monsters. They appeared like shimmering golden pinpricks falling from the sky—narrowly avoiding Arabella and Jessamine.

Jessamine loosed arrow after arrow, all the while forming her own weaves of magic. "If you die, I'm going to hire the best necromancer money can afford, bring you back, and kill you myself."

Arabella released bolt after bolt of magic, weaving more together as she did. "I'd be offended if you didn't."

Then the fengrine were upon them.

Arabella charged forward with her sword, bringing up a weave from the earth. Instinctively, she laced it with her magic, like a massive thorny vine, and pushed it forward with her mind as a fengrine leaped toward Jessamine, who released an arrow at its maw.

The massive wolf-like creature jolted to a stop as the vine of magic punched a hole up its chin and through its snout.

Arabella cursed.

She'd missed its skull, which could be a deadly mistake.

Before she could weave another band of magic together, Jessamine loosed an arrow at its eye, which it swiped away with its paw. As it did, Arabella leaped forward, spinning and bringing her sword down on its shoulder. The blade cut clean through flesh and down to bone. The creature roared, pulling its head back, trying to pull free of the magic through its jaw and snout, holding it to the earth. With a swipe of its massive leg, Arabella went flying.

She crashed to the ground, rolling back to her feet. Glancing at her hand, empty of its weapon, her gaze snapped back to the fengrine—and her sword still embedded in its shoulder.

Quickly, she moved her arms in a swirling motion, and more thorny vines of shimmering gold sprouted from the earth around the creature. Then she lowered her hands, and the thorns lashed across the fengrine's back, tightening, and forcing the creature to lower itself to the ground.

Nearby, two more fengrine growled, lips pulled back in a snarl as they approached. Arrows and golden bolts of magic continued to rain down on the creatures from the wall above them, keeping the creatures from approaching Arabella and Jessamine.

It took all of her strength to hold the weaves in place, and her arms trembled as the fengrine fought against the weaves coming from the ground beneath it, keeping it in place.

"I can't hold it for much longer," she said, glancing at Jessamine, whose chin dipped in understanding.

Arabella released the weave through its jaw and snout.

Jessamine launched an arrow at the creature's wounded shoulder, which punched deep. It roared, which rumbled through the ground beneath them. Then she formed weaves of magic into something akin to a spear and released it in a band of air. It soared straight through the creature's opened mouth and deep into its throat.

It swallowed and tried to shake its head before it fell to the ground in a heap.

Arabella's weaves snapped free, retreating into the earth.

"One down," Arabella gasped.

"Eleven more to go," Jessamine said as she looked down at her empty quiver. She turned back to the wall, shouting, "I need more arrows!"

But no one heard their calls.

The archers loosed arrow after arrow down at the fengrine at the base of the wall, the creatures' claws breaking away chunks of stone as they tried to climb. Even the enchantresses were at maximum capacity—every female releasing countless bolts of magic at the creatures spreading out along the wall.

Nearby, several lifeless bodies crashed down to the earth.

With a growl, Jessamine threw her bow and quiver to the ground.

"Take this," Arabella said, tossing her sword to Jessamine, which she caught in a deft grip.

Arabella loosed a band of air, wrapping it around her sword embedded into the dead creature's shoulder and pulling it back toward her. She caught the hilt as black blood spurted from the creature's shoulder, splattering across her face.

"Gross," Jessamine hissed from somewhere behind her.

Arabella cursed under her breath and wiped her face with the back of a hand, spitting.

Some demons' or monsters' blood was poisonous to humans and enchantresses. Best not to learn the hard way whether fengrine's blood was deadly to mortals.

Arabella bit her cheek, her gaze swiveling from the wall to the tear in the ward.

"I've got an idea," she said. "Watch my back."

But before she could move, there were two thumps behind her. A sudden gust of wind lifted her braid off her shoulder.

"We're coming, too," a familiar voice said.

Turning, Arabella spotted two priestesses who couldn't be more different in both physique and temperament. Brynne was as tall as she was strong—a solid wall of muscle, quite unlike Arabella's lean physique. At her side was her far shorter counterpart, Cora, who had a fair complexion similar to Jessamine's.

Both were armed heavily, two swords in each of their fists, their black leather consuming the sun's rays above them.

Arabella smiled and nodded. "Follow me."

Then they were all running toward the rift in the ward, diving out of range of the fengrine's swiping claws and gnashing teeth and narrowly avoiding the arrows embedding into the surrounding earth.

Sounds faded into the distance as Arabella weaved around the grass plain until she was before the ward. A distant part of her noted that the wind blew more strongly through the tear.

"If you close it, you'll lock the fengrine in with us," Jessamine shouted from behind her.

Arabella nodded. "We'll have to trust Iris and the others to take them down. It's that or wait for more creatures to come through."

"We've got you," Jessamine said before turning and facing the wall and the remaining fengrine.

The enchantresses and archers had killed a few more, but far too many remained and were trying to climb up the walls.

A flash of movement had Arabella's gaze following Brynne as she strode to the other side of the rift in the ward—closest to the forest. Brynne's broad shoulders took up much of the tear, and she held her massive blades aloft. Cora started to join her, but Brynne shook her head firmly.

"Stay with Jessamine. There are more fengrine on your side. Maybe we'll get lucky and no more will come," Brynne said, to which Cora nodded reluctantly.

Then Jessamine and Cora took defensive stances around Arabella on the side of the ward nearest Shadowbank and Brynne on the opposite.

"Here goes nothing," Arabella said before she opened herself fully to the earthen magic saturating the ground.

There were many reasons why the villagers remained so far from civilization—and so close to the home of so many demons. The ground was as fertile as it was full of magic, which would be ideal for humans and mortal magic wielders... if it wasn't for the demon and monster attacks. Today, Arabella planned to capitalize on the magic and use it to her advantage.

Magic filled her veins, flowing up her arms like river rapids as she pulled more and more into herself until she couldn't hold another drop. Enchantress magic was the richness of spring and blooming life. It was earth and hope for tomorrow.

So much magic coursed through her that it was painful. Tears formed at the corners of her vision. Slowly, she spun the earthen magic into long strands before banding them together in what eventually resembled a massive patch two stories high—one she hoped would allow the ward to sew itself back together. She wove and wove strands together, far more than she ever had before. With all her strength, sweat pouring down her face, she moved her arms in sweeping motions until at last the patch was complete.

Behind her, there was the pounding of feet, but she didn't dare to turn, didn't dare to take her attention off this task. Her sisters would protect her. If she didn't repair the ward, more monsters could come through—or worse, demons.

With the motion of her arms, the golden weaves hovering in the air floated forward as though wading through deep waters. Ever so slowly, it moved until it hovered at the center of the tear in the ward.

It was too short.

She needed several more weaves to make the patch large enough so the ward could meld with it and repair itself.

"Open yourselves to me," Arabella called over a shoulder.

She needed to borrow the magic of one enchantress if she was to have the strength to finish this patch.

"I'll go," Cora called. "I'm the weakest warrior. It should be me."

Jessamine and Brynne said nothing, and Cora was beside her a moment later.

Arabella swallowed thickly as she heard the heavy breathing of a fengrine and gnashing of teeth.

A hand was on her shoulder.

"Take what you need," said Cora.

Beside her, Cora's magic swirled in a current, as golden as any other enchantress, but it was laced with lavender. The latter was an essence that was just Cora. Each enchantress had a piece of themselves in their golden magic, and each felt different.

Arabella reached for Cora's well and drew it into herself.

Energy flooded her veins alongside the whirlpools of power she'd pulled from the earth and still held suspended in the air.

Rivulets of sweat plopped to the ground, and Arabella's breaths came in ragged gasps. Something warm leaked from her nose, and it was then she realized it wasn't sweat but blood streaming from her nose and ears. But she didn't dare stop.

Under any other circumstances, there would be a dozen enchantresses lending their power to one wielder to repair the ward. But everyone was required to defend the village. Even with Arabella's abilities, far more powerful than most enchantresses, she had precious little time until she passed out from burnout. Even with Cora's well, Arabella's mind swam, growing dizzy from the effort it took to hold so much power and weave it together, not releasing a single strand.

Slowly, she added more to her patch, lacing in several rows at the top.

"Got it!" Arabella rasped, her voice hoarse even to her ears. "Now just to—"

But her words were lost to the sound of snapping fengrine jaws somewhere behind her.

Arabella positioned the patch at the center of the tear in the ward, holding it with all her strength, waiting... waiting...

Come on, she thought. *Take.*

If the ward didn't take to the patch on her first try, she wouldn't have the strength to create another.

Just when she thought she couldn't hold on a moment longer, there was a flicker of purple-blue light as it sparked outward, latching on to one of her golden weaves. Slowly, the ward's rippling sides stretched and melded with the patch until it had fully taken around the patch.

"You did it!" Cora said from where she clutched Arabella's shoulder, her hand shaking.

In an instant, Arabella's grip on the magic snapped. She was a conduit between the earth, the patch, and Cora. When she released the magic, it ripped through her before receding into the ground beneath her and into Cora. They crashed to the ground, the force of the retreating magic sending them back several feet.

Pushing off the ground, Arabella looked up to see the patch still held and remained in place. But the tear wasn't closing fast enough. It inched back together far too slowly.

As four more fengrine appeared from the line of nearby trees beyond the ward, her heart dropped. But Brynne stood tall, the grip on her blades strong and sure—not an ounce of fear in her posture. Meanwhile, both Arabella and Cora shook like leaves in the autumn wind. Using so much magic had taken every ounce of strength she had.

Beside her, Cora turned over, heaving on the ground.

They hadn't hit burnout, but they'd been close—close enough that they'd be wrung out and sick in their own ways. Blood still streamed down Arabella's face from her ears and nose. She tried to swipe it away, but it was no use.

Arabella looked from where Brynne loosed her magic at the two fengrine to where Jessamine launched her attack on a pair of fengrine. Beyond them, several fengrine had made it up the wall and were leaping over soldiers into the village.

Bodies of the beasts littered the grassy plain, and she should feel relief. But all she could feel was dread lacing through her tired limbs as the forms of fengrine disappeared into the village and screams of humans rose into the air.

"We've got to defend the ward with Brynne," Arabella choked out. "If we don't, everything we did to patch it will be for nothing. Those fengrine will rip through it."

Cora nodded, but when she tried to get to her feet, they wobbled and she fell back to the ground.

Arabella stood on unsteady legs, extending a hand to Cora, who took it.

Beyond the rippling ward, Brynne faced down the first fengrine, but the other three were spreading out. Soon, she would be surrounded. She didn't stand a chance.

Arabella reached for the magic of the earth, hoping to use it to lend her strength, but it snapped back down. She was too weak to coax it out.

There was another magic she could take, she knew. But did she dare?

"Cora," Arabella shouted as she was running to the second fengrine Jessamine fought, the other lying in a heap on the ground. "Go help Brynne."

Cora nodded before dashing for where Brynne stood on the other side of the ward.

Before Arabella had gotten far, Jessamine launched herself into the air, bands of wind releasing beneath her feet. She soared above, a sword held between her hands, blade aimed earthward— at the fengrine's neck.

There was no time for Arabella to react as the creature raised one of its legs and its claw swiped sideways, batting Jessamine away like she was nothing more than a gnat.

"No!" Arabella screamed as Jessamine went crashing several yards away.

Her head bounced off the ground once, her body limp. Sensing vulnerable prey, the creature turned and bounded toward her.

Even if Arabella was at full strength, there was no way for her to reach Jessamine in time—not if she ran and not with her enchantress magic. It took far too long to weave bands of earthen magic together.

She took a breath.

Revealing her secret would be worth it if she could save her friend.

So, she reached for the whispering shadows, toward the darkness that had been there for as long as she could remember.

Dark magic was forbidden. It was something only the witches, sorcerers, and demons dabbled in, she knew. Not even the powerful fae dared to touch the darker forces in this world. It was a magic that would get Arabella killed simply for the ability to use it.

But she stretched out a hand, closing her eyes as she felt for the shadow of the lumbering fengrine, the one beneath its taloned paws. The shadow of the lowering sun stretched out far longer than it would at midday. She latched her senses around it and *pulled*.

Opening her eyes, she watched as the creature's legs tangled and it fell to the ground in a twist of limbs.

There was a flash of movement, and a bolt of magic soared through the air. Conscious again, Jessamine sent her magic toward the creature. Arabella watched as the bolt struck true, running clean through the beast's heart.

It didn't raise its head again.

Jessamine leaned on an elbow, brows drawn together as she looked at Arabella. But if she'd seen what Arabella had done with her dark magic, she didn't say a word.

Light flashed, and Arabella turned, relief flooding her chest as the ward closed fully, Brynne and Cora soaring through the gap before it sealed shut.

On the other side of the ward, the remaining fengrine growled, jaws snapping. But this time, the ward held. It kept the beasts at bay.

Arabella fell to her knees, relief flooding through her. "We did it."

"Fuck, we did," Brynne said, wiping sweat from her brow with the back of a muscled arm, swords clutched in her hands. She nodded to the repaired ward. "Nice job, Arabella. That was impressive."

Something between a cough and a laugh escaped Arabella's lips. "I couldn't have done it without all of you."

But her relief was short-lived.

The battle had cast a light on an undeniable truth—if the enchantresses were barely strong enough to face down one pack of fengrine, they were doomed the moment the ward truly fell and the demons came in hordes to feast on human flesh.

She swallowed thickly, turning her mind toward the fengrine that had made it over the wall, hoping the others had ended them.

One thing at a time.

First, they had to see to the damage of this battle with the fengrine. Then they'd figure out who would be the next offering to the Devourer, the demon of the forest.

They had three days until it would be back.

Then she'd worry about the fate of Shadowbank.

Chapter Three

ARABELLA

Not every darkness was the same.

The descent past the dormitories, past the kitchens and mess hall, and down into the depths of the Quarter was a cold one, as though the earth had hardened itself for the demons it would house in the depths of the dungeon.

Arabella walked at Iris' side as they entered the dungeon. Inhuman screams echoed down stone corridors, and she steeled herself for what was to come. Wordless, they strode down a dark stone corridor, past door after door that she knew from experience had countless devices to restrain and torture the demons and monsters of the shadows. It was the dark side of being an enchantress—to study the demons, themselves.

Ignorance wasn't bliss. It was glean whatever knowledge they could or be killed.

Some cells weren't separated from the hallway by massive magic-imbued wooden doors but by twisting metal bars with spikes as sharp as dragon teeth. Gremlins, gargoyles, small ogres, and countless other creatures leaped from the backs of their cells, launching forward and reaching their arms, claws desperately grasping.

Iris didn't flinch, and neither would she. But Arabella's heart skipped a beat at how close the ogre was to reaching them—mere inches away from grabbing on to their arms. Blood dripped onto the floor from the spikes on the cells' bars. The demons and beasts seemed uncaring if it injured them if it meant getting back at their captors.

Arabella trained her eyes forward, on the muscled back of the Head Enchantress. Time had demanded much of Iris' mind and body, and she had hardened herself to withstand what came. Arabella must do the same.

Eventually, they came to a door larger than the others.

Two heavily armed enchantresses dressed in traditional black leathers stood at attention, fists on their hearts. Neither flinched as more inhuman screaming sounded from the cell behind them. They opened the door, which creaked open on sturdy, magically enforced hinges. The door was as thick as Arabella's waist.

"Head Enchantress. Enchantress Arabella," the enchantresses murmured, heads bowed in deference.

Arabella nodded to them, following Iris inside.

As they entered, the smell of searing flesh assaulted her senses.

Arabella swallowed back bile. Something inside of her twisted at the almost pitiful sounds of the fengrine screaming even though she knew it was a beast of the forest, a *demon*, and didn't deserve her sympathy. This creature had killed dozens of civilians inside the walls of Shadowbank today. It had earned this outcome. And yet, she had to school her features as the smell of roasting flesh rose into the air more strongly when two of her sisters pressed a heated metal rod into the fengrine's side.

The wolf-like beast thrashed against the chains holding it down before collapsing to the stone floor, which was slick with its black blood.

It was the easiest way to identify a demon—by the color of its blood.

Demons and enchantresses had been enemies since the beginning of this world. Some theorized that enchantresses had been created by a goddess who'd taken pity on mankind as demons fed on their mortal flesh and desecrated the lands. But it was the very reason for Arabella's existence in Shadowbank—and the existence of every enchantress in every city and village—to protect those without magic from the wild shadows.

The witches and vampires couldn't be relied upon to provide aid, and the fae didn't bother with their realm, keeping to themselves on the other side of the gateways. Thus, it was to the enchantresses that the citizens looked to keep them safe. Because none would willingly entrust a sorcerer to protect them—not unless they wished death upon all those they held dear.

Dozens of her sisters had died over the years, and too few humans had been found to have the gift to replace them. It was one reason for the failing ward. There were too few enchantresses to protect the village and fewer still with giftings in repairing or reinforcing wards—or the knowledge for how to create them at all. Arabella was one of the few with the ability to repair the ward.

The enchantresses stopped their administrations on the fengrine and approached Iris, bowing their heads and holding heated pokers in gloved hands.

"We've confirmed it is, indeed, a fengrine," said one enchantress with a gift to sense the different types of demons. "It's not a shifter demon. That said, there's no way to communicate with it."

Iris nodded. "Well done. Learn what else you can. Report what you find to Enchantress Arabella."

They bowed their heads.

In the last few years, Arabella had become a sort of second-in-command to Iris. Arabella liked to think it wasn't because the Head Enchantress had been like a mother to her, having found her at the edge of the forest twenty years ago when Arabella was just a girl. Iris had allowed her to stay in the Quarter like one of the enchantresses—even before she showed signs of being gifted. Most assumed her position was because her powers were second only to Iris and that was why Iris had unofficially placed her as second-in-command. But deep down, she knew why it was.

There was nothing Arabella wouldn't do for the Circle, the only family she had.

Iris knew it, too.

The Head Enchantress turned on a heel and headed back down the corridor and toward the staircase. Before following Iris, Arabella looked to the enchantresses in expectation, and the enchantress placed two vials in her hand.

"Thank you," Arabella said, pocketing the vials and turning on a heel.

Arabella strode back through the cell doors, which the two enchantress sentries closed behind her.

"What do you hope they'll find?" Arabella asked when she'd caught up with Iris.

That they haven't found before, she didn't add.

"I want to know how these creatures keep multiplying," Iris said, her eyes fixed ahead, determination as cold and unyielding as the dungeon itself in her words. "How are they made? What other abilities do they have?"

"Could our time be better spent elsewhere?" Arabella pressed gently. "We need to send more of the sisters to the capitol—"

While there was some value to extracting information from the demons that could communicate, there were other ways they could seek to protect Shadowbank.

Iris waved a hand in dismissal. "Even if I wasn't afraid of their deaths along the deserted roads, we don't have the time for them to travel to the city, find the information we need, and return before the wards fall."

None knew how long the wards had been in place around Shadowbank, but they suspected it had been there for hundreds of years. Over time, ever so slowly, the ward had weakened until holes began appearing. And without the knowledge they needed to repair the wards for good or to replace them, they were living on borrowed time.

"Should we consider evacuating?"

Demons stretched out hands toward them from their barred prison cells as Iris halted, her shoulders hardening as she turned back toward Arabella. Her silver braid slipped over a shoulder—a braid similar to the one Arabella, herself, preferred. But unlike Arabella's headdress of overlapping silver chains and teardrop on her forehead, the Head Enchantress wore a golden crown of ivy. The metal of the crown starkly contrasted the black twisting bars of the cells, which had dried, crusted demon blood on the spikes.

"You mean well, child," Iris began, ignoring the reaching claws and talons, "but the dangers on the road are as plentiful as the ones here. At least here, we know the terrain."

Arabella dipped her chin, and it took all her concentration to keep her eyes on the Head Enchantress and not the creatures reaching for them. Creatures that would tear them apart if given the chance.

She'd pressed Iris as far as she could today. They were all exhausted after the battle, and weariness marked every line of Iris' features, making her appear older than her eighty years. Like her, Iris had blood and dirt on her face and leathers.

Before Iris could turn back toward the stairs, a hoarse laugh rumbled from a nearby cell, quite unlike the roars and screaming of the creatures throughout the dungeons.

Turning, Iris took a step toward the cell. As she did, the creature's skinny arm lashed out. In the blink of an eye, Iris wove together a wall of air, which the creature's fingers bounced off of, bones cracking. It hissed, pulling its arm back through the bars and cradling its hand, blood flowing down its arm from where one spike had grazed it.

Arabella blinked, unable to comprehend how Iris had pulled weaves together so quickly. One day, she hoped to be able to do the same.

The creature jumped backward in its cell out of their reach and made a sound like the hissing of a cat. Overly large cat-like ears protruded from a wide head. Its snout was also cat-like, but its skin was covered in thick green scales and there were spikes along its backbone. It could skitter up walls as deftly as a cockroach, and she knew from experience it feasted on small animals and children.

"Gremlin," Iris said. "Are you that eager for your death?"

Suddenly, Arabella's shadows rippled around her feet, darkening. Being down in the deeper darkness awakened something in her magic, and it took all of her focus to keep her shadows from stretching out into the cell.

She hadn't had a chance to speak to Jessamine about what she'd done to stop the fengrine, and she could only hope that Jessamine hadn't seen her shadows tangle the fengrine's legs. But Iris was far more powerful, and a single moment of lost control would mean Arabella would never leave these dungeons again.

As though sensing her magic's restlessness, the gremlin—no taller than Jessamine—stared at her with narrowed pupils.

A long tongue slashed out into the air before disappearing again.

"So, the wards are weakening?" the creature asked, its voice like broken pottery grinding together.

Arabella crossed her arms. "What gave it away? Your new houseguests? Or that we just *talked* about it?"

Iris' gaze shifted to Arabella before flicking back to the little demon. "What do you know of it?"

Still cradling its arm and broken fingers, the gremlin said, "I was there when the wards were built."

"You lie," Arabella said, sighing in exasperation.

It wasn't the first creature to make up stories to try to bargain for its freedom.

"It cost many enchantresses their lives. The ward," the gremlin said, its unnatural green eyes seeming to glow in the dark.

For some reason, Arabella paused. "What do you mean?"

"There aren't many of the older ones left, are there?" the gremlin asked.

Iris was one of the oldest enchantresses at eighty years of age.

The elder enchantresses had died in battles with demons over the years. That's why there were none left—and just the young remaining. At least, that's what she'd been led to believe...

Iris turned on a heel, heading for the stairs. "You speak nonsense."

Arabella hesitated, eyeing the gremlin. But her shadows lashed out like the tail of an agitated feline, threatening to roam free across the dungeon, and she hurried after the Head Enchantress. Best they return to what remained of the daylight before she truly lost control.

More than that, she needed to find Jessamine, and *soon*.

At the top of the stairs, beastly screams echoing up faintly, Iris turned back to her. Arabella paused, fear flooding her chest as she wondered whether Iris had sensed her shadows. Instead, Iris wrapped her arms around her, pulling her in for an embrace. Instinctively, Arabella returned the gesture, closing her eyes.

Although Iris was shorter than her, it felt like she enveloped Arabella. Her mere presence had always filled every room she entered. Her foster mother smelled of eucalyptus and cucumbers, and Arabella leaned her head on Iris' shoulder, allowing herself this moment of weakness. Every other minute of the day, she had to be strong. She had to be an example for the other enchantresses so they didn't succumb to fear. But at this moment, it was just her and Iris. Like it used to be all those years ago.

"You've done well, my child," Iris said, arms holding fast. "You were everything I hoped you'd be."

Iris pulled back then, looking up to Arabella, her dark green eyes flickering between Arabella's.

"I'm sorry I couldn't protect you," Iris continued. "But I knew you could do it, and so you did."

Arabella swallowed thickly, a faint tremble making its way to her arms. "I couldn't have done it without Jessamine and the others."

Iris harrumphed, clearly displeased by the mention of Jessamine.

Taking a breath, Arabella dared to ask the question she'd been wanting to voice for months.

"How much time do we have?"

Iris released her but paused, her hand cupping Arabella's cheek, her thumb swishing back and forth across her skin—seeing past the mud, blood, and gore. "I can still see the little girl you were. Lost, confused, but never scared."

Arabella leaned into the touch. "I'm always scared."

"Perhaps," Iris said. "But you never let it stop you."

"Nor do you."

Not once had she seen Iris do anything but stare a challenge in the face and leap for it, wrestling it into submission.

"Tell me, Mina," Arabella said, using the private name she'd given to Iris as a small child. "How much time does Shadowbank have? Weeks? Days?"

"Months," Iris said, not dropping her hand. Instead, she stroked it over Arabella's hair.

Arabella nodded, her heart dropping.

They had mere months left of relative safety before her family, her entire village, would be in grave danger. And what was she without her family? Just a lost girl wandering through a forest, unwanted and unloved. She couldn't become that girl—not again.

Throw me into a pit of monsters, Arabella thought as she studied the woman who'd taken the mantle of mother in her life. *But don't leave me.*

"My precious girl," Iris said. "I ask too much of you, I know. I wish things could be different." She dropped her hand then, shaking her head as though clearing her thoughts. "Well, then. There's much to do before the day ends."

The Head Enchantress turned on a heel and said over her shoulder, "Don't you dare go to the healers' quarters to lend your strength, Arabella."

The drop in her title had Arabella pausing.

"But—" she began, but Iris had already resumed speaking.

"Get some rest at once. You look like you're about to fall into a pool of shadows on the floor."

Arabella made a sound that was somewhere between a laugh and a cough. What exactly did Iris mean by that? Did she know? Had she seen her shadows in the dungeons? Instinctively, Arabella clutched both the shadows beneath her feet and the vials in her pocket.

"Yes, Mina," she managed.

Without another word, Iris disappeared down the halls.

Taking a shaky breath, Arabella turned and headed for the dormitories in search of Jessamine.

HOURS LATER, Arabella was clean, dressed for sleep, and weaving through the hallways of the enchantresses' living quarters —the middle levels of the Quarter, a large stone building for the enchantresses. Only the temples on the top floor were above ground. Everything else was beneath the very earth the enchantresses drew their magic from.

Young enchantresses moved from one door to another, weaving through the hallway by lantern light or by the light of golden fire magic around them. Many had just come from the washing chambers and were wrapped in robes, their hair wet and dripping. Some had the hardened seriousness of battle still in their eyes, as though they didn't realize they were safe now—their postures suggesting they were ready to fight at a moment's notice. Other women strode down the hall, talking and laughing, as though the day were like any other.

But all moved as they saw her, parting to either side of the long stone hallway.

"Enchantress," they whispered, heads bowing.

Arabella offered a smile, an objection on the tip of her tongue, but she swallowed it. No matter how many times she'd insisted that they treat her like any other enchantress, it seemed to only reinforce the awkward formalities.

That was, except for her quarlet.

The women in her quarlet were her innermost circle.

She turned the corner and entered her shared room, which had several beds across the room. Interspersed throughout were simple wooden drawers for their belongings and a single table with matching wooden chairs.

While she could have had her own room years ago, as could Jessamine, Brynne, and Cora, they'd all chosen to remain in the dormitories.

Arabella scanned the room.

Cora and Brynne were in the corner on a single bed. Brynne had an arm wrapped around Cora, and she whispered something into Cora's ear, which made her laugh. Arabella couldn't help but notice countless scrapes down both of their arms, which were visible in the long shirts they wore to bed. One of Brynne's eyes was swollen shut and a large scrape ran across her cheek to her forehead and was partially healed over.

Scarlett had moved back into their room and was already asleep.

"Arabella!" Cora exclaimed, turning toward the doorway. "I was hoping you'd return before lights out. You can take my bed."

With Scarlett back, there would need to be two people on one bed for all of them to fit.

"What's it like being the savior of Shadowbank?" Brynne said, not taking her gaze from Cora.

Her dry tone had the corner of Arabella's lips quirking up.

"Lonely," Arabella said, equally dryly. "Where's Jessamine?"

The bed closest to the door was void of the very person she was looking for.

"She's getting cleaned up," Cora said. "She'll be back soon."

Reluctantly, Arabella lowered herself onto the bed beside Jessamine's.

Weariness seeped into her bones. If she allowed herself to close her eyes, she'd be asleep in an instant. The cost of using so much magic earlier that day was a feverish hunger and exhaustion, and she'd cleared four plates of food before she'd had the energy to return to the living quarters and get cleaned up. The blood had stopped seeping from her nose and ears—one of the final signs before burnout and unconsciousness—but her body felt like she'd been wrung out a few too many times.

Even so, she couldn't allow herself to rest. Not yet.

"What's going on?" Cora asked, sitting up in bed. Her blonde hair was loose around her shoulders, and her bangs that she normally clipped back in battle were down. Her large eyes were filled with kindness and concern, as they always were. She was the exact opposite of Brynne and Jessamine, who were skeptics of all good things in the world. This woman believed in the best in people and wanted the best for others.

"I'm fine," Arabella lied. She considered her next words, glancing at Scarlett's sleeping form and then back to Cora. "After today, we have only two days until..."

Until the Devourer was back for its offering.

"Did the healers find anything?" Arabella managed.

Cora shook her head. "Nothing. Her memories are just... gone."

Like all offerings before her, Scarlett had no recollection of what had happened or where she'd been for the last ten years. The Devourer clearly didn't want anyone to know just what it was or where it lived. None dared to venture into the forest to rescue the enchantresses who'd given themselves as offerings. Even if anyone knew the location of the Devourer's home, those who entered the wild shadows rarely returned. There were far too many demons in every form that could be imagined.

Although the enchantresses were strong, the demons were stronger.

It was an ugly truth that few enchantresses dared to acknowledge. If they did, if word got out, there would be panic in the streets. The humans would become desperate. Perhaps they'd flee to the nearest cities and be demon fodder on the open roads.

Arabella's magic—even Iris' magic—paled compared to the other beings walking this land.

It was why Arabella had made her secret agreement six months ago—the one she didn't dare tell anyone about.

Shadows twisted beneath her. It was like a tickling sensation on the pads of her feet. She willed them to still. There had been far too many close calls today.

"How's she holding up?" Arabella asked, nodding to Scarlett.

"She's in shock, but she's okay," Cora said. "She needs sleep as much as you do."

"I'm fine," Arabella insisted.

"Keep telling yourself that," Brynne muttered.

Arabella leveled a flat look at her friend. But before she could respond, footsteps sounded behind her, and she spun around.

Jessamine stood in the doorway, one hand holding up her towel and a lantern in the other. The fact that she wasn't using magic and instead relied on a lantern was a clear sign of how exhausted she was. They'd all spent more energy than they ever had before—and it was barely enough to hold off a mere dozen fengrine.

"You're back," Jessamine said, her tone unusually guarded.

Striding into the room and closing the door behind her, Jessamine grabbed her sleeping shirt and headed for the dressing room in the back corner. In a minute, she was dressed and walking to her bed, toweling her long blonde hair.

When Jessamine settled on the bed beside her, Arabella said, "How are you feeling?"

The words sounded forced even to her ears. But Brynne and Cora had turned their attentions back to each other.

"Tired," Jessamine said.

Like Brynne and Cora, Jessamine's arms were covered in long scratches from the fengrine's claws. Most likely, she'd been partially healed—just enough so the healers wouldn't expend too much energy and had some remaining energy to see to the other wounded.

"Did the Head Enchantress find anything?" Jessamine asked.

Arabella shook her head. "It was confirmed they were fengrine. Not shifter demons."

Jessamine sighed. "Too bad they aren't the kind that can speak. That would've been far more useful."

Rubbing her clammy hands together, Arabella fixed her eyes on the stone ground and said, "Thanks for having my back today. It was all kinds of idiocy to jump down from the wall. But... thank you."

There was a snort beside her before Jessamine said, "You'd have done it for me."

It was true.

She hated that she had to voice the next words. She hated that she felt any doubt about her best friend, but Jessamine might have seen her shadow magic. And if she had, there was a chance that—despite their friendship—she could turn her over to Iris or the town. Perhaps Arabella would be thrown down in the dungeons alongside the gremlin, fengrine, and other demons. That was if she wasn't killed outright in some large spectacle or exiled back to the forest she'd once come from.

So many encounters with demons that wielded dark magic and changed their forms so that they looked like men had made the villagers skittish. She couldn't blame them. But they desperately needed more magic to protect Shadowbank, and Arabella wasn't about to disregard anything that could help protect her family and home.

Still... she had to know if Jessamine had seen what she'd done to the fengrine.

"Did you notice anything... different during the battle?" Arabella asked carefully, raising her eyes from the floor.

Jessamine's green eyes were focused on the far wall before she turned to face Arabella.

"Should I have seen anything?"

Arabella bit the inside of her cheek.

Was this Jessamine's way of letting her off the hook? Had she sensed the shadows twisting beneath the fengrine? If so, was she fine with it this once since it was to save her life? Or had she truly not seen anything?

Shoulders lifting and dropping in a shrug, Arabella said, "There was so much going on. I was curious if you'd spotted... anything out of the ordinary."

Slowly, Jessamine shook her head. "Nothing that bears repeating."

Relief flooded Arabella's chest, and she released the breath she'd been holding. Allowing herself to feel how tired she was, she lowered herself onto the bed and pulled the blankets up. But rather than succumbing to exhaustion, her thoughts cycled between the wards and the Devourer.

She had to focus on one crisis at a time, and the one with an immediate deadline was the one that meant she could lose one of her sisters for ten years to a demon. And she'd never let that happen if there was something she could do to protect them.

Tomorrow, she'd find the two people who might be able to help. If they didn't have answers, Shadowbank would be at the mercy of the demons.

Chapter Four

ARABELLA

Arabella sat in a booth at the House of Obscurities, clutching her tankard as though it held the answers she sought.

All around her, tables filled with patrons—everyone eager to escape their reality after the battle with the fengrine the day before and the Devourer had returned Scarlett. In addition, the ward near the ports on the far side of Shadowbank had weakened, and there were rumblings of the creatures of the deep that were far too eager to come upon their shores.

Musicians set up their instruments, and the drummers pounded a steady beat for the dancers who'd just taken the stage in the larger room beyond the bar. As the dancers moved, beads and shining metal disks woven into skirts or belts tinkled as they spun and reflected the flames from lantern lights.

Across the table from her, Jessamine tipped her tankard back before saying, "Has the Head Enchantress picked the next offering?"

Things still felt slightly off between them, but Arabella tried to chalk it up to exhaustion or stress—or both.

Arabella shook her head. "She's probably hoping someone will volunteer before she's forced to pick."

"I might volunteer."

Although Jessamine's words were soft, they rang like a bell over the music, the thumping feet of dancers, and the chatter of the crowd.

Arabella's throat tightened, but she managed, "No one's going to be volunteering this time."

Jessamine was one of the best fighters in all of Shadowbank. Having her taken by the Devourer would be a tremendous hit to Shadowbank's defenses, especially with the weakening ward.

As Arabella finished her drink, a woman wearing an apron and with hair brighter than the lanterns' flames, appeared with two full tankards.

"Nemera," Arabella said. "It's good to see you."

Nemera smiled, and her entire face brightened like the glimmer of the sun's rays across the water as it rose. Freckles dotted across her nose and cheeks, and her eyes crinkled at the corners.

"This round is on the house," Nemera said. "Looks like you could use it."

They murmured their thanks.

"Is Rowan here?" Arabella asked. "I need to speak to him."

After what she learned of the Devourer so far, this was her first lead to learn what she could of the demon.

Nemera nodded over a shoulder toward the stage and the large sitting room beyond it with countless tables and chairs, most of which were filled. "He's helping someone in back. I'm sure he'll be around soon."

Arabella thanked her, and Nemera weaved in and out of standing patrons back toward the bar.

She and Jessamine drank in silence for several minutes, watching the dancers on the stage between the bodies of muscled farmers, sailors, and other laborers as they moved around the room.

At last, the person Arabella wanted to see appeared, striding back toward the bar.

"I'll see you later," Arabella said to Jessamine, swallowing the last of her drink, before pushing to her feet.

A hand grabbed her wrist. Turning, Arabella was surprised to see Jessamine holding her.

"Don't do anything I wouldn't do," Jessamine said dryly, a knowing look in her eyes.

"Me?" Arabella said with mock offense. "I would never."

Releasing her, Jessamine raised a brow but said nothing further.

With a nod of farewell, Arabella wove between patrons toward the bar. Eventually, she found an open space and waved to the male with hair as black as a moonless night and skin paler than the moon.

"Rowan!" Arabella said, smiling.

The male wore a matching apron to Nemera's, but he also had donned practical trousers and sturdy boots—prepared for a long night of catering to short-tempered patrons. He returned her smile with a closed-lip grin as he made his way over to her, wiping his hands on a towel.

"Hello, Arabella," Rowan said. "What can I do for you?"

"I was hoping I could speak to you," she said. "In private."

His brows furrowed, but he nodded toward the stairs behind the bar. "This way."

She followed him to the second floor of the House of Obscurities where some of the staff lived and where patrons could rent out rooms for more private shows.

Rowan pulled her into a quiet alcove, which had several wooden buckets and mops. Immediately, the sounds from below quieted to a distant roar, and it felt like Arabella could finally hear her thoughts again.

He glanced over a shoulder, seeing no one else winding down the hallway before he turned back to her and smiled widely. When he did, she spotted two elongated canines.

Arabella crossed her arms. "When was the last time you fed?"

The vampire ran a hand over his hair. "Nemera likes to make me work for it."

Despite the stupidity of that statement, Arabella snorted and rolled her eyes. "Her being a tease could get her killed."

A vampire bite was addicting, courtesy of the venom that vampires often injected into their prey when they fed. It wasn't the type of high that could be had from drugs. Instead, it was a high that filled a vampire's prey with uncontainable lust. At least, that's how Nemera had described it to her. The need for the other's body would overcome both the vampire and their mortal of choice. That was if the vampire didn't lose control and drink their prey dry.

But she knew one thing for certain—vampires' elongated fangs appeared when they were hungry.

"Don't worry," Rowan said, offering her a sheepish grin. "I'm in control still."

Arabella nodded. "Be careful. I don't want anyone else to discover what you are."

Or all of her and Jessamine's efforts to protect them would be in vain.

In the months that Arabella had been researching how to repair the ward, she'd had to seek the many races of this world. She quickly learned there were few enough within the walls of Shadowbank. Outside of enchantresses, shifters were the most common to live among humans, at least those not demon-born, but they had little magic outside of their ability to change from man to beast. The fae didn't bother with their realm, keeping to themselves on the other side of the gateways. There were those who dealt in dark magic, like witches and vampires, but most human cities or villages forbade them entry and hunted them down.

In Shadowbank, Rowan was the only vampire she knew of.

"You had a question for me?" Rowan offered.

"Do you know anything about the Devourer with your... background?" Arabella asked carefully.

Rowan shook his head. "Not much, I'm afraid. I'm from the city. So, all the demons out in the country are new to me. The ringleader captured me during the daylight after I'd been turned and kept me in the cage until... well, you know what happened. I didn't have a chance to learn about just what's in the forest."

Her heart dropped.

"I'm sorry," he added. "But maybe if you tell me what you know, it might spark something."

She thought back to her encounter with the Devourer yesterday. She didn't dare reveal that she'd wanted to kill the Devourer despite the bargain that was in place. But she recalled just what had happened and what powers it had displayed.

"It's fast. Male, I think. It moves in shadows, and it can imprison its prey in some type of bands of magic."

Her thoughts once again strayed to what she'd felt when it was behind her.

It made me lust after it. But how?

She couldn't form the words to tell the vampire this.

Lines formed between Rowan's brows. "It's not a sorcerer?"

"I don't think so," she said. "It was powerful, but not as powerful as sorcerers are rumored to be."

He ran a hand over his hair, mussing it. "That doesn't ring any bells. I'm sorry. I wish I could be of more help."

"It's not your fault," Arabella said, sighing. A thought occurred to her, and she added, "You don't happen to know anything about wards, do you?"

Again, Rowan shook his head.

It was an effort to swallow back the lump forming in her throat.

"Thanks anyway," Arabella managed as tears welled in the corners of her eyes.

How can I protect my family? The wards are failing, and an offering must be given tomorrow.

Time wasn't on her side.

A hand was on her shoulder, squeezing gently.

43

"If there's anything I can do to help, don't hesitate to ask," Rowan said gently. Then he nodded to the hallway. "You can stay up here as long as you need. Come down when you're ready."

When his too-quiet vampire footsteps disappeared downstairs, she waited a moment before she hurried down the hallways of the sleeping chambers and several staircases to the back of the large room with a stage full of dancers. A song had ended, and the audience was clapping as she strode along the back wall of the room. Turning down another hallway, she headed for the back door, grabbed a cloak hung on a rung at the door, and slipped out.

She couldn't risk Jessamine or anyone else seeing her leave. Not with who she planned to see next. She had hoped that Rowan would know more about the Devourer—or the failing ward—but there were no other options left to her.

The objects in her pocket weighed heavily as the sun gave way to dusk as she weaved down the streets of Shadowbank, donning the cloak.

She passed countless buildings made of stones and brick—as hardy as the people living within them. The homes on the outskirts of the village were small and had barred windows and doors. But at the center of town, the buildings turned to two-story structures with shutters and potted plants outside windows. Horses and carts moved along the cobblestone streets along with many people pulling carts behind them and shouting about the sales of their wares.

Pulling up the hood of her cloak, she ducked into the dark alleyways leading to the Wolford District. Few ventured to the poorest parts of town near the docks on the far side of Shadowbank. Not unless they were looking for a fight—or the unscrupulous type.

As she walked, women leaned out doorways, wearing low-cut dresses that would do little against the night's cool air, calling to her. But she kept her gaze trained ahead. Several figures opened their cloaks to reveal countless pockets filled with what they claimed were gold watches, though were far more likely to be made of something else entirely. With a flick of her hand, a gust of wind pushed the pickpockets-turned-merchants to the side of alleyways, keeping straying fingers in their own cloaks.

Eventually, Arabella came to a nondescript wooden door. It looked the same as every other door in the alley, the warped wood unmarked. She raised a fist, banging thrice on the door. A hush settled over the alleyway. No beggars lingered, and no sex workers leaned out of doorways. It was entirely void of people.

She raised a fist to knock again when the door creaked open to a darkened room.

Arabella paused for a moment before striding into the room.

"Hello?" Her voice felt like a knife slicing through the hushed darkness.

For a moment, all was silent. Then the door slammed shut of its own accord, enclosing her in darkness.

"I wondered when you'd make your way to me." A voice rasped into the blackness. It was hoarse, as though claws scraped against glass, but it also held an air of artificial youth.

Even in the darkness, she felt the stirrings of a deeper black swirling around the edges of her senses. But Arabella didn't reach for her enchantress magic that could illuminate the space in an instant. Instead, she sought her shadows, the ones beneath her feet that whispered excitedly like awakening children. The shadows around the room whispered to her as well, revealing the presence of another magic wielder stepping through them. She could feel sandaled feet moving across the stones, though the space was utterly silent.

"You're getting rusty," Arabella said as she reached for the shadow where she'd felt a footstep. Then she *pulled* at the shadows as though pulling a rug out from under their feet.

But there wasn't the telltale sound of feet shuffling or a body falling to the floor.

Instead, a chuckle rumbled through the room, penetrating the darkness.

A presence hovered behind her, and there was the press of a chin on her shoulder.

"I don't think so, girl," Lucinda, the former witch's apprentice, rasped into her ear.

Arabella spun on a heel to face her, but the shadows wrapped around her arms, pinning them to her sides.

There was a snap of fingers and dozens of candles flicked to life across the small room, illuminating a stone mantle and the face of an ageless woman.

"You haven't practiced," Lucinda hissed, smelling strongly of cheap incense.

Arabella gritted her teeth, pulling at her restraints of shadows. "You know I can't at the Quarter."

"Make time to get away, then," Lucinda said with a wave of her hand.

"As if I do nothing all day," Arabella grumbled.

"Excuses," said Lucinda. "Have you brought it with you?"

"Release me, or you'll crack the vials."

At once, the shadows dissipated, and Lucinda held a hand free of wrinkles toward her, palm upwards. With slight reluctance, Arabella pulled the vials of demon blood from the inner pocket of her leather coat and placed them in the former witch's apprentice's hand.

"As agreed," Arabella said.

It was what they'd settled on six months ago.

Arabella was one of the few people with access to the dungeons that housed the captured demons in the Quarter. Even amongst the enchantresses, there were few permitted down there. As such, she was one of the few people with access to demon blood.

And witches coveted demon blood for their spells.

Magical wielders had access to many types of magic—elemental, like enchantresses, but also spirit magic, magic of the dead, blood magic, and other dark magics. Some magic wielders chose not to train with the enchantresses and apprenticed under a witch to see if they possessed the gift for the darker magics. If they couldn't tap into the magic or weren't strong enough, they were dismissed, so far as Arabella knew.

As a witch's apprentice, Lucinda must have been lacking in some type of magic. But she'd been strong enough in her abilities to have been taken on by the powerful Witch of the Woods.

"What do you do with the demon blood, anyway?" Arabella dared to ask.

"That information was not part of our agreement," Lucinda replied as she stashed the vials up her sleeves.

Arabella took a deep breath. "I have questions."

"You usually do."

"I've asked you about how to repair the wards, but I've never asked you about creating one," Arabella began. "Is there a way for witches to create a ward?"

It was clear the enchantresses wouldn't be able to create a new ward with the resources they had. But what about the witches? What would be possible with dark magic?

"There is," Lucinda said. "But what use would it be to the enchantresses? You couldn't repair it in a few hundred years when it starts to fail, too."

A problem for a future day, she thought. It would buy the villagers more time in safety.

But Lucinda was right. If the witches could even be convinced to create a ward, there wouldn't be a way for the enchantresses to maintain or repair it since their magics were so different. That was aside from the fact that bargains with witches were usually more dangerous than they were worth. Even bargaining with a former witch's apprentice was foolhardy at best. But Arabella's shadow magic had been growing, and it was either she learned how to control it or be discovered.

"Come," Lucinda said, flicking a wrist. The door opened, and she strode out into the dark alley.

With a sigh, Arabella followed her down several narrow alleyways into the pits of Shadowbank until they were in a forgotten alcove between buildings near the port. Discarded barrels, crates, and other garbage littered the ground, and the stench of sulfur and dead fish hovered in the air. This area had become a sort of practicing ground. There was nowhere safe to practice shadow magic, but this was the best option they had.

"Strike me," Lucinda said, settling into a low, wide stance.

"I don't know if I can after yesterday—" Arabella began.

Without waiting for her to finish, Lucinda moved her arms in a swirling motion, similar to what many enchantresses did when using their elemental magic. Only the most experienced could form weaves with a mere thought, like the Head Enchantress.

Shadow speared toward Arabella, two bolts spinning directly toward her chest.

She tried to move, but even a day later, her legs were lethargic and slow after battling the fengrine. In an instant, she knew she wouldn't get out of the way in time.

Desperate, she reached for the shadows at her feet, pulling them out from beneath her. Her hip slammed into the cobblestones as the spears of shadow narrowly soared over her head and crashed into a barrel behind her. When she looked back, she noted two distinct holes the size of her thumb in the thick wood.

"Are you mad?" Arabella hissed.

"You're a one-trick pony," Lucinda said. "Stop trying to use the shadows beneath someone's feet to trip them. Though I've never seen a shadow whisperer do that to themself."

Slowly, Arabella got to her feet, rubbing her aching hip.

"Try something else I've taught you," Lucinda continued. "Move into the shadows. Form a shield. *Anything.*"

"I can't do any of those things even at full strength," Arabella grumbled. "But I need to ask you about—"

Two more spears of shadow shot out of Lucinda's hands and toward Arabella's chest.

Arabella's mind went blank. For a moment, she froze. She

stared down the shadows as sharp as a blade's edge that flew toward her. After everything she'd done to fight the fengrine and save Shadowbank, was this going to be the moment she died? Was she about to be bested by two arbitrary bolts of shadow?

But no matter what she did, no matter how much she tried to will her arms, her body to move, to do *anything*, she couldn't move. She was utterly spent.

Before the bolts could collide with her chest, they veered skywards hissing into the night air.

Lucinda made a tsking sound in the back of her throat. "If you hadn't paid today, I might have let you die, stupid child. You owe me two more vials next time you see me."

Air heaved in and out of Arabella's chest.

"The Devourer," she said, gasping, not wanting to think about how she'd manage to get more demon blood so soon. "What do you know of it?"

Lucinda started moving her arms in sweeping motions, the shadows gathering between her palms, but she paused at Arabella's words.

"Little of use," Lucinda said.

Arabella raised her hands, preparing for Lucinda to try to kill her again. "Tell me what you know."

Shadows hovered between Lucinda's hands as she said, "It's an immortal demon, a hybrid creature that's new to this world."

"How new?"

Lucinda shrugged. "The last millennium."

"Time is relative," Arabella muttered. In a louder tone, she said, "What does it do with its offerings?"

"I don't know."

Arabella chewed on her lip. "Can it be convinced to accept something else instead of an offering?"

"Unlikely."

Arabella wanted to growl, to ring Lucinda until she gave a response longer than a few words. But a thought occurred to her.

49

Instead, she said, "Can the Devourer repair the ward? Make a new one?"

Lucinda swirled her hands and then the shadows were dancing up her right arm and over her shoulders. The motion was almost playful. "It's my turn to ask questions."

Arabella frowned, uncertain what she could tell Lucinda that the former apprentice didn't already know.

"Who are your parents?" Lucinda asked as shadows continued to dance along her shoulders and down her other arm. "Just where does that magic of yours come from?"

Arabella started. "I've already told you. I don't know."

"Perhaps not right now," Lucinda said, her eyes on the shadows skittering across her fingertips. "Not without help."

Suddenly, Lucinda extended her fingers toward her, and shadows flew through the air before colliding with Arabella's forehead.

On any other day, she would've been able to dodge out of the way of the shadows or fend them off. But as she was, she could do nothing as the shadows penetrated her mind, peeling back her conscious thoughts and plunging into the dark.

"Stop it," Arabella said through gritted teeth, feeling the sharp edges of Lucinda's magic scrape against her mind.

"Or what?" Lucinda said, her hands still outstretched toward Arabella as she took one step forward and then another. "Haven't you always wanted to know? Are you not curious about where your abilities come from?"

"No," Arabella hissed, feeling the spikes of the shadow press into her mind, sifting deeper. Images of her growing up with the enchantresses streaked across her mind's eye, unbidden. "It's enough to know my family now."

It was the truth.

She didn't care to know where she came from so long as she could keep the Circle safe and control her abilities. Whoever her parents were, they'd either abandoned her or were killed by the demons of the forest. They'd been foolhardy enough to venture

KISSED BY A DEMON

into it, and they'd paid the consequences. What else was there to know?

Lucinda's magic spread in her mind like thorny vines, splintering across her thoughts until it overwhelmed her, and she dropped to a knee.

"Stop," Arabella said, her voice near to pleading.

Lucinda was right—there was nothing she could do to make the woman stop. She could only hope that her ability to supply this woman with demon blood was enough for her to want Arabella to live, to release her.

But she wasn't stopping. The vines spread, and more images flashed across her mind's eye. She saw the first time she'd met Iris —when her hair was still brown and streaked with gray. Iris had strode through the gates when Arabella stumbled out of the woods and through the wards. Exhausted, she'd fallen to the ground, eyes fluttering shut. But she'd remained conscious long enough to see the Head Enchantress' worried eyes as she stood over her. The next she knew, she woke up in a warm bed with clean clothes, and her new life had begun.

Lucinda's shadowy vines stretched out, reaching for the moments before Arabella had stepped through the trees—

Panic twisted her chest, and she could no longer form words.

Lucinda was going to kill her. She'd rip the memories from Arabella no matter the cost.

This couldn't be happening, Arabella thought. *Please make it stop. Someone make it stop.*

Arabella held her head between her hands, tears streaming down her cheeks.

"Stop!" someone shouted from down the dark alleyway.

A flash of light as bright as the cresting moon pierced the darkness, soaring through the air and piercing the former witch's apprentice in the shoulder.

Suddenly, the thorny vines in Arabella's mind loosened, retreating in an instant, sliding from her in prickly, slimy tendrils.

The pressure in her forehead popped, and she blinked back her tears.

Jessamine stood behind Lucinda with bands of golden magic extending from the earth and several more golden bolts hovering above her shoulders. Bolts like the one that had pierced Lucinda's shoulder.

Blood trickled from the wound in Lucinda's shoulder where the magic had gone clear through, and the former witch's apprentice held a hand to staunch the bleeding.

"How dare you?" Lucinda hissed, her eyes fading from their usual blue until they turned a deep midnight black.

There was a hissing before shadows rippled up from the earth, from underneath crates and barrels, forming a looming cloud over the cobblestones around Lucinda.

"You've spelled your doom," Lucinda said before she released her shadows at Jessamine.

"No!" Arabella screamed, but her voice was lost to the sounds of colliding magic.

To Arabella's shock, before every one of Lucinda's strikes of shadow, Jessamine was one step ahead. She moved to the side, dodging blow after blow a breath before it came. Then she loosed her magic, and in movements too fast for Arabella's tired eyes, Lucinda was on her ass on the ground, glaring up at Jessamine.

"Best you piss off into the shadows you thrive in, you wretch," Jessamine said. "Before I change my mind and decide to kill you."

Blood leaked from a corner of Lucinda's mouth. "Enchantresses don't take life."

"I consider the code of my order as more of... a suggestion. Guidelines, if you will," Jessamine said. Then she leaned down and added in a lower, menacing tone that Arabella had never heard, "I think you'll be far easier to kill than a fengrine."

Lucinda rose to her feet, unhurried, her eyes promising retribution. Turning, she glared at Arabella. "I won't forget this."

Lucinda strode back the way they'd come without another word.

When Arabella turned back toward Jessamine, her friend hadn't dropped her weaves. Instead, her eyes narrowed, and she crossed her arms.

Arabella ran a hand over the back of her head, feeling the strands of hair that had come free from her braid. "It's not what it looks like—"

"Don't lie to me," Jessamine snapped. "I saw what you did with the fengrine. How? And what are you doing here with *Lucinda?* Are you trying to get yourself killed?"

"Lucinda and I came to an... understanding," Arabella began.

An understanding that is officially over.

Jessamine didn't move from where she stood before Arabella, arms crossed, eyes narrowed. Despite their significant height difference, it felt like she loomed over Arabella.

"I give her demon blood in exchange for lessons."

"What kind of lessons?" Jessamine demanded.

"I have elemental magic, like all enchantresses," Arabella began. "But ever since I was a child, I've also had an... affinity for the shadows. And in the last few months, I've been struggling to control it."

Jessamine stiffened.

"I don't know what it is. I've never done any type of dark magic, but it's like I can sense shadows and things in them. Yesterday, I used the fengrine's shadows to trip it before it could get to you."

Jessamine remained quiet, her eyes flicking back and forth between Arabella's.

"Twenty years. I've known you for more than *half* of your fucking life. And not once have you shared this with me. Not *once.*" The anger filling Jessamine's eyes dampened somewhat and was replaced by sorrow. "I won't turn you in, Arabella. If that's what you're worried about. I don't think you're a demon or a danger to anyone. Maybe to yourself, but that's out of sheer stupidity."

Arabella winced even as her breath whooshed out of her.

Jessamine wasn't going to turn her in.

Relief rushed through Arabella as sweet and overwhelming as anything she'd ever felt. Just as suddenly, guilt filled her senses, twisting her gut. She had been wrong to doubt her friend. It was clear she should have trusted her sooner.

I didn't have to bear this secret alone.

"I want to be friends," Jessamine continued. "And for me, that means talking about the deeper stuff. I don't want to just joke around, but I want to be there for you. And I can't do that if you don't tell me what's going on—or what I can do to support you."

"I'm sorry."

The words came out as a hoarse whisper.

Golden weaves dissipated around them as Jessamine stepped forward and wrapped her arms around Arabella's waist.

"I'd be scared, too, if I had magic I didn't understand," Jessamine said. "But don't you fucking dare keep secrets like this from me again, okay? Not about the important stuff."

Tears welled in Arabella's eyes, coursing down her cheeks in quiet rivulets. She nodded into Jessamine's hair. "I won't. I promise."

As they walked back to the Quarter and went to bed, reality settled on Arabella's shoulders.

Both Lucinda and Rowan had been dead ends—neither the former witch's apprentice nor the vampire could help her. Neither knew a thing about wards or the forest demon.

The Devourer would come tomorrow, and there was nothing she could do to overpower it or strengthen their wards to keep it from coming in. But did any of this with the Devourer matter if the wards would fail in months if Iris was right? The winter would mean death for countless if the ward fell during the darkest, coldest season when the most demons emerged from the forest—starving for human flesh with so many animals going into hibernation. Would only the offering be alive after all of this?

An idea struck her.

There was a way she could save the villagers.

If the Devourer had forced the early, powerful enchantresses of this village generations ago into an agreement that sacrificed one of their own just to appease it, it must have powerful magic. She gambled that its magic might be strong enough to fix the ward.

But what could she offer it that it didn't already have? She didn't even know what it was or why it wanted an offering.

All at once, she knew what she must do.

She'd make a bargain with the Devourer.

She'd be its next offering and offer the rest of her life to it if it could fix the ward.

Others would have to repair the ward. While she was one of the strongest magic wielders, others could repair it. But perhaps more than that, many of the enchantresses had families in Shadowbank—people who loved them and would miss them. People who would die in a few decades with their far shorter lifespans. Arabella had only the enchantresses. She would be the least missed out of everyone.

But if she struck a bargain with the demon, there would be no going back.

Bargains were currency, and they were binding. A broken bargain could bring the wrath of the Yrenes upon her. But even if they didn't draw the hellish creatures to them, the magic of this world would force them back together.

Careful not to wake Jessamine, Cora, or Brynne, Arabella rose from the bed, dressed, packed a bag, and left a note for her friends. They'd try to stop her, which she couldn't allow. There was no way she'd let her family volunteer and put themselves at risk. Not when there was something she could do about it.

Without knowing what kind of dark creature it was, it would

be a risk whether it could help them. But it would be worth it if the ward could be repaired.

For my family, I can do this. I will *do this.*

Without another word, she snuck out of the village, passing coins to one guard who opened the front gates for her. Eyes on the line of trees before her, she strode forward, weaponless but not defenseless.

The shadows rumbled around her, slowly acquiescing to the rising sun.

Come to me, she thought. *And I'll make you a bargain you can't refuse.*

Chapter Five

ARABELLA

Arabella strode into the forest on the third day, welcoming the wild shadows.

Every instinct inside of her screamed to run, to turn around and flee this place before the monsters noticed her presence. But that was exactly what she was there for—to find a monster. Or in this case, a demon.

A pack over a shoulder, she walked until all she could see were trees in every direction, the walls of Shadowbank long behind her. She forced herself to move with her usual practical stride, not allowing herself to show fear despite her racing heart.

She would not be prey.

"I'm here," she called into the trees, which swallowed her words into its eerie silence. Even the shadows did strange things, seeming to ripple outwards. She pushed her hood back, revealing her face and the chains woven into her hair. Let the demon see her.

"You want your offering? Come get me."

A chill crept through her leathers and sent a wave of gooseflesh up her arms.

"I've brought no weapons." She spoke into the surrounding trees, dropping her pack to the ground and opening it. She'd filled it with as many potions and tinctures as she had clothes. Who knew what medicines demons had? And what if she needed tinctures to heal after... Well, after whatever it intended to do with her.

While her fingers itched for the reassuring weight of her two swords, she worried that if she was armed and the Devourer appeared, it may think she'd come to kill it rather than broker a deal.

So, she reached for her magic instead, weaves at the ready. But as the minutes turned to hours, her grip on the weaves loosened. There had been faint rustling of small forest animals, but it had otherwise been painfully quiet.

Had the Devourer already seen her, found her lacking, and turned away?

It had accepted only female offerings for the last several decades—young women, specifically. Thus, it seemed this creature preferred females and those of childbearing age. Did it have other preferences?

Arabella wasn't unbecoming. She was lean and of average height with a muscled build. She had thick, dark hair to her mid-back and dark eyes. It was rare that anyone had refused her advances, which she'd assumed meant the average person found her attractive. But would *this* creature? Would it not only accept her as an offering but also be willing to make a bargain?

Now isn't the time to second-guess yourself, she thought.

Hours later, she sat on the ground, yanking on her braid. If only she knew where its home was, she'd have traveled straight for it even with the risk of encountering other demons of the forest. It was better than sitting and waiting for something to find her.

Suddenly, there was rustling in the trees, and she stood and spun.

It was quiet once more.

She scanned the trees. A moment later, a flash of movement caught her eye, and she turned toward it.

Was it a demon of the forest coming to feast on the flesh of a foolish woman who dared to step into its territory? Could it be the very demon she sought or something else entirely?

"I'm here to make a bargain," she said, hoping like hell it was the Devourer.

A chuckle rumbled from deep in the surrounding trees, and for a moment, it felt like her blood froze in her veins. Her heartbeat rang in her ears when she felt it—more power than she'd ever sensed in her time as an enchantress. Sheer power emanated from whatever this demon was, billowing out into the trees. It wasn't visible to the human eye, but Arabella could sense a darker magic roiling and rumbling around her as it moved.

As movement flashed around her yet again, she realized she could sense whatever it was as it moved from shadow to shadow unnaturally fast—just as she could a few days ago. Could it manipulate shadows like her?

A deep voice spoke from somewhere in the trees. "I knew you'd return." The sound moved in a circle as though it came from all around at once. Whatever it was, it was closing in. "What could an enchantress offer that I'd desire?"

She swallowed, hands opening and closing into fists. "Are you the Devourer?"

"That's what the humans call me," came the voice.

It sounded similar to the creature she'd encountered a few days ago, but she couldn't be certain. And she wasn't about to make a deal with a rogue demon. Somehow, she needed to make sure this was the Devourer.

"What's the name of your last human offering?"

There was a chuckle and then, "Scarlett."

She breathed a sigh of relief. So, it *was* the creature. At least, she didn't think another demon would know that. At least, she wouldn't be killed in vain by a random demon. If it happened, it would be on purpose—or out of spite.

"I'll be your next offering," she said, her throat dry. "In exchange for—"

"There's no exchange." The creature's words rippled through

the shadows and into the quiet forest air. "Other than the one that has already been agreed to."

"I wasn't done speaking." She fisted her hands at her sides, willing them not to shake. "In exchange for my services and compliance for the next ten years, I want a way to strengthen Shadowbank's ward."

She hated admitting the village's weakness, but she held on to hope that this creature wouldn't be able to do anything with this knowledge since it had agreed to the ten-year offerings—which included leaving the villagers in peace.

"You offer something that has already been promised."

Its tone was matter of fact, bored.

There was another flash of movement, and then a figure stood before her.

The first thing her eyes landed on was a male chest as wide as a mountain and dressed in what appeared to be a black long-sleeved shirt and matching vest with crossing laces. Gaze shifting upward, she noted hair as dark as hers but with ringlet curls instead of her soft waves. Slowly, she looked upward until her gaze connected with the demon's.

Only, it wasn't a demon—or at least it didn't appear like one. No, it was a handsome male dressed entirely in black. His eyes were as lonely as the sea, and she found herself wanting to reach out and touch his light brown skin, which appeared soft, and run her fingers through his hair before pulling him down to her.

How strange.

She'd never been this drawn to a person so soon after meeting them before, and never one that was part demon.

I mustn't forget that.

Unable to stop herself, she said, "You're... a man."

A wicked smile traced his lips. "Not all demons have fangs and claws."

She realized then she had expected a creature of bones like nightwalkers or a clawed beast that walked on all fours like the fengrine. She'd expected something inhuman. But this demon wasn't that way at all. In fact, he was the most handsome male she had ever seen.

She shook herself. "Do we have a deal?"

His smile dropped, and he was once again all cold detachment. "No. You've offered me nothing more than what I already possess."

She stiffened at the reminder that she was his for the next decade. A thought struck her. "You have my services during my term as your offering. But you do not have my compliance."

He raised a brow.

"I will make your life hell for the next ten years unless you agree to this."

He chuckled, turning his back toward her as he strode toward the deeper part of the forest. The gesture said one thing: he didn't find her a threat. Else, why expose his back to her?

"A feisty one," he said over a shoulder. "This next decade shall be interesting."

She was losing him. He was going to take her to his home and soon, and then she'd lose any bargaining power once he locked her away.

There was a rumbling in the shadows, and she sensed he was about to lurch back into them, but she said, *"Wait!"*

The word sounded like a plea, but—luckily—he paused.

"I'll give you everything. I offer you the rest of my life. Not just ten years. You won't need to take any other offerings. I'll comply willingly... if you can fix the ward or create a new one."

She'd never see Jessamine, Iris, or any of the other enchantresses again. The thought was like a stake to the heart. She'd never get the chance to say goodbye.

I have to save them, my family. That will make this worth it.

She'd be alone, but her family would be safe.

A look of what she could only describe as hunger passed through his eyes before one of indifference replaced it. "You would offer me the rest of your days?"

He made a show of considering it, glancing at the trees and taking a few steps as though deep in thought.

Then he looked to her, his dark eyes blazing, and said, "No."

Her mouth hung open.

No? That was it? No counteroffer? No explanation?

She started to protest, but he said, "I'm not interested in any further bargains with mortals."

A weight settled atop her shoulders and wrists before it disappeared.

The magic of bargains.

"Now, little enchantress, for the next ten years, you're mine."

In a swirl of motion, he was before her, pressing a cloth to her mouth. She blinked as sleep took over, her eyelids growing heavy.

Her knees went out, and a large arm scooped her up before her world turned black.

A LOUD CREAKING sound pulled Arabella from unconsciousness before she was lying on the ground, her boots touching stone floors.

Her first thought was to wonder if she was in a prison cell. Was that how Scarlett spent her days?

"You drugged me." Her lips tingled and moved slowly. She pushed herself to a seated position, trying to blink back the sleepiness lingering at the corners of her mind.

"None know the location of my home. I intend to keep it that way."

The voice was everywhere and nowhere, both eerie and melodic.

Looking around, she was in what appeared to be the entryway of a large, stone castle. The space was cloaked in shadow with only wisps of light coming through windows several stories up. Across the space was a massive staircase that led from the entryway to a landing that then had two branching staircases going up in different directions. But even more than the dated decadence was the silence. The place felt... abandoned.

Instinctively, she reached for her enchantress magic, preparing to defend herself, but something burned at her neck before she could even form a weave. Pain lanced through her as her skin throbbed in protest. Then a weight on her neck that she hadn't realized was there cooled as soon as she released her magic. Gasping, she drew her fingers up to it, recognizing at once what it was.

A collar that suppressed elemental magic.

It was so rare that not even the Circle had it in the Quarter's dungeons. How had a demon gotten a hold of it? One thing was certain—she wouldn't be able to use her enchantress abilities until she could get this thing off her, and she didn't know how it was removed.

"Are you that scared of me that you put me in a collar?" she demanded, fury roiling in her veins.

The creature was nowhere to be seen. But once again, she could feel him at the corner of the room, lurking in the shadows.

Blinking, she realized she could still use her shadow magic. It appeared the collar didn't stop the darker magics—it only kept her from accessing the earth, air, and other elements. Which meant the demon didn't know what else she could do. It was a minor victory, but a victory all the same.

She tried to stand, but her legs twisted in her bag's straps, and she collapsed into a heap on the floor.

There was a soft chuckle from the shadows. "This is simply a precaution until we can learn to... trust each other."

"It's hard to trust someone after this kind of first impression," Arabella said. "First you refuse to make a bargain, then you drug me and strip me of my powers."

He didn't respond, only moving from one shadow to the next, never staying in one place for long.

"The women you take—what do you use them for?" she asked, finally managing to stand.

The terrified part of her needed to know what she was in for

—and when the agony would start. Because there was no way an offering was made to a forest demon without there being some sacrifice. Would there be torture? Bloodletting? Hard labor?

In the back of her mind, she recalled how Scarlett didn't look unwell or undernourished. But if this wasn't just one long, torturous imprisonment, just what did he have her here for?

Suddenly, his presence was behind her.

Jumping, she spun around.

His dark eyes grew to the deepest midnight as though his pupils consumed the rest of his irises until most of his eyes were black just like Lucinda's had.

There was something magnetic about him now, even more than before. His sharp, chiseled features hardened further, and his light brown skin glowed as though emitting the sun's rays. Muscles broadened, and it felt like his wide shoulders were larger than they had been in the forest. His beauty was so overwhelming that it became painful to look at him.

Heart racing, she found herself unable to draw a full breath. Her chest heaved, and her breasts pressed uncomfortably against her corset, hardened nipples rubbing against the fabric.

A deep yearning filled her chest. She wanted to learn the feel of him—the hills and valleys of the muscles along his biceps, down to the narrowing in his forearms, and even farther down...

Unbidden, she reached out, her fingers touching his shirt.

He was a mystery to her, and she wanted to unwrap him and learn every curve, every part of his body. Better yet, she wanted him to unwrap *her*.

Suddenly, her leathers felt far too tight.

Realizing her hands had started moving up and down his sides and reaching for the waist of his pants where his shirt was tucked in, she pulled back as though scorched. She shook her head as though that would dispel the lust clouding her thoughts. What was *wrong* with her? This was a demon—her captor, *not* a lover. Even knowing that, it felt like her self-control had been sucked into the shadows, devoured, and spat back out onto her boots.

Maybe if she put some distance between them, some sense would return to her.

She took one step back and then another. Something hard scraped against her back, and she realized she'd backed into a wall. When she looked up, he was before her once more, and she jumped.

Damn rabbit, she thought. He was so fast and moved soundlessly.

His arms were on either side of her, pinning her against the wall. There was no escaping him and this strange magnetism. His presence was everywhere, encircling her like morning mist on a scorched hillside. She was surrounded by muscles and waves of sheer power.

Slowly, his hand moved until he held her chin between his thumb and forefinger. He smelled of mint, citrus, and pine.

"You're far more skittish than I thought you'd be after our first encounter." He studied her as though assessing a prized stallion before a smirk traced his lips. "I can also sense you're far more willing."

"I don't know what you're talking about." Even as she spoke, desire stirred within her, heat gathering in her core. "What are you?"

She had to focus hard, *too hard*, on voicing that question.

Why were her thoughts muddying? All she could think of was what his hands would feel like roaming over the length of her and those sinful lips and tongue on her most sensitive flesh.

"No guesses?"

The words were a caress against her neck.

"The kind that has a habit of accosting females and drugging them, clearly."

She hoped her tone would have him stepping back, but he didn't move, didn't release her chin. Instead, he studied her intently with those unnaturally dark eyes.

Another wave of desire coursed through her, rolling over her like the ocean's tide, and she quickly looked away from him. It was all she could do to keep her hands at her sides, his body bracketing her in. She was a breath away from pulling him into her and grinding against him.

She was an enchantress. Enchantresses were sworn to protect humans from demons of the wild shadows. There could be no attraction between them.

"Eyes on me, little enchantress."

"Obedience wasn't part of the bargain," she said, eyes fixed on the stone wall across the room. "You didn't repair the ward, so I'm going to be a thorn in your side for the next decade."

A chuckle rumbled through him, and he was so close that she could feel it vibrate in his chest.

"Be careful. I like a challenge," he said, gently turning her head. "But I will have your obedience. One way or another."

He leaned forward, tracing his tongue over the sensitive flesh on her neck. A shiver rolled through her. Then his lips were moving, kissing up and down her neck, her collarbone, nipping at her skin. When he released her chin and wrapped an arm around her lower back, pulling her body so she was pressed against him.

She yearned to touch him, to feel the warmth of his skin, but she refused to give in to this. He hadn't agreed to her bargain, and she wouldn't make this easy.

All the while, his lips and tongue moved across what little skin was above her black leathers, and she could feel herself growing wet. Hell, her undergarments were likely soaked.

A distant part of her wanted them *off,* wanted nothing between them—nothing but flesh against flesh, his skin on hers. She didn't care if they fucked on the hard, cold stone floor as long as he was inside of her, filling her with his cock.

What in the hell was she *thinking*? She didn't want this demon.

She realized suddenly that his cock was very large and very hard. It pressed into her stomach from beneath his pants.

Realization dawned.

He wanted her, too.

That thought sent hot bolts of lust through her. This feeling was unlike anything she'd ever experienced. It was an all-consuming desire she'd never felt before.

She also knew that even if she'd had her enchantress magic, even if she could control her shadows, there was no overpowering this demon. His power far exceeded hers, and her abilities were insignificant in comparison. He could force himself on her, and she'd have no way of stopping him.

At that moment, it was a kind of relief to allow him to move her body, to touch her as he wished. Then she didn't have to fully acknowledge how much she didn't want him to stop.

The demon's lips moved to the other side of her neck before skirting down. There was a prickle on her skin and then the sound of tearing fabric. Cool air kissed her breasts, and her nipples pebbled.

Glancing down, she saw the leathers of her top and corset were cut neatly down the center.

"What... have you... done... to my... corset?"

Her breaths were ragged gasps as her hips tried to move of their own accord, to rub against his hard body. But she forced herself to remain still.

"Gotten it out of the way."

His voice was deeper than before, almost inhuman. Leaving her neck, he kissed his way down her collarbone, in the dip between her breasts, to the sensitive flesh beneath one of her breasts. His tongue flicked back and forth, and she longed for him to pull her nipple into his mouth and *suck*.

Some distant part of her wondered what had gotten into her, and she knew she should care. It had to be some kind of magic.

A hand encircled her neck, pinning her in place against the wall. Desire made her mind swim, but she refused to be used so easily. Bringing her hands up, she tried to pull his hand from her neck. But no matter what she tried, he was as immovable as a mountain.

As she fought, his other hand encircled one of her breasts,

squeezing it before his mouth closed around her nipple. Something between a sigh and a moan escaped her lips. The idea of him using her body to slate his needs heightened her desire.

She brought her arm down, landing a hit to his cheek with her elbow. He merely grunted and released her breast before grabbing both of her wrists in a single hand and holding them above her head.

"You can try to pretend you don't want this," he purred in her ear. "But I can scent your desire."

As he spoke, he reached a hand down and pressed a single finger between her legs right where she could feel the swell of her clit against her pants. He moved from her clit to her opening and back in a slow, steady motion. To her shock, she nearly orgasmed, a wave of pleasure almost crashing over her from a *single touch*.

Over. Her. Pants.

"Such a wanton little thing," he rumbled. "So eager for my hand."

Pressure built in her core and between her legs. Although she'd never come with a man while fucking before, she knew what was happening. She'd come enough times from touching herself that she could feel her body cresting, hovering at the edge.

"I don't want this."

Maybe I want this.

A wicked smile brightened his features, contrasting his fully black eyes and the dark beauty that had her blinking back tears.

"Keep telling yourself that."

She should be mortified. Instead, her hips moved of their own accord in time with his touch even as she pulled at his hold on her wrists—to no avail.

"That's it," he said. "Fuck my fingers."

She teetered on the edge, about to tip over. Then the pressure of his touch increased, and she couldn't hold on any longer. She thrust into his hand—once, twice, three times—and then she was coming undone.

An orgasm crashed into her, and she cried out as she rode his hand. He sucked on her breasts as though he was a starving man at a feast. Some sound escaped his lips, and she thought it was a moan, but she couldn't be sure. All she knew were the waves of pleasure crashing over her as she took in one ragged breath and then the next.

But the waves of pleasure didn't stop. They kept going, far longer than she'd ever experienced. She bucked against his fingers, ravenous for his touch. As she did, something inside her chest hummed. It was like the tingling of the earth after a thunderstorm when the magic was raw and wild. Another moan escaped her lips, and then he was before her, catching it with his mouth. The energy inside her chest crested and hummed louder in response, and somehow, it increased her pleasure.

Something slipped from between her lips. A crackling blue light floated in the air between them, illuminating the dark entryway. It flowed out of her, and he pulled it into his mouth. As he did, another orgasm hit her, and it was all she could do to remain standing, her back arching as she screamed in pleasure. The blue light poured out of her lips as her pleasure peaked. He captured it with his lips. As he did, the brown color of his eyes returned, his pupils shrinking until they were once more almost human.

His hand dropped from her pussy, and she bit her cheek to stop herself from protesting. Her whole body ached, all but screaming for his touch.

It wasn't enough.

All at once, she realized what he was.

"You're... an erox."

The offerings the founders of Shadowbank had agreed to weren't just for any demon. It was for an immortal demon that fed off sexual energy. And she was at his mercy for the next ten years.

The corner of his lips quirked up in a wicked grin.

"Indeed."

His eyes skirted down to where her breasts were bare before him and then back up. "Welcome to your new home. As of today, you—and that fine pussy—are mine."

Chapter Six

ARABELLA

The erox escorted Arabella up the stairs and down several long hallways in complete silence. Her bag had disappeared, and she held the remains of her top together. Beside her, she purposefully ignored the way his muscled arms swayed as he walked.

She wondered what he'd look like with nothing on.

Stop it, she chastised herself, holding on to the anger swirling in her chest. It was far better to feel that than allow herself to think about just how much she wanted this demon to touch her —and how he was the only male she'd ever orgasmed with.

Stopping before a large door, he opened it, revealing a canopied bed with dark curtains and... were those ropes at the four corners?

"Welcome to your new home," he said, voice infuriatingly sultry. "This is where you will stay. You may decorate the room however you'd like."

She couldn't help but note that, while his voice held a hint of allure, his eyes were stone cold. They were so distant compared to the molten desire she'd seen swirling in them only minutes ago.

He pointed to a wardrobe along one wall. "Your new clothes

are in there. You will no longer wear your enchantress garb when I am at the castle."

Frowning, she strode to the wardrobe and opened it to reveal a wardrobe full of short dresses that would go to her mid-thigh at best, many of which were at least somewhat see-through. There were some floor-length gowns as well along with sweaters and cloaks.

"Where are my undergarments? Corsets? Busts? Pants?"

In a flash of movement, the shadows in the room crackled, and he was before her. His hand encircled her neck, and his other arm wrapped around her waist, pulling her into him. Her heart raced, and her back arched into him.

What is happening to me?

"I will have access to your body. That is my rule." Fiery embers replaced the coldness in his eyes. She wondered what would happen if they were fully aflame. "I can feed off you regardless of if my cock is involved. But... we will see how long you last without it."

Mischief sparked in his eyes, full of suggestion. It was all she could do not to close the distance between their lips.

"That won't be a request you'll hear from my lips." It took significant effort to ignore the way her pussy clenched at the thought.

"Oh no, little enchantress. You must *beg* for it."

Her face flushed.

That would never happen.

She was an enchantress, and she'd been taught since she'd been found outside the forest that demons were the enemy of mankind. Hundreds of enchantresses and humans over the years had died because of them. But on a personal level, this demon had refused to bargain with her, had refused to help Shadowbank. She felt tricked, and she couldn't forgive that.

No matter what her body seemed to think of him, she wouldn't give in to him or his magic. He would have to force her every step of the way to feed on her, and she'd *never* ask for his cock. And all the while, she was going to learn everything she could about his magic to help save Shadowbank while not violating the agreement as his offering.

"What happens if I don't wear these?" She gestured to the dresses behind her.

A wicked smile spread across his face. "Then you will walk around naked."

In an instant, she grew wet between her legs.

It was as though she hadn't orgasmed multiple times.

She pursed her lips in an attempt to keep her expression neutral.

He took a step back, putting distance between them.

"Eat, rest, bathe. I will see you tomorrow."

To her surprise, a bowl of what must be stew was on a table beside the window. Steam wafted up, and her stomach growled in response. How had that gotten there? She'd seen no one else in the castle, and he'd been with her the whole time.

The glass-paned window revealed a starry night sky. Somehow, an entire day had passed. Scanning the rest of the room, she noted a large bathing chamber in the corner of the room.

Something occurred to her, and she turned back to him.

"Wait, I don't even know your—"

In a swirl of motion, he was gone, and the door closed behind him.

"Name."

Sighing, she glanced between the wardrobe and the table beside the window.

What have I gotten myself into?

THE NEXT MORNING, Arabella woke up to the smell of eggs and potatoes. She rose from the bed, stomach already rumbling. In fact, she was so hungry that it felt like she'd battled the fengrine all over again and needed to eat to regain her strength. Was that the cost of the erox feeding on her? She supposed she'd find out soon enough.

She sat down and ate. While the food was rich, she already missed her food in the village.

One of the main reasons the villagers stayed in a land so unfriendly to humans was because the ground was fertile. It was perfect for crops—so long as the workers could defend themselves from any monsters that appeared from the surrounding forest. The ward wasn't big enough to extend out over the farms. As such, working out in the fields was one of the most dangerous jobs in Shadowbank.

Rising, she donned one of the frilly dresses from the wardrobe, cursing. Even though she had every intention of fighting him during her time here, she wasn't about to risk having to walk around the castle naked. What if she finally encountered servants? Or worse, what if she encountered other demons?

As she ate her breakfast, cool air kissed her skin, and goose-flesh rippled along her pale arms. After a minute, she donned a long sweater as well.

Now what?

Was she expected to wait in her room until Mr. Nameless sought her out? Surely, he couldn't expect her to remain in here all day, every day.

She paused, noting her pack on a lounge chair by the door. Glancing inside, all of her tinctures were still there, but her leathers and other clothes were gone. She rolled her eyes.

This was ridiculous.

Why didn't he simply schedule a time with her each day to consume her essence and allow her to exist in peace—and clothed in her leathers—for the remaining hours? This had to be some twisted attempt to strip her of her identity. But his efforts would be in vain. She may not remember her childhood, but she would always remember the family that had taken her in. The family she was here to protect.

Spotting her head chains in her bag, she grabbed it and wove it into her hair before braiding her dark waves. She couldn't help but wonder, if he'd taken her leathers and stripped her of the items that identified her as an enchantress, why leave her headpiece behind?

Slipping her feet into her black leather boots, she strode out into the hallway. She paused on a carpet that ran the length of the entire hallway with at least ten doors to what she presumed were similar suites.

Which way?

She wasn't even sure where the front door was nor where the kitchens were. She'd been so preoccupied with what happened between them in the entryway that she neglected to remain aware of her surroundings. Now, light streamed through the windows throughout the hallway, making the space feel... peaceful—if a castle with a demon as its host could be called such a thing.

Glancing either way, she didn't spot a single servant walking by. Where was the castle staff? Who had made her breakfast and dropped it in her room without her noticing? She wasn't the lightest sleeper, but neither was she a heavy sleeper. Surely, she would've awoken at the sound of her door opening.

Sighing, she turned and strode down the right hallway. It was as good a direction as any. She opened each door she walked by, glancing inside. Most were indeed unoccupied suites, many of which had furniture covered by sheets. There wasn't a speck of dust in any of them.

As she moved, the shadows tickled the edge of her senses. At this time of the day, the shadows were fewer and pressed more lightly on her mind. But as she moved, the shadows wiggled as though small footsteps trod on them around her. Turning, she glanced around the suite she'd just opened the door to and saw no one. There wasn't even a sound. Glancing back into the hallway, there was no one there either. And yet, as she walked further into the castle, the hairs on the back of her neck prickled as though pairs of eyes followed her as she moved.

Fucking creepy.

It was something Jessamine would say if she were here. The thought of her friend had her chest clenching and hot tears forming at the corners of her eyes. Swallowing back the tightness in her throat, she took several deep breaths.

Now wasn't the time to succumb to the overwhelming sense of loss creeping in at the corners of her mind. There would be time for her to mourn the loss of time later. Right now, she had to get her bearings. Once she got a lay of the castle, she would do whatever she could to learn about the demon's magic. Perhaps there would be a library. There had to be something she could use to figure out how to repair and strengthen the ward.

After she'd gone down what seemed like a dozen hallways, she paused, leaning against a windowsill that overlooked the castle grounds. There was an area of gardens and walkways, beyond which was the massive forest as far as the eye could see in all directions. Leaning forward, she tried to spot any break in the trees, but there was none. Shadowbank could be beyond her line of sight or in another direction she couldn't see from this vantage point. She moved down more hallways. Even after looking north, east, west, and south, she still couldn't spot a break in the trees, though there was a body of water on one side of the castle.

There was no sign of the village.

Clenching her hands into fists, she strode into the nearest room. Unlike the countless others she'd seen, sheets didn't cover the furniture in this room. The window shutters were closed, and the fireplace had half-burnt logs inside of them. Frowning, she moved to open the shutters. A plume of dust billowed into the air, and she coughed, waving a hand. There was a quilt atop a four-poster bed that had likely once been beautiful in its ornate patterns, but they were subdued by a layer of dust—as was the fabric overhanging the canopy. Both the quilt and curtains seemed to have once been a deep maroon. But now, it was a gray-purple color.

As she walked, she wondered why this room felt so different

from the others. It wasn't just the layer of dust. It was as though someone once stayed here, and no one had touched it since.

Who could have lived here? Scarlett would have inhabited her quarters recently. There wouldn't have been enough time since her departure to accumulate this much dust. Had it been the offering before Scarlett?

She strode over to the wardrobe.

I wonder if this person was required to wear dresses, too.

Had their pussy been open to the air, ready for their nameless lord's pleasure at a moment's notice—if they begged for his cock? Or had they been content to be fed on and nothing more? Had they wanted to be touched by him and not fucked? The thoughts brought her back to last night and the multiple orgasms he'd given her after hardly touching her.

Pulling the wardrobe doors open, she found an array of beautiful gowns from decades past. The style of the cut and the type of fabric implied they were of the fashions from decades (or even centuries) ago. It was the first time she thought to wonder just how old this erox was.

"Find what you were looking for?" a male voice hissed.

Jumping, she smacked her head on the top of the wardrobe. She rubbed her scalp and turned to the erox.

Something in his tone had her heart thudding in her chest, the hair on the back of her neck standing on end. Instinct had her standing on the pads of her feet, ready to run.

"I didn't hear you enter," she said.

"No, you wouldn't."

Even the shadows hadn't whispered to her. Perhaps she'd felt too many strange presences in the castle that it cluttered up whatever ability she had to detect this demon's nearness.

She swallowed, feeling the weight of the collar around her neck.

As the day before, she couldn't help but notice that he was strikingly handsome. The sun from the open window seemed to kiss the light brown skin peeking through his white long-sleeved shirt. The laces hung loose, revealing the top of a large, muscled chest. He also wore tight black pants that left nothing to the imagination along with knee-high leather boots. Curly black hair came to his shoulders in neat spirals, blocking the sun from his face. But even without seeing his face, she knew he was furious.

Anger billowed off him in waves, seeming to thin the air.

She couldn't form words as her eyes locked with his shadowed gaze, and he stalked towards her.

"Get *out.*"

The two words were so filled with menace that it made her heart skitter, and she backed toward the open door.

"You didn't tell me I couldn't walk around the castle—" she began, but he interrupted.

"If I see you enter this room again, you will live to regret it."

She wanted to ask just what he meant, but she only backed away. She realized then that she was nothing more than prey and he the predator.

"I'm in a generous mood. So, I will give you a chance to run." His voice was low as he stalked toward her. "I'll give you a thirty-second head start. If you make it outside, I won't punish you for entering this room."

Just what did that *mean?*

She didn't know where she was nor where the main entrance to the castle was, but she wasn't about to wait around. The menace in his dark gaze had her fear spiking and her heart racing.

Turning, she ran.

She raced down the hallway, making several turns.

Where is the door? Where is it?

After turning down more hallways, she found herself before a massive set of stairs that led down to what appeared to be an entryway.

The entryway from last night.

At the opposite end of the room that was as long as it was tall —sweeping multiple stories upwards—was a large door. She ran down the stairs, feeling her dress billow behind her, her ass visible to anyone looking.

I'm going to make it, she thought.

She was almost at the landing at the center of the staircase when she heard pounding footsteps behind her.

The erox.

He could move as quietly as the shadows themselves. But instead of doing so, he moved loud enough for her to hear. Realization dawned. He wanted her to hear him—to know how close he was... and how she was utterly helpless.

He was toying with her.

Her foot hadn't so much as touched the landing on the grand staircase when arms wrapped around her, and she went down. The air knocked out of her in a rush, but it wasn't hard enough to hurt. Instead, the motion was surprisingly gentle. Legs were on either side of her back as she lay on her stomach, and one of his hands wrapped around her wrists, pinning them behind her. His body shifted, and she felt the tickle of his breath against her ear.

"You're a naughty little thing—going around the castle without my permission." Instead of the anger she'd expected to hear, the sultry tone had returned to his voice. "But you obeyed my orders to wear a dress."

For a moment, it felt as though a gust of wind swept through the room, caressing her legs.

"How should I punish you?"

He leaned upright, and she could no longer feel his breath against her ear.

Despite herself, desire swam through her at his nearness, building between her legs until her breaths grew ragged. She knew exactly what she *wanted* him to do, but she wasn't about to say it.

There was a light touch of his fingers between her legs, tracing her inner thigh.

"Do you want me to fuck you, little enchantress?"

Yes.

"No." Her heart skittered in her chest, but she refused to give in to this demon no matter what he made her body feel. The attraction she felt was all from his magic. It couldn't possibly have anything to do with her.

But some part of her knew she was lying... or at least, it wasn't entirely true.

"I told you before," he continued, a finger moving lazily across her inner thigh. "If you want my cock, you must ask."

She bit her lip as his finger drew close to her pussy but didn't touch where she needed it, where she craved him.

"Since this is your first full day here, I'll ask a second time. Do you want me?"

Unable to speak the lie, she shook her head.

Then a single finger swept over her clit and into her wet folds, and she gasped. She felt him move and glimpsed him rubbing his fingers together, seeing the evidence of her lie. He tsked.

"Even now, your body knows what it wants. Yet you deny yourself." He leaned back down toward her, pressing a finger into her mouth, and she tasted her salty desire. "Suck it."

For a moment, she did as he said, wrapping her tongue around his large finger. Realizing what she was doing, she stopped and bit down on his finger *hard*.

Like hell was she going to just do what this demon said. He'd refused to bargain with her, and he'd have to suffer the consequences.

He'd have to suffer her.

Pulling his hand free, he grabbed her hair in a fist and pulled back. She grunted as her head snapped back. Though once again, it wasn't rough enough to truly hurt. But the prickle of pain along her scalp stirred something deep within her. Some part of her liked that he took control of her—that for once in her life, she didn't have to make decisions on behalf of an entire village or on behalf of the Circle. Instead, he moved her body as he pleased, doing with her as he wanted, and the release of control felt intoxicating. Almost as intoxicating as feeling his body pressed against hers.

"Never do that again," he hissed. Then he leaned upright and said in a casual tone, "I've never encountered an offering so wanton as you—nor one so intent on convincing themselves that they don't want this."

That was impossible. The enchantresses who were offerings before her would have resisted him, and so would she. She was an enchantress—sworn to protect the realm from monsters like him. She couldn't—*wouldn't*—give in to a demon.

"Your body is mine." Releasing her hair, he swept a finger across her wet pussy again. "And I take care of what is mine." His fingers slowed, moving in lazy circles. It wasn't the pressure she craved, and he knew it. "But you know what I need to hear before I'll grant you any release."

Desire swirled through her so strongly, making her heart race and muddying her thoughts. She found her hips moving as she tried to grind against his fingers. She was on the cusp of coming already. His words had her on the edge.

"Ah-ah." He removed his hand from her center, though he still held her wrists in his other hand, pinning them behind her back. "You know what you must do, little enchantress."

"Arabella," she managed, her voice sounding breathy. "My name is Arabella."

He rumbled somewhere above her. "A lovely name for a lovely little thing."

Something warmed inside her at hearing that he found her attractive.

A thumb found her ass, and he traced her entrance. To her surprise, she gasped, and the desire swirling through her grew hotter.

"You may call me Elias. When we are fucking, you will call me sir or master."

Another finger was on her pussy, just barely pressing inside of her, the other tracing circles around her ass. She groaned.

"Are you on birth control?"

The question surprised her. Could demons impregnate

females? She hadn't thought it possible. It took her a moment before she said, "Yes."

"Good."

Her bare legs pressed into the cool stone of the landing.

They were in the middle of the large entryway, and if servants were tending to the castle, they could walk by. They'd see her short dress hiked up obscenely and the master of the castle pinning her to the ground with her arms behind her back.

She heard a shifting of fabric as though he unbuttoned his trousers. Then he pulled her hips upward, arching her toward him while keeping one hand on her wrists. Her face pressed onto the ground. The position should feel degrading. But it only made her grow wetter.

Was he really going to fuck her after saying she had to beg for his cock?

"Last chance," he said from somewhere above her. "Ask me nicely, and perhaps I'll give you what you want."

The cool air against her pussy had her hips rolling as she waited for him to press into her, to feel the head of his silky cock.

"If you want me, you'll have to take me," she said.

"Soon, little enchantress. Soon."

Hands still holding her wrists, she felt him shift before she heard a faint slapping sound and felt him stiffen behind her. Looking over a shoulder, her eyes widened as she saw his hand wrapped around his enormous cock. His cock wasn't long but wide, and it curved up at the end.

She licked her lips as she watched his hand move in steady strokes.

"You wish you were touching me, don't you?"

She swallowed thickly, turning her head back so that she was looking away—unable to move from where he straddled her.

"I could be fucking your pussy," he purred. "You could have had several orgasms by now. Instead, you get to listen as only one of us finds release."

His movements grew more jagged, quickening, before they stopped. She frowned, about to look over her shoulder again, when large hands flipped her, and she was on her back.

"What—" she began, but his legs were on either side of her, pinning her down.

Then he grabbed her wrists again, holding them over her head. His other hand returned to his cock, moving in faster strokes.

Her mouth watered as she watched a bead of moisture form at the tip, and her hips thrust upward and into his ass. She pressed her legs together, desperate for a release, for any kind of friction.

"Not so fast," he purred as he leaned down, his lips a breath away from hers. But he didn't kiss her. Instead, he leaned back upright, working his length.

His body stiffened, and his hand moved in jerking motions. Then warmth splattered across her stomach and chest as he came. She watched as his eyes rolled back and fluttered closed before he released a heavy exhale. The sight of it had her hips moving again, brushing against him.

Releasing her, he removed a handkerchief from his pocket and wiped her clean of his seed before he rose to his feet and tucked his cock back into his pants.

Still on the ground where he'd left her, she sat upright.

"You won't get my cock until you prove you can obey me," he said. "I don't need your pussy to feed. Though, of course, your pleasure would taste far sweeter." He turned to leave, then paused and looked back at her. "One more thing—you're forbidden to touch yourself unless I tell you otherwise."

Without another word, he turned and disappeared—gone in an instant. He was so fast, she could hardly see his movement. Then she was alone in the foyer.

For a moment, she lay there on the ground, sexual frustration making her thoughts spin. Then one thought pushed to the forefront.

Fuck him so very much.

How *dare* he toy with her like that? How dare he be angry at her for going into a room *he* didn't tell her was off-limits and then try to chase her out of the castle like he was an animal?

Like he was a demon.

Anger unfurled in her chest, spreading throughout her whole body, until it was all she could feel. Some distant part of her knew it was better to feel that than admit what she truly felt—that she wanted him to fuck her. Dissatisfaction swirled through her mind distantly, and her body ached to be filled, but she quickly squashed it.

One thing was certain. There was no way he was telling her what she could or couldn't do with her body, and there was certainly no way she'd be listening to some demon... or wanting one.

I'm an enchantress, and enchantresses don't want *to fuck demons.*

Somehow, this—her sacrifice—would all be worth it.

She reminded herself that she'd protected her family from one evil. Although she'd sought to both protect them from the Devourer and fix the ward, she'd at least achieved one of the two things she'd set out to do. Even without the bargain to repair the ward, by coming here, she'd kept Jessamine and the others from volunteering and giving up ten years of her life. Plus, she'd see her family again—in a decade. Now, she'd use her time there to search for something to repair the ward.

She had to focus on that. But even as she tried to turn her thoughts, her mind strayed to the erox and how much she wanted to wrap her lips around his thick cock.

Running a hand over her face, she stood and headed for her rooms and the bath, determined to wash every trace of this demon off of her.

There was no way she was going to fuck him—or as he put it, to *beg* him to fuck her.

KISSED BY A DEMON

He might wear the face of a man, but beneath it was the heart and desires of a demon—to consume and devour and ravage all life.

He was something she could never want.

Chapter Seven

ARABELLA

Arabella decided this demon would be an idiot to not have a ward.

With a castle in a forest overrun with demons, beasts, and other dark creatures, he was basically guaranteed unwanted house guests without one.

And if he had one, she was going to find it.

The next morning, she ate breakfast in her room, pocketed an apple, and headed outside immediately without looking down any of the hallways. After what had happened yesterday, she hesitated at the idea of searching for a library if it would result in the erox accosting her on some staircase again.

Even if the idea of it stirred something in her core.

As she pushed through the doors, cool autumn air kissed her bare legs, and she held her sweater closer to her. The day would warm as it went on, she knew, but she yanked on her short dress before walking down the gravel paths. There weren't cobblestone streets like there was in the center of Shadowbank, but there also weren't dirt paths. Gravel sidewalks and wider paths that might have once been intended for horses and carts were well maintained. But as she walked, she was surprised to once again find no servants or staff. Not for the first time, she wondered just how this castle functioned if it was only the demon and an offering. Would she eventually be expected to clean it in her free time when he wasn't feeding on her essence?

Focus, she thought as she passed several one-story stone buildings. The doors were closed, and she didn't hear animals inside. Perhaps they were once storage buildings. But she didn't dare stop to check. If she was going to get in trouble again, then it would be once she found what she sought.

As she walked toward the trees, the paths branched off to the right toward what must be gardens. Bushes, flowers, and other smaller shrubbery wove in a winding path off into the distance.

Darting behind a large oak tree, she glanced over a shoulder, wondering if the demon had spotted her. Wondering if he had followed her. But she could see nothing behind her, and she didn't sense any movement in the shadows.

Reaching for the collar at her neck, her stomach sank. She certainly wasn't helpless, but dressed as she was without her magically enforced leathers, no weapons, and unable to touch her elemental magic... well, it made her feel far too exposed. And that was aside from the fact that her pussy was enjoying the cool fall air as much as she was.

Clenching her fists at her sides, she turned back toward the trees.

When the demon had brought her here, she'd been drugged and mostly unconscious. But she'd been lucid enough that she thought she'd felt the ripple of a ward when they drew near to the castle. Though she couldn't be sure.

As she glanced to the sky above, she didn't spot the purple-blue dome, the telltale sign of an elemental ward. It was possible that wards created with other magic looked differently, weren't perceptible from other types of magic wielders, or were invisible entirely.

Before she could enter the crop of trees beyond the gardens, she heard a rustle coming from behind her. Spinning, she spotted the demon in the gardens. He wore tight trousers and tall boots as he had the day before, but he was shirtless. His chest was covered in a light sheen of sweat as he leaned over one of the rose bushes with what appeared to be small shears...

Was he pruning the garden?

Arabella froze in place.

For reasons she couldn't explain, the sight of an immortal demon doing something as mundane as caring for plant life had her staring blankly at him.

"I haven't yet decided whether I should feel offended by the look on your face," the erox said without turning to look at her.

The way the light of the rising morning sun flickered off the sweat on his neck made his light brown skin appear to shimmer.

She crossed her arms, careful to stay far away from him—and his magic.

"I've never seen a demon garden before."

"Have you ever met a demon?" he said as he snipped off a dead branch.

"Yes," she replied, irritation growing in her voice. "And it seemed like their most prominent hobby was death by claws or fangs."

He turned to her then, brow raised. "Not all demons are intelligent or can see past the hunger."

"And all lack self-control," she said, thinking not just of the countless times shadow monsters had tried to eat the flesh off of her but also of the last time she'd seen the erox on the staircase.

Something flickered in his eyes, but she couldn't quite identify the emotion.

"I can't speak for others of my kind, but I can say that I've exercised quite a lot of control with you thus far," he said, his voice low. Then he turned back to the bush, removing more dead leaves and branches. "If I hadn't, you'd already be dead or under my spell."

"You haven't killed me? Oh, how sweet," she said, sarcastically. "So, what—you like your offerings to choose you after you've kidnapped them? How noble. Excuse me if I'm not impressed."

"My presence affects all mortals, but I don't take anyone's free will."

"Can you?"

With his powers, she very much believed he could make her lose herself completely to the lust. She'd come far too close already. Even from this distance, something in her urged her to step forward, *needing* to be near him.

"Yes."

"Am I supposed to be thankful that you haven't turned me into a mindless sex doll?"

He chuckled humorlessly but didn't respond.

Why would a demon care about whether its prey had free will? No matter what he said, she knew she was nothing more than a food source to him. Perhaps more importantly, why was she trying to instigate him? She should be trying to excuse herself —to get away so she could try to find the ward and study it.

A thought occurred to her.

What if she couldn't learn a damned thing about the ward with this collar on? What if the reason she couldn't see the ward was *because* she didn't have access to her enchantress abilities?

Somehow, she'd need to get it off. And if she couldn't do it on her own, she'd need to gain this creature's trust enough so he'd take it off himself. Hadn't he said himself the day before that it was a temporary precaution until they learned to trust each other?

As if she'd trust a demon.

"What happens to me when you feed?" she eventually managed.

If she was going to be forced to be in this demon's presence, there were a few things she needed to know. For one, she needed to know just what his magic would do to her.

Lifting his head, his eyes narrowed on her as though he was considering her—truly looking at her and deciding just how much of his energy she was worth. His gaze took in her sweater, short dress, tall black leather boots, and enchantress head chain. The way his eyes raked over her did something inside her chest, and she had to bite the inside of her cheek.

It's just his magic. Calm down.

She wondered if this was what it had felt like for Nemera when she'd been bitten by Rowan.

The erox placed his shears down, grabbed his shirt from the ground, turned, and walked out of the gardens without a word.

To her utter annoyance, she followed him. "Where are you going?"

"A question for a question," he said. "You want answers? So do I."

She followed him until he strode into an open grassy area past the gardens.

Tossing his shirt onto the ground, he said, "What is your specialty?"

Arabella blinked. "My what?"

He lowered himself into a fighting stance, his hands raised but weaponless. While he didn't wear a sword, the erox had a single blade strapped to his thigh that he didn't reach for. She noted a plain black handle and wondered why, of all things, he'd chosen to keep a single knife with him.

"What are you doing?" she asked.

"Fight me," he said. "I find it's the most effective way to learn another person."

She smiled. He wouldn't have to ask her twice.

Without a second thought, she struck out at him.

It wasn't that she agreed with his approach. She, too, thought a lot could be learned from watching how someone faced an opponent. But there was so much anger swelling in her chest from the fengrine attack, the failing ward, for how Lucinda had tried to pull her memories free, and for the simple fact that she was here— and her family was still in danger. And the opportunity to punch the demon who'd jacked off on her was too good to pass up.

She jabbed at him and swung her leg up in a kick.

It was at that moment she recalled she wasn't wearing anything beneath her dress.

Halfway into the kick, she tried to pull back, attempting to cover herself. Before he could deflect her kick, she stumbled backward. Her cheeks heated as she yanked her dress down and thought of just how much of her he must have seen. Stifling a groan, she thought longingly of her leathers.

"I was second to the Head Enchantress," she answered as she launched into a series of punches and jabs—not eager to flash her pussy at him again.

He dodged her blows with ease.

"The ward was a large part of my responsibility," she continued, her cheeks still warm.

"Were you a healer?" he asked, continuing to pivot and avoid her strikes.

Why wasn't he attacking? She could tell he was holding back, but why?

"No," she said, breathing easily. "All enchantresses can do at least some healing magic, but I suck at it. Now, it's my turn to ask you two questions."

Ignoring the itch in her fingers for her swords, she launched a series of punches at him, one that Brynne had taught her years ago when they'd been training in hand-to-hand combat.

Not a single one landed.

"Will I lose years of my life from you feeding on me?"

"No."

She breathed a sigh of relief, again thinking of how Scarlett had looked so healthy when she'd emerged from the forest.

"Why do you take offerings?"

She jabbed at him again and again, but she kept her feet firmly on the ground.

"To sustain my life," he said. "Why did you volunteer?"

"To save my sisters from this fate." As she spoke, she didn't hide the disgust from her voice. "Why do you hide what you are and where you live?"

It was like her words unlocked something in him, and the erox unleashed himself.

His movements were so fast that her eyes could barely keep up with him, and it was all she could do to bring her arms up in time, narrowly blocking attack after attack.

"I don't wish to be found," he said as he closed in on her.

She ducked underneath the swing of his left arm, but before she could spin out of the way of his other arm, he landed a punch to her side. Hissing at the pain blossoming in her ribs, she said, "That's not an answer."

Launching herself at him once more, she tried to strike him, but she felt him shift, felt the shadows around her move. It was then she realized that he'd backed her toward the line of trees at the edge of the grass. Suddenly, she felt a presence behind her, and she rolled forward. There was a whoosh of air where her head had just been, but she rolled back onto her feet and face him before he was swinging again.

"Do you lack confidence in your fighting skills so much that you resort to magic?" she said, tsking. "And after all the effort you went to in order to take my magic..."

"Maybe I like my offerings docile," he said, never stopping moving.

"Maybe I like my partners not to be a leech."

There was the slightest flicker of one nostril and a swirl of anger in his eyes before he landed a blow to her side. It knocked the wind out of her, and she staggered backward.

"Tell me what you really think, little enchantress," he said, voice harsh. "As though your kind hasn't murdered countless."

"Demons," she rasped, feeling herself growing fatigued from the effort it took to dodge his blows. "I kill the demons. Not people."

She flipped in the grass, trying to create distance between them, trying to get away from the shadows and into the grass beneath the sun. Her shadows retreated beneath her feet, but so would his. He'd have no way of surprising her again.

"And what if they are sentient?" Sweat slid down his neck and between his pecs. "What if they're just desperate for food, just like you humans?"

"Then they'd have asked nicely," she said through gritted teeth as he landed a punch to her shoulder. "But I doubt even you would take kindly to being on the menu."

For the first time, she thought to wonder whether the magic of the bargain would prevent her from trying to kill the erox. She'd agreed to stay with him for ten years. But if their sparring was any indication, the original agreement with the founders must not have included not harming the other.

Which could mean that he might be able to kill her if he wished.

"It's my turn to ask a question," she said. "Because you didn't actually answer my last one. What magic do the erox possess? You take essence. So, what do you do with it?"

His eyes flashed up to hers then, no longer fixed on her abdomen and trying to anticipate her movements.

Slowly, he stood to his feet. "You'd be foolish if you thought I'd tell you everything of my kind. But I'll tell you this—all erox can move through shadows and are stronger than humans. All are immortal." He strode toward her, sweat running in rivulets down the sides of his face.

Instinctively, she took a step back and then another, but he didn't stop approaching her.

"However, some erox have their own special abilities."

"What's yours?" Arabella asked as the heat from the sun lessened.

"It's my turn to ask a question," he said, and it was then she realized he'd backed her into the shadow of the castle. Her back scraped against unyielding stone.

Not again, she thought.

"Are you a virgin?"

His eyes flickered between hers as though he was actually interested in the answer, and something like butterflies fluttered in her stomach.

"No," she said. "I doubt I need to ask the same of you."

She needed to create space between them before her thoughts grew fuzzy and his magic made her lose all common sense. But as yesterday, her heartbeat quickened, and her breaths grew ragged.

Anger swirled in his gaze. "I take it you've learned what you like."

Pulling her hands up, she pushed against his chest, but he might as well have been one of the oak trees in the yard for as much as he moved. Then she felt large fingers trailing up her thigh and lifting it toward him until he was pressed between her legs.

Her thoughts muddied, but she didn't move her hands—even as a distant part of her wanted to let go. To let him make the decisions and use her body until they were both unraveling.

"Back up, demon," she said, but the words were as wobbly as her conviction.

He leaned a hand against the castle wall, never letting go of her thigh with the other. And she was all too aware of the press of her clit against his leg. It was an effort not to thrust her hips against him and feel the delicious friction right where she needed it.

The corner of his lips quirked up.

"One more thing about my magic," he began, and she felt her head tipping back as though her chest was drawn toward his. "My offerings are only overwhelmed by lust when they're attracted to me. Those who aren't can feel the lust, but... they can resist it if I allow them their free will."

"I don't want this." The words came out in a whisper, and they tasted of lies. But she kept her hands between them, feeling the firmness of his chest against them... and wanting to rake her fingernails down his...

Nope, she thought, ending that thought before it could truly begin. *He's lying. I could never want a demon.*

As he spoke, his eyes lingered on her lips. "Keep telling yourself that, little enchantress."

Suddenly, he released her and moved back toward the grass, retrieving his shirt. She ignored the disappointment swelling within her as he pulled it back on.

"I have things to do this afternoon." Pausing, he looked back and said over his shoulder, "And don't even think about going near the wards."

Then, just like the day before, he disappeared in an instant.

It took several minutes before her thoughts settled enough for her to move. But as she did, her clit tingled uncomfortably between her legs.

Fuck him and his magic.

Glancing around, wondering if perhaps he lingered nearby, she paused, but there was nothing in the shadows and no one in sight.

She glanced toward the line of trees, wondering if she dared to approach them despite what he said.

Tomorrow, she thought. *I'll try again tomorrow.*

She'd return when he wasn't suspecting she would. Going now would be far too obvious, and perhaps he'd threaten to make her walk around naked again.

With a sigh, she strode back toward the castle, all the while refusing to believe that the desire blossoming in her had anything to do with what she truly felt.

For a demon.

Chapter Eight

ARABELLA

The next morning, Arabella blinked awake to the rising sun.

Sheets twisting around her, she stretched and blinked sleepily, rolling onto her side.

Her thoughts turned to the ward and her sparring with the erox in the grass the day before.

Perhaps I can study the wards today.

She hoped she'd be able to find time to get away from him and slip into the woods. Her family needed her, and her heart twisted at the thought of Iris, Jessamine, and the others. It was strange sleeping by herself for the first time in years, and she missed the reassuring hum of their chatter at night as she slipped off into sleep. Homesickness struck her so strongly that she wrapped her arms around herself and bit the inside of her cheek.

She was nothing without her family. Nothing but a scared little girl with no place in the world to call home. Even her parents hadn't wanted her. And while she didn't care to learn what her life had been before Shadowbank, the fact that they'd left her lingered in the back of her mind. Once again, she was without a home or people who loved her. But she'd chosen this. This sacrifice would be—*was*—worth it. Still, she wondered if the Circle realized she was gone or if they missed her for more than her ability to fix the ward. Could they love her if she wasn't useful? But her being here had proven she was useful. No one else would have to sacrifice a decade of their life to the Devourer, at least not this time. Hopefully, in ten years after she found a way to repair the ward, her family would welcome her home. Hopefully, they would have missed her while she was gone.

I'll be back, she thought. *I'm going to save you.*

But there was one thing between her and helping her family—the erox.

He had known she wanted to see the wards. Was she that obvious? Her attempted bargain had likely given her away. But she had the uncomfortable feeling that he'd find her today, and any chance of studying the wards would have to wait. He hadn't fed on her in a few days, and while she didn't know how often the erox needed to feed, she suspected he'd need to feed soon.

Hadn't he said something about the essence being better or lasted longer if he fucked with his prey? Or something? Even so, she recalled that he said he didn't need to fuck her to feed. And damn him, she wouldn't do any such thing.

But even as she thought it, desire spiked deep within her core, and she groaned. Her body felt like a bowstring strung far too tight.

She reached a hand down into the sheets where her night-gown had bunched up to her lower back, her pussy bare. She ran a finger over herself, feeling the wetness already gathered there. A whimper escaped her lips. Hand moving in a lazy circle, she thought of the erox. She imagined the shape of his cock and what it might feel like. She imagined his brows drawing together as moans escaped his lips when he thrust into her.

Her fingers moved more quickly. She brought a second hand down, fingering herself, while her other hand moved in steady up-and-down motions on her clit. Even as she drew toward climax, it wasn't enough. Her hands were far too small, far too *her*.

She wanted him to use her body, to fuck her until they were both sated.

A soft moan escaped her lips as she came, head tilted back, the image of the erox in her mind. As she came back down, irritation bubbled within her as she realized the orgasm hadn't dampened the molten desire in her core. She desired him just as much as before.

Moving toward the bathing chambers, she paused, spotting what appeared to be a note on the table beside the window. She walked over to it and picked it up.

I'll see you at breakfast.

No signature. No request. Just a bold assumption she would do as asked.

Prick.

But there was no food in her room this morning, and if she had any hope of having breakfast, it was with him.

Crumpling the note, she tossed it down onto the table before turning toward the bathing chambers. Even though she'd bathed the night before, she took a warm bath before donning yet another of her "uniforms." This dress was black and went to her knees. Once again, she wore her boots and a sweater. Pausing in front of a mirror, she pulled her long black hair back, braiding it and putting her enchantress headdress on, the gemstone resting at the center of her forehead. As she finished her hair, she noticed something atop her table in the mirror's reflection. She spun on a heel and went over to it.

Her heart raced as she stared at the note. It was no longer crumpled in a ball. Instead, it had been smoothed out and placed on the tabletop. Had someone been in her room while she bathed? Was this castle somehow enchanted?

Taking a breath, she strode for the door. If he was standing outside, she was going to give him a piece of her mind. He might be some high and mighty erox, but that didn't give him the right to enter her room while she was undressed. She swung the door open and looked down either end of the hallway.

Empty.

What the...?

There was a piece of paper on the floor of the hallway. Reaching down, she picked it up. It was a simplistic map of the hallways that detailed how to get to a dining hall. She huffed before following the map down two floors and several long hallways. Eventually, she stood before a large two-story door. As she reached for the handle, the door creaked and opened inward. She dropped her hand, clenching it into a fist.

Magical castle with its bloody self-opening doors and notes that move on their own.

They had a lot to discuss.

But even as she had several sharp words on the tip of her tongue, they were forgotten as she looked across the room, spotting the erox at the head of the table... reading a book.

The room boasted a massive table that could host at least thirty guests along with stained-glass windows filling up an entire two-story wall. The room was bright as sunlight streamed in, leaving streaks of color across the chairs and table.

She stalked over to Elias, ignoring enormous bouquets at intervals across the table. When she stood before him, he continued to read his book, not bothering to glance up at her. She crossed her arms.

After several moments, he flipped a page and pressed a bookmark into it before closing the book.

"Good morning." The words were mundane ones and yet filled with *suggestion.*

"Why?"

He looked up at her then, an eyebrow raised.

"Why did you come into my room this morning while I was bathing?"

Slowly, he leaned forward and placed his book on the corner of the table. "I did no such thing."

Liar.

He gestured to a chair beside him. "Sit. I'm sure you're hungry."

As if in response, her stomach grumbled, and she realized suddenly that she was, indeed, starving.

She sat down, reaching for the fork beside a plate filled with chicken, a biscuit, and roasted vegetables. She ate them wordlessly. The food tasted delicious—hearty and full of flavors. Glancing up, she spotted a tray of eggs and fruit she hadn't noticed before. She scooped both onto her plate before eventually going back and finishing both.

As she cleared her third plate of food, she looked up, spotting Elias pushing his plate with chicken and a biscuit toward her.

Realizing she'd been eating like an animal, she dusted her hands on her napkin and wiped her mouth. She floundered for some sense of pride, which she'd tossed out the window the moment she dove face-first into breakfast. She ate the way she had after repairing the ward during the fengrine attack and had used so much magic. Her body must still be exhausted from it plus the erox feeding off her...

Magic always had a cost, and those whose cost was an increased appetite were the lucky ones.

Ignoring the blush creeping into her cheeks, she said, "Where are your servants?"

Elias blinked, surprise streaking across his features.

"What servants?"

"Who cleans this castle for you?"

He waved a hand, dismissing her. "Magic."

As if that explained it. Perhaps the castle really was sentient.

She fought the urge to run a hand over her face in frustration. Instead, she said, "What other rules should I be aware of?" Elias looked at her and opened his mouth to speak, but she continued, "There are rooms I'm not supposed to enter that you never told me about. I have to wear your silly dresses. What else?"

He put an elbow on the table and leaned toward her. His forearm was muscled like the rest of him. Veins bulged in his arms where his shirt was rolled up. Her eyes lingered a moment too long, and she had to tear her eyes away, forcing them back to his.

"You are required to wear one of the dresses I've left in your wardrobe."

"Yeah. Got that."

His lips drew into a thin line before he continued. "You will do what I say when I say any time we are intimate. If you don't listen, your pleasure will cease."

First, she had to beg for his cock. Now, he's a control freak, too?

"You may not leave the castle grounds, but you're free to go where you please—except that room in the guest quarters—during your time here if I don't require your services."

"My pussy, you mean."

A spark flickered in his eyes, and he leaned back in his seat. "Your pleasure, little enchantress. I told you, I don't need your cunt to feed. It's... a sweeter pleasure if I do, but it isn't necessary for me to survive."

"So, you don't need me to orgasm or to fuck me for you to feed. But what do you get out of having control over my pleasure?"

"Call it a... preference of mine. It has less to do with feeding as it does turning me on," he said. "And I do need you to orgasm to feed. That is one of the rules of the magic."

Desire spiked in her so hot that it was an effort not to reach down and touch herself right then. Even after her release earlier that morning, her body craved to be touched—and not by her small fingers.

"I see."

She couldn't manage one more word, or she feared she'd give away just how much her body craved him. Even so, she squirmed in her chair, feeling her dress hike up her thigh as she did.

Once again, he leaned forward, an elbow on the table, until he was close enough that she could see the faintest flicker of his pupils. "I can scent your desire."

Her heartbeat quickened.

"I don't know what you're talking about."

"I can also tell that you touched yourself this morning without my permission." His eyes burned with desire as he looked at her. "That is another of my rules. You'll never touch yourself without my permission. If you need to be satisfied, all you must do is ask and obey."

"What if I don't want to obey?"

As though out of sheer rebellion—or sheer foolishness—her hand skated down her body, lifting her dress, and stroking her clit.

The fire in his eyes burned hotter. "Then you will go... wanting."

She touched herself, pressing one finger inside of her and then two.

His gaze slid down to the edge of the table, where it blocked his view. "If you cannot obey, little enchantress, there will be consequences."

"Oh?" she said, continuing to finger herself, her head tilting back in pleasure. "But you need me to come to feed, don't you?"

There was a flash of movement, and she was in his arms, being carried across the large banquet hall and toward a stone wall. Sofas were against it, and he dropped her atop one.

She began to protest, but his hands locked around her ankles. Before she knew what was happening, he'd grabbed ropes she hadn't noticed from beneath the sofa, tying her down.

When he went to do the same to her wrists, she panicked and struck out with her fists. "No! You won't tie me down like... like..."

But he was too strong. Her protests died as she fought in vain against his iron grip, tying each of her wrists down until they were stretched out on either side of her. Her legs, too, were spread wide. And her dress had hiked up in her pointless fight to stop him.

For a moment, she thought about lashing out against him with her shadow magic. But even if she was more than a "one-trick pony" as Lucinda had called her, she thought that this secret was best kept for now and only revealed when it truly mattered. When she found a way to repair Shadowbank's ward. Because she knew when she did, she would do everything she could to help her family, and he would try to stop her.

So, she pulled against the restraints and glared up at him.

"You will learn to obey me, little enchantress," he purred as he reached a hand down and ran it over his hardened cock that bulged against his tight black pants.

Unable to stop herself, she bit her lip as she eyed him. She couldn't take her gaze off him as he stroked his hand up and down.

"You bet like hell I—"

Suddenly, he was before her pressing a gag into her mouth and tying it behind her head. Then he hiked her dress up so she was bare before him. Her nipples grew hard from the cool castle air. She held her chin high, unwilling to yield. But even as she did, desire coursed through her, and she wondered just how much her stubbornness was worth it.

In a single motion, he was above her, legs straddling her.

"You had a chance to prove to me you could listen." He reached for the laces at the top of his pants, slowly untying them. "Instead, you outright disobeyed me. You *asked* for this. What comes next is your doing."

He pulled his cock from his pants.

As she'd seen on the stairs, his cock curved slightly upwards, and veins bulged along it. His tip was pink, and a bead of moisture already glistened at the tip.

He moved his hand up and down his length, his eyes never leaving hers.

"When you apologize and learn that to listen is to have pleasure, you'll know that resistance is pointless." As he touched himself, his breaths grew ragged. "I can give you everything your heart desires. If only you submit to me."

Despite herself, she found her hips moving, her hands pulling against the restraints. She arched her back upward, trying to press into him.

"Ah-ah," he chastised, leaning out of her reach—away from where she craved him. He pumped himself as he spoke, voice low. "You've got beautiful breasts. I look forward to when I can run my hands over them again and suck those tight little nipples."

She moaned into the gag, closing her eyes.

A hand was under her chin. "Open your eyes. You *will* watch this."

Damn her, but she listened.

"Good girl."

Then he moved until he was between her thighs and his cock was so close to her pussy. She made a sound that was far too close to a moan, but the gag muffled it. Again, she strained against the restraints, arching her pussy toward him.

To her surprise, he fisted his cock before running the tip over her clit and then down to her entrance.

She moaned then.

Molten heat surged through her core, and her wrists ached as she pulled against the restraints, her back arching.

Fuck, she was close to coming already. But could she hold out? He said she had to come for him to feed. The darker part of her thought: *Do I want to hold out?*

This creature had her nearly wrapped around his finger.

Was what he said yesterday true? Was the lust she was feeling really because she felt some attraction to him?

For a moment, she truly considered whether she wanted to give in to him. She wouldn't be giving her heart away, after all. It was just her body. And it wouldn't prevent her from doing all she could to protect Shadowbank.

But as he stroked his cock over her again, and she yearned for him to press into her, to feel his hard length fill her, she made her decision.

No, she thought. *He refused to help Shadowbank and fix the ward, so he's going to have to rip this orgasm out of me if he wants to feed.*

But she grew wet as he pulled his cock back and reached out with a hand, his fingers running over her wet folds. Her clit was so swollen, and as he stroked up and down, she moaned into the gag. But she kept her hips firmly on the sofa. She wouldn't move, wouldn't let him know how much she wanted this. And she wouldn't make her orgasm easy for him—even though she knew if he kept touching her like that, she was going to come.

Suddenly, he pulled back before slapping her clit. She cried out, gasping. Then his fingers returned to their lazy strokes across her clit and skating around her entrance. Her body wound tighter, and the echoing sting of his slap only increased her desire. When he did it again, it took the last of her restraint to keep her body from moving against him.

I'm going to come, she thought, her mind frantic as she tried to hold back.

His eyes locked with hers, and she knew he could sense it, too.

Releasing his cock, he removed the gag from her mouth while the other moved deftly over her clit, stroking her where she needed him.

Leaning down, his lips captured hers as pleasure cascaded over her.

Desire swelled in her chest even stronger than before, and she moaned into his mouth. There was a shift in her chest like some piece of her from deep within had been pulled free, coaxed slowly up her chest and into her throat. Blue light crackled between their lips for a moment before he pulled it into him. As he did, his eyes became a matching shade of blue, and she watched as the light went down his throat until it flickered in his chest and disappeared.

Hunger swirled in her stomach alongside the desire.

His hand moved, and she could feel him pumping his cock even as he touched her and a second orgasm rocketed through her. The entire time, his lips never left hers. Her essence leaked from her lips, only heightening her desire.

His movements became more jagged as his pleasure grew tighter. Then he was coming, spilling his seed on her. Warmth splattered on her breasts and stomach. She kissed him hungrily, wanting to taste his pleasure. He pulled more of her essence from her. When he finished, he pulled back, looking down at her.

Once again—just like on the stairs—this should be degrading. She shouldn't want him. But the more she tried to fight this attraction, the more she felt herself succumbing to it.

A cloth was in his hand, and he cleaned both her and himself before tucking his cock back into his pants. He lowered her dress so she was covered, but he didn't release her from the bindings.

Suddenly, she felt herself growing tired and darkness creeping over her vision.

She tried to stay awake. But as her eyes fluttered closed, she thought she saw a trace of worry flash through his gaze. Then everything went black.

SOMETIME LATER, she awoke.

She was still on the sofa, but she'd been untied, and there was a thick blanket over her. She sat upright, and a wave of dizziness passed over her.

"What—" she began, but the erox was before her.

"Drink this." He passed her the cup of tea that smelled of vanilla and chamomile. "It has honey in it."

Then he put a plate of crackers, cheeses, and grapes on a side table beside the sofa.

She took a drink of the tea, sighing with pleasure. He picked up a cracker and offered it to her. Taking it, she ate in silence for a few minutes. Slowly, the dizziness faded.

"What happened?" she asked.

"When I take your essence, I'm also feeding on your desire. But if my kind feeds too often or takes too much, mortals can grow weak." He passed her cheese. "Essence replenishes with rest and sustenance. It only harms you if I take too much too quickly or too much if you're weak. You need to eat more to keep up your strength."

After a moment, he added, "Were you under some kind of exertion before you came to me?"

Images of the battle with the fengrine came to her mind's eye.

"Yes," she said, knowing that coming close to burnout could weaken an enchantress for days or weeks after depending on how close they came.

He nodded. "Each person has a different stamina, and I'm learning yours. You must eat enough at each meal, especially protein." He met her eyes. "I'm sorry I weakened you so quickly. I'll be more mindful going forward."

She blinked.

Had the erox just apologized?

A swirl of emotions passed through her, none of which she had any desire to name at that moment.

Once she finished the plate of food, Elias leaned back in his chair, picking up the book he'd been reading earlier that morning. She leaned back into the sofa, listening to the sound of birdsong beyond the stained-glass windows and sipping her tea. Eventually, she dozed off again. When she awoke the second time, he was still there, reading his book.

When she turned to him, he said, "Are you hungry?"

She shook her head and voiced a question that had been burning inside her since he'd brought her to the castle.

"Since I will be here for the next ten years, what am I expected to do during the day?"

"You may do as you wish," he said. "So long as you remain within my borders."

And so long as I don't go back into that one room.

"I'd like to practice archery." As she spoke, she could have sworn she saw surprise on his features.

"As you wish. You shall have all you need when you go outside." Then he added, "You will be granted your leathers when you are practicing with weaponry or when otherwise appropriate. But I expect you to change when you return."

She nodded. That seemed reasonable... or as reasonable as such things could be for a demon.

Closing his book, he stood. "Lunch will be in your quarters this afternoon. Dinner will take place here after the sun sets. Don't be late."

Then he disappeared, moving inhumanly fast through the castle.

As she returned to her room, she noticed her leathers had been cleaned, repaired, and placed on her bed. Changing, she donned the outfit she'd worn for years and had become accustomed to. It felt like home. As she strode toward the front doors, courtesy of yet another map that appeared at her door, she couldn't help but think of how gently the erox had cared for her after she'd woken up. Such gentleness she hadn't expected from a demon she'd been taught to fear.

Could he be different from his kind?

For a moment, she wondered if the demons of the forest weren't so unlike her after all. But that was ridiculous.

She was an enchantress, and he was a demon.

They couldn't be more different.

Chapter Nine

ARABELLA

Arabella found her way to the palace gardens, where she lingered for a moment to study the changing colors of the leaves—the deep burgundy and bright oranges and golden yellows. Autumn was fully upon them. Normally, it was a season she longed to linger in and enjoy the scents of falling leaves. But in Shadowbank, it was a time of preparation and fear of what the winter would hold—and the demons that would emerge from the forest, hungry.

Slowly, she made her way past the gardens to an open area where a target had been set up. It was at the edge of the castle grounds, nearer the woods, and a quiver of arrows and a bow rested several yards away from it.

While she preferred her two swords, she'd been trained in all weapons. Every enchantress had to be adept at archery, as they were often called to the wall. But only the strongest enchantresses could release both bolts of magic and arrows at the same time, especially with any accuracy. Jessamine was far more skilled than she was in this sort of multitasking, but Arabella could hold her own.

Once she learned how to repair wards, she would need to leave this place to give this information to Iris and the others in Shadowbank—before the bargain's magic wrapped around her and made her return. Since she couldn't touch her enchantress magic and her shadow magic was fickle at best, she'd have to rely on her ability with weapons. If she had any chance of making it through the forest, she had to keep her skills sharp.

Picking up a bow, she nocked an arrow, aimed, and released. There was no hesitation. No questioning. It struck one of the target's innermost circles. It wasn't the perfect center, but her aim was solid. She released arrow after arrow, enjoying the familiar sting in her fingers from pulling the bowstring and the ache in her muscles as she pulled and released.

As she drew and released arrows, there was a faint prickle of eyes on her that she'd come to expect. It felt like there was someone nearby, someone watching. But as every time before, when she turned to look, there was no one around.

When her quiver was empty, she collected the arrows. She returned to her starting point and then walked back so that the target was significantly farther away. For some reason, she needed to test the boundaries of her skills.

Eventually, one of her arrows went wide. It flew past the target and into the line of trees beyond.

With a sigh, she put her bow down and headed for the trees. Even this close to the castle, it wasn't long until shadow swallowed her and the trees closed in. The forest floor was covered in moss and leaves. Above, the canopy blocked out the sky. But she knew the darkness, and she felt along the shadows, scanning for her arrow. After some time, she spotted it—embedded into the trunk of a large tree several paces ahead. As she strode toward it, she felt a pressure, like a tugging beneath her skin, and stopped.

Was she at the edge of the ward?

There wasn't a translucent wall before her of a purple-blue hue or any other sign that a ward was present. Was this what mortals saw? She hadn't thought to wonder before that moment whether mortals could even see a ward.

Reaching for her collar, she pulled, but it held fast. Feeling around it, it was like it had been welded onto her. There were no clasps or hinges that she could detect, which meant it was likely put on using magic. If only she had access to her enchantress magic. Then she'd be able to see just what this sensation meant and what magic was used.

For a moment, she remained where she was, uncertain whether to turn around and abandon the arrow or grab it. The erox had told her to stay away from the ward... which she hadn't actually intended to listen to. She'd planned to study the ward, but she'd lost herself to the rhythm of pulling and releasing arrows just now. Now, she couldn't even be sure that this *was* the ward. It certainly had the pull of magic.

Looking up, the arrow was so close—mere paces ahead of her and embedded into a tree.

There was a shift in the trees as though the forest held its breath, and all sounds of small forest animals stopped. Then there was an unmistakable crunching of leaves.

She wasn't alone.

Instinctively, she reached for one of the sheaths at her belt only to realize she had no weapons. She'd brought none with her, and she'd left her bow.

Her heart raced, and she looked around, trying to locate whatever stalked the surrounding trees. But all she could see was countless trunks, low branches, and twisting roots along with ground. Reaching for her shadow magic, she sifted through the surrounding darkness, sensing a prickling darkness that weighed on her.

The hairs on the back of her neck stood up, and she took one step back and then another.

I'm behind the ward, she thought. *It can't reach me here.*

She hadn't asked the erox what kind of ward he had, and she knew there were countless different kinds. Some kept demons out, others kept a certain type of magical creature or magic wielder out, and yet others were spelled to only let certain people in. Some were even imbued with an invisibility cloak, not allowing those on the outside to see in. Just what kind of ward was this? And was she, in fact, before the ward?

One thing was certain—whatever was out there was close. But either the monster couldn't reach her or it wouldn't even be able to sense her.

She hoped.

Her boots crunched in the pregnant silence as she continued to back away. It felt like she waded through water as she forced one foot to move and then another. Every instinct told her to freeze, to stand still, but she fought it with every step she took. Even if she was behind the ward, it would be best she put some distance between herself and whatever stalked the forest.

A dark figure appeared between the trees.

She inhaled sharply, heart pounding in her ears. It wasn't a beast on all fours prowling toward her. Instead, it was tall and shaped like a man and stood a dozen paces away, silhouetted in the trees.

It was anything but human.

Its black cloak swirled along the ground as though stirred by a phantom wind, and trails of black smoke trailed out from the tips. A hiss skittered through the surrounding trees.

She reached for her elemental magic, but she slammed against the invisible wall as the collar burned simultaneously. She hissed in pain.

The creature's head turned toward her at the sound, and a magnetic energy latched on to her, its hook sinking into her mind. Her thoughts blurred as she felt its gaze, its intention, settle on her from beneath its black cloak. In the silence of the forest, she felt something stir in the air and in herself. Something beckoned her, calling to her spirit, ushering her forward.

Her feet began moving of their own accord.

The shadows beneath her feet hissed and whispered as though agitated. But her mind honed in on a single thought: she needed to see this creature for herself. She walked until there was a *pop*, and a distant part of her wondered if she'd passed through the ward.

A stream of dark magic lashed out.

There was no time to shield herself or move or think before oily tendrils of magic snapped around her neck, snaking upwards until she felt it slide inside her ears and eyes. She tried to move, tried to scream, but her arms fell to her sides and her whole body went slack. It was as though poison moved through her veins, rendering her unable to move or utter a word. Then all at once, her mind went blank.

The dark figure raised too-human hands and pushed back its dark hood, revealing the face of a man. He was the most handsome man she had ever seen—with ivory skin and eyes as deep and fathomless as the night sky. His jawline was as sharp as an axe, and he had a fine nose and a strong chin. Like his cloak, his auburn hair seemed to move in a phantom wind or perhaps like he was underwater.

As he stepped toward her, she noticed he was shirtless beneath his cloak and wore tight britches that highlighted muscled legs.

She couldn't move, couldn't think. All she could do was look into the dark eyes of the man who approached her.

As he grew close, his beauty became even more vivid. It was as though she stared into the sun but couldn't look away. Tears filled her eyes as she looked at him, blinking through the blinding magnetism.

Some part of her screamed that this wasn't a man, but she didn't care. He was approaching her. She *wanted* him to approach her, to touch her, to consume her. She had to be by his side.

"What has stumbled into my woods?"

The words sounded like the hissing of a snuffed fire, somehow both warm and sharp.

Then he was before her, and she couldn't find the will or ability to speak. She just looked up at him. Something akin to desire swirled within her at his nearness. But even as it did, she felt some darker part of her mind draw forward.

She was unworthy of him. He was a god, and she was nothing but the decaying earth under his shoes. He deserved to be worshipped in temples, for followers to fall to their feet and praise the very ground he stood upon.

Next to him, she was nothing, less than nothing.

Shadows writhed and twisted beneath her.

"Such a pretty little thing," he purred.

I am yours, her mind seemed to say. *Do whatever you want with me.*

The man with beautiful ivory skin and auburn hair leaned forward. Hands closed around her shoulders, and her arms remained slack at her sides. Something sharp pricked her skin. Talons, she realized, protruded from otherwise smooth hands. Distantly, her mind registered pain.

But rather than the pull of attraction or desire, a dark allure swirled within her. Suddenly, memories ripped through her mind. She started to cry out at the push of images slicing through her thoughts, but the man pressed large lips into hers, capturing her scream with his mouth and pulling something from her.

A crackling blue light appeared between their lips, hovering in the air.

He's taking my essence, she realized.

Then she slackened in his grip, submitting to him.

Memories of the first time she met one dancer in the House of Obscurities seared across her mind's eye. Charun, his name had been. She watched herself as though disembodied, seeing how she'd approached him and how he'd tried to seduce her. He'd tried to win her affection, but all she could offer him was friendship and physical intimacy. In the past, she'd never felt ashamed of the time they'd spent together, pleasuring each other. But now, a deep, overwhelming shame surfaced. Why had she never formed a romantic connection in Shadowbank? So many of her sisters had found partners.

Something was wrong with her.

She was incapable of finding love.

But it was more than that. She was incapable of loving anyone at all. She was broken—a shell of what an enchantress should be. It shouldn't come as a surprise that all she could offer anyone was her body. She'd live out the rest of her days without knowing romantic love and unworthy. Charun was the only person who had any type of romantic interest in her, and it was filled with pity. No one else could find her tolerable as she was. She was selfish. Worthless.

Self-loathing swelled within her, and she cried out again, tears streaming down her cheeks. The man sucked in her shame, pulling it into him as though he tasted the finest wine. As he did, she could feel herself growing wet with desire. A tingling sensation grew between her legs.

Use me, she thought. *End me.*

She recalled pieces of her childhood, which were spotted with gaps. There was so much she couldn't remember, and for good reason. Her parents hadn't wanted her. They'd discarded her like the garbage she was, and she'd been left to fend for herself, wandering in the woods.

Iris and the enchantresses had felt sorry for her when they found her. But there was no love or affection—only obligation. She could see their faces, warped and shadowed, lips drawn upward in disgust. Their sympathy turned as they decided how she'd be useful. It was that or throw her out like everyone else. Why keep someone incapable of love? Best to use or discard her.

Tears streamed down her face, but the male before her paid them no mind.

He would take care of her now. She was his, and soon she would be no more. He would end her suffering.

Distantly, she registered a hand on her breast, squeezing painfully. Then the hand was between her legs, moving roughly against her clit through her leathers. Her body was frozen, and all she could do was receive what he gave to her. Something like an orgasm ripped through her senses, and she whimpered as his tongue ravished her mouth, engulfing all that she was.

As more memories ripped through her mind, the male continued to kiss her, pulling and pulling her essence until her knees grew weak and gave out. It squeezed her shoulders painfully, keeping her upright. All the while, her body felt feverish, and she both loathed and longed for him to touch her again.

Her mind grew fuzzy, and a strange numbness settled over her even as pain tore through her mind. Shame crashed over her like a breaking wave until she was drowning, unable to take another breath.

She couldn't last much longer. This would all be over soon.

It had to be.

A cry tore through the forest, breaking through the torment ensnaring her.

The beautiful male looked up, hissing and releasing her.

She fell to the ground, her body crumpling in a pile of leaves on the forest floor. Her vision blurred as she spotted another figure above her. The newcomer stood between her and the beautiful male in the dark robes as though protecting her. She could feel power swirling around them both and crashing together. A thunderous clap sounded through the forest as their powers came together. The figure in the dark robe's power was as black as the shadows swirling off him while the male above her had power as blue as a clear summer sky.

Don't, she thought to the man who stood above her. *He was helping me. He'll make it all go away.*

But she couldn't speak the words, and she felt so tired. Her eyes grew heavy, and she slowly gave in to the weight that had settled over her.

My family doesn't love me, she thought. *Did I ever truly have a family at all?*

Then hands were under her back and legs, picking her up and moving quickly.

"Stay with me," came a voice from above her. "Don't close your eyes just yet."

There was a deep hissing sound behind them, or perhaps it

was around them. But it wasn't the sound of one voice. It was many. And it was coming for them. She couldn't find the will to care. But she leaned into the powerful chest, head bobbing forward. A tugging sensation across her skin brought her back as they must have passed through the ward. She felt the person holding her continue to run, and then she was suddenly lying on the ground, grass tickling her cheek.

Above her, the male moved his hands in a swirling pattern before blue light gathered between his palms.

Strange, she thought distantly. *He weaves magic just like an enchantress.*

Brows furrowed, he said, "This is going to hurt."

And then he plunged the light into her chest.

ARABELLA SCREAMED as pain surged through her. It felt like every muscle, every ligament in her body was being stretched to its limits and shot with lightning. Somewhere above her, she saw a familiar, handsome face. Reaching out, her hand closed around a wrist, and she clung tight as the pain swept through her in unyielding waves.

All at once, it was gone, and her mind cleared.

Blinking, she sat upright. She was at the edge of the forest in the grassy clearing near the target that had several arrows embedded in it. Beside her, the erox sat on the ground, slumped over. He had one arm on a knee as his chest heaved, and he swiped a hand over his damp brow.

"Welcome back, little enchantress," he said, a hint of relief in his voice.

Then it all came back to her—the creature in the forest, its painful beauty, and the memories and feelings that had coursed through her.

Tears streamed down her face, unbidden, and she swiped them back with a sleeve.

"What was that?" She couldn't disguise the fear lacing her voice nor the trembling in it. Tangling her fingers in the grass, she tried to hide the shaking of her hands.

"An Alabaster." His eyes were fixed on the line of trees—and likely where the monster and its kind lay beyond. "They usually travel in packs. You're fortunate this one was alone—at least initially. Otherwise, I wouldn't have gotten to you in time."

"What's an Alabaster?" In all her years as an enchantress, she'd never heard of such a creature.

"They're a..." He hesitated as though searching for the right words. "A cousin to the erox. A demon. But instead of feeding on sexual desire, they feed on shame, particularly sexual shame."

Realization dawned.

That must have been why she'd thought of Charun, her former lover from Shadowbank. She'd never felt ashamed of her casual sexual relationship with the dancer, but she had been self-conscious of how she'd never been able to fall in love like so many of the enchantresses. It made her feel alone, reinforcing the image of her as a child, emerging from the forest by herself. With no family, no one who loved her. She didn't dare touch the feelings she'd had of Iris and the Circle.

"Sometimes, the Alabaster use your memories and feelings when they feed," the erox continued. "Other times, the Alabaster will weave shame into existing memories where it hadn't been before. Once you believe the shame is your own, they can feed off it."

Nodding, she wiped another tear from her cheek. "Can you change my memories and feelings?"

"I can only amplify feelings and desires that are already there," Elias said. "And I can erase memories, but I can't change the ones you have."

Not sure if she believed him entirely, she eventually said, "Thanks. For saving me."

To her surprise, she'd clung to him when she'd thought she'd go under. He was a stranger to her, a demon, and yet she'd held on to him like a harbor in the storm.

"Why were you outside the boundary?"

The sharpness in his voice had her looking up. His eyes fixed on her, hot and inescapable.

Running a hand over her braid, she said, "As ridiculous as it sounds, I was hunting down a rogue arrow. But I didn't go outside of the ward on purpose. With the collar, I can't see it, only feel it. And once I saw that demon, my legs were moving without my willing them to..."

"What do you mean your legs moved? You didn't go outside the boundary of your own accord?"

Slowly, she shook her head. "I stopped just before it, I think." She fisted several clumps of grass. Seeing it, she forced her hands to relax. "I think I felt its magic on this side of the ward, and then it lured me out. Is that possible? I thought wards protected those inside them from the magic on the other side."

"It shouldn't be." He sighed. "All wards weaken over time. The magic that powers them wanes, and they have to be... charged up again. Or taken down, and new wards must be put up. If there are repeated attacks on a ward, they weaken more quickly. I'd thought this ward had many more years before I'd have to worry about that. But..."

He remained silent for several long moments, and her heart raced.

He knew about wards. She was right! He'd also officially confirmed that he had a ward around the castle grounds. The bad news was that this ward seemed to be weakening, too. Could he know how to repair it? Was this ward similar to the one around Shadowbank?

"You're never to go near the boundary again," he said, interrupting her thoughts. "If you go through it, you're to turn around immediately. Do you understand?"

"Yes."

As she watched him, she couldn't help but notice that he

looked different. He was always handsome to her, but now... sort of like the Alabaster... he looked *painfully* handsome.

"You look different."

He rose to his feet. Were his legs trembling? He always seemed so strong, so resolute. But now, he locked his knees before extending a hand to her. "You nearly died. It took a lot of my strength to heal you and fend off the Alabaster."

How had he fended off the Alabaster? She couldn't be sure what had happened, but she thought he'd wielded some sort of magic.

When she took his hand to stand, her knees wobbled. "Your appearance changes when you have more or less essence?"

He gave her his arm, and they walked toward the castle.

"The less essence an erox has, the more beautiful we appear to mortals. It makes us... irresistible to you."

If she wasn't struggling to put one foot in front of another, she might have been tempted to kiss him and to have him kiss her on every inch of her naked skin. She *felt* drawn to him at that moment. As it was, she could barely remain on her feet.

When they entered the castle, he brought her into a side room and helped her onto a chair. Going to a nearby wardrobe, he shuffled through some drawers before grabbing a box and turning.

"Eat this," he said, passing something to her.

She studied the small brown object in her hand. "What is it?"

"Chocolate. It'll help you recover."

Her eyes widened. "You have chocolate? It's so rare and expensive. How'd you get your hands on this? Surely, you don't have vendors coming through the woods alongside the Alabaster?"

"I have my ways," he said. "Despite what you mortals think, I don't spend every waking moment within this castle." Darkness spread through his eyes, and he grew quiet.

"What's wrong?"

She didn't know why she asked. Whatever worried him wasn't any of her business. Even so, she wondered just what plagued the mind of an immortal.

"Nothing."

Just like that, he closed the door on whatever was happening behind his eyes. It was silly of her to want to know. She shouldn't have asked.

When she finished the chocolate, he passed her another piece. As she ate, she noticed how her mood gradually improved. The despair lingering at the edge of her thoughts and the shame that felt rooted within her stomach dissipated. But she was ravenous.

"Are you hungry?" she asked.

He'd been leaning on the windowsill of the room, eyes fixed on some point beyond her vision. Turning, his eyes seemed to feast on her as his beauty drained all the light from the room.

At once, she realized her mistake. She held her hands up. "I didn't mean—"

"I might be a selfish creature, but I'm not so heartless as to feed off you in your weakened state. Be at ease, little enchantress. I won't take any more of your essence today."

While she was relieved that she'd have some time to recover, some distant part of her felt disappointed.

He left the room, returning sometime later with two plates of food. He placed it in her lap, and she ate greedily. As they ate, he watched her from his seat across the room.

When they'd both cleared their plates, he said, "I will escort you to your room."

He extended his elbow to her, and she took it without a word. They walked up the massive staircase in the entryway, and she made a point not to look at the landing as they strode past.

As they walked, guilt twisted in her stomach. It was her fault that they'd both nearly died. She should have turned around when she sensed the demon was close by. Sure, she hadn't known for certain if the sensation she'd felt was the ward, but she'd lingered far too long when she knew a creature of darkness approached. She knew better. Her teachers had trained her better. And her actions nearly had her killed. If the erox hadn't been nearby, she would have been dead, or perhaps they both would be.

Together, they strode down hallways in silence until she was before her door. He lowered his arm, and she let hers slip free.

For some reason, the gentleness of the touch had something inside her chest aching.

She turned to him, feeling words coming out of her in a rush. "I'm sorry about passing through the ward. I didn't mean to—"

Before she could finish her sentence, his lips were on hers, his fingers slipping into her hair. She gasped, her arms wrapping around his waist of their own accord. Every time they'd kissed, it had been when he'd fed on her. But as his velvet-soft lips ran over hers, she didn't feel the calling in her chest or the thrum as her essence moved. Instead, his tongue ravished her mouth as though to explore every inch of her.

It didn't feel like he wanted to dominate her.

As he pulled her close, one of his thumbs running over her cheek as his tongue wrapped around hers, she thought she sensed relief emanating from him. As though he'd feared he might lose her.

For the first time, she kissed him back willingly, breathing in his scent of pine and chaos. As she did, the tiredness in her bones became a distant memory.

"Don't scare me like that ever again," he rasped between kisses, gripping her hair almost to the point of pain. All she could do in response was to pull him close so his chest and stomach pressed against hers.

When lust stirred in her chest, the one she was slowly becoming familiar with every time she was near him, she felt his lips tear from hers. He stepped back and bowed at the waist.

"Good night, Arabella," he said before disappearing into the darkness.

She touched a finger to her lips. "Good night."

Elias.

Chapter Ten

ARABELLA

Arabella rounded the corner, about to enter the banquet hall where they'd eaten breakfast the previous day. Some strange part of her was hoping to catch the erox reading his book at the head table.

I'm not seeking his company, she thought. *I'm simply bored.*

Before she could enter the room, however, he was already striding out of it. As ever, he wore all black. But this time his boots were of a far sturdier leather, and he tied a cloak over his shoulders. He offered her a brief nod as he moved down the hall.

"Good morning, little enchantress," he said over his shoulder. "Your time is yours for the rest of the day. I'll call on you tomorrow."

She hurried after him. "Where are you going?"

Turning, he headed toward the sweeping staircase and the entryway.

"I have something I must see to."

On his heels, she strode down the stairs behind him, dress flowing upward with the movement, and she had to hold it down. "Can I come?"

She stopped mid-stride, blinking. Had she just asked to spend time with the erox on purpose? She must truly be bored. It certainly wasn't because of their last interactions the night before.

He took another few steps forward onto the landing of the main staircase before turning to her. His eyes swept over her boots, dress, and sweater. "Not in that. You'll freeze."

She blinked. "I can go with you?"

"Is there a reason you shouldn't?"

She hesitated. "No..."

Was she just a prisoner here? Was that how he saw offerings? If so, shouldn't he insist on her staying within the palace walls? In the past, he'd insisted that she remain within the wards, but that was when she was without him.

"Are you so untrustworthy that you must remain in your quarters?"

She flinched as though slapped. No one had ever called her word into question. When she'd been in the Circle, everyone knew that once she committed to something, there was no going back.

"Of course not."

"Then go change into your leathers. We ride in fifteen minutes."

With a smile, she hurried back up the stairs and toward her room. She shouldn't be so pleased by his reaction, but it surprised her. In minutes, she was in her enchantress leathers and boots.

Outside the castle, she walked around until she located the stables, which were in a small building made of dark gray stone similar to the castle itself. Inside, there were a dozen stalls, most of which were empty except for two. Massive war horses that were far taller than any she'd seen in Shadowbank were already saddled, and the erox had the reins of both, guiding them outside. He passed her the reins to a beautiful black mare.

Smiling, she patted the creature's neck. "Hello, beautiful."

Beside her, he mounted his horse with ease. She paused, eyeing her mare with trepidation. It was slightly smaller than The erox's horse, but not by much. She'd never ridden anything so big, let alone mounted one so far off the ground. There'd been no need since she never left Shadowbank and didn't need to transport goods.

Reaching for its side, she grabbed the saddle and put her foot in one stirrup. She pushed off the ground several times but couldn't get the momentum to lift herself. Elias started to dismount, but she quickly said, "I'm fine." Then she heaved herself up, catching the saddle and swinging into it.

Unable to help herself, she glanced at the erox, who averted his gaze and turned to the forest, ushering his horse forward.

"You will listen to me without argument or objection when we are outside the ward," he said, not looking back at her. "Is that understood?"

"Yes."

"These woods are crawling with supernatural creatures. Most should stay away when I'm with you. So, don't leave my side." He nodded to her saddle. "You have weapons if you need them."

Glancing down, she noted several long knives, which she eyed appreciatively before grabbing them and putting them in sheaths on her legs, arms, and throughout her enchantress leathers. It felt good to be armed and wearing her leathers again. Belatedly, she realized the knives fit perfectly in her sheaths. Did he already have knives of the correct length? Had he had them made for her, or did they belong to one of his previous offerings? Either way, he'd made accommodations specifically for her.

"Where are we going?" she asked, both fear and excitement to be traveling through a forest she'd been taught to stay away from her whole life mingling in her veins.

Fear lurked in the back of her thoughts at the idea of possibly encountering the Alabaster again, but she felt... safer with the erox by her side.

What has gotten into me?

"About fifteen miles east of here, there are a few cottages. I wouldn't call it a village, but there are a few things I must get there."

She didn't press further, sensing she'd get no more from him.

There was a tugging on her skin, a pulling in her chest, as they passed through the ward. Immediately, her whole body tensed, preparing herself for an encounter with a demon. There was no guarantee the creatures of the forest would stay away with an erox beside her, but she could sense his power. It billowed around him in dark, lapping waves like ocean tides at midnight. Perhaps if there were any creatures that didn't travel in packs, like the Alabaster, it would deter them from approaching. She also wasn't powerless—she had to remember that. Though her shadow magic was unreliable at best.

They rode in silence for what felt like hours. She thought about trying to fill the quiet, to ask the erox of his family or how he liked to spend his days. But she found herself content with the wordless journey.

The horses seemed familiar with the forest terrain, and she let her black mare follow his massive white steed. The larger horse's coloring was like a beacon in these dark woods. She tried not to worry about being spotted. But she held on to weaves of power, keeping one hand free of the reins as she kept her eyes on the surrounding woods.

Eventually, they came to a clearing in the trees, which gave way to rolling green hills. There were a few farms and a small outcropping of buildings. He rode for the cluster of buildings, moving with familiarity. They eventually came to a small stone building, and he dismounted and tied his horse to a nearby post. She followed suit, narrowly avoiding stumbling forward as she hit the ground.

Turning, she patted her horse. "You are tall, my darling. Very tall."

The horse whickered but didn't object as she tied it beside Elias' mount.

He strode inside the stone building, and she followed. As the door opened, a bell chimed and a thousand scents assaulted her senses.

"Since when do erox get sick?" she mumbled, pulling a mask over her face that was attached to her hood as they entered.

She hated apothecaries.

The would-be healers poisoned folk as much as helped them, especially since most didn't have proper training and treated patients based on superstition rather than what methods had been proven. By the looks of this establishment, the owners of the establishment had collected hundreds of different plants and herbs with bottles and jars of every color filling the walls. There were a number of jars with what appeared to be pickled animal parts also filling the shelves.

The erox ignored her, turning toward the woman who strode through a door leading to what must be the back of the shop and into the main room. She was tall with a confident walk and many wrinkles on her tan face. If Arabella had to guess, she'd say that the woman spent many hours working under the sun.

"Madam." He offered her a slight nod.

"Good morning to ye," she said with a heavy accent Arabella didn't recognize. "What brings you in this time, Mr. Whitlock?"

Whitlock?

Arabella's eyes flicked to the erox, but he kept his gaze trained on the woman. She realized then there was so much she didn't know about him. For reasons she couldn't explain, that saddened her.

He pulled a small parchment from his pocket and handed it to her.

With a glance at the parchment and then to Arabella, the woman turned and began bustling about the room.

No introductions, then. That was fine enough by her. She supposed Scarlett must have been the last person with Elias—if he'd allowed her to accompany him. So, the sight of a new companion may have been surprising. But just what was he here for? And how many times had he been here previously?

As the woman moved, Arabella studied the shelves, noting a few poisons.

Foxglove. Hemlock. Rhododendron.

"You've got a keen eye, Enchantress."

Arabella turned.

The woman's eyes trained on her as she gestured to the shelves behind her. "I really should move those to the back." She shrugged. "But so few people come by these days, and most of my work is house calls."

"You've seen an enchantress before?"

"I met Mr. Whitlock's other companion," she answered simply. "And I've seen one or two others in my life. Though folk rarely venture out this far."

"How do you survive so close to the woods and with no wards?" It was a question that had been burning in the back of her mind.

"We have no enchantresses to protect us, and there are few of us left. Perhaps the beasts of the forest know we aren't worth the effort—with just the old and thin remaining. We'd be tough meat."

Guilt twisted Arabella's chest.

While it was true the role of enchantresses in the continent was to protect humans, there simply wasn't enough to send to every single town. And if the dwelling was as small as this one, well... it likely wouldn't have been on any official map. None would think—or even know—to travel this way.

"But," the woman added with a sly smile to the erox, "we've had some good fortune of late."

He merely nodded.

In minutes, the woman had collected everything from the list. Arabella recognized remedies for common colds, nausea, insomnia, and even pain medication. Did the erox get sick? She would've assumed that consuming essence would have healed his kind from any maladies.

The woman wrapped each of the glass bottles and jars in towels so they didn't clink together, and then the erox passed something to her.

"Good day to you," he said simply before turning toward the door.

Arabella offered the woman a nod as well. She might not be a fan of apothecaries, but this woman was making the best of her situation. Without enchantresses and proper healers, there were few other options but to attempt to find remedies themselves.

Once outside, the erox packed the supplies in his saddlebags before mounting. Arabella did likewise, struggling once again to mount her very tall mare. As they rode through what must be the center of their town, she spotted a small child wearing old rags in the shadows of a building before a thick canopy of trees surrounded them once more. She swallowed back the guilt for leaving them. This place was even more defenseless than Shadowbank.

They neared the castle as the sun began its descent in the sky above the leafy canopies. As they moved through the ward, she could see streaks of pink and orange and took her first deep breath in hours.

Somehow, they'd managed not to encounter any demons.

The erox dismounted and strode over to her.

"Are you hungry?"

She nodded.

"Come. Let's eat in the gardens."

They returned their horses to the stables, removed their saddles, and saw to their needs. Arabella thought to wonder who took care of the animals most of the time.

The erox disappeared into the castle, gesturing for her to go into the gardens where flowers bloomed along winding stone pathways. Not long later, he returned with a basket and a large blanket, which he laid in open grass near the flowers. Then he set up a variety of foods for them—cheeses, dried meats, fruits, nuts, and biscuits. He even brought a bottle of wine, uncorked it, and poured her a glass. She ate hungrily, enjoying all the different tastes mixing on her tongue and the sharp tang of the red wine.

After some time, she broke the silence. "How long have you been going to that village?"

"A few years."

Beside her, he popped a grape into his mouth.

"Are you sick?"

He frowned and turned to face her. "No. Why do you ask?"

She shrugged. "You purchased medicines. I wondered if you were getting sick."

"The erox do not suffer common illnesses like humans or lesser magic wielders."

It was as she suspected.

"What is it for, then?"

"You."

He said it so frankly that all she could do was blink for several moments. Realizing her mouth hung ajar, she snapped it shut before opening it again.

"You got medicines for me?"

First, he'd taken care of her after he'd taken too much essence the other day, then he'd saved her from the Alabaster and gave her chocolates and food to regain her energy, and he'd allowed her to journey with him to the apothecary when she'd asked. Now, he not only prepared a picnic for them, but he also bought medicines for her. And that kiss... Why kiss her if he wasn't taking her essence? Could it be some manipulation on his part to have her infatuated with him so that she was under his control?

None of this should matter, and it *didn't* matter.

She was an enchantress, and he was a demon. There was nothing between them nor could there ever be.

"Of course. You're part of my household, and I care for what's mine. If you're sick, I need to be prepared."

"That's kind of you."

The sun felt warm on her skin and leathers, and she tilted her head back, sighing. It was far warmer than yesterday as though autumn had receded for one final echo of summer's warmth. In fact, it was getting hot.

130

Rising, she said, "I'm going to take a walk. Would you like to join me?"

Lines formed between his brows, but he nodded and stood, following her.

A pleasant breeze lifted the small hairs curling around her face, and she allowed her feet to move across the garden, the open grassy area where they sparred, and then to the lake beside the castle.

The water was utterly still as though it was a mirror to the sky above. It seemed as beautiful and serene as the day itself. As she looked along the coast, there were no docks or boats nearby. Not that an erox would host guests. But the water looked serene. It was a temptation she couldn't resist. She slipped her boots and leather jacket off and headed for the water. She sat on the shoreline and stuck her toes in.

The water was a cool kiss against her skin, and the sun warmed her shoulders. But soon, she grew warm and the water too tempting. Standing, she pulled off her leather pants so that she was in only her shirt, corset, and undergarments. She took a step into the water and then another until she was up to her knees, enjoying the squish of sandy earth beneath her feet. A sadness squeezed in her chest as she thought about just what magic she could have sensed from all around her if she'd had access to her elemental magic.

Beside her, the erox removed his shoes and tossed them farther back up the shore. She turned fully toward him.

A rare smile as warm as the autumn sunshine brightened his face. His hair was pulled back, revealing high cheekbones and the start of a beard. He wore his usual tight pants and tall leather boots, but he'd rolled up his shirtsleeves past his elbow, leaving muscled forearms open to the sun.

"Eyes up here, little enchantress," he purred.

She swallowed, tearing her eyes from his arms. "I don't know what you're talking about."

"I'd thought you would have had your fill of bad ideas," the erox said, nodding toward the lake. "Or perhaps you have a death wish."

She gestured to the water, which was motionless outside of little ripples from the small waves at the shoreline. "I think a swim on a warm autumn day is a wonderful idea." A thought occurred to her, and she hesitated, groaning. "Don't tell me there are monsters in the lake, too. I thought it was just the ocean and bay."

He smirked. "The forest—and everything in it—isn't a safe place for mortals. Even my wards can't fend off all water creatures."

She raised a brow. "Are the erox completely useless?"

As she spoke, he stood and grabbed the corners of his shirt before pulling it over his head.

All at once, it felt like time stopped.

His chest was as chiseled as his arms, and he had large pectoral muscles—which was covered in a fine layer of hair as dark as that on his head. His hip bones stuck out the top of his pants along with the start of a line that led down, down...

Time resumed normal speed as he reached for his pants, loosening his belt.

Her heart raced, and she turned away from him, water sloshing as she faced the lake.

I'm an enchantress. Enchantresses don't fuck demons.

I'm an enchantress. Enchantresses don't want to fuck demons.

She replayed the mantra over and over in her head, hoping that with repetition maybe she'd believe it.

Water sloshed behind her, but she didn't dare turn around. "I thought you said it was a bad idea."

"It was." The words were a rumble over her shoulder. She could feel his body close to hers, nearly touching. "But I know some creatures that live in these waters. They won't approach you if I'm nearby."

They'd be able to sense his magic, too.

She felt the brush of his breath along her neck before he leaned down, his lips tracing along the sensitive skin. In an instant, she was aflame. It was all she could do not to whimper at the simple touch.

His hands found her waist, pulling her in. She felt so tempted to tilt her head back, close her eyes, and let him sweep her away.

What happened the other night, the kiss in front of her bedroom door, would only happen the once. It was a lapse in judgment. It would not—could not—happen again.

Even as she held on to the thought, she found herself reaching back and gasped as her hands touched his bare thighs.

He was naked.

Chapter Eleven

ARABELLA

All that was between them was her undergarments and top.

Arabella lowered her hands to her sides. She would fulfill her role as his offering and nothing more. They did *not* need to fuck for him to feed.

"Can you obey me?" he rumbled from where he stood behind her. One of the erox's arms wrapped around her stomach while the other hand slipped across her chest and up her neck. His kisses trailed up her neck, finding the shell of her ear.

A shiver ran through her, and she bit her lip.

"Show that you can do as I say," he said, one of his hands moving until stopping beneath her breasts. "And I'll give you as many orgasms as you'd like."

Fuck.

So far, all he'd had to do was barely touch her, and she'd been unraveling. How long could she hold on? Could she give her body to this male—this demon?

"How do you know I want anything you can give me?"

He spun her around to him, his hand beneath her chin, forcing her to look up at him. His grip was firm, but it didn't hurt. Despite herself, she couldn't look away from his dark, piercing gaze.

"I can smell desire on you, little enchantress. Your body doesn't lie."

"It's your magic," she said, belatedly recognizing it as the admission it was—that she wanted him. "It's making me do things I normally wouldn't."

A smirk traced his lips, and he stroked the side of her neck with his thumb before leaning forward and whispering into her ear. "My magic can't create something that isn't there. It can only deepen an existing attraction." He leaned back, their eyes connecting again. She tried to look away, but he held her chin once more—forcing her to meet his gaze.

"Only I can fulfill your every fantasy. But first, you must trust me with your body. Can you do that?"

Heat surged through her as her desire spiked. To her shame, something flitted in her chest as his eyes darkened and fluttered closed for the briefest of moments as he took a breath. Something about the rise and fall of his chest mesmerized her. But she didn't dare look down and see his hard length. The length she could feel against her stomach. She had to keep her eyes above his chest.

Better yet, she had to stop this.

Floundering for a way to break this connection, she said, "Was Scarlett like this?"

Was she willingly offering you her body like I crave to?

"No."

She was so shocked that she realized she was gaping and snapped her mouth shut. "No?"

"There was no sexual chemistry between Scarlett and I. Over time, we formed an understanding. For my part, I enjoyed her company. But she provided me with a way to sustain my immortal life, and nothing more."

She bit the inside of her cheek.

He could be lying to her, telling her what he thought she

wanted to hear. He could have fucked Scarlett senseless and enjoyed every moment.

Or he could be telling the truth.

Could he have just fed on Scarlett without ever touching her sexually? She'd have to come for him to consume her essence, but she could've touched herself. If that was true, did attraction to him mean this could be something more than the tugging of dark magic?

"You just want physical connection after years of abstinence," she said.

The words tasted bitter, and it took far more effort to voice them than she cared to admit.

He shrugged, a shifting of muscled shoulders that glistened in the late afternoon sun. "I can't deny I haven't longed for the feel of a warm body pressed against mine these many years. But I won't take just anyone." His eyes dipped down before rising back to meet hers. "I want you." He leaned in, biting her ear. "And you want me, too. All I ask is for your obedience."

"What does obedience mean to you?"

Why was she asking this question? The answer didn't matter because she would not obey him, let alone fuck him.

"When I tell you to move, you move. When I tell you to remain still, you will do so. When I tell you that you don't come until I say, you hold on until the moment I give you the word." His eyes glittered as though he knew he had her, which he most assuredly did not. "I will use your body in any way that I like. I will explore the length of you until I know everything that makes you squirm and scream. And by the end, you *will* be screaming my name."

A whimper escaped her lips.

Keep it together, keep it—

Slowly, she reached up, entangling her fingers in his soft curls. Then she wrapped her arms around the back of his neck and pulled him down to her for a kiss. As his lips met hers, he moaned.

Never in her thirty years of life had she heard a sound so magnificent, so alluring as that.

She wanted him to make that sound again.

"Say you will be mine," he whispered between kisses. "Say you will obey me, and you can have everything you wish."

He couldn't mean... no. He was just asking for her body.

She should say no. But she was his offering for the next decade. Would it be so bad for them to pleasure each other during their time together?

She thought of Shadowbank and its failing ward. If she was going to study the ward, she needed to get this collar off, and no matter what she'd tried when she was in her room alone, she couldn't get it off. So, if she had any hope of accessing her elemental magic, she'd need to gain the erox's trust so that he removed it himself. Maybe if he trusted her enough, he'd change his mind about helping reinforce Shadowbank's ward, and then she wouldn't have to sneak away to help her village and face the demons of the forest alone.

Her thoughts shifted to the countless demons and dark beings she'd faced when protecting Shadowbank. All she'd ever known was life against them—kill or be killed. It wasn't just a mindset she'd been taught in her upbringing amongst the Circle. It was a reality she'd lived for two decades amongst the mortals in the village. So many times she'd come close to death or had to save one of her sisters from these monsters. But she'd never spoken to a demon before and witnessed some sense of humanity.

The erox was still a demon, but he'd protected her from the Alabaster and gotten her medicine. Surely, he couldn't be like all the other demons she'd faced. Perhaps he was different.

Perhaps what was between them was different.

Despite every objection she had, her body knew what it wanted. It had since the beginning. No matter the words she'd uttered, she wanted him.

If she was going to abandon everything she had known and

been taught as an enchantress, then she was going all in. She wanted all he could offer her.

In the deepest corners of her mind, she knew she wanted a lover that could control her—that could dominate her body and fuck her so hard that she forgot her name. She didn't want a gentle lover and never had. She wanted a male who wasn't afraid to make decisions and take control. So often, she was the one in charge of others, protecting and delegating. But in this, she wanted nothing more than to submit to a strong male—for him to use her body in any way he'd like.

And he was offering her just that.

She pulled back from him, her eyes flickering between his. There was a hint of earnestness there. Could that be hope she detected as well?

Then she uttered four damning words.

"My body is yours."

He growled with pleasure. Then his hands were on her corset, unlacing it with deft fingers. He removed it and her shirt, tossing both to the shore. Then he tore her undergarments with ease and tossed them aside. His lips found hers, and he *feasted* on her as though he were a dying man in need of air. As he kissed her, he took a step forward, forcing her back toward the shore until there was grass beneath her feet.

"Lie down."

It wasn't a request.

"I want to get my fill of you."

She did as he said, lying back in a bed of grass along the shoreline, revealing all of herself to him. Utterly naked, his eyes soaked her in as much as she did him. His cock was wide and curved upward. She bit her lip, knowing that it would stroke her in just the right place when he was inside her. Her eyes traced down his muscled thighs, marveling at the size of him. He was perfection. It was as though he'd been sculpted just for her.

Lowering himself until he kneeled above her, he leaned down, his lips tracing paths up her neck and down her chest before suckling her breasts.

She made a sound somewhere between a moan and a whimper.

In the past, her times with lovers had never made her feel like this. It had been nothing more than a quick coming together of bodies. But now, she was so filled with lust, with a desire for him, that it made her mind swim.

She needed him. She needed to feel him inside her. But he continued his lazy trail of kisses down her stomach, lingering at her hips and sinking his teeth into the soft flesh. The idea that it would leave a mark on her spiked her desire hotter.

Her hands were in his hair, and she thrust her hips upward. "Please." The word was a mere whisper but held so much weight.

He paused, looking up at her.

"So eager," he said with a soft grin. "Does my little enchantress feel unsatisfied?"

Should she say yes? Would that displease him if she implied she didn't like what he was doing? Because she did. Far too much. But she needed more.

"I want you to touch me."

"Mmm," he purred, lowering himself over her and nibbling on her hip once more. Then he pushed her legs apart, spreading them obscenely wide. His eyes rounded as though he'd never seen anything so beautiful and then narrowed, a growl rumbling from deep within his chest.

Ever so slowly, he lowered himself until she felt the tickle of his breath on her clit. Leaning in, he kissed where her leg met her inner thigh, his tongue tracing where his lips had been. So very close and yet nowhere near close enough. But she didn't move. He'd asked for her obedience, and she would give him that. Or try to—this once. Because damn her, she wanted everything he could give her.

Then he was on her.

He didn't wait, didn't go slow. He feasted on her like a man starving. Immediately, her desire spiked hotter. She gasped as she felt his tongue ravish her clit, moving in swift but steady strokes—up and down and back. It drove her wild.

She realized then she'd let no one go down on her before. It wasn't because she didn't like the idea of it. To have someone between her thighs, it felt like she'd be exposing the deepest part of herself to another person. And the idea of that was far too vulnerable. But now... she hadn't even thought to object as he spread her wide.

It felt right.

As he licked her length, his hands roamed across her body, pulling at her hips and ass as though he couldn't get her close enough. It felt so intimate even while her every carnal instinct pulsed inside her and demanded she fuck his face and then kiss him until they were both breathless.

Pleasure spiked hotter, and her fingers tangled in his hair as a whimper escaped her lips. Unable to stop herself, her hips began to move in time with his tongue.

She was close, oh so close. If she let herself, she would fall over the edge.

"Can I come?" she whispered as a breeze tickled her bare skin in the afternoon sun. Opening her eyes, she looked down. His black curls appeared a deep blue in the sunlight, and it reminded her of the depths of the ocean, of cool waves and dark pleasure.

There was a distinct shake of his head as his hands gripped her thighs and pinned her in place. She couldn't move away from the delicious flick of his tongue even if she wanted to. And she did *not* want to. But his refusal surprised her—and the fact that he was well and truly feasting on her, unwilling to come up for air. She was going to come all over his face.

He looked up then. His normally dark eyes had darkened even further. His irises looked black as his pupils expanded, engulfing everything in shadow.

She should be frightened, but all she could see was the naked lust in his eyes and the faint sheen of sweat on his shoulders.

Shifting, he lifted one arm so that his hand rested at the base of her stomach, pressing down, and the other moved toward her center. Fingers lazily trailed her entrance, and she groaned.

"That's my good little enchantress—asking for my permission," he purred as he lowered his head back down. "Do you like what I'm doing?"

"Yes."

She was a breath away from coming, her core tingling, yearning for release.

Of course, she liked what he was doing. Was that not obvious?

One finger slipped inside her, and she gasped, back arching. He moved in a come-here motion, pulling her ever closer to the edge. His other hand pressed down on her stomach, which only enhanced what his finger was doing, heightening her every sense.

Panting, she teetered on the edge. She couldn't last much longer.

"Come for me, little enchantress. Fuck my face."

Then his tongue was moving over her clit again, steadily moving up and down. All the while, his finger worked, moving deep inside her, pulling her again and again toward the edge. The pressure building within her heightened, and instead of fighting it, she was swept into the current.

She came undone around him, crying out as she fucked his face and he fucked her with his fingers. Wave after wave of pleasure crashed over her until she was lost to time. Broad shoulders blocked out the sun before she felt the press of his lips, a tongue in her mouth. She tasted herself on his tongue, and then she felt his magic ensnare her, pulling. It was a gentle ushering forward, coaxing her essence out of her chest, up her throat, until it was filling her mouth. Just as he'd feasted on her clit, he feasted on the bright blue essence, sucking it from her lips. As he did, he kept fucking her with a finger before slipping in a second, and another orgasm had her gasping into his mouth, his name on her tongue. Her essence glowed brighter, and then he was moaning. She captured the sound with her lips, eager to consume as much of him as he was of her.

"I want to roll you over and fuck you on this beach," he rasped, his fingers easing out of her. "But I promised I would take my time with you. And damn it, I will."

Even as her mind and body floated, feeling weightless, she detected his weakening restraint. A distant part of her wondered how an erox could so quickly lose himself. He'd only pleasured her. She hadn't even touched him yet.

Slowly, he rose to his feet and extended a hand toward her. The afternoon sun cast shadows on his naked body, making the curves of his muscles appear even larger.

Without the feel of his warm body against hers, her chest ached. Not letting herself think what that could mean, she accepted his hand and stood. Smiling, he backed into the water.

"Follow me."

And damn her, she did.

Chapter Twelve

ARABELLA

E lias guided her into the water until it sloshed around her hips.

The water was only to his mid-thighs. Arabella tried not to let her eyes linger too long on those large, muscled legs and what they led to. She could feel his presence beside her like a physical sensation. His nearness wrapped around her senses, making her feel warm and treasured.

How strange, she thought, *that a demon could make me feel this way.*

She stuffed the thought down. She was being silly. It was just the orgasms talking.

As he moved in front of her, guiding her around a bend in the shoreline into an alcove in the water where several boulders protruded from the shoreline, her eyes flickered down to their entwined fingers.

She blinked, surprised by the sight.

"Have you been fucked in the water before?"

Just like that, heat filled her core, and her breaths grew shallow. She inhaled slowly, trying to steady her racing heart.

"No," she said, thinking of the bay beside Shadowbank and the dark waters that held darker creatures beneath them. Unlike the shore here, the bay had a steep drop-off into the deep. It wasn't safe to swim there. "But not out of preference."

He nodded, seeming to understand. When he turned to her, there was a mixture of lust and curiosity in his eyes—which were still the color of a moonless night.

"Would you like to?"

She paused, surprised by the act of him asking her preference. It wasn't that she was unaccustomed to sexual partners checking in, but he'd seemed so keen on control. So, why offer her the opportunity to deny him something? She couldn't deny she wanted to feel the length of his cock inside her as water sloshed around them, a cool boulder at her back.

With a wicked smile, she said, "Can't you smell the answer?"

"I want to hear it from your lips." He pulled her toward him, gathering both of her hands in his as he walked backward into the alcove. She followed him, toes squishing in sticky sand. "Because when we start, your body—all that you are—is mine."

"Yes," she said as her eyes flickered between his. Then she added, "You aren't what I expected."

"Neither are you, little enchantress."

She realized then that he never used her name. To her surprise, she wondered what it would sound like on his lips. She had a feeling she'd like it all too well.

Her hand slipped free of his, and she pressed his chest. He allowed her to move him and walked until his back was against a massive boulder along the shoreline. The water was still to his mid-thighs. Her eyes flicked down, and she could see that he was still very hard.

He'd had his taste of her. Now, she wanted her taste of him.

"What are you—" he began, but he fell silent as she lowered herself to her knees before him until the water was all around her and there was nothing between her and his cock but the autumn air. The surprise in his gaze was deafening. Leaning forward, she nipped his hips, enjoying the feel of his soft skin between her teeth.

"This isn't—" he tried again, but his words turned into a gasping moan as she kissed and licked the skin right next to the base of his cock.

This demon was an eager lover. And she wanted to be the reason he made those sounds again.

Raising her hand, she grabbed the base of his shaft, marveling at the softness of his skin and how hard he felt in her palm and beneath her fingers. Slowly, she started stroking him, and he made another noise that she took as encouragement before she licked his cock from base to tip. She could have sworn she felt him *shiver*. But how could that be? This was an erox. Surely, he'd had dozens —or even hundreds—of lovers over the many years of his immortal existence. Why would her touch affect him in this way? She must be mistaken. It had been the movement of the lapping water around them and nothing more.

Then she wrapped her mouth around him, unable to wait a moment longer. His cock was wide, filling her mouth. He was like velvet against her tongue, and she sucked and flicked her tongue as she moved. He tasted as decadent as sin, and he *was* sin to her.

The two of them were something that could never—should never—be. A defender of the realm and a demon should never be found in common circles, let alone fucking each other. But she couldn't stay away.

As she worked, he moved his hands down from where he'd clutched the boulder behind him to her neck and shoulders. She could feel his eyes on her, hot and wanting, as his fingers tangled into her hair. Surprised this male who was so keen on control had let her have her way with him, she slowed her movements to an agonizing pace, wanting to draw out the pleasure just as he had with her.

Somewhere above her, he growled, fingers tightening in her hair. Then without a word, he fisted her hair and began to fuck her mouth in earnest. It was all she could do to hold on and take small, gasping breaths. He moved like a male who hadn't seen the light of day in years, hungry and desperate for any glimmer. She was his sun, and he orbited her. Circling and circling until he, too, finally gave in. But what reason did he have to hold back? He was a demon. No rules were keeping him from taking whatever—and whoever—he wanted. And by the feel of his cock hitting the back of her throat, he wanted her.

Pleasure built between her legs at the feel of him taking control, using her body to sate his needs. Damn her, she wanted to be used by this man—this demon.

Soon, he became impossibly hard and his movements more jerky. Then he released her hair and pulled himself out of her. Looking up, her eyes locked on his. If she thought his pitch-black eyes were hot before, they were like molten lava now. Something inside of him had been brought to life, and it was like this was the first time she was truly seeing him. With a grin, she traced her tongue over her upper lip, marveling at the lingering taste of him.

With a growl, he picked her up, her legs wrapping around his naked hips, and moved her so her back was against the boulder.

"You've pleased me," he purred as he held her. "And for that, you can have my cock."

Heat surged through her, and she swore that the smell of her desire must be heady because his impossibly black eyes flickered with a deeper desire, fluttering closed as he breathed in before opening them again.

"I asked you this once before, but I'll ask you again," he continued, as though he narrowly resisted the temptation to fuck her that very moment. "Are you on something to prevent pregnancy?"

She nodded.

She'd been taking herbs for years to prevent her from getting with child. Being a mother was never something she'd wanted to pursue, and she'd made every effort to ensure it wasn't in the cards for her.

"Good," he said as he positioned her above his cock, her back against the boulder. "Do you want me to come inside you, little enchantress?"

Licking her lips, she said, "Yes."

"Do you want me to fuck you?"

She dipped her chin, her heart racing.

"I need to hear you say it."

Taking gasping breath, she opened her mouth before closing it again. Gathering the shreds of her courage, she said, "I want you to fuck me. Hard."

With a growl, he held her up effortlessly with one hand and grabbed his cock in his other hand. He nudged her opening with the tip of his cock. Both of them moaned. He moved the head of his cock around her folds, sliding easily. She was slick with desire, so ready for him that she felt ready to scream—to beg until he fucked her like he'd promised.

"Say please," he purred.

She moved her hips, straining for his cock, wanting to feel him inside her. But he evaded her. For a moment, she felt his cock at her ass, and a desire she'd never felt before hit hard.

One thing at a time, she reminded herself. Her focus splintered into all the ways she wanted her body to be used by him.

"Please."

She couldn't hide the desperation in her voice—the sheer need.

A smile spread across his lips.

Then he sheathed himself inside of her.

She cried out at the feel of him pressing deep into her. He was everywhere, widening her, pressing at her walls.

"This pussy is mine." His lips were against her ear as he thrust into her, and she was all too aware of her breasts pressing against his chest. The sensation had another moan escaping from her lips. "And it feels so good."

Logically, she knew that her body was hers and could never truly be anyone else's. But in that moment, it didn't matter. She wanted to be owned by this man, to be *dominated* by him, body and soul. She wanted everything he could give her.

Hands wrapping around his neck, she pulled him in and

pressed her lips to his—needing to taste him as he thrust into her again and again. It reminded her of the ocean, the salty sea breeze, and the dark allure of a moonless night. She knew if she let herself, she could get lost in him. But was she ready for that? She could give him her body, and she could desire him with every fiber of her being. But she could never give in fully to him—not with her heart.

But even as she thought this, his tongue ravished her mouth, twisting around hers and sending a bolt of pleasure down to her core even as his cock curved against her G-spot. She was going to come again. He'd been fucking her for a minute, and she was a breath away from unraveling again.

Did she still need his permission?

She pulled away from his kiss, gasping. "You... I..." His cock plunged into her again, and her back pressed hard against the rock. It wasn't painful, but he rocked into her so deep that a whimpering sound escaped her lips.

"Can I come?"

The words were softer than she'd intended them, almost a plea.

With a wicked smile, he said, "Come for me as many times as you can."

That was all the encouragement she needed before she let go.

Pleasure racketed through her, a powerful wave that washed over her, and it was all she could do to hold on to him. His lips were on hers again, his tongue inside her mouth as it felt like a breath was being sucked from her chest. Sky-blue essence flowed between her lips, and he ate it hungrily. As he did, his black irises faded somewhat back to his usual brown. But she could tell he was far from finished with her.

"What does it taste like?" she asked, breathless. "My essence."

"Like a constellation—powerful, brilliant." He didn't stop fucking her, but a thoughtfulness crossed his eyes, and he slowed his pace somewhat. "No one has ever asked me that before."

That seemed strange to her. Wouldn't his offerings be curious about the experience of his consuming essence? Did it drive him closer to release, or did it simply sate his need to feed and survive?

His tongue ran up the length of her neck until he nipped her ear.

"I don't know how to explain it. It's like... tasting your skin, the feel of your pussy on my tongue... I'm tasting you, but it's deeper than that. I can feel your core, the heart of who you are—a small sliver of it—and..." He trailed off, thrusting into her. She could see his control was on a knife's edge. If it tipped, he'd lose himself in her.

"You are decadent." He seemed to gather himself before saying, "Everyone tastes different. The darker the heart, the greasier the taste. But you..." He paused, his fingers gripped her hips tighter, never tiring. "You're unlike anything I've ever tasted. You are strength and resilience and hope and desire."

Then it was like he pulled release from her, demanding her pleasure, as he consumed more essence from her in a kiss that deepened until it felt like she was cascading through clouds.

"I can't get enough of you," he said.

His admission sent her core aflame, and she reached a hand down, stroking her clit.

"One day soon," he began, his eyes moving down to where their bodies joined. "I want to watch you touch yourself—just where I tell you. I want to watch your body move as you teeter on the edge, and then I want to be the reason you come."

She held on to his neck with one hand, not stopping the movement with her other hand on her clit even as she moved her hips in time with his thrusts. Leaning in, she pressed her lips to his, eager for him—for this erox—to taste her desire for him. For some reason, she needed him to feel her pleasure in this moment. She needed him to know that she couldn't get enough of him. As she came again, she moaned into his mouth, and he ate it all just as he ate her essence, the two mingling together.

Suddenly, his movements grew jerkier, and his grip on her hips tightened.

"I'm going to come," he rasped before he pounded into her with abandon. He slid in and out of her folds with delicious wet slaps until he cried out. She found his lips, eager to taste his pleasure as he'd tasted hers.

Warmth filled her core, but his thrusts never slowed, and his lips found her neck, biting *hard*.

"You are mine, Arabella."

Her heart raced at the sound of her name on his lips.

His cum spilled out of her, and she could feel it running down her ass. Even after coming several times, the feel of it sent a swirl of pleasure through her.

"I will have every part of you," he said, his words full of raw emotion and promise.

The idea of time with him should scare her. It should be revolting.

It wasn't.

Unable to think about that now, she kissed him, and they fucked late into the night.

Chapter Thirteen

ARABELLA

T he next morning, Arabella dressed and headed to the stables.

Her black mare stood in its stall, spotting her immediately when she entered and stomping a hoof against the ground as she approached. As she glanced around, she noted fresh hay and food in each of the stalls.

"Hello, darling," she said as the horse stretched out its nose to her. She ran a hand over it, petting it in long strokes. The creature nuzzled into her hand, and she smiled. Pulling out an apple she'd pocketed from breakfast in her room, she offered it to the horse, and it snapped it up eagerly.

As the horse sniffed her in search of a second apple, a flash of movement in the corner of her eye and a soft thump had her spinning on a heel. When she turned to look, there was nothing there. She could have sworn she'd heard footsteps, too. But the stables were empty except for herself and the horses. Nothing seemed amiss either. Only a single saddlebag was off its shelf where the others were stored.

How strange.

Walking over, she grabbed the saddle and placed it back with the others. It must have fallen.

Footsteps sounded behind her, and she turned, seeing Elias.

Had he been the one she'd heard a few moments ago? But why would he then enter through the main entrance at mortal speed?

As ever, he stood tall, his wide shoulders taking up the entire doorframe. While she was tall and lean, he had a wider build with large muscles cording up and down his arms and legs—all of which were *very* visible through his pants and tunic. Her eyes skirted down to where his shirt was unlaced at the top of his chest and then back up to his beard, which was full and well-groomed. He'd grown it out recently. Like his hair, it was as dark as a starless night. The sight of it—and the thought of it scraping against the soft skin at the tops of her thighs—had her thoughts spinning.

"Ah, good. You're here," he said, busying himself in the stables.

"Good morning to you, too."

Suddenly, she wasn't sure how to act or what to say. There had been little need for words the day before when they'd fucked in the lake, inside the castle, and in her bedroom. Today, she was pleasantly sore, and something warm swirled in her stomach. And even though she'd decided to be with him sexually despite everything she'd been raised to believe and knew to be true about demons, she still had some reservations that she couldn't shake. Namely, he was a demon—a dark creature she'd been taught all her life to seek and kill before it killed her or the humans she protected. Still, she very much intended to fuck him again, but it would *just* be fucking and nothing more.

Not for the first time, she wished Jessamine were here. She wanted to confide in her friend and get her advice. What would she think about Elias? He was different from any other demon she'd met. Would Jessamine think the same, or would she tell Arabella she was out of her mind for spreading her legs willingly for an erox?

She wondered if Jessamine would even speak to her again when she returned home in a decade. Arabella wouldn't have her memories of her time with the erox, but would she remember why she'd chosen to sacrifice herself without saying goodbye or the bargains she'd tried to make? How far back would the memory wipe go? Did her fighting the connection between them matter when she wouldn't remember it, anyway?

Unless she convinced the erox not to take her memories.

If their roles had been reversed, Arabella would be furious at Jessamine for leaving and not saying goodbye or for sacrificing herself. If she ever saw Jessamine or the other enchantresses again —so long as Arabella found a way to keep the wards from falling —they may not speak with her out of anger for what she'd done. And if they found out what she'd done with the erox, perhaps they wouldn't speak with her out of disgust at *who* she'd done.

She should feel some regret for her time with the erox yesterday... but she didn't. And that made her feel even more guilty.

As the erox moved about the stable, preparing packs and saddlebags, she said, "Are you leaving?"

"We," he said as though that answered everything.

"We?"

"We're leaving." He looked up at her for the first time that morning. The way his eyes connected with hers, it felt like the crashing of waves against each other. Then he held up a letter with a broken wax seal.

"I just received an invitation," he said. "There's a ball in the Twilight Court, and I'd like for you to come."

She gaped.

He wanted to bring her to one of the fae courts?

The fae were magical creatures who looked like humans but were far more elegant and powerful. The difference was far greater than the pointed ears. They were fast, deadly, and had access to powerful magic that far exceeded any abilities of the enchantresses. Some fae were rumored to have access to dark magic.

Few humans would ever see a single fae in their entire life. They lived in a separate realm that was tied to this one by mystical bridges, known as gateways. Only the most powerful creatures could use the gateways, as they required a significant amount of magic to open. Outside of the gateways, it was possible to get to the fae realms by creating a portal. But no human nor enchantress had that ability. Neither did most demons so far as she knew. Only the goblins, a reclusive race that hadn't been seen in centuries, could portal without a gateway. It was this ability that had led to their assumed extinction, as they'd been hunted down and used for this gift.

"Why do you want me to come?" she asked. "What's the occasion for the ball?"

"Is it not enough that I want to have you on my arm for an evening?" he said, mischief alighting in his eyes.

Was he flirting with her?

"No," she said flatly. "You don't do things without a reason."

He shrugged. "It's true that I want you on my arm."

She watched Elias as he moved around the stables, packing saddlebags.

"But your presence at my side isn't for just anyone to see. I'd like for you to meet the queen of the Twilight Court. She is said to value curiosities. No enchantress has ever traveled to there, and I'd like for you to... *enchant* her."

She rolled her eyes. "Cute."

Never had she heard of this queen, and she couldn't help but wonder why no enchantresses had ever been invited.

"What do you hope to gain by parading me around?"

Despite her skeptical tone, she couldn't help the excitement coursing through her. Going to the fae court would be an opportunity of a lifetime. She knew what her answer would be, but she wasn't about to let him know that yet.

"She has something I want," he said. "Something I hope she'll be willing to part with."

She chewed on her lip.

The little she knew of the fae was through the Circle. What she did know was that fae didn't care one lick for mortals, particularly humans. They saw them as less than, and the fae only came to the mortal realm if they needed something—usually, to take something. Such encounters had led to battles against the fae, but never a full-on war. The fae were far too powerful for mortals to have a hope of winning. At least, that's what she understood. She'd never seen the fae herself. Even with the help of magic wielders like enchantresses, the powers of the fae would likely far exceed anything the mortals could muster. Unless the humans recruited the power of the sorcerers, which would never happen.

Given that, why would Arabella's presence inspire the queen to part with something valuable when the fae looked down upon mortals? This plan seemed faulty at best. And what could the erox want so badly to journey through a gateway and risk the wrath of the fae queen if his request offended her?

Regardless, Arabella could use this chance at the ball to steal an object of power—something that could strengthen Shadowbank's wards. Maybe the answer wasn't studying the erox's wards around the castle. Maybe it was a matter of getting more power instead. She doubted such a thing would be left in the open for anyone to see, but the fae's arrogance could mean they'd flaunt their power and any objects that could enhance their power, such as an amplifier.

There was so much she didn't know about the fae or what the erox intended. But this could be her only chance to enter the fae realm. It was worth the risk.

I must protect my family, she thought. *I'm nothing without them.*

"When is the ball?" she asked.

"Tomorrow night."

She nodded, crossing her arms. "I'll go with you, but on one condition."

He raised an eyebrow.

"I want you to ravish me at the ball."

To her delight, his mouth hung open in disbelief. After a

moment, he snapped it shut, shaking himself before his eyes found hers again.

It was one of her most secret dreams—to be ravished in some dark corner at a ball. Before today, she'd never thought she'd actually go to a ball (or leave the boundaries of Shadowbank at all). But it had been a fantasy of hers for a long time, and if their time together the day before had shown anything, it was that there was a deep attraction between them.

However, she would respect his decision if he'd said no.

"*That* is what you want?" His tone reflected his facial expression—a mix of shock and lust. "You could ask me for anything—jewels, weapons, a favor... and you asked for what I've already given you freely?"

Something inside of her stomach fluttered, and she bit the inside of her cheek.

Frankly, she hadn't thought to ask for anything else.

"Since you find my offer insufficient, I'd like to be fucked at the ball *and* for you to help repair Shadowbank's ward."

Even before he spoke, she knew what his answer would be.

"No." His expression turned cold, impassive.

Sighing, she tried again. "Then I'd like you to answer three questions—truthfully. Any three questions I want to ask at any time."

She'd been burning with curiosity about his past, and this seemed the best way for her to learn exactly what she wanted to.

"And to be ravished at the ball?" he asked.

She nodded.

With a flicker of disbelief in his gaze, he said, "You have yourself a deal. But..." His voice dropped, filling with suggestion. "I will fuck you whenever and wherever I want at the ball—with or without an audience."

The idea of an audience shouldn't excite her, but desire shot down to her core. She bit her lip to keep any sounds from escaping her lips.

There was a flash in the shadows, and he was before her. His eyes skirted down the length of her, and her breath came in ragged gasps. His hand was at her side, moving down the thin fabric of her dress to her hips, and then his fingers were between her legs. She gasped as his other hand was at her lower back, pulling her into him. His fingers ran gently against her folds. He pulled his hand back and held it in the air between them. The tips of his fingers glistened with her desire.

"So needy. Did I not satisfy you yesterday?"

Then his fingers pressed to her lips, and she opened them. His eyes held dark expectations, and she sucked on them willingly.

"I want you to taste your desire—to know how much your body yearns for mine." He grabbed her hand, slowly bringing it to his crotch and placing it over his hard length. Her fingers closed over him, and he moved her hand up and down. He was fit to burst through his pants. "And I want you to know just how much I burn for you."

Pulling his fingers from her mouth, he grabbed her neck, pulling her into him. As he kissed her, claiming her mouth as his tongue swept across hers, her desire heightened and her eyes fluttered shut. When he pulled back, she gasped, sucking in cool air—and wishing he hadn't stopped. She wanted him to take her, all of her.

"Do you want me to fuck you in these stables, little enchantress? To bend you over a bale of hay and take you from behind?"

Now that he said it, she wanted exactly that. But did she dare admit it? He already had her wrapped around his fingers.

"Or," he continued, "perhaps I shall make you wait until the ball."

Slowly, he released her neck and took a step away from her. She craved his touch, feeling like the wanton creature he accused her of being.

"Why punish us both when it's clear you want me just as much as I want you?" she said, a hint of desperation in her tone.

What was wrong with her? But damn her, she *needed* him.

His eyes flicked down to the bottom of her knee-length dress where he'd touched her only moments before, deep in thought. What was he debating? She could see indecision and desire warring in his gaze. Then he closed the distance between them, his hand encircling her neck above her collar.

It brought to mind her plan to gain his trust enough so that he removed the collar so she had some hope of studying the wards around his castle. But she was careful to keep her expression neutral and keep her eyes fixed on his.

"You've pleased me in agreeing to go to the ball. So, perhaps I'll reward you for your good behavior." He walked forward, forcing her to take several steps back until her leg brushed against something hard and scratchy. Glancing down, she spotted a bale of hay.

Was he really going to—?

He flipped her around, pressing her down in a smooth motion so her stomach was against the hay. Fingers were at her thighs as he raised the back of her dress, pulling it until it was around her waist. Baring her to him.

She wore no undergarments, and her pussy was exposed in the cool air. A boot kicked against hers, and she was forced to spread her legs wide. She could feel his gaze raking over her, lingering on her wet pussy.

"Don't move."

She did as he bid, not daring to even turn her head for fear he'd stop whatever he was doing. Was he removing his trousers? But there was a sound like water moving and... was he washing his hands?

A few moments later, he returned, and a hand was at her lower back.

"You will have to wait for my cock until the ball. But I'll satisfy your needs before then."

She tried to steady her breathing as she readied herself for the feel of his fingers between her legs. For him to finger-fuck her in the open stables with horses in stalls nearby. Instead, one of his hands moved on her back as though trying to soothe her before something hard pushed into her. She gasped, trying to move on instinct. But a hand pressed into her back, keeping her bent over, and his feet were on the inside of hers. Unable to rise, she was forced to remain with her legs spread obscenely wide.

"What are you—"

The hard object thrust into her and pulled out.

She gasped, once again trying to move, her brain not fully comprehending what was happening.

"Shhh," he whispered as though quieting a spooked horse before something pressed deep into her again.

Her desire leaked between her legs, and any objections she had were lost. She managed a glance back, noting his hard cock pressed tightly against his pants, but he was fully dressed. In a hand, he held a brush by its bristles. Her mouth hung wide.

He was fucking her with the handle of a *brush*?

She should be outraged, disgusted. Instead, she stifled a moan as he pushed the handle into her again. The entire time, his other hand moved in soothing circles on her back.

"That's it," he purred. "You've got such a pretty cunt. Give in to me. Let me pleasure you."

She did just that. Body relaxing, she arched her back into him.

Slowly, he moved the hand on her back down until fingers traced against her clit, moving in too-gentle strokes. The touch wasn't enough. She needed *more*.

"Let me fuck you like the needy little thing you are."

His words had the pressure between her legs building even higher, and she teetered on the edge.

"I need..." she began, the words a faint whisper.

She wasn't sure what she was asking for.

"You want more?" he rumbled. "Say it."

He moved a finger against her clit, the touch so soft.

"Harder."

ROSALYN STIRLING

She gasped as the pressure of his touch increased. But he moved in a long, torturously slow stroke.

Teeth were on her neck, sinking into soft flesh, and she knew there'd be a bruise.

"I want everyone at the ball to know who you belong to," he said.

Another moan escaped her lips as he timed the thrust of the brush with his too-soft strokes against her clit.

His chuckle was farther away as he pulled back. And finally, his fingers stroked against her clit with the pressure she needed.

"Come for me."

All it took was several thrusts of the brush into her pussy as he moved up and down her clit with deft fingers, and she was coming undone.

She cried out, and somewhere around her she distantly registered the stomping of hooves and neighs. But her pleasure washed over her in wave after wave. The orgasm lasted far longer than it had any right to. Then he was flipping her so her back was against the hay. His lips were on hers, and he never stopped fucking her. As a second orgasm crashed into her, he pulled her essence into his mouth. It was brighter than before, pooling between them like a brilliant blue cloud. His eyes glowed, matching her essence as he breathed it in greedily.

"Come for me again," he whispered into the space between them.

It had to be his magic because she felt herself cresting for a third time as he never stopped his ministrations. It was good. Too good. He kept kissing her even after he'd feasted on her essence. It was as though he enjoyed her touch, her kisses, as much as she did his. Perhaps he wanted her for more than her essence, and the thought had her moaning. Her fingers tangled in his hair as she pulled him down to her. She needed to feel him—all of him. Hands moving, her fingers roamed beneath his shirt, her nails scraping against his chest. He moaned into her mouth.

And that sound was all it took.

She came again as he continued to fuck her with the brush handle and his fingers.

"Elias."

The word sounded like a prayer as pleasure racketed through her.

When she came back down, gasping and blinking, he slowly removed the brush and pulled her dress back down. He pulled her upright, and if he hadn't wrapped an arm around her back, she might have fallen as her knees buckled.

"That was..."

Words failed her. She should feel humiliated by what he'd just done, but it was quite the opposite. She'd never fucked anything besides a cock or fingers before, and the idea of other things filling her was officially on the table.

"You were incredible," he purred, sounding as though he meant it.

To her utter surprise, he pressed a gentle kiss to her forehead. "I'll see you tomorrow, little enchantress. Prepare yourself for a journey to the gateway."

Releasing her, he turned to leave the stable before pausing and looking back at her.

"I left something on your bed for tomorrow. I hope you like it."

Then he left the stable and didn't look back.

Chapter Fourteen

ARABELLA

Arabella hadn't known what she'd expected exactly.

Perhaps part of her had thought there'd be a horse-drawn carriage for the journey to a fae ball. Logically, she knew such transportation was impossible through a dense forest.

But she couldn't help sighing as she looked up at the saddled horses and then down at her gown.

A dress had been spread out on her bed, just as Elias had said. Intricate black lace and shimmering beads of the same color were interwoven throughout the gown, and it hugged her curves sinfully. Unlike many of the shorter dresses she'd worn around the castle, this one went all the way to the ground. The neckline skirted just above the swell of her breasts with an intricate bodice that narrowed at the small of her waist. It was the most gorgeous dress she'd ever seen.

It was also ill-suited for long journeys on horseback.

"Absolutely not." She eyed the saddle of the black mare. "There's no way I'm wearing this and riding at the same time."

Nearby, Elias was also dressed in all black, his back turned to her as he sifted through saddlebags. His black trousers were tailored tightly to his muscled thighs, leaving nothing for the imagination, while his long-sleeve black shirt was made of the finest materials and hung loosely around his arms. But what drew her eye was the black leather corset that was tied together at the front and accentuated his wide back and narrow waist. The corset had satin throughout as well, offering varying shades and textures of black.

It looked like a fancy version of the clothes he wore most days.

They were a gorgeous pair, and the outfits blended exceptionally well. To her surprise, both outfits had a timeless fashion. Given the contents of the room that had been covered in dust—and the outdated fashion of the clothing in the wardrobe—she had assumed his taste in clothes would be equally outdated. How could he know current fashions from this remote forest castle so far from civilization?

However, the fashion of the fae could be entirely different from humans.

Although she didn't want to remove her black dress, she carefully pulled it over her head before folding it and packing it in her saddlebags. Cold autumn air kissed her skin as she stood, and she resisted the urge to shiver as she stood in just her undergarments.

Elias turned to look at her. He blinked. "I won't be fucking you just yet, little enchantress."

She would not dignify that comment with a response. So, she offered a brief glare before pulling her enchantress leathers out of a saddlebag and swiftly donning them and her boots. She also pushed the knives Elias had given to her during their last ride into sheaths around her body.

"Need I remind you there are still monsters in this forest?" she said. "I will not risk the chance of fighting one and not having the full use of my legs."

There was a soft chuckle, but he didn't object as he donned a cloak.

It was then she noticed he had a sword at his hip. The sheath bore intricate silver and black etchings that swirled the entire length. Out of

163

the top of the sheath, there was a glint of bright metal. She wondered if his sword was made of silver. Certain monsters could only be killed by a blade made of pure silver, but she couldn't help but wonder whether his weapon was made of a common steel or something more.

"Oh," he said, grabbing something from his cloak. "I have something for you."

Closing the distance to her, he extended a hand to her, in which he held a knife with a simple black leather hilt. It was unremarkable to the eye, but her shadows hummed beneath her as soon as she wrapped her fingers around it.

"What is this?" she asked before gesturing to the knives in hilts at her thighs and waist. "You already gave me these."

"This blade is different," he said, his eyes lingering on it for a moment too long. "It's imbued with magic to ward away creatures of magic."

Fae, she thought.

"I'd hate for something to happen before I can steal you away at the ball," he said, a hint of forced playfulness in his voice.

Frowning, she nodded as she stashed it in a sheath at her side, beneath her leather jacket.

"That reminds me," he began before reaching for her. His fingers touched the metal collar around her neck, which warmed against her skin. She gasped, nearly jumping back before she heard a click. Then the weight she'd become accustomed to dropped to her collarbone, and Elias' fingers were at her neck. He pulled the collar from her, offering her a small smile.

The energy of the earth rushed up to infuse her senses. It was sunshine and wild green life just like Shadowbank. But in the middle of the forest, the energy all around her was also laced with stringy darkness, like veins of sickness traced through the ground, corrupting everything that grew from it. Even the energies in the air crackled with a sharpness unfamiliar to her.

"Can't have you unable to use your magic if we have any hope of impressing the queen," he said.

Threads of magic flowed up from the earth through her, and she knew her eyes glowed golden in the way they did when she held a lot of magic. She allowed herself to fill with fury at having been kept from the elemental energies surging all around her. Even as heat rippled in her chest, there was a strange fluttering in her stomach as her gaze settled back on Elias.

"How do you know I wouldn't attack you once I had my magic back?" she dared to ask.

"Call it a suspicion."

"Are you that confident in your cock? That I'm that besotted?"

While her tone held a hint of playfulness, something in her demanded that she challenge him in this. Why take the collar off her now? Did he wait until all of his offerings showed some semblance of obedience before removing it? It couldn't be until his offerings fucked him, as he claimed he and Scarlett were never intimate in that way. Did he collar everyone?

I did it, she thought. *I got him to remove the collar.*

When they returned, she would study the ward. If she didn't find another way to strengthen Shadowbank's ward in the fae realm.

"You asked me what essence tasted like," he said as he took a step back. "And yours tastes of freshly fallen snow, among other things. Only someone pure of heart tastes like that."

Nodding, she found her brows drawing together.

He thought she was pure of heart? She didn't know why this surprised her, but she turned from him quickly and pushed onto her mare's back and grabbed the reins.

He also mounted his horse before turning toward the woods without another word. As he rode, she studied his back and allowed herself to feel his magic from the lenses of both her enchantress abilities and that of her shadow magic.

Perhaps he had released her from her collar simply because they would see the fae queen soon and his magic far exceeded hers.

This could be a power move and nothing more. Certainly not a showing of trust.

The ride through the forest took several hours, during which they had only the briefest encounters with creatures of the forest. Small, prowling things that moved on all fours had approached them; but as soon as they'd sensed Elias' power, the creatures turned and fled. The entire time, she kept a hand on the hilt of a knife sheathed at her hip and was ready to lash out with her power.

As they traveled, she wondered if she would know when they had reached the gateway. Was it a crack in the air that was only visible when opened? Would a squadron of fae guard it? Would there be monsters around it, waiting for some unknowing traveler to pass through before ambushing them? Her heart raced, and she could barely contain the excitement coursing through her. She was about to be the first enchantress to travel to the fae courts and pass through a gateway. So far as she knew, anyway. But when they stopped in a small opening within the massive forest, she knew at once they had arrived.

The moment the gateway was near, it was like the earth itself screamed in agony.

A soundless, ear-splitting tremor ripped through her mind. The sound was so loud, so overwhelming that for several long moments, she couldn't breathe. Beside her, Elias casually dismounted his horse and looked ahead. Though to what, she didn't know. It was suddenly difficult to focus.

Could he not hear this?

It was like the grinding of glass and the shrieking of souls had formed a dissonant chorus. The sound stretched through her senses with sharp talons, scraping through her very being. Pain split her head, and she gasped, hands on her temples. The world around her swayed, the trees blurring in and out of focus.

She registered Elias' voice somewhere nearby, raised in agitation. Shadows moved around them, but she couldn't see them. All she knew was the pain consuming the very marrow of her bones. Screams ripped from the earth and sounded like they were coming from...

It took every ounce of strength to look up.

Her eyes fell upon a dark fissure in the air. A crack had formed mid-air before a stretch of rocks that led to a waterfall beyond. It wasn't a large waterfall, but a tumble over those rocks could easily lead to a broken arm—or neck if you were unlucky. When she looked upon the crack, it felt as though she looked into the antithesis of the sun. A dark star or a black hole that swallowed every ounce of light. Tears formed in her eyes, and the pain seemed to split her skull. Tears fell freely down her cheeks. She bit back a moan of agony that threatened to escape from her lips.

The land rioted against this invasion, this magic, between worlds. It didn't want the gateway here. It didn't want *them* here.

"Enchantress."

It was Elias. He was somewhere nearby. But she couldn't look up anymore. She wasn't even sure she could remain upright.

She couldn't take it much longer. The sound, the sensation... It was all too much. The earth never stopped screeching its devastation and fury in her mind. Her muscles grew slack, and her grip around the horse's reins loosened. She slipped from her seat on the saddle. For a moment, she felt herself free-falling to the ground, but before she felt either the dark bliss of unconsciousness or the hard ground, arms caught her.

"I've got you," a male voice rumbled.

Some part of her knew she should feel scared or repelled by the owner of this voice. Somehow, with him, she knew she was safe.

Tears streaming down her face, she allowed the pain to overtake her, and she felt herself slipping into darkness. Before it took her, her magic—the one of shadows and secrets—rumbled and roared to life as she sensed his dark magic cascading around them, encircling them in a powerful wave.

At that moment, her shadow magic reached out and touched his. It was the smallest of caresses. But she felt him shift, seeming to start as his gaze fell upon her. For a moment, the gateway's cries softened as though it was curious as to just who stood before it. Then darkness took her, and she knew no more.

ARABELLA JOLTED UPRIGHT.

The all-consuming pain and the screeching in her mind were gone. But her head throbbed, and nausea turned her stomach. Leaning over, she heaved, emptying the contents of her stomach.

Her ears rang, though there had been no sound.

Rubbing her temples, she tried to steady her breathing. Blinking, she realized she was no longer atop her horse. Looking around, she was in a grassy meadow. A forest stretched behind her in a line from horizon to horizon as though some powerful entity had drawn a line and demanded it stop. Compared to the forest that surrounded Shadowbank, this one held no menace. She couldn't sense any dark creatures of the forest lingering nearby.

Rolling grassy hills went on for miles opposite the line of trees. In the far distance, she spotted movement and realized there were carriages moving in a single-file line. The incomers approached a wall as dark as the night sky and spanning six stories in height, which stretched on for miles. It encircled what could only be the capital city of the Twilight Court. Above the wall, she counted at least six spires from a castle and made of an equally dark stone, though it shimmered as though there were traces of silver in the walls itself. If she could see the castle from miles away, it must be unfathomably huge once closer to it.

For a moment, she paused, frowning.

What did the fae have to fear that would have inspired them to build such a wall? It far exceeded anything built by the hands of men—certainly exceeding the wall of Shadowbank. Demons stood no chance against the fae's magic. So, what could they be trying to keep out?

Despite her questions, she breathed a sigh of relief.

They had made it.

"I know why enchantresses haven't traveled to the fae realm before," she muttered, wiping her mouth with the back of her hand.

Even if there had been an enchantress foolhardy enough to face that unearthly gateway, they wouldn't have stood a chance at passing through it without being carried through... which was exactly what had happened to her.

Once again, the erox had saved her.

He's using you, a dark part of her mind whispered. *He only needs you for a deal with the fae. That's why he bothered to help you.*

"Such drama," Elias murmured above her.

Her gaze snapped up to Elias, who kneeled in the grass beside her, one corner of his mouth quirking up. She opened her mouth to snap a retort back, but she closed it.

Had he just made a joke?

She shook her head, uncertain what to make of that.

"Did you know?" she demanded.

He raised an eyebrow.

"That the gateway does this to enchantresses. Did you know?"

He shook his head. "I was as surprised as you were."

She released the breath she hadn't realized she'd been holding, glad he hadn't willingly tricked her. Behind her, the horses whinnied, and she was thankful they had made it through safely as well.

The erox passed her a handkerchief and water skin. She took it, cleaning herself and rinsing her mouth before standing and breathing in the cool air.

"You can change inside or in the forest." He gestured to the shadows amongst the trees.

She hesitated, suddenly very much wanting to remain in her leathers. What if other things could make enchantresses ill—or worse, kill her? It would be wise to be able to move freely in her leathers and be ready to take on whatever the fae had in store for her. But damn, did she wish she could wear the beautiful black gown. Perhaps one day she could.

"I'll stay in this."

If the fae wanted to meet an enchantress as a sort of novelty, then they'd get the full experience. She was garbed from head to toe in enchantress black leather and also wore the headdress of silver chains and a teardrop gemstone that came down her forehead.

Let them see me as I am.

She pulled up the hood of her leathers.

For a moment, Elias eyed her, not saying a word. Then he nodded, grabbed the reins of the horses, and said, "Ride or walk?"

"Walk."

Despite being able to see the carriages on a beautiful, paved road in the distance, it took them a while to get to what appeared to be the main road, which was smooth cobblestones. Once there, they joined the line of horse-drawn carriages, which had intricate golden or silver swirls throughout large wooden doors with hand-sculpted carvings. Even the wheels bore intricate designs in often black metalwork. Horses were brushed and had intricate plaits.

Looking at the spires of the palace, she couldn't help but gape, realizing just how much of a country girl she was. Compared to other towns in the human realm, Shadowbank had been considered, at best, a small port village with multiple districts and a modest trade business. To most, it was a mere remote village. She had thought it a large place, though she'd never traveled to the capital. But the visible fae grounds in the Twilight Court far exceeded the size of the entirety of Shadowbank—let alone adding in what the size of the fae city and castle must be as well as all the territory surrounding just what was visible to her.

As they drew closer to the walls, she could see a midnight-blue city surrounding the base of the castle on a hill with silver roofs and spires. It was the most beautiful, most decadent place she'd ever been. The castle itself was a mixture of the darkest blue and silver hues, winding up turrets and towers into the clouds—far past what her mortal eye could see. Perhaps the fae with their gifted sight could spot where it ended. But as they moved closer, she lost view of the city beyond massive stone walls.

Beside her, Elias smirked.

"Quiet," she said.

"I didn't say anything."

"You didn't have to."

All around her, power bloomed from within carriages. In Shadowbank, she had been one of the strongest magic wielders. But here? Here, she was a small fish in a large ocean of predators —and proud ones at that. No one besides her and Elias either rode on horseback or walked on the road. All rode within carriages as though not even the eyes of lesser magic wielders could glimpse them.

With all the decadence surrounding her, she suddenly questioned her choice to wear her leathers. But she held her chin high as they neared the palace.

"Have you ever traveled outside of Shadowbank?" Elias asked.

The question surprised her. He'd never asked her about her life.

"No," she answered honestly. "The enchantresses found me wandering at the edges of the forest when I was young and took me in. When I showed signs of magic, they trained me in my gifts, and I've been with them ever since."

He nodded. "It's fortunate they found you. I've never heard of a child surviving the forest alone."

"Neither have I," she said as she gathered courage to ask what she said next. "What brought you to the forest? Do other erox live there?"

She hoped he wouldn't insist that this was one of her three questions he must answer.

Gravel crunched beneath his shoes, which were made of dark leather, matching the coloring of the rest of his attire. It was as dark as the magic billowing around him like a controlled tempest of power and temptation.

"I came upon it," he said, uncaring or not noticing how his presence was like a shard of the universe had implanted itself within him, as fathomless and dark as the space between stars. "But the erox do not live in a single territory like the fae. We are... a rare species. Most of us try to assimilate into the society we choose to call home. I separated myself from humans."

"Why?"

There were only two carriages between them and the guards before the castle gates.

He sniffed. "It's far more difficult to harm others when they aren't nearby."

Turning to face him, she tried to decipher just what he meant by that. But his face remained neutral, his eyes fixed ahead.

Then they stood before the guards. She knew they were fae by the gracefulness of their movements, even if she couldn't see their pointed ears behind helmets. The way they moved their bodies looked like they were amidst a fluid dance.

"Name," said the guard standing before them.

The female was as tall as Elias and had muscled arms and legs that were visible in sections throughout her minimalistic navy-blue armor. It wasn't the bulky armor of human soldiers but covered only sections of her body. She imagined it allowed her—and other soldiers—to move more nimbly. Behind her, a squad of guards of every gender stood with spears or swords. Atop the wall, more guards stood at the ready with longbows and crossbows. Power pulsed in every single one of them. Their magic wasn't as strong as Elias', but they far exceeded the enchantresses' abilities.

"Elias Whitlock," he said before gesturing to Arabella. "This is my companion."

The guard studied a scroll, scanning the length of it before eyeing Elias with narrowed eyes. "State your purpose."

"To attend the ball, of course. It's been many years since I've seen Her Majesty."

For a moment, she thought the fae wouldn't admit them entry. But she eventually offered a curt nod and gestured for them to pass. Wordlessly, Elias strode forward with his steed at his side. Arabella did likewise, and her mare followed.

The city was even larger than she'd estimated from outside the walls.

The line of carriages moved with swift efficiency through immaculate streets. Eventually, she and Elias mounted their horses and rode through busy streets of sellers calling out from shops in midnight-blue buildings that shimmered faintly with silver.

As they neared the castle, there were fewer buildings, and the ground swept upward toward a winding road that led to the castle, which was set higher than the city proper and provided a view of the surrounding city. It was then she noticed movement in the dark sky above. There were silhouettes illuminated by the stars. After a moment, she realized they were dark, winged figures flying to and from what she thought were turrets and spires.

Her heart raced. She'd never seen winged fae before. What must it be like to soar in the skies, far from the reaches of the worries far below?

Even while she thought of Shadowbank and how she could help save the ward, some part of her longed for freedom from all of this—to truly explore the world without having to make decisions that could impact countless others. To be free.

She shook her head to clear her thoughts. Such a thing wouldn't be in her future. That was, unless Shadowbank's ward fell, and there was nothing for her to return to in ten years.

Like the city wall, there were guards stationed outside the base of the castle, where there were several massive entry doors and a large area of open grass to park the dozens of carriages after they'd dropped off their occupants at the main doors.

"What's the occasion?" she asked, noticing how none of the fae entering the castle wore visible weapons. Could they be so confident in their own power that they didn't fear an attack? Did the queen have rules against weapons at her ball?

For a moment, Arabella's hand hovered over one of her knives, which was sheathed on her leg, wondering whether to leave it in her saddlebags.

"Keep that with you," he said, seeing her hand and gesturing to the knife with the black hilt he'd given to her earlier that was tucked away in her jacket. "As for the day, it's the queen's nine hundredth birthday."

For a long moment, she rode in mute silence, unable to fathom an existence for that long. She'd heard the fae could live to be several thousand years old, but even living to be nine centuries was beyond her comprehension.

Enchantresses lived slightly longer than humans, but usually around one hundred fifty years. Meanwhile, the erox beside her had unlocked immortality. She couldn't help but wonder how one became an erox. But if the price for eternal life was feeding, what was the price for not feeding? Just what happened to the erox if they didn't have access to essence or chose not to feed? Perhaps more importantly, how did they manage self-restraint to not kill every single person they fed on?

How many erox didn't bother to restrain themselves?

That was the question she should have been asking as an enchantress in the first place. And how to kill them.

There'd be time to learn such things later. For now, she had to focus on the fae and the ball—and finding something she could use to help strengthen Shadowbank's ward.

Once at the door, Elias dismounted, securing the sword at his waist, and passed his reins to a fae servant. He then went over to Arabella's horse and offered her a hand, face void of expression. Pausing, she eyed the hand dubiously. After a moment, she took it and slid off her horse. But before she touched the ground, she felt hands at the small of her waist, lowering her to the paved road. She blinked, uncertain how he'd moved so quickly.

The way he moved... it was like she was something precious to him. Why else handle her with such care? Could it be for show?

That must be it. Demons were incapable of any emotions beyond hunger—no matter what Elias said.

Elias.

It was then she realized she'd started calling him—and thinking of him—as Elias.

Demon, she corrected herself. *He's a demon.*

Why was that becoming so difficult to remember?

Another fae servant took her black mare wordlessly. Then Elias extended his arm to her. She looped her arm through his and walked through the massive open doorway and into a ballroom.

Unlike the castle walls, the inside of the room appeared like stones made of silver with veins of black webbing across the divots and cracks. Multiple chandeliers each the size of Shadowbank's main hall table hung from the ceiling across a room that glowed like the inside of a star with countless gemstone teardrops of every shade of blue as well as countless translucent stones.

The first thing her mind registered was that it was bigger than four of Shadowbank's main halls together. It was even larger than the dining hall at Elias' castle. Several hundred people could comfortably fit within the room even with the dance floor at the center and tables at the outskirts of the room.

Beautiful fae moved in a swirl of colorful fabrics at the center of the dance floor to the sweeping notes of a flutist and the harmonic melody of a violin. Other musicians played in a band atop a small platform just beyond the dance floor.

The female dancers wore massive ball gowns, glittering lace dresses, or trim trousers of the finest fabrics along with flowing tops or corsets so tight that many bosoms threatened to spill out. Male dancers had a large variety in their attire as well. Most wore brightly colored jackets adorned with pins and brooches and trousers tight enough to leave little to the imagination. Though some wore gowns or skirts. A few wore masculine corsets, similar to Elias'.

But none had her heart pounding at a simple touch on her hand as the erox did.

"The queen and her court are late, it would seem," the erox said as he eyed the empty dais at the far left of the room with a massive silver throne at the center.

"How do you know her court hasn't arrived? They could be among the dancers."

He chuckled. "You can't miss them."

She frowned. "What do you mean?"

"You'll see."

He gestured to where there were fountains of blush-pink liquids in a corner of the room, and she followed him. He grabbed two glass goblets and ran them under the fountains, filling them before passing her one.

"Is fae alcohol safe for mortals to drink?" she asked, eyeing the cup.

He nodded. "As long as it isn't poisoned. And I doubt such a thing would occur. Anyone with less than charitable intentions would act with more discretion."

She raised the cup to her lips.

It tasted like a blossoming flower, decadent and rich.

"It's also strong. Go slowly."

She smiled, turning to him. "Is that concern I detect, Mr. *Whitlock*?"

"Naturally," he said, his tone emotionless. "I care for what's mine."

He claimed to not be able to stay away from her, but did either of them really know each other? They'd hardly shared more than words.

She sighed.

"What?" When he turned to her with narrowed eyes, she saw darkness ripple there—the first emotion she'd detected since they arrived. "Is my presence such a burden to you? I daresay you've enjoyed my company on multiple occasions. Else, why would you make your request of me this evening?"

Her heart hammered, and her thoughts swam as she thought of their rendezvous in the water and in the stables... She wondered just how he would fulfill his half of the bargain tonight.

"Such interactions require little social engagement," she said, glancing toward the pairs of dancers at the center of the room. Some spared her lingering looks, eyeing her leathers and headdress. She tried not to think about it. They were interested in the attendance of an enchantress and nothing more. Still, she eagerly gulped her drink to steady her nerves.

Elias placed his full glass down on a nearby table. "What is it you wish to discuss?"

In the warm, golden light of the room that reflected the last rays of the sunset beyond the massive glass windows a story or two up, the deep black of his hair and beard appeared almost blue. Everything about him radiated darkness, from his outfit to his hair to his eyes to his magic.

He was everything she shouldn't want.

"I want to learn more about the male I'll be spending the next decade with."

Not that she'd remember their time together when this was all over.

"Ask me what you wish to know."

"How old are you?"

"The next full moon will mark three hundred years since my birth."

She blinked. He was two hundred seventy years older than she was.

"Happy almost birthday," she said, considering her next question. "How did you become an erox? Or were you born this way?"

A faint smile touched the corners of his lips. "And here I thought you wanted to know my favorite color."

"I'd like to know that, too. But I suspect it's black."

He glanced down at his outfit. "How could you tell?" With a glance to the dance floor behind her, he said, "I was thirty when I was turned. You must be turned to become an erox."

"Do you ever age visibly?"

"No. Once you become an erox, you're frozen in time to the age of your body as a human."

That explained why he appeared to be a similar age to her.

"Since we are getting to know one another, I'd like to know more about you as well," he said. "Did you always aspire to become an enchantress?"

The depth of the question surprised her. Why would he care about such a thing?

"Once I showed signs of having a magical gift, it was expected of me to join the Circle," she said. "I never thought of doing anything else."

His eyes locked with hers, sympathy echoing in his dark irises. "You love them."

It wasn't a question.

"They're my family. I'd do anything for them."

"And so you have."

She didn't respond, unsure of what to say.

"Do you know how old you are?"

She shrugged. "I suspect I'm in my early thirties, but I'll never truly know without my birth parents to tell me the date of my birth."

"Does it bother you that you never knew them?"

"I always thought it should," she answered honestly. "But no. I have a family and people who loved me."

What bothered her was not knowing why she was in the forest the day they found her and how she'd survived.

"Did you have a family before becoming an erox?"

"I did. They are dead now."

"I'm sorry." She couldn't imagine what it must have been like for him to outlive his family. If she outlived those in the Circle, it would break her heart.

"Does this mean you've used all of your questions?" he asked.

She shook her head and placed her glass down on a tray of a server who walked by. When she didn't spot pointed ears, she thought to wonder whether he was human.

"You answered freely and didn't specify that our conversation was a part of the bargain."

Dark eyes alight with mischief found hers. He leaned forward until his beard scratched against her cheek. "I also seem to recall something else that was a part of our bargain."

Shivers traced down her spine, and desire immediately swirled between her legs.

Leaning forward, she ran her teeth lightly over his ear. "And here I'd thought you'd forgotten."

Hands were on her waist, putting distance between them.

"Ah-ah. Best you behave. I agreed to fuck you, but I never promised I'd let you come."

She bit the inside of her cheek, holding back a retort. He'd shown that he meant every word he said, the controlling bastard. But she wanted everything he could give her, and she wasn't about to ruin living out one of her fantasies sometime this evening.

Suddenly, she could feel countless gazes on them, and she realized the song had ended. Fae on the dance floor clapped. Compared to the raucous cheers in the House of Obscurities, the polite applause was downright subdued. But as they clapped, bodies angled toward them, and eyes scanned both her and Elias, lingering on her leathers.

"Let me guess," she began, swallowing thickly. "Not only am I a novelty at this little gathering, but there are no other erox here either."

"Unlikely." His eyes flickered between hers, clearly sensing her anxiety at so much attention. "Eyes on me, little enchantress. They're simply as entranced by your beauty as I am."

She started. Did he just call her beautiful?

His words quelled the uneasiness in her chest somewhat. Ignoring the feel of nearly every eye in the room on them, she fixed her eyes on his, feeling... safe.

Then he extended a hand toward her, his other hand behind

his back. As he did, he bent at the waist in a slight bow. "Would you join me for the next dance?"

No, she thought. Not only would she have the eyes of every fae and important dignitary on them, but they'd witness her woeful inexperience in dancing. She'd never been trained in court dances nor did she know anything about the fae's culture and traditions. At the same time, the idea of dancing with Elias at a fae ball was temptation incarnate.

"You'll have to lead me through the dance," she said, taking his hand. "Ballroom dancing wasn't part of my education."

He smiled, a true, brilliant smile full of delight. "It would be my pleasure."

As he led her through a flurry of bright skirts and trousers to the center of the dance floor, she leaned into the sway of her hips. She wouldn't look timid in front of these people. She might be scared shitless, but she refused to look it. They'd give everyone a show—and hopefully get the queen's attention. They'd see just how strong enchantresses were.

And how uncoordinated.

As the music started, a slightly faster tune than the last song, Elias took one of her hands in his, wrapping the other around her waist and pulling her close. Around them, the other dancers swayed in identical steps with much more distance between their bodies.

Elias led her just as he'd promised, guiding her through spins and intricate steps that had her heeled boots moving quickly to keep up with him.

The most dancing she'd ever done was in taverns with friends or lovers. But it required little skill. In fact, it required only enthusiasm. But the twirls and steps that Elias moved her through were far more complex. The pattern repeated like a chorus, but the verses of the song had different movements that had her turning and spilling, which was far from graceful with the grips on the bottom of her boots.

As they moved, the feeling of eyes never left. But she found herself caring less and less about the attention as her eyes locked on Elias'. His heartbeat under her fingertips as he spun her into him and she placed a hand on his chest. Had his heartbeat quickened at her touch?

No. That couldn't be right.

Before she knew it, the song ended. All around them, fae clapped politely. But she didn't have eyes for them. She looked up into Elias' eyes, her hands resting on his chest from the final spin. His hands lingered at her waist. Both of them breathed heavily, and she knew it had nothing to do with the physical exertion of the dance.

"Look who it is."

The voice nearly blended into the sound of applause.

Elias' eyes fixed on something behind her, and she turned toward the voice.

All at once, the breath whooshed out of her. The man standing before them was, objectively, as beautiful as Elias. His light brown skin contrasted eyes so dark they seemed to be pure black.

His beauty was so sharp, it was painful, and she felt herself drawn to him. Desire swirled in her chest. Before she could take a step toward him, Elias blocked her with an arm. She shook her head, dispelling the magic.

The magic of another erox.

Chapter Fifteen

ARABELLA

All sounds dulled as her senses focused on the male before her.

He wore pants and a shirt of pure black, just like Elias. But he also had a jacket with pins of what must be some type of military achievement. Instead of the tall black boots, he wore black dress shoes. He was of a height with Elias and equally muscular. But his shaved jawline was as sharp as the look in his eyes.

Arabella crossed her arms and forced herself to look away, to not make eye contact. "One of you is more than enough."

She turned her narrowed gaze on Elias as if to say, "*Did you know?*"

"Brother," Elias said, ignoring her glare. "I didn't expect to see you here."

He has a brother? I thought all of his family were dead.

"I decided it'd be worth the trip," the new erox said, his eyes fastening on her. "Just what do we have here?"

The stranger closed the distance between them, placing a finger under her chin and studying her as though she was a prized horse at auction.

She slapped his hand away. "I'm spoken for."

Internally, she groaned at her choice of words. She didn't want to imply that she was Elias', but it seemed the quickest way to tell this man to piss right off.

The man raised an eyebrow before his gaze settled on Elias. "Another one of your offerings?" When Elias didn't respond, he added, "Still busy feeling sorry for yourself, I see."

Elias gestured to doors at the far end of the room that led to a terrace. "Let's speak outside."

Around them, the dancers began moving to the steps of the next song. She thought the male was going to object, but he shrugged before striding toward the door, and they followed.

"You have a brother?" she whispered to Elias as they walked.

He waved a hand in dismissal as though this was a trivial question. "It's what the erox call each other. We're not of the same bloodline."

That explained some of it.

Once outside, a gentle breeze lifted the edges of her hair. She took a deep breath, attempting to center herself. In different corners of the garden and along the terrace, there were fae dressed in glittering gowns and bright jackets and britches, leaning in to whisper to each other and laughing. Others strode through the garden to get up to... Well, probably exactly what she wanted to do with Elias.

And shouldn't want to do.

But all were far enough away that she didn't think they could hear. At least, Elias must think they were safe from fae ears after he spared their surroundings a brief glance.

The erox turned to face them, a devious smile lighting his face and lingering in his gaze. "It's good to see you, Elias."

A slow smile spread over Elias' face, and the two males embraced.

"How long has it been?" Elias asked.

"At least a decade," the male replied. "Too long."

Releasing each other, they turned to her.

"It's been years since my path crossed with an enchantress. You may call me Breckett," the erox said, offering her his hand.

Slowly, she took it with one hand while the other rested atop the hilt of one blade at her hip. For reasons she couldn't explain, she wanted to reach for the blade Elias had given to her at her side.

"Arabella."

"That's a lovely name," Breckett said.

"Thank you. I chose it."

Breckett's brows arched. "Is that so? I'd very much like to hear your story."

"Why are you here?" Elias asked, bringing the male's attention back to him.

Breckett shrugged. "It's been years since I've been to the fae realm, and the queen sent an invitation. I didn't think you'd leave your little prison—I mean, *palace*—in the woods. Otherwise, I'd have extended an invitation for you to join me."

Arabella snorted before covering her mouth with a hand and clearing her throat. Elias spared her an annoyed glance.

"I received an invitation as well," Elias said. "I suspect it's the usual."

"Naturally," Breckett said as his eyes roamed over the terrace and gardens.

She frowned. "What do you mean? Does the queen want something from you both?"

Breckett ran a hand through his short black hair, which made the front stick up in spikes. It should have made him look ruffled or unkempt. Instead, it made him look even more charming.

"Immortality," Breckett said in a bored tone. "The fae are always eager to see how they can live a few more millennia."

"Why not make her an erox?" she asked.

"That's exactly what she wants," Elias said, crossing his arms and leaning against the terrace railing.

"First, she's female," Breckett said as though this was the most obvious thing in the world. "It's rare females survive the transition. Only males have a near guarantee of becoming an erox. It's also never been done with a fae."

"Only the foolish choose this life."

Elias' words were so quiet that she nearly missed them.

She turned to Elias. "You won't make the queen immortal, but you want something from her."

That's the real reason you brought me.

Breckett's gaze snapped to Elias, his black eyes alighting with curiosity. "Just what is my brother hoping to acquire from the queen of the Twilight Court?"

Elias made a show of dusting off the sleeve of his shirt. "Nothing you need to be concerned with."

"How am I supposed to aid you in your quest if I don't know the destination?"

She could feel Elias stifling an eye roll, his annoyance palpable.

"I didn't ask for your help."

"Yes, but that doesn't mean you don't need it."

Raising a hand, Elias rubbed the bridge of his nose with his thumb and pointer finger. With a sigh, he eventually said, "I require an amplifier."

Arabella's heart drummed so fast that, for a moment, her heartbeat swirled in her ears, blocking out all sounds.

Elias was searching for the very thing she needed to save her people. The very thing she'd hoped to get from the fae. But what did he want it for? Why hadn't he mentioned this earlier?

Breckett stiffened and glanced around the terrace. For a moment, it felt like even the wind held its breath. Two fae exited the ballroom at the other end of the terrace before disappearing into the gardens.

"What for?" Breckett asked, failing at an air of casualness as he glanced at his nails.

"Alabaster nearly broke through my wards," Elias said, not looking at her. "I must strengthen them."

Arabella swallowed back a lump forming in her throat even as her stomach turned.

He needed to strengthen his ward as well. Was that why he hadn't agreed to help her enforce Shadowbank's ward when she offered him the bargain—because he sought the very same thing? With all his power, was he unable to do the very thing she needed?

Breckett's gaze turned skyward, toward the twinkling stars and planets in the sky above, which were entirely unlike any constellations from home. He seemed deep in thought for a moment before he said, "They attacked her, didn't they?" He gestured toward Arabella. When Elias didn't respond, he shook his head, a laugh escaping his lips. "You haven't changed. You're still as soft as ever. Desperate to protect everything and anything."

Arabella frowned, turning to Elias, whose face was expressionless as he locked eyes with Breckett.

Elias? *Soft?* That was ludicrous. The male wore indifference like a second cloak outside of rare moments of warmth during their moments of intimacy. As for protecting others—he'd taken villagers from Shadowbank for decades. No one trying to protect others stole people from their homes and took ten years from their lives before depositing them without memories back at the border.

"Perhaps not," Elias said. "But I'm hoping the queen will be... sympathetic to my request."

Breckett eyed Arabella, his full attention settling on her once more. "An enchantress for an amplifier?"

Just what did he mean by *that*? Surely, Elias wouldn't *give* her to the queen. Would he?

"She might kill you for asking," Breckett said, his voice lowering further. "Are you sure it's worth the risk?"

Elias nodded. "I have to protect my home."

Lines formed between her brows.

Could he be like her—desperate and single-minded to protect his home? And just what was this queen like that she'd consider execution of those who asked something of her? Were all the fae like this, or was it just the Twilight Court?

Slowly, Breckett strode over to her. She took a step backward and then another until her back brushed against something hard. Leaning forward, he placed his arms on either side of her, resting his hands on the terrace railings until he bracketed her.

"You are beautiful with your dark hair and..." Breckett's eyes skated down her body. "Other assets. But I daresay it won't be enough to sway the queen."

Suddenly, Breckett's beauty sharpened, and her chest tightened to the point of pain. It took all of her mental energy to resist the magnetic pull toward him. His black eyes seemed to engulf her, and she tried to pull her gaze away but found herself unable to.

A moment later, she wondered why she was resisting. He was so beautiful and awaited the touch of her lips against his. All it would take was rising on her toes, and she'd close the distance between them. All at once, she yearned to touch him and feel the warmth of his skin, to have him bend her over the terrace railing and take her from behind...

Slowly, she felt herself leaning upward, raising her chin until there were mere breaths between them. Breckett's black gaze settled on her lips as she neared his, expectant.

A blue light burst between them, throwing Breckett back several feet. He landed in a crouch, his gaze snapping to Elias.

Elias' eyes were bright blue, the color of her essence.

What was that light that had blasted them apart? It had been some type of powerful magic, but had it come from Elias? She thought he'd mentioned some of the erox having unique gifts. What was his?

"Touch her without my permission, and you won't live long enough to regret it."

Breckett rose to his feet before dusting off his black coat. "Fuck, Elias. Will you just say that next time? I didn't realize you were attached to this one."

Elias was still tense, his entire body stiff and ready to spring. "Why didn't you feed before arriving?"

Arabella blinked.

That was why she felt attracted to Breckett—because the erox needed to feed. That must be why his eyes turned black.

Breckett waved a hand. "There wasn't time." He gestured to her. "Would you object to a brief taste? Just to tide me over?"

"I would mind."

There was no give in Elias' voice, as impenetrable as stone. For some reason, his protectiveness surprised her.

With a shrug, Breckett said, "As you'd have it." With a gesture toward the gardens and the sound of giggling females, he added, "I'm off to find a willing partner. I'll find you later."

Spinning on a heel, he turned and disappeared into the massive hedges.

"That was fun," she said, eyeing the dance floor beyond the massive windows. "Let's never do that again."

"Sarcasm is unbecoming," he said.

"How many of you are there?"

Elias shrugged. "I've known some erox over the decades. Breckett is one of the few who isn't merciless in his feedings. Too many feed to the point of gluttony and kill every victim. But Breckett feeds until satiated and often erases memories after. He *usually* only takes willing partners."

She took a deep breath, steeling herself for the question she was about to ask.

"I'd like to use one of my three questions that you must answer truthfully."

He raised an eyebrow.

"Did you want to become an erox and be immortal?"

Elias sighed as though expecting this question. Turning, he leaned on the terrace railing, studying the hedges as though he'd find whatever answer he was looking for in there. She walked over to him, resting her hands on the railing as well, not daring to speak.

She waited in silence for what felt like several minutes before he said, "No. I was on death's door and turned without my consent." He turned to her then. "You have two questions remaining."

So, her demon hadn't chosen this fate for himself. Somehow, that changed everything.

Behind them in the ballroom, there was thunderous applause. They both turned toward the sound.

"The queen has arrived," he said, extending an elbow to her.

She took it, allowing him to guide her off the terrace and back into the warm silver light of the ballroom. The moment she laid her eyes on the dais, her jaw dropped.

There were five males with scaled wings that resembled the wings of dragons and wyverns. Their wings extended several feet above their heads, and each male was at least a head taller than Elias. While there was a variety of different colors to their wings, most were of a black hue, matching the dark color of their hair.

At the center, a woman wearing a dark blue gown laced with shimmering silver as bright as the moon lowered herself onto the throne. The entire room knelt, bowing heads. Arabella quickly did likewise before standing with the crowd as they chanted, "All hail Genoveva Grimwald, first of her name, Queen of the Twilight Court."

As Arabella stood, her eyes connected with one of the winged males at the end of the dais, who had rich black hair and eyes alight with curiosity.

She averted her gaze and took a breath.

It was time to impress a fae queen.

Chapter Sixteen

ARABELLA

"Don't speak unless directly spoken to by the queen," Elias said as they made their way to the dais. Many fae stood in a line before them, all eager to greet the queen.

Arabella nodded, stuffing down her irritation.

She wasn't a child, and she didn't intend to make a fool of Elias as he bargained for an amplifier. Not when she hoped to acquire one herself. The thought of an object that could increase a magic wielder's power as much as tenfold—so far as she'd heard—made her stomach twist.

Unless there had been some miracle since she'd left, the enchantresses still needed this artifact at Shadowbank to repair their wards.

Did she dare beg the queen for a second amplifier? Would she be sympathetic to humans? But Arabella had nothing to offer more than her presence—that was if Elias didn't bargain the remaining years of her decade with him away. Perhaps he could give what time remained in exchange for an amplifier. But he'd still need a willing offering to feed on to survive.

As the fae in front of them parted one by one, she chewed on the inside of her cheek, uncertain what to do.

I have to save my family.

Then they were before the queen.

If Arabella had thought the other fae were regal, they paled in comparison to the majesty of the woman who sat before her. Up several stairs to a large dais, the throne was made of twining metal that formed some type of constellation she didn't recognize. But the queen outshone it in her gown of the deepest blue and shimmering silver, which hugged her every curve. To Arabella's eyes, Genoveva wasn't more than a decade older than her. But according to Elias, she was nine hundred years old.

Flanking her on either side of the throne were five winged males, all of whom were a wall of muscles, magic seeming to gust around them even though she knew it was visible only to the eyes of magic wielders. But the air was so thick with power, for a moment, she forgot to breathe. Even Elias' magic was a fraction of what these fae possessed. The males were also armed with a variety of different weapons strapped to their waists and thighs.

The male on the far right, standing somewhat behind the other four, eyed her with the same expression as before—devious curiosity.

At her side, Elias lowered to a knee, and she did likewise, dropping her gaze to the ground.

"Stand," the queen said, her voice as sharp and cold as icicles.

Slowly, Arabella raised her eyes to the queen's.

Genoveva had dark brown eyes as welcoming as a hailstorm.

"Your Highness," Elias said. "It's always a pleasure to be in your presence. Thank you for your invitation to join in your celebrations. May your next nine hundred years be equally prosperous and peaceful under your sovereign reign."

Arabella was careful to school her features into a look of neutrality. But the entire time, she wanted to turn and glare at Elias. Since when was he an ass-kisser?

Since he needs an amplifier.

"Erox," Genoveva said. "I'm pleased you accepted my invitation. How are things in the human realm?"

"The humans continue to innovate and change in their short lives," he said. "But I often remain at my home, which is remote. Breckett, who is also in attendance, can comment more on what the humans have been up to than I can."

"Ah yes. The pirate. I'm sure he will regale me of his journeys." Genoveva waved a hand, and a server brought a glass of what Arabella guessed was wine. For the first time, the queen's full attention settled on her like a physical weight, and she resisted the urge to squirm. "Who do we have here?"

"This is Arabella, an enchantress from a human village," Elias said.

Uncertain of what to do, she bowed her head to the queen. "It's nice to meet you, Your Highness. Your lands and home are beautiful."

"Never has a human entered my city before," Genoveva said, her icy gaze settling on Elias, not bothering to acknowledge Arabella's words. "What is the meaning of this?"

"I know Your Majesty has a keen eye for the... unique," he said. "I have brought her here for your pleasure so that you might know of some of the human magic yourself."

"Don't waste my time with such trivialities," the queen said. "Unless her magic rivals the fae, I'm not interested in weak humans or their weaker magic."

Anger coursed through Arabella.

She knew she was far less powerful than nearly every single person there and the closest thing to a human with her life of one hundred fifty years, but she was still a person and should be treated with dignity. More than that, they needed this amplifier—two, in fact. And she wasn't about to let this opportunity slip through her fingers.

Grabbing weaves of her magic, pulling them from the earth beneath the castle, which was as rich and decadent as the palace itself, she laced them together with the thread of magic from her own well. It was so unlike the lands between Shadowbank and the rest of civilization, which now felt laced with decay. She gathered several more weaves, tying them around the original ones she'd laced together. When she released her magic, a single blue rose floated in the air. She grabbed it and offered it to the queen. The blue wasn't as dark as the queen's gown, but it also didn't occur in nature.

"A small token of my appreciation," she said, extending the flower to the queen. "It will not wilt for many years, and if you crush the petals, it will emit starlight."

The queen eyed the rose but did not take it. Arabella held it and stood there for several long moments before the winged male from the far right of the dais stepped forward and accepted it. With a wink, he returned to where he stood before.

Once again, anger burned through her. She didn't care how old or how powerful this queen was. This female didn't have a right to treat other people this way. She could feel Elias at her side, reaching for her as though to calm her. But when his hand brushed her lower back, the shadows at the feet of the queen roiled and twisted. As they did, wordless whispers filled her mind.

Who does she think—

Suddenly, she realized the male holding her rose didn't move. He watched Arabella with slightly widened eyes as they flickered between her and the shadows at her feet. Fear sliced through her. Did he see the shadows at the queen's feet moving? Was shadow magic forbidden amongst the fae as well? Could she have just secured death for both Elias and herself by revealing she was a shadow whisperer? Just as quickly as her anger arose, it abated, and the shadows quieted. But she knew the male had seen what she'd done.

Even the queen sat on her throne more stiffly than before.

As though seeing her for the first time, the queen's gaze fell on her, her eyes narrowing. "Who are your parents?"

The question was so sudden, so unexpected that Arabella started.

"I don't know, Your Highness," she said carefully. "I was raised by the Circle."

The queen waved a hand in dismissal. "A common human order." She tilted her chin up as though scenting something in the air, her nose slowly arching upward before her head angled toward Arabella. "You don't smell like an enchantress. Your scent is... something I've smelled before."

Just what did that mean?

Heart pounding, Arabella willed control over her shadows. Perhaps the queen had seen Arabella's taking control of the shadows at her feet. She hadn't been about to do something to this fae female, had she? She'd never let her anger get a hold of her in that way before. She'd also never been treated so dismissively before.

But she didn't know what to make of the queen's words.

Before she had to think of a reply, Elias spoke, his words coming more quickly.

"I've also come to request your assistance, Your Majesty," he said. "The wards of my home need strengthening to keep out the scavengers of the woods. I hoped to acquire one of your amplifiers to—"

"Have you reconsidered my request?" Genoveva interrupted, taking a sip of her wine.

Elias' lips thinned before he said, "As I've told you before, it's dangerous for females to become an erox, and no fae has ever been turned. The stakes are too great."

"That's for me to decide."

He licked his lips, clearly debating. After a long moment, he said, "I'm sorry, Your Majesty, but I cannot."

"Then my amplifier shall remain in my possession. Good day." With a flick of her hand, they were dismissed.

Arabella's heart dropped, and an overwhelming sense of sorrow filled her. Elias only sought to protect his home, which was the same as what she wanted for Shadowbank. That was something she could understand—admirable, even. But the queen's response also dashed any hope of help for Shadowbank. If she wouldn't assist an erox, she certainly wouldn't show empathy for a remote human village.

Arabella stood immobile for a long moment before Elias gently took her arm and guided her away. When they'd found an empty spot along the outer wall of the ballroom, she let out a sound that was somewhere between a growl and a sigh. "You failed to mention the queen is... unpleasant company."

To her surprise, Elias turned to her, wrapping a hand around her waist and kissing her.

"Thank you."

She gaped. "What for? We didn't get the amplifier."

Disappointment, she could understand. Anger and frustration she had expected. But gratitude and a display of affection? Immediately after being rejected by the queen? This had been nowhere in the realms of possibilities.

"No," he said. "But I knew it was going to be a reach. I appreciate your help all the same."

"I nearly lost my shit."

"But you didn't."

She shook her head. "You're strange, Mr. Whitlock."

"Perhaps." He sighed, running a hand over his curly hair, which was tied back in a neat knot. "I don't know how I'll get another amplifier now."

Me either.

"Could you pull the ward's borders back?" she offered. "With less territory to protect, it will strengthen the remaining ward."

It had been an idea the enchantresses had considered for Shadowbank. Unfortunately, this idea was nixed almost immediately, as there was no logical place to pull back the ward with the stone walls along the border of the town and the port on the opposite side. If they didn't protect the walls, the monsters of the forest could climb them and wait in the town for the moment the wards weakened and then fell for good. On the other hand, if they didn't protect the ports, any creatures of the deep might prevent what little economy the trade brought in. That, and the boats in port could be the last point of refuge—and escape—if the town was overrun by forest demons.

"I could," he admitted. "But that's a last resort."

Taking her hand, he nodded toward a hallway at the opposite end of the ballroom where a few couples had disappeared down. "Come. Let's stretch our legs."

Rather than extending an arm to her, he took her hand, lacing her fingers through his, guiding her across the outskirts of the ballroom and expertly navigating drunk fae and rogue dancers. Something warmed within her chest, but she shook her head to clear it. The gesture meant nothing. He was just holding her hand to make sure he didn't lose her in the crowd.

And yet... the more she learned of this demon, this male, the more she was coming to like him—genuinely like him. He had shown character. It took someone with great conviction—and perhaps a death wish—to turn down a fae queen.

He didn't want to make more of his type of demon.

Was there such a thing as a moral demon?

What he'd done took courage. The queen could have ordered his death, and Arabella doubted anyone would blink an eye at such an order. Not to mention, his refusal was at the expense of an amplifier.

When they passed through the archway into a hallway, the sounds of lilting music and echoing laughter became background noise. For the first time in hours, she could properly hear her thoughts. As they walked, there were long, sheer curtains blowing in front of open windows, twisting and swirling into the hallway like champagne clouds.

Somewhere ahead, she heard the distinct sound of laughter like the tinkling of bells carried on the wind.

Elias guided them down several more hallways, twisting and turning until they found an alcove with a balcony behind sheer curtains, the same color as the countless they had passed earlier. There was a long chaise lounge chair at the center of the space—as if this room was often used for quick trysts. A balcony was at the far end of the room with intricate railings that overlooked the garden.

Her cheeks blushed as she thought of what lovers would be doing around quiet corners of hedges. Then her eyes flicked to Elias, who grabbed both of her hands and guided her slowly into the quiet alcove.

"Is this you fulfilling your half of the bargain?" she dared to ask, her voice breathless.

A corner of his lips curled up. "Do you still want me to... how did you phrase it... *ravish* you?"

She licked suddenly dry lips.

Before she could respond, he flicked a wrist, and her shirt was undone, her breasts were in the open air. Her leathers were unlaced, and her shirt was pulled indecently down. His mouth found one of her nipples, suckling and pulling the sensitive bud into his mouth. His hands were on her sides, his thumbs gently stroking the sensitive skin beneath her breasts.

She laced her fingers around his neck before grabbing the tie that held his hair back and pulling it loose. His black curls fell to his shoulders, and she ran her fingers down them, enjoying the coarse softness. He moved to her other breast, giving it equal attention.

"How...?" she began, struggling to find her voice. "What's your unique magic?"

Pausing, he looked up at her, running a thumb over his lower lip.

"You want to have this conversation now?"

She glanced down at her breasts. "You magically undressed me, *again*. A girl can't help but be curious just *how* you're doing it. And what else you're capable of."

"Is this your second question?"

"Yes."

His hands dropped to her waist before he grabbed her, spun them around, and tossed her onto the chaise lounge chair as though she weighed no more than a saddlebag. With a snap of his fingers, her leather pants were suddenly at her ankles.

"I'm immortal," he said as he took a step toward the base of the lounge, his eyes fixed on her pussy. "I feed off the sexual desires of others and take pieces of my partners' essence to survive."

Another step.

"I can wield essence as a weapon or give it to others as a power source."

Echoes of images from the confrontation with the Alabaster glanced across her mind, and she suddenly understood. He had wielded the essence he'd taken from her to fend off the creature. She also recalled the pain in her chest when he'd somehow revived her after the Alabaster had fed off her and nearly killed her.

He'd saved me, she realized.

It wasn't just that he'd rescued her from the demon in the forest, but he'd used his magic to save her life.

Once at the base of the chair, he leaned down, his hands on either side of her legs.

She didn't know why, but she suddenly felt nervous. Her heart raced as she heard the laughter of other couples down the hallway, beyond the sheer curtains that separated them from passersby.

He made a tsking sound as he grabbed her knees, pressing them apart. "I want to see all of you."

Leaning down, he traced kisses from one knee up her inner thigh, ever so slowly, to...

"What else?" She swallowed thickly as he pressed a kiss just beyond her clit.

She had to know. If she got too distracted, he might choose that what he told her was enough, and then perhaps she'd never know all he was capable of.

"I can make myself appear irresistible to my prey when I'm famished." His words were a tickle of air against the sensitive skin of her inner thigh. "And I have some control over the thoughts of my prey. I can... make them more amenable to my will."

She knew this. He'd revealed as much when they'd sparred in the grass outside the castle.

"How much have you used this ability on me?"

He glanced up, a look of surprise on his dark features. "Not once."

She frowned. "Really?"

A smile lit his face. "You have required little encouragement."

She bit the inside of her cheek.

Best not to think about that now.

"Do you have other—?" she began but was cut off as he leaned forward, running his tongue up the length of her, from her pussy to her clit. A moan escaped her lips.

"Are there not other things you want to do with your time this evening than... talk? I've answered your question."

"There are many things I'd like for you to do with your tongue," she admitted.

"Good." His hands gripped her inner thighs, spreading her even wider. "Then don't move your legs again until I tell you to do so."

All she could do was manage a nod before he was between her thighs once more, licking her clit as though he were a starving man and she was his only source of nourishment.

And... she supposed she was.

He flicked his tongue up and down her clit with just the right amount of pressure that it had her pleasure building swiftly. He never slowed, never faltered. Soon, she found her hands tangling in his curls as she held him still and moved her hips against him.

Taking control.

She knew she'd have hell to pay for this later—that this male thrived when in control. But for the first time since she'd been with him, she wanted one moment to be hers alone, where she could control her fate. Or in this case, her pleasure.

He moved as though to protest, but she held him in place. It wasn't hard enough to hurt or hard enough that he couldn't break free of her grip if he didn't want to. But it was hard enough to show that she wanted him right where he was.

With a rumble against the soft flesh between her legs, he kept going. He didn't quicken his pace nor did he slow. She moved against him, fucking his face and moaning as her pleasure built. But before it could crest, he was moving. The motion was so fast that she couldn't track it with her eyes. He flipped her so that she was over him, kneeling on either side of his face as he lay on his back on the lounge chair. Somehow, her pants were no longer around her ankles but in a heap on the floor.

"You want to be in control, little enchantress?" he said, eyes full of challenge. "Then fuck my face for real."

She opened and closed her mouth.

She'd dreamed of this very moment for years, never daring to ask her sexual partners for what she wanted most. Never feeling safe enough to come with just anyone. But now? At this moment, she knew exactly what she wanted, what she needed, and it was this male between her thighs. She wanted to use him and to scream his name as she came again and again.

Hesitant at first, she began to thrust her hips. His tongue moved in the same, long strokes with the same delicious pressure. At this angle, she could feel the scrape of his beard more than before. It scratched and tickled against her inner thighs. The sensation wasn't unpleasant. Instead, it made her move faster.

Her pleasure built higher and higher, and she spared a glance down at where he lay between her legs. His eyes flashed up at her then, a brilliant blue instead of the deep brown, nearly black coloring she'd grown fond of.

He was losing control, she realized. And so was she.

Eyes never leaving him, she came, her pleasure blossoming from deep within her before crashing outward like a tidal wave. She cried out before covering her mouth with her hand as the sounds of conversation echoed down the hallway and then quieted to stifled giggles.

In a flash of movement, he sat up with her straddling his lap, his hand moving hers from where she held it over her mouth.

"Let them hear," he said. "Never hold back, not from me and not for anyone else. I want to hear your every sound of pleasure."

He kissed her, pulling essence from her lips in long strands, stealing her breath away with it. It heightened her desire for him.

She was far from finished.

"I want you," she said, loud enough for whoever was in the hallway to hear.

He smiled—a genuine smile that made her heart skip a beat. His eyes flicked to the ground. "On your knees."

She disentangled herself before lowering to the ground, never breaking eye contact. As she did, he pulled his shirt over his head and unlaced his trousers just enough so that his massive cock was free, impossibly hard without her ever having to touch him.

As though sensing her thoughts, he said, "It turns me on to touch you, to feel you come."

She bit her lower lip. "I feel the same way about you."

His eyes somehow darkened even with the essence swirling through his irises. "Open your mouth."

She did so. He grabbed the root of his cock at the same time as he grabbed the back of her neck before sliding into her slowly, inch after inch until he filled her whole mouth. He didn't press to the back of her throat.

"Tap my hip twice if you need to stop."

She managed a small nod before he moved in and out, a sound of pleasure escaping his lips.

"I like you on your knees," he said as he thrust into her.

With one hand, he continued to hold her neck while the other hung at his side. His eyes ate up the sight of her as she took him. She flicked the tip of his cock with her tongue as he pulled her mouth back. He moaned, eyes blinking rapidly as though clinging to shreds of control.

"Do that again, and I'm going to come in your mouth."

She hesitated, not sure whether she wanted to see him unravel or to let him continue with whatever plans he had for her. Instead, she allowed him to move her so that she took him deeply, her lips sliding over his cock.

Pleasure built between her legs once more, and she felt on the verge of coming again. If she lowered her hand and touched herself just the slightest, she'd unravel.

His nostrils flared, and he said, "So needy again, are we?"

He pulled out of her, spinning her around and bending her over the lounge chair. She lay on her stomach, her ass and pussy bare to him, and she could feel his wet cock pressing on her ass.

"What would you like, my little enchantress? Do you want me to fuck you in that wet pussy? Or are you eager for me to take you in that little ass of yours?"

Oh fuck. She wanted both.

"My pussy," she said. "And touch my ass."

He growled before thrusting into her. She was so wet that there was no resistance. Then one finger was twirling against her ass before he pressed into her. One knuckle. Two. And then he paused.

"That's good," she said, uncertain she could take anymore just yet.

Just as his hips began to move, she heard the shuffling of foot-steps in the hallway before a rustle of curtains. Turning, she spotted one of the warriors who'd stood behind the queen, his massive black wings filling the entryway. The one who'd taken her blue rose.

"I could hear you two hallways down," the male said.

Her heart pounded, and her instinct was to cover her breasts. She was completely naked from the waist down and her shirt was undone while Elias was shirtless, his cock sheathed in her. But her eyes skirted the length of this stranger, noting the distinct bulge of his cock in his pants.

He liked what he saw.

Behind her, Elias didn't bother to move, to cover up—to

cover her up. Instead, he continued to thrust inside of her, his gaze shifting from the stranger and down to her ass.

"Have you come to join us, Prince Hadeon?" Elias asked as he fucked her ass with a finger.

She bit her lip, stifling a moan.

Then her mind registered Elias' words. This winged male was a *prince*? She thought the males were the queen's guards by the way they stood behind her.

Hadeon's lips quirked. "That's up to her. I'm not attracted to other males."

Elias' hand tightened at her hip, his other hand never leaving her ass. "Tell me, little enchantress, do you want a third? Or should I tell him to get lost?"

She considered for several moments; her desire heightening with the feel of Hadeon's eyes on her.

"I want him to watch."

Hadeon smiled, and he strode across the room until his wings rested against the wall before them. So he had a clear view.

"As you wish."

Then Elias thrust into her with abandon, the sound of his hips slapping her ass filling the small alcove.

"Touch yourself, little enchantress," Elias demanded.

She did so, reaching a hand down to her wet pussy, running a finger up and down in the way she liked.

She wouldn't last long. With the feel of Hadeon's gaze, hot and lusting, and Elias fucking her pussy and ass...

Fuck. It was ecstasy.

Crying out, she held on to the chair, feeling her legs wobble beneath her as she came. Elias wasn't far behind her, his thrusts growing shorter and hungrier. In a sudden motion, she was on her back on the chair, and he fucked her pussy as he kissed her. As he came, he pulled essence from her, and she wrapped her hands around his neck, bringing him closer.

Warmth filled her as he spilled his seed, and she thrust back

into him, wanting to feel him even deeper as the last of his pleasure subsided.

"Ravished?" he asked, his voice breathy.

She smiled, nodding.

Slowly, they disentangled, and she stood. Turning to Hadeon,
she didn't bother to cover herself. Beside her, Elias' cock was hard.
Ready to go again. Likewise, he didn't cover himself.

"What brings you here, Prince?" she asked, a challenge in her
eyes.

Slowly, he leaned forward, pushing off the wall and taking
several steps forward. He was so tall and his wings so wide that it
blocked out much of the starlight from the balcony.

"I've come to make a bargain."

Chapter Seventeen

ARABELLA

Dressed once more, Arabella and Elias studied the prince with eyes full of suspicion.

"What is it you wish to bargain for?" Elias asked.

The prince was far taller than Elias, his massive shoulders wider than most doorframes and with a wingspan wider than he was tall, though he kept his wings tucked in tightly to his back. Like the queen, he had fair skin, more olive in tone than hers, with dark, upturned eyes. Like Elias, his eyes were sharp, hinting at the quick mind she suspected was behind them.

"You want an amplifier, do you not?" Hadeon studied his nails.

"What do you want in exchange?" Elias asked, his tone neutral.

Meanwhile, Arabella's heart tried to beat right out of her chest. Why would this male offer them the very thing his mother had refused to give them?

"How did you get it?" she asked, interrupting Hadeon before he could speak.

"Smart woman," Hadeon said. "It's a treasure I acquired in my time going on missions for my court. It's not from my mother's private archive if that is what you're asking."

She nodded. It wouldn't do if they left with an amplifier only to be chased down and implicated for stealing a valuable artifact from the fae queen.

"As for what I want," Hadeon began, his eyes locking on Arabella. "I like to make... investments in those who I find intriguing."

"The fae don't give anything freely," Elias countered.

"Perhaps not," Hadeon said. "But I'd like to see where the two of you go. And if I need a favor from either of you in the future, I hope you'd be amenable to it."

There it was.

His request was as dangerous as he was. She could feel the raw power emanating from him even as her shadows twisted and stirred in his presence. His abilities far surpassed any of the fae in the ballroom, all the fae guards, and perhaps even Elias' essence-based magic. It certainly surpassed hers. Only his brothers on the dais seemed to have a similar level of power—them and the queen, of course. She wouldn't be surprised if he could take down a battlefield of soldiers with a flick of his fingers. But she thought to wonder just what kind of power this fae had. Was it elemental like the enchantresses? Could he wield storms or bursts of fire?

With such power, what could he possibly want from them? Only Elias had anything of value to offer, and he'd refused immortal life to the queen. More than that, would becoming an erox mean anyone's powers before turning would be void? Perhaps all the queen's or Hadeon's powers would disappear the moment either became an erox—if they didn't die in the transition. She couldn't see a good reason for Hadeon to risk losing such power.

"Why?" she dared to ask. "You already know Elias' answer about turning anyone. So, why help us?"

Hadeon's sharp eyes flickered between hers before he said, "I'm the least favored son of Genoveva Grimwald, Queen of Twilight Court. If I'm to find my way in this world, it won't be through traditional means."

She nodded, ignoring the heat of Elias' glare.

There was every chance this male could be lying to them. Clearly, Elias didn't believe this fae's words. But why would Hadeon meet with them? Could he be trying to manipulate them somehow? For some reason, she found herself accepting his answer. Even her shadows seemed satisfied by this, their stirring seeming to subside.

"How many amplifiers do you have?" she asked.

She knew the question showed her hand. She hadn't outright refused to give him a favor at an unknown future date, and it showed she was willing to consider it. It gave him the upper hand.

The prince raised an eyebrow. "One."

Fuck.

That meant only Elias' home or hers would be protected.

Unless I take it.

The traitorous thought struck her like a cord, and she froze, uncertain what to think. Could she betray Elias after all they'd been through? She had slowly grown fond of the male, but stealing from him would be the ultimate act of betrayal. Even if she did, could she find a way back to Shadowbank? He'd made certain she hadn't seen the journey from Shadowbank to his castle. She wasn't even sure what direction it was in.

Would he be willing to let me have it?

If she asked for it—revealing her heart to him, not holding back—would he still refuse? The wards around his castle were stronger than Shadowbank's. Or could they share the use of the amplifier?

For the sake of her people, she had to try.

At that moment, she knew she had to be the one to make the deal with Hadeon. If he refused to let her take it, perhaps it would mean that the amplifier would be hers by right.

"No," Elias said. "Unspecified favors are powerful, and you know it."

"I'll do it," Arabella said.

Elias' gaze snapped to her, but she didn't turn to look at him.

"I'll be *amenable* to helping you at a future date within my lifetime so long as it doesn't harm those I love, doesn't require killing or endangering any humans, and doesn't violate any bargains I've already made."

Hadeon looked between her and Elias. "Done."

With a flick of his wrist, a shape appeared.

A round, black orb hovered in the air, reflecting the light of the moon and stars. It was as dark as a moonless night and as deep as the sky and whatever lay beyond. Instinctively, she reached for it. Elias caught her wrist before she could grab it.

"I'll take her bargain," he said.

Hadeon shook his head. "It's too late. Her offer has been accepted."

Elias' grip tightened on her wrist. "I won't make Arabella suffer for the actions I've taken for our home. Accept my new offer, and let her be free of this bargain."

Our home.

Is that what he felt? That the castle was her home, too? The thought made her insides twist.

It's not my home. Shadowbank is.

"There's nothing I can do," Hadeon said as he strode toward the curtains. "Good luck to you both. We'll meet again soon." Then he disappeared down the hallway in long, confident strides.

Elias removed a handkerchief from his pocket, grabbed the amplifier, and pocketed it with a hand before he turned to her, fury in his eyes. He never let go of her wrist with the other.

"What have you done? You've risked yourself. And I can't... I can't..." His grip was tight, and she tried to pull away. "Protect you," he finished at last.

Unable to see the vulnerability in his eyes, she looked away, studying the stone walls and hardening her heart. "I did what I felt I had to."

Suddenly, a hand gripped her chin turning her toward him. He pressed his lips to hers in a kiss so urgent, so hot, it took her breath away.

"I'll get you out of this bargain," he said, his voice hoarse. "I *will* protect you."

She managed a nod, pulling her wrist, and he released her, the gesture reluctant. Guilt swam through her, but she clung to her conviction and the need to protect her people as she turned back toward the hallway where Hadeon had disappeared.

As she walked back toward the great hall and the sound of lilting music, she made a decision.

I'll talk to him first. If he refuses to give me the amplifier or share it with Shadowbank, I'll take it.

As they strode under the archway before the ballroom, Breckett appeared. He glanced them once over before saying, "Leaving so soon?"

"The queen has refused my request," Elias said.

Breckett's eyes narrowed. "But...?"

Eyes scanning the room as though assessing for threats, Elias said, "We got what we came for."

"How very interesting," Breckett said. "The queen requested the usual from me. I suspect she did from you as well?"

Elias nodded, his hand enclosing over hers where she'd looped her arm through his, as though reassuring himself she was by his side. "Did you refuse?"

Breckett shrugged. "For now. I don't want a reason for him to seek me out."

Arabella frowned. "Who?"

Taking a step forward, Elias strode into the hall, directing them toward the main doors that led to the lawn and the horses beyond.

"Mind if I join you?" Breckett said, striding beside them. "It's been too long since I've visited your gloomy castle. Perhaps I can brighten things up."

As they strode onto the cobblestone street with lines of carriages, Elias said, "Who are you hiding from?"

"I wouldn't call it hiding. Just... taking time for personal space and reflection."

Arabella suppressed a smirk.

"Fine," Elias said.

"Excellent! I'll get my horse."

A fae servant brought their saddled horses to them, and they quickly mounted. Then they were off, exiting the castle grounds and riding through the illuminated city streets of the Twilight Court.

Her time in the fae lands hadn't been what she'd expected. But the majesty and decadence were unparalleled. Even the streets brightened by lamps filled with flameless lights—powered by some fae magic—were a wonder. Shadowbank had been a far darker place once the sun had set. But this city was lit as though it was midday, alive and bustling with people. Part of her was sad that she'd never have the chance to explore it.

Before she knew it, they were on the rolling hills once again, headed toward the trees—and the gateway beyond. Her stomach turned at the thought.

As before, the gateway tore through her mind with its soundless screeches, the earth crying out. And as before, Elias carried her through after she blacked out. Once on the other side of the gateway, she woke up and vomited what little fae wine she'd drunk. Elias' hand moved in slow circles on her back, and she tried to ignore the gesture.

I must prepare myself for what's coming.

She couldn't allow her heart to feel anything toward this male. If she was forced to steal the amplifier, he may just kill her once he found out.

Unless she killed him.

The dark thought shot through her with sudden ferocity. If she ended Elias, Shadowbank would never have to fear the erox coming to take another offering. They would be free to live out their human lives in relative peace, only needing to worry about the monsters coming from the forest and protecting the walls and port.

But could she do it?

I'm an enchantress. My loyalty is to my people.

She'd sworn an oath to protect humans. How could she do anything else? Somehow, in her time in the forest, she'd forgotten that. She'd allowed herself to become distracted by this handsome male and his talented dick and tongue.

But no more. She would do what she must.

Elias helped her back onto her horse, and she offered him a nod of thanks before riding toward the castle. Behind her, both of the erox did the same, the sound of their horses' hooves close behind her.

Chapter Eighteen

ARABELLA

A rabella found a window in one staircase leading up to a turret that overlooked the lake and sat there, legs swinging in the open air as she sat. Dawn was likely still some time away, and her gaze lingered on the starry night sky. The constellations were entirely unlike what she'd seen in the fae realm, and she couldn't help but wonder if the fae lived on a different planet somewhere far away.

She wasn't sure how long she sat there for. But eventually, she felt footsteps in the shadows before Elias appeared behind her.

"May I join you?" he asked.

She nodded and turned her gaze back to the lake, which reflected the fair moon.

They sat in silence, both wearing their attire from the ball.

Now is the time, she thought. *Ask him.*

But her courage flickered like the lantern behind her.

Beside her, Elias rubbed his hands together. "When you look at me, what do you see?"

Frowning, she turned to him. "What do you mean?"

"What do you see?" he repeated. "A demon or a male?"

She started, taken aback by the question—and the vulnerability she felt behind it.

"Where did this come from—?" she began, but he was already speaking.

"Don't evade the question," he said. "Please. I need to know."

"Why does what I think matter to you?"

"It doesn't." His words were clipped, and he kept his gaze fixed on the lake.

She crossed her arms. "And that's why you're asking? Because it doesn't matter?"

His gaze snapped to her. "I notice *everything* about you. The way your shoulders relax when you're dressed in your leathers. The delight in your eyes when you're in nature. The way you look at me when I taste your essence. It's a look of wonder and revulsion. And..."

"And what?"

"Forget I said anything." He stood and turned toward the stairs.

"Wait a minute." Rising to her feet, she hurried after him. She moved a few stairs ahead of him so she stood in front of him, cutting him off. "Why does what I think matter to you?"

His eyes flickered between hers. They were a warm brown—not the black irises as they so often were. There was a dark smoke in his gaze rather than the flames that had burned at the ball in that alcove. Even as she studied his eyes, he searched her gaze for... something. But she wasn't sure what.

"I can't stand the idea of you finding what I am despicable."

Her heart pounded despite herself.

"I'm just your offering," she began. "What I feel doesn't matter."

"I want..." He snapped his mouth shut before he could finish the sentence. After a moment of silence that seemed to stretch on, he continued, "You're different. And despite myself—no matter how hard I try—I care what you think about me."

Unable to stop herself, she said, "Did you care what Scarlett thought of you?"

She knew she sounded jealous. But some part of her needed to know if he was this way with everyone—with all of his offerings. Scarlett was a beautiful woman with a sharp wit and kind demeanor. Any man would be lucky to spend time with her.

He hesitated. "I enjoyed her company. Over time, we became friends. But I didn't care what she thought of me. And she certainly had *opinions*, which she didn't hesitate to let me know. But with every word you speak, I feel like I'm hanging on the edge, wondering when the ax will fall. When the mistrust in your gaze will turn to outright hate." He ran a hand through his tangled curls.

A question hung in the air between them, and the answer shouldn't matter. But she *needed* to know.

"In the ten years I shared with her, I never fucked Scarlett. I never even touched her." His hands opened and closed as though he didn't know what to do with them. "And yet, I can't keep my hands off you."

She didn't know what to say. She'd thought Elias tolerated her company—that she was nothing more to him than an offering that he'd used to survive and then fucked when he felt like it.

"My entire life, I've been taught to fight and kill the monsters and demons who pose a threat to the humans that I'm oath-bound to protect. I've been taught these creatures are heartless murderers who kill for pleasure and feed without remorse. But you... You're nothing like I expected."

"We aren't all the same," he said. "Some of us never asked for this."

She opened her mouth, ready to ask him just how he became an erox, but closed it. Now wasn't the time.

"I have tried to fight off whatever this is," she began. She knew she should stop herself—to keep the words close to her chest before they slipped into the space between them. But she couldn't. "I can't stay away from you either."

His gaze flicked up to hers, hot and full of hope.

"But we can't." Her words came out in a whisper, her eyes

falling to the dark stairs between them. "This... Us... We can never be."

A hand was beneath her chin, and he pressed gently until she met his eyes.

"Who's here to tell us otherwise?"

Again, her heart hammered in her chest, and it was a struggle not to lean forward and press her lips to his. He was so close. Instead, she took an unsteady breath and then another.

"A demon and an enchantress," she began, her eyes flickering between his. Brows drawing together, she shook her head as though to clear herself of the pull she felt toward him. "It's forbidden."

His other arm wrapped around her waist, pulling her close until their bodies pressed together. "Then why does it feel so right?" He leaned down until his lips pressed against hers. His lips were soft, and the kiss was gentle, yearning. She could feel how he desired her, how he wanted more, and yet he held back.

For a moment, she closed her eyes and leaned into him, fingers gripping the edges of his corset, holding him close.

Realizing what she was doing, she pulled back, releasing him. But he didn't let go of her.

"The amplifier," she began. "What do you plan to do with it?"

Frowning, he said, "If the ward is beyond repair, then I'll create a new one."

"How much power is in the amplifier?" she asked. "Is there a limit?"

He released her then, grabbing a small, dark orb from his pocket. "I tested it when we returned. It seems there's limited power in this amplifier. I haven't tried using it yet though."

"How much power?" she repeated. Then she added, "Is there enough for two wards?"

She dared to look at him then, to let him see the need in her eyes—the sheer desperation she felt to protect her family.

"Shadowbank is in danger," she continued. "If something

isn't done soon, the ward will fall. There are months left at best. Before I offered myself to you, a pack of fengrine attacked. Many died. There aren't enough enchantresses to protect the walls and the bay."

His gaze flickered between hers, and she thought she saw indecision warring in his dark eyes. Slowly, he ran a hand through his curls, tangling them further. Then his grip around the amplifier tightened.

"There isn't enough magic for two wards," he said, his voice low. "I'm sorry. I must protect my home."

She pulled back, taking a step down the stairs, her head shaking in disbelief.

"Are you really that selfish?" she demanded. "There is no one here. It's you, me, and now Breckett. We could go anywhere. We could go far from these woods and be safe from the demons with your magic. But in Shadowbank, there are hundreds of people who will die in a matter of months."

"I can't leave," he said.

"Why?" When he didn't respond, she demanded again, nearly shouting this time. "Why?"

"Because I can't!" he snapped back, his voice growing louder.

"That's not a reason, and you know it. What are you so afraid of that has you refusing to leave these woods? Who are you afraid will find you?"

"Him."

The fear in his voice had her pausing, the tides of her anger lowering slightly.

She had guessed at his reasons for not leaving the woods, and she had theorized he was hiding from something—or someone. And she was right.

"Who?"

"I can't tell you."

She growled and turned, using her enchantress magic to grab the lantern from behind Elias before plucking it from the air and walking down the stairs. She could use her magic to light the way, she knew, but she had grown accustomed to having lanterns at night after her time wearing the collar.

"Why do I bother talking to you when you can't even be reasoned with? When you can't bother to be *honest* with me."

As she spoke, she felt more than heard his footsteps behind her.

"Wait," Elias said, his hand finding her shoulder. "Please."

The plea in that one word had her pausing and turning around. Glancing up, she couldn't help but note the stiffness in his body, the way his shoulders drew up, and how it looked like he held his breath.

"You're afraid of him," she realized. "What has he done to you?"

"Please," Elias said. "Don't ask. I... I don't know if I can..."

His words trailed off, and his eyes shifted around the staircase, never settling in one place for long.

He can't speak of it. Just what could frighten a demon? Could a demon even be traumatized?

She swallowed thickly.

"I'm sorry for whatever happened to you," she said. "But I can't justify trying to protect a few lives over hundreds of innocent ones."

And if you won't give me the amplifier, then I'll be forced to take it from you.

Slowly, resolution settled in her chest, knowing what she must do.

"Give me time," he said, his voice softer than she'd ever heard it. "I want someone to know. I just can't speak of it yet."

She turned back toward the stairs. "I'm tired. I need to get some rest."

"Can I walk you?"

Not looking back at him, she said, "I'd like to be by myself this time."

She thought she heard his soft assent as she padded down the stairs, her boots clicking against the stone.

Tears streamed down her cheeks. She allowed herself this moment of weakness before she must harden her heart. In her mind's eye, she kept seeing the look of raw vulnerability in Elias' gaze, and no matter how hard she tried to clear it from her thoughts, it lingered.

I'll do what I must, she thought.

Perhaps he wasn't innately evil. Perhaps he was more human than even some of the people she'd encountered in Shadowbank. But he couldn't be reasoned with.

And she wouldn't let him be selfish with the amplifier just to protect himself.

She'd made the deal with Hadeon, and she'd take the amplifier that was hers by right—one way or another.

Chapter Nineteen

ARABELLA

T he next morning, Arabella bathed, combed her hair, and packed a bag. Then she donned the beautiful lace gown that Elias had picked out for her for the fae ball. Moving quietly through the castle, she stored her bag behind an alcove near the castle entrance before heading to the dining hall where she heard the faint echo of male voices.

She could only hope that Elias hadn't used the amplifier yet on the castle's ward.

When she entered the room, all discussions stopped.

Beneath her gown, she was as naked as the day she was born. The morning was cool, and she knew her nipples pebbled even as her breasts swelled at the top of the gown. She strode forward, eyes only for Elias. His dark gaze feasted on her, roaming up and down the length of her body where the dress hugged every curve and left nothing to the imagination.

Once at his side, she rested a hand on the table before leaning and whispering into his ear, "I wanted a chance to wear the gown you picked out. But I admit... as lovely as it is, I'd much rather you take it off me."

Blackening eyes locked on hers, molten. He stood in a smooth motion, sweeping her off her feet and into his arms.

"I'll see you later," he said over his shoulder.

"Yes, yes," Breckett said, waving a hand in dismissal. "But don't wait too long. We have a ward that needs seeing to."

Relief swelled in her chest.

They hadn't used the amplifier yet.

In a motion too fast for her mortal eyes to keep up with, Elias leaped from shadow to shadow until, suddenly, she was in front of a massive oak door with metal swirling patterns across it and rounded arches.

Elias' room.

He'd never permitted her there before.

His eyes glowed bright blue, and the door opened of its own accord before shutting behind them. Flames flickered on in countless candles throughout the room. In the hearth at one end, the logs crackled as orange flames billowed upward. But she had eyes for none of it.

At the other end of the room was a massive, four-poster bed with curtains as black as Elias' eyes were now. He flicked a hand and ropes with handcuffs appeared at each of the corners.

In a panic, she said, "I want to try something different."

She couldn't let him tie her up. She couldn't be at his mercy. Not with what she needed to do.

He raised an eyebrow.

Licking her lips, she nodded toward the bed. "I'd like to have you... in any way I want. Let me be in control this once."

Black eyes heated, and he considered.

"Please."

Fingers entwined in hers as he guided her across satin carpets toward the bed. But rather than a quick tangling of bodies, he turned and sat on the edge of the bed, holding her hands.

"Thank you for what you did last night with the prince," he said. "You shouldn't have endangered yourself. I *will* find a way to undo this bargain. For that, you can have your way this time. Use my body as you wish."

She let out a breath she hadn't realized she'd been holding.

"I'm sorry for how things ended last night," she said into the space between them. "Perhaps we can find another way to protect Shadowbank."

They were empty words. She didn't think he would. Not truly. But she thought this was what he expected her to say.

With a curt nod, he said, "Perhaps."

After a moment, she pressed a hand to his chest. "Lie down."

He moved back on all fours until he lay in the center of the bed. One by one, she tied his wrists and ankles until he was stretched out before her, his hardened cock visible through his pants.

She pulled up her dress so she could crawl onto the bed toward him. When she was above him, legs straddling either side of his hips, she leaned down, kissing and licking his neck, enjoying the satin softness of his skin. He tasted faintly of soap and smelled of pine and citrus. The touch had her breath quickening, and she reminded herself this wasn't for her pleasure. She had to focus.

Leaning up, she allowed her fingers to trace lines over his chest before she reached for the knife strapped at her thigh. It was the same knife with the black handle that he'd given her the day before. She twirled it between her fingers.

His eyes widened ever the slightest, but the look disappeared as quickly as it had appeared. So quickly she thought she must have imagined it.

"While I don't have the magic you do, I know another way to remove your clothes quickly."

With a flick of the blade, she cut his shirt neatly down the center. His chest rose and fell more rapidly. She allowed the blade to graze his skin.

"I'll remember this," he said, his voice a deep purr.

He won't forget the day of my betrayal.

She stuffed the thought back down. There'd be time enough for guilt later—after she'd given the amplifier to the Circle and returned to Elias' castle. The magic of their bargain wouldn't allow her to be away from him for long after all. She forced a smile, unable to take her eyes off his warm brown skin as she re-sheathed her knife in the holster on her leg. "I'm sure you will."

Leaning down, she ran her tongue over one nipple and then the other. As she did, she allowed her hands to roam across his chest and down his sides. She noted a bulge in one of his pockets. A small, round bulge the size of an amplifier.

Too easy.

Elias growled. "Such a tease."

"You like it," she murmured as she leaned up, her fingers lazily tracing the waist of his pants. His hips thrust into the air, but she didn't touch where he craved most.

"Look who's needy now."

"Quit playing with me—"

"Ah-ah," she scolded. "You said I could use your body in any way I'd like."

His mouth drew into a thin line, clearly struggling with this loss of control.

She traced kisses across his chest, moving lower down his side to his stomach. She ran her tongue over where his hip bone dipped to his pants.

"I have my third question."

"Oh?"

"Yes." As she kissed him, she moved her body against his, feeling the press of his cock against her stomach. He tried to thrust up into her, but she leaned back, not giving him the pressure he sought. She allowed the warmth of her breath to wash over his stomach as she said, "I want to know how an erox can be killed."

His whole body stiffened as she reached for the button of his pants, moving torturously slow. Her heart raced, and she forced herself to focus on the task at hand. Even as his body was rigid, his eyes fixed on her, and his chest rose and fell more quickly.

"Why do you want to know?"

She released one button and then another, allowing her fingers to skate against his skin, enjoying the feel of the coarse hair there. "There is another erox in the castle. I need to know how to defend myself."

"Breckett would never—"

"He's already tried to feed on me."

"I would kill him if he dared to touch you."

"Only if you're there. What if he tries to feed on me when you're not around?"

Elias' lips drew into a thin line, and his eyes moved between hers, searching for something. His fists opened and closed, but he didn't fight the restraints.

All at once, realization dawned.

This demon trusted her—even after their fight last night. The male she'd met when she first came here would never have allowed her to tie him down in this way. Nor would he even have considered sharing this information. But as she waited above him, she could see indecision warring in his eyes.

She released another button. "You promised to answer three of my questions honestly."

"That isn't fair," he said, watching where she worked on his pants. There were only two more buttons between their bodies.

His eyes closed as though in pain as he said, "Decapitation. Ripping the heart out of the chest. And a silver blade imbued with the magic of shadow and earth called a syphen. The erox are made with this type of blade, and they can be killed by it."

She frowned. "I've never heard of a syphen."

"The blades were made by the shadow fae long ago before they were wiped from existence. There are few blades left." His eyes were filled with hesitance and... was that hope?

"Now, you know," he said, eyes rounding. Was that hope in his gaze? Fear?

"Protect yourself, my little enchantress. I'd hate to lose you."

Her heart twisted, and she reminded herself to move. She released the last button, pulling his pants down to his knees.

She couldn't go back now.

For a moment, she paused, trying to memorize his willing

body beneath her. Then she wove strands of weaves together, pulling power from the earth and air and braiding them together.

"There's something I'd like to try," she said. "Do I have permission to do anything I'd like to your body?"

"Yes." Elias' brows drew together. "But what are you—"

She pressed a finger to his lips. "Patience, lover."

Then she willed the weaves to move, and they soared through the air in a circle. The erox's eyes followed them, clearly sensing her magic. But he didn't move. She allowed one of the weaves to lower toward him before she gently inserted it into his ass, moving ever so slowly. It was a trick she'd learned years ago that had served her well with lovers—and had them begging for more. As she'd expected, Elias moaned and pulled against the restraints on his wrists, his head tilting back.

"I didn't expect that," he gasped. "Don't stop."

She did as he asked, moving the weave in and out, fucking his ass with the gentleness he'd shown her at the fae court.

His cock was impossibly hard and so large. She wanted nothing more than to position herself above him and sheath him deep inside her.

Instead, she grabbed a cloth she'd brought with her and inserted it between his teeth. As she did, he moaned, and it was muffled into the gag, which she tied around the back of his head. He thrust up into her, his cock rubbing against her stomach, his eyes pleading.

Now, she thought. *I must act now.*

Still fucking his ass, she swirled her other weaves in the air and then brought them down on him in featherlight touches all over his body—his chest, stomach, hips. She moved one between his legs, caressing his balls, which earned her another moan.

Then she wove together the thinnest weave she could manage. She hoped he wouldn't notice it with the many others she had around them. With careful precision, she plucked the amplifier from his pocket with her weave and stashed it in a pocket she'd sewn into the back of her dress. She released that one weave but held on to all the others, continuing to fuck Elias in his ass and touch him everywhere.

Leaning down, she moved the gag from his mouth and pressed a kiss to his lips, holding his face in her hands. She should let go and do as she'd planned. But she hesitated, not wanting this moment to end.

His eyes locked with hers, and the sheer vulnerability in his gaze nearly stopped her heart.

"I love you, Arabella. I never want to be parted from you again."

A choking sob escaped her lips as she released his face, tears streaming down her cheeks.

This was the very thing she'd been wanting her whole life—to be loved, to feel like she had a family who accepted her for her. But she'd had that with the Circle. And she couldn't have both Elias and the enchantresses, not if she was to protect her home.

He frowned, brows drawing together. She shook her head, unable to form words. A thousand emotions rose to the surface, but she slammed them all back down and locked them behind a mental door.

Then she pushed the gag back into his mouth and wove four more complex weaves as strong as the sturdiest ropes. Before he could recognize what she was doing, she locked each of them around his arms and legs for additional restraint. She knew they'd be a mere nuisance with his power being so much greater than hers. But every extra moment it gave her to escape would have to be enough.

She grabbed the blade from her leg and held it above his chest.

There was genuine fear in his eyes as he looked up at her in disbelief.

She'd never forget that look for as long as she lived.

But why would he look at her with such fear? He could only be killed by decapitation, ripping his heart out, or a magical blade. This was just the blade he'd given her. It was just—

Realization dawned.

Could it be? No... It wasn't possible. He wouldn't...

But the look in his eyes was raw and true, and she knew he'd given her a shadow fae dagger. A syphen. The very weapon to kill an erox had been in her possession, and she'd never realized.

As his eyes flared a bright blue, she knew she had less than a moment before he overpowered her.

For my people, she thought. Then she grasped the dagger in both hands, closed her eyes, and brought it down.

Elias screamed.

But when she opened her eyes, she saw the blade was embedded in his sternum.

She released the breath she'd been holding.

I couldn't do it.

Despite the threat he was to her people, she couldn't kill him. But as he drew several ragged breaths, she knew she'd injured him greatly. She withdrew the knife and stood.

"I'm sorry," she whispered as she tied off the weaves. They'd last for perhaps a few minutes at best before he broke through— depending on how badly a syphen would injure him. Perhaps less. "I need the amplifier to protect my people. They'll die if I don't. I tried to ask you, but you wouldn't listen. Once they have it, I'll return, and you can do whatever you wish to me."

Without another word, she turned and fled the room, a bloodied knife clutched in her hand. She raced down hallway after hallway, heading for the front entryway. He would heal, but she wasn't sure how long it would take with an injury from this magical blade. Likely longer than a regular blade. But would it be long enough for her to get away?

She grabbed her bag from where she stashed it and ran outside. In the stables, she threw a saddle over the black mare and guided it out. She heard a cry from somewhere inside the castle, and fear tightened her chest.

He'd told her that he loved her, and she'd stabbed him in the chest.

I'm sorry.

Her dress was too tight to allow her to sit on the saddle properly. With the blade, she cut the sides of her dress, making a slit to her mid-thigh on each side, Elias' blood still warm on the metal. With a slam, she pushed the blade into a sheath she'd tied to her waist and grabbed the amplifier from the hidden pocket in her dress. Power bloomed in her mind, coursing up her arms and filling her chest to bursting. So much power. Even her shadows stretched out beneath her with inky tendrils.

Then she mounted the horse and galloped toward the woods, hoping it was toward Shadowbank.

For the first time in her life, the dark creatures of the forest didn't scare her. Not nearly as much as the demon who would soon be at her heels. If Elias caught her, she may not live until sunrise. Even with the power of the amplifier, she may not have the strength to fend him off.

As another scream sounded from within the castle, she clutched the reins, blinked back tears, and rode into the forest.

Praying that this would be worth it.

Chapter Twenty
ARABELLA

A rabella weaved between the trees on horseback, riding recklessly fast. Elias' scream echoed through her mind, and she choked back a sob.

He's a demon. Demons are incapable of love.

Even as she repeated this mantra, she knew it was far from true. She'd seen this male show kindness toward humans in the remote village where they'd bought medicines. She'd seen his friendship with another erox and allowed him an escape from whatever challenges he had in his life. And she'd seen him stand up to a fae queen, refusing to make her into an erox—a demon that could hurt humans.

Why did he give me that stupid blade? Why didn't he protect himself better?

But she knew the answer.

I love you, Arabella. I never want to be parted from you again.

She'd never hear those words from him again.

Clutching the amplifier, she was tempted to hold the knife in her other hand, but she held on to the reins, afraid she might fall off as the horse galloped over the dark forest ground. Above the leafy canopies, she thought she saw some light peeking through, but she couldn't be sure whether the sun had started to rise. She prayed they would avoid rocks or fallen logs—anything that could lead to the horse's broken ankle or leg. Such an injury would mean death for her. Elias would find her within the hour.

As she rode, she allowed her shadows to stretch out, and they moved from beneath her and the mare's bodies, reaching into the trees beyond her line of sight. If a monster was headed toward them, she wanted to know. The horse whinnied and shook its head, slowing and stomping its hooves. She stretched a hand forward and stroked its neck.

"Shhh," she whispered. "It's just me."

But the horse couldn't hear her. It was agitated by her shadows. It must have never experienced this type of magic before—whatever her magic was. So, she pulled the shadows back in. After a minute, she soothed the horse enough for it to resume its pace.

Sighing, she strung weaves of her enchantress magic together, sharp as fae arrows, ready to release them at a moment's notice. She may not be able to sense anything nearby without her shadows, but she'd be ready to respond to any threat. She'd have to be.

Rustling sounds in the trees had her head turning toward shadows to her left, but she couldn't see anything in the dark. Was that the wind? But no... the trees were too thick here. More sounds came from her right, and she directed her weaves in that direction. When there was a crack of a branch and the distinct sound of heavy footsteps, she released one weave and then a second.

Elias could move soundlessly. Was he moving this way so she could hear him? He may want her to know he was coming for her as he had the day he had on the stairs landing. She didn't allow herself to think of what happened after, focusing only on how he'd stalked her. He could leap from shadow to shadow.

"Please," she called toward where she'd released her weaves where she still heard heavy footsteps. "Just let me go. I have to help the Circle, but I'll come back immediately after. I swear it."

There was no response to her words.

Tightening her grip on the reins, she urged her horse to

move faster, giving it a hard kick. It couldn't go any faster through the trees. It was a miracle the horse hadn't broken an ankle or been injured yet. But if they couldn't go faster, that meant one thing.

She would soon be caught.

When she noted a second set of footsteps, her heart beat so hard in her chest that it made her head swim.

Elias had brought Breckett with him.

She didn't stand a chance.

Weaving as fast as she could, she released more of her shards of wind and earth, sharp as an icicle, into the forest on either side of her. She was hesitant to use the amplifier, not knowing if there was a limit to the magic within the object. Every drop she could save for Shadowbank, she would. So help her, she was going to make what she'd done worth it.

She released weave after weave into the forest, sweat pouring down the sides of her face.

Suddenly, there was the sound of grunts, deep and guttural. She frowned. That didn't sound like Elias. Could it be Breckett?

The footsteps were coming closer, the rustling of forest floor debris becoming louder. Soon, more footsteps sounded, and she knew she had been surrounded. She slowed her mount, pulling back on the reins as a massive shadow blocked the trees in front of her. With a yank, she turned the horse, trying to flee in another direction, but another shadow appeared. She turned again, but shadows were everywhere.

Then the shadows moved.

Massive creatures with wrinkled skin and a single deep-set eye surrounded her. They walked on two legs like humans, but they were at least four times the size and had sharp talons extending from the fingertips on either hand.

Ogres.

She'd never seen an ogre before, though other enchantresses had faced the creatures in attacks on Shadowbank in years passed.

The one in front of her had massive tusks extending up from

a mouth that could easily clear her head from her shoulders in a single bite. It smiled, revealing countless smaller, sharp teeth.

For a moment, her mind was utterly blank. She stared at the monsters, and they stared back at her. Time stretched on—seconds feeling like hours. Saliva dripped from the mouth of the ogre with tusks, and one to its left wheezed heavily through flat nostrils. Another ogre, this one on her right, had what she could only describe as antlers atop its head. More of the monsters appeared in the darkness.

She was alone and vulnerable. There was no ward to protect her now.

Then time resumed, and she moved on instinct.

Unwilling to use the amplifier, she released more weaves in every direction, moving her arms in swirling motions to help her create them more quickly.

One of her weaves pierced the ogre to her right in the chest. It fell to his knees, fingers touching black blood seeping from its wound. More weaves went wide or merely grazed the shoulders or thighs of the ogres. There had to be six of them lumbering toward her.

When one ogre closed in, reaching toward her, she knew there wasn't enough time to form another weave. Instead, she extended the shadows beneath her and her mare and lashed out. They wrapped around the shadows of the ogres and *pulled*. It was as though the ogres had pulled the rug out from under them as they went crashing down.

She could hear Lucinda's voice even as she did.

You're a one-trick pony.

Perhaps she was, but it gave her precious moments. She created and released several more weaves, hitting two of the creatures in the chest. She hoped it was enough to kill them.

The horse whinnied, kicking up onto its back legs. Desperately, she clung to the reins, but she lost her grip and fell.

This was the end.

She knew it at once.

She'd not be able to mount again, and it wouldn't be possible to outrun these creatures on foot. But she wouldn't let them take her alive.

Hesitating, she glanced down at the orb clutched in her fist and leaped to her feet. She could either die or risk using the amplifier. She had a moment to consider and then made a decision. She'd use only enough to kill these creatures. If she didn't survive this, she'd never be able to give the amplifier to the Circle. As she opened herself to the orb, an inky slime of energy coursed up her arm, slid over her chest, and stole up her neck until darkness fell over her vision. Fear iced her senses, and she tried to release it, but there was no letting go. It had seized her power, lacing it through the amplifier and keeping it in place with its oily energy. She screamed as something squeezed her chest, tightening over her neck. Then it was gone.

When she opened her eyes, every sense was heightened. She could see there were more ogres in the trees beyond the line of the creatures closest to her. Those were an arm's reach away. But as she reached for her magic, she felt her shadows sing, felt something crack open in her chest. It was like she took the first breath of fresh air in her life, the cool ocean breeze of deep winter. It made her enchantress magic, of earth and air, pale in comparison.

She didn't need weaves nor did she need to summon the magic. It was there, within the invisible chasm torn open in her chest—a well of magic she'd never realized had always been there. Raising an arm, she pointed toward the ogre that wrapped a meaty hand around her wrist and released. Shadows exploded in its gut, forming a hole several feet wide and blasting it backward into the trees and onto more of its kind. Gore splattered her face, but she ignored it, turning toward another ogre that had seized her horse and yanked violently on its reins, pulling it away from her and deeper into the forest. Another ogre took its place.

But it didn't matter now. She had her shadows. She *was* darkness. Nothing could stop her.

She released blast after blast of night into the surrounding trees, allowing the inky tendrils of the amplifier to plunge deeper into her. Two more ogres fell. Somewhere in the distance, she felt more than heard the rumbling of more heavy footsteps. But she became the darkness, pulling shadows beneath the trees and sending them in spinning arcs, as sharp and thin as a needle, outward.

Time passed. She couldn't tell how long. But even as the bodies of ogres piled up around her, more came. Using her magic felt sticky sweet, and she couldn't get enough. As she blasted more shadows, she saw an opening in the trees and dashed forward. She didn't know where the horse was, but perhaps she could find her way home on foot. And if any of the creatures came too close, she'd cut them down.

But as she ran, footsteps thundered behind her. The ogres were surprisingly fast for creatures of their size. The taller ones had to duck underneath massive tree branches several stories high, while the smaller ones wove in and out of the trees with agility.

She pulled from the amplifier, willing her legs to go faster, her strides to be longer.

But as she did, the oily tendrils fastened to her neck tighter. At that moment, she knew if she wasn't careful in pulling its magic into her, it would claim her. She would be nothing but a shell of herself, a slave to this object. And if she was going to destroy herself, she wanted to wield the amplifier to save her people—not use it against these monsters. She worried she'd used too much of its energy already.

All at once, she closed the door to her magic from the amplifier. It resisted, claws latching on to her chest and neck. With all the energy remaining in her, she ripped it from her, forcing it back down her arm and into the orb at her fist.

Her feet tripped over a protruding root, and she went down. Three more ogres moved in. But she was spent, gasping and leaning on a knee. It felt like her body had been wrung out and left to dry. Was that the cost of using an amplifier?

Swallowing back bile, she shoved the amplifier into the pocket in her dress and retrieved two of the knives from the sheaths on her legs, ignoring the blood that had dried on one.

As another ogre reached for her, she lashed out with the blades, slicing up an arm from wrist to bicep. The creature made an inhuman screaming sound, deep and guttural. Black blood sprayed her face. As she wiped her eyes, two arms wrapped around her from behind. She fought with every remaining ounce of energy she had. It would take too long to make weaves, and her shadows had retreated to those beneath her feet, which were several feet below her on the forest floor as the ogre lifted her off the ground. All that remained to her were her knives and her wit.

But she was spent, and the creature gripped her so hard that she was forced to drop her blades. They fell to the ground with a faint thud.

In the trees, she sensed a magic wielder approaching. Their power rippled in waves far more powerful than Elias, Breckett, or any of the fae she'd encountered. Even Hadeon. It was like a thunderstorm crackling through the forest with the strength of the entire fae court.

Then they appeared before her.

It was a man, or it looked like one. But it didn't feel human. Blond hair came to his mid-back as straight as the edge of a longsword. His nose was as sharp and chiseled as his jawline, with high cheekbones as unforgiving as the look in his eyes. Eyes that demanded obedience and had seen armies fall leveled on her. Only his clothes were soft—as fine as any fae clothing that encircled his body and extended to the forest floor.

She knew he could lift a hand and blow the forest off the map if he so chose. Yet he stood before her, assessing the trail of bodies in her wake and then her gore-covered gown.

"Just what do we have here?" he purred, head cocking to the side.

Hand outstretched, he made the slightest flick of a finger, and something small squirmed on her back before the amplifier was free of her pocket and flew through the air and into his open palm.

"No!" she cried, but the ogre held tight as she fought.

It was no use.

Nodding to the ogre, he said, "Bring her."

Again, she fought, trying to break free of its grip, but something hard struck her atop the head and blackness took her.

WHEN ARABELLA BLINKED her eyes open, she immediately wished she hadn't. Her head throbbed, and her vision swam. She leaned forward to be sick but was stopped short. The sickness retreated, replaced by shock as she glanced around. She was tied to a stake in the ground and surrounded by dozens of tents set up in the forest beyond which she could feel the lumbering footsteps of ogres before she saw their bald heads with wisps of hair over the top of tents.

Where am I?

Then it all came back to her—the ogres in the forest, her shadow magic exploding out of her, the inky tendrils of the amplifier, and... the male who'd billowed magic about him like clouds of steam from a volcano in the heart of winter.

Instinctively, she reached for her enchantress magic, and then fear froze her movements. It was... gone. Just gone. Then she reached for her shadow magic and breathed a sigh of relief. She still had access to one of her powers.

Even as relief washed over her, she could feel the familiar weight of a collar and nearly groaned.

She pulled against her restraints, and the coarse rope dug into her wrists.

"I wouldn't bother," came a masculine voice from behind her.

A male appeared before her. It wasn't the male she'd seen before who exuded power; and the way he'd walked, his chin as high as the clouds, implied that he was sure himself. This male wore nondescript leather armor and had pale skin and dark brown hair. His features were average—somewhat attractive with his sharp jawline and fit body. If she'd seen him in the streets, she probably wouldn't remember him. He would make the perfect spy. The most notable thing about him was the pull within her chest toward him and his blackening eyes.

An erox.

She knew the telltale desire stirring between her legs at once. It wasn't the fire that Elias set off within her, but the pull was strong enough that she'd be helpless to fight it even if she wasn't tied to this stake.

"The Sorcerer has placed a collar on you. You won't be able to touch your magic until he says so."

"Piss off," she hissed, trying to get her feet underneath her. They weren't tied together, and she slowly rose to her feet, sliding her bound hands up the stake until she stood.

"Ah-ah," the erox scolded her. "Is that how you greet your hosts? And after killing so many of our ogres. You'd best be playing nice and pray for mercy from *him.*"

The pull toward the male before her grew stronger as he took one lazy step toward her and then another until he was so close that their bodies nearly touched.

She turned her head away, unable to resist him more than that, but his hand gripped her chin painfully, forcing her to face him again. Then without their lips touching, an orgasm ripped from her, and the male pulled essence from her lips. Whimpering, tears ran down her cheeks as the blue energy twirled and twisted in the air between them before he breathed it in. His head tilted back as though savoring the most delectable wine.

"That's not how we treat our guests, Orson," a familiar male voice said from behind him.

Orson turned on a heel, bowing his head. "As you say."

Power rippled like waves of a stormy sea around the male who stood before her. He wore the same long robes as before, his unbound blond hair as straight as the horizon.

"What brings an enchantress into these woods? And with an amplifier, no less."

For reasons she couldn't explain, she kept her mouth shut. Danger rippled off him as surely as power. Instead, she fixed her eyes on the forest floor, trying to ignore the labored footsteps of countless ogres around her. There had to be hundreds...

"How did you get the amplifier?" the male asked, his footsteps coming closer. "Are you from the village beyond the forest?"

She could feel the weight of his gaze as he strode across the tent toward her.

The village? Does he mean Shadowbank?

He clapped his hands together. "I forget myself. Most here know me as the Sorcerer. But you may call me Magnus."

A sorcerer.

As if she wasn't terrified enough, fear rippled through her. No wonder power billowed off him. Sorcerers were some of the strongest magic wielders in existence. They could access any magic they wished—or had giftings in—earth, spirit, air, blood, light... It didn't matter. But to access such magic, they first had to open themselves to the dark magic of the deep to extend their wells. It was unlike her shadows, as what sorcerers drew was the very source of everything evil. The blood veins of the creatures of the deep—the monsters none dared awaken.

Sorcerers could use different magic at once. He could snap his fingers, and she would die from across the room.

Again, she reached for her enchantress magic but was met with a wall of resistance, her mental fingers moving through nothing as the metal around her neck heated painfully.

When she didn't speak, Magnus said, "I see you're overwhelmed by everything. How could you not—?"

"Why?" She looked up to him then with narrowed eyes, her eyes locking with his blood-red eyes.

This sorcerer had stolen the very thing she'd taken from the male she'd...

Well, she'd certainly not fallen in love with Elias. She couldn't. But she'd dashed any hope of them coming back together and finding any type of happiness once he found her. Because it was only a matter of time. Her life would most likely be forfeit.

But more important than her relationship with Elias was the fact that Magnus had stolen the hopes of Shadowbank.

His brows rose, though his face remained impassive. "Why what?"

"Why do you have an army this close to the human village?"

From his earlier question, she guessed she'd found her way toward Shadowbank. The odds were slim, but maybe she'd gone toward her home. Still, she had no notion why this many ogres and a sorcerer—and at least one erox and countless other males—would be here of all places.

Magnus shrugged if the too-graceful rise and fall of his shoulders could be called such a thing. The grace of his every movement made her wonder just how old he was.

"I'm searching for something," he said. "Someone close to me stole something precious. And I want it back."

She nodded. It wasn't an answer, not really. But she could... sympathize with his predicament.

Or Elias could.

Magnus waved a hand, and the bindings on her hands loosened and dropped to the ground. "Come. Join me in my tent. You must be hungry."

He turned, showing his back as he walked away. Clearly, he didn't see her as a threat. It was likely because he thought she couldn't access her magic, and she was weaponless. She'd dropped her blades in the forest—including the syphen. Could he not sense her other ability?

Uncertain what else to do, she followed him. She didn't have any desire to have another rendezvous with Orson or the ogres.

Soon, she stood before a massive tent, which had the fabric

pulled back to the entrance. Inside, there was a lush rug over the uneven forest floor along with a bed, table, chairs, washing basin, and a collection of pillows on the ground.

So much decadence for temporary living quarters in the forest.

When he sat down on the pile of pillows, she realized it was an area to lounge. Stretching long legs out, he leaned an elbow on a pillow as red as the irises studying her face.

She gestured to the tattered remains of her dress and the dried gore and blood all over her. "I'd hate to ruin your pretty pillows."

Chuckling, he flicked his wrist. A breeze swept through the tent. Looking down, her eyes widened. Not only was her skin clean and completely clear of evidence of the battle, her dress was repaired—no slits in the sides or tatters. It was as beautiful as the day she'd first seen it. Even her hair was clean and braided, and she reached up, touching the teardrop from her enchantress headdress.

"That's much better," Magnus said, gesturing to the pillows.

Without a word, she sat.

A figure strode through the entrance to the tent with what appeared to be a tray of food. As the male approached, another wave of desire hit her, and she flinched away from him.

Another erox?

The male said nothing as he placed the tray between her and Magnus before walking away. The tray had an assortment of nuts, seeds, cheeses, and dried meat. Her stomach rumbled, but she kept her hands folded in her lap.

"Please," Magnus said. "Help yourself."

Even though her body hurt everywhere and her exhaustion seeped into her bones from using so much magic—and she needed the sustenance to regain her strength—she didn't move.

The sorcerer shrugged before reaching for a nut and popping it into his mouth.

"I imagine you must have an interesting story," he continued.

"No ordinary enchantress comes into possession of an amplifier —and a shadow amplifier at that."

"It's a shadow amplifier?" she asked before she could stop herself. Realizing what she'd done, she glanced away, studying the nearby fabric walls of the tent.

"Indeed. Some amplifiers work for all magic, but there's a toll to be paid. Other amplifiers only work with specific types of magic. And everything in between."

There was a flash of movement, and he held the small black orb between his fingers.

"This one," he continued, "has an addictive property."

That explained the difficulty in stopping using it. Her lips narrowed into a thin line.

Fucking Hadeon. That bastard should have told me.

But he hadn't, and she still owed him a favor after all this. *If she survived.*

"I see this has come as a surprise to you," Magnus said. "Be careful using this one. It also brings out your darker desires. That's how it's powered. The more you give in to your dark desires, the more power you'll have access to."

She swallowed thickly. "I'd like it back."

The sorcerer didn't move from where he lounged on the cushions as she outstretched her hand, palm upward.

"I'm being polite, Enchantress." As he spoke, his red eyes darkened, and the light in the tent seemed to snuff out, though she could still see the movement of flames in the nearby candles. "But do not mistake that you remain alive only because I say. Become too difficult, and I'll send you back to be a plaything for my ogres or erox. Do you understand?"

She licked suddenly dry lips and nodded.

"Good. Now, I'll ask again—where did you get the amplifier?"

Fists opening and closing, she considered. She didn't want to mention Elias' involvement for fear the ogres would travel only a few miles into the forest and discover his castle—and weakening wards. Even with his power, the wards likely wouldn't hold with this many foes. But did she dare reveal Prince Hadeon's involvement? What would his wrath—or the wrath of the Twilight Court—be? She was certain he didn't want their deal known, else why seek them out when they were in the lovers' quarter of the fae castle?

"I got it from the Twilight Court," she said carefully. "I stole it."

"You couldn't have gone through a gateway on your own. Who did you work with?"

Damn it. How did he know what they did to enchantresses?

"I..." she began, opening her mouth before closing it. "I traveled with Breckett."

It wasn't untrue. She *had* traveled with him. Best to lace her answers with truth.

The sorcerer leaned forward, all pretense of relaxation forgotten. He appeared like a predator ready to pounce, closing in on his prey. "You know Breckett?"

She shrugged. "Not well. He was passing through."

Why was he so interested in Breckett?

"Why did you steal it?" he asked.

She didn't dare mention Shadowbank's weakening wards—not that it would do much to stop a sorcerer. But what would an all-powerful sorcerer believe she might be after?

"I wasn't about to pass up the opportunity for more power than any enchantress has ever dreamed of."

He leaned back on the pillows. "Our meeting is fated. It just so happens I'm in search of Breckett. Where can I find him?"

An image of Breckett at the banquet table with Elias ran through her mind, and she stuffed it down.

"He and I parted ways after the gateway," she lied. "Once I had the amplifier... Well, as you can imagine, I had to leave rather quickly—put as much distance between me and the fae as possible."

Magnus' eyes narrowed. "Did he say where he was going?"

She shook her head.

"What direction did he head in?"

"I'm not sure."

Eyebrow raised, the sorcerer leaned back further. "Why would he agree to help you through the gateway? It doesn't seem like there'd be much for him to gain."

She licked her lips, carefully forming the lie. "He needed to feed. I offered my body and essence to him in exchange for safe passage."

Magnus sat in silence for a few moments and then snapped his fingers. Two figures appeared in the tent's opening.

With a soft groan, she realized that they, too, were erox.

The beauty rippling off both males was so overwhelming that she felt the flesh between her legs grow wet, which—she suddenly remembered—was entirely naked beneath her gown. All they'd have to do was spread her legs, and she'd be ready for them.

Scenting her desire, both males turned their gazes to her. One had skin as black as night, and the other had pale skin with an olive hue and dark brown hair. Both of their eyes were entirely black, and she knew she should avoid meeting their gazes. They both needed to feed. But even as she fixed her eyes on the pillows beneath her, the pull toward them was tangible, and she felt her head dropping back, her eyes fluttering closed.

"Careful, boys," came the voice of Magnus. "This one is my special guest."

She felt the weight of their gazes shift and nearly sighed in relief.

"Gather a team and search the woods. Breckett was nearby. I want him alive. Understood?"

They nodded, glanced at her one more time, and disappeared from the tent.

Magnus flicked a wrist. Suddenly, she was lifted from the cushions by bands of air that wrapped around her and pinned her arms to her sides. Feet dangling over the ground, she floated toward the center post of the tent. Then the phantom wind had ropes swirling above and below her. She yanked against the air, trying to break free, but she might as well have been pushing against a mountain. The sorcerer's strength was unfathomable. And for reasons she couldn't understand, she knew not to use her shadow magic—not yet.

The streams of magic moved her like she was a rag doll. It tied her arms above her head and feet to the base of the large wooden post even as she yanked against it, earning her rope burns for her efforts.

"If you're telling the truth," the sorcerer said, his back to her, "you have nothing to fear. My soldiers will find Breckett, and then you'll be given the option to join us. I always have a place for power-hungry magic wielders at my side. But if I find you're lying…" He spun on a heel, striding across the tent toward where she was tied in the center. Raising a finger that glowed at the tip, light reflected off the beads along her bodice. "I will let my erox feast on you."

Then he pressed his finger against her chest.

A scream tore through her throat. It was like an ember from the core of the earth had been pressed to her chest—like he'd branded her with a single touch. Steam rose into the air above where he touched her skin, and the air filled with the scent of cooking flesh. But even as he stood before her, she could see magic billowing around him in rippling, unyielding waves, and he used but a drop of it.

He trailed the finger down, leaving behind a trail of red, angry flesh, which immediately raised and blistered. If she could breathe, she might have retched from the pain. Instead, she clenched her teeth, feeling like her chest was being split open. Glancing down, she watched as he ran his finger down her stomach, her once beautiful gown tearing down the center, a line of smoke trailing up from the edges and blood dripping onto the carpet in large, red rivulets. He stopped just before her pussy as what remained of her dress fell to her ankles.

He surveyed his work and the line of red, angry flesh before his eyes settled on her breasts and then on her pussy. "I can see why Breckett was so distracted to let a little enchantress take an amplifier that's within his reach."

"Don't call me that," she said, pulling against her restraints. The rope bit into her wrists.

The picture of Elias' face appeared in her mind's eye—and the many times he'd called her that. She didn't regret her actions to try to save her people, but she regretted hurting him. If only there had been a way for him to protect his home and for her to protect hers...

Magnus raised an eyebrow. "Have I hit a nerve?" Turning toward the tent's entrance, he said, "Someone will be back soon when we've either found Breckett or... Well, let's hope for you that we find him, and soon."

Tears streamed down her cheeks when the sorcerer disappeared, pain and shame rippling through her.

What have I done?

Chapter Twenty-One

ARABELLA

Something coarse bit into her wrists, the pain slicing into the black oblivion, and Arabella jerked awake. Glancing around, she noted the light from a single lantern at the tent's entry, and she groaned.

Her arms had lost feeling hours ago—sometime between the stretch of daylight hours and when they'd once again succumbed to the domain of the moon and stars. But she must have enough blood flow to feel the bite of the ropes in her wrists as her body slackened in sleep.

Males strode past the tent entrance, and she held her breath. One male paused, the angle of his chin highlighted by that single lantern as he turned slowly to peer into the darkness at her. She pressed her knees together, waiting for the crushing desire to overwhelm her senses. The flickering of the telltale signs of a hungry erox tickled the edges of her mind, but there was a shout beyond the tent and the male disappeared.

In the hours that had stretched by, she'd lost count of the number of males who had passed the tent and spared lingering glances her way. She was slowly coming to understand one unyielding fact: the sorcerer had built an army of erox and other creatures of the wild shadows.

She'd known of the ogres, but she'd also seen glimpses of trolls and winged gargoyles. Shadowbank didn't stand a chance against this army if they turned toward it.

That should have been her first thought.

Instead, her first thought was on one thing—was Elias okay? Had he and Breckett been found? Even while she hoped for their safety, fear twisted her gut. If they hadn't found Breckett, then this was going to be a very long—or very short—night.

She swallowed past the tightness in her throat.

Would she be raped by erox after erox, a willingly unwilling participant as they fed on her until her essence was depleted and only her corpse remained? She couldn't let herself dwell on that. If she did, she would succumb to the fear tightening her chest and the panic at the edges of her senses.

Think, she thought. *How can you escape?*

The collar was still around her neck. She had no access to her enchantress magic and couldn't form a blade of air to cut her restraints. But she had her shadow magic.

Magic she'd never been able to truly use without an amplifier.

The amplifier had sliced something open in her, and there was a pathway that hadn't been there before—one that stretched between her fingertips and that dark well deep within her being. Before, she could sense the shadows and what lay within. But now? Now, it was like the shadows were an extension of her, if only she could reach out and touch them. Even her body itself felt different.

Could she possibly wield them again? She'd not just tangled the shadows at someone's feet, but she'd slain ogres. Surely, she could cut herself free. But she was so impossibly exhausted from using so much magic, even with the amplifier's aid. And she'd had no food and precious little sleep.

She had to try.

Reaching for her shadows, she stretched a mental hand out, fingers splayed. She reached deep within her, past her senses of the earth and surroundings, past her hopes and fears, down to her very core—to what made her uniquely *her*. Magic wielders were more than their magic, but their magic was also an integral part of the gears and cogs that turned the levers and powered life itself. She was her magic, the same as she was a compilation of her dreams and experiences. They were all a part of her. And there was one part she'd never been able to reach before.

But she wasn't the same woman she'd been before. She'd learned so much of herself and of others from one being, one male. One demon.

Just like magic was part of a person, the type of magic that person possessed didn't inherently indicate goodness or evil. It was about *how* that magic was wielded and the intention behind it.

She'd been so blind.

Stretching out further, she reached to the innermost parts of herself. As she did, she thought perhaps something caressed the edges of her fingertips. It felt like she was trying to put water in a box one droplet at a time, and the drops leaked through the corners until the entire thing was a sodden mess.

Sweat rolled down the sides of her face despite the cool air of the evening.

Focus. Now wasn't the time to become frustrated.

Again, she stretched out mental fingers toward the dark depths of her mind, toward the shadows that had always seemed to be interlaced with her very being. For a moment, it felt like she'd touched something, like the strumming of a single cord on a harp. At that moment, she knew she had to give more of herself. This wasn't enough if she hoped to tap into the well. She allowed her mind to fall completely into the darkness, letting it fill her, and dove into the chasm that the amplifier had ripped open in her chest.

The shadows beneath her feet rippled and moved.

She swam through sands the color of secrets. But as she moved, reaching ever forward, something blossomed within the deep—a faint flickering of a gray as though the moonlight illuminated a rain cloud in the sky. As she reached toward that well of power, she tried to grasp it, but it slipped through her fingers. Once more, she tried to grab it. For a moment, it felt like she'd caught something as a strand of shadows rippled upward in the endless, formless landscape. Shadows twice as dark as her shadow.

"Hello, Enchantress," came a voice from the tent's entrance.

Her eyes snapped open.

The candles in the lantern had burned low, but she could see the darkened faces of four erox—two of whom were the males who'd spoken with Magnus earlier. Her heart dropped into her stomach, and any hold she'd had on the shadows slipped between her fingers.

Pulling against her restraints, she shook her head.

"Please," she begged, gooseflesh rippling along every inch of her bare skin. "Leave me alone."

Three of the males stalked toward her, the fourth closing the tent's opening behind them.

"We spent the day in search of Breckett with no sight of him," said the one with fair skin and brown hair.

A strangled relief in her chest had her exhaling a shaky breath. They hadn't found Elias or Breckett.

But her relief was short-lived.

"The sorcerer gave us permission to do *anything* we wanted with you," he continued. "While we won't kill you just yet, there are plenty of ways to pass the time."

He nodded to two of the other erox who kneeled before her, each wrapping their hands around one of her ankles. She pulled against them even as desire washed over her, making her breasts tighten and her nipples harden.

If she didn't fight now, it would be too late. She'd be under their spell, a willing participant in their plans.

The third male sliced the bonds tying her legs to the post, and the other two pulled her legs until they were spread wide. She yanked on her bound wrists again and again until they were bloody, but it was no use. The fourth erox closed the distance

248

between them. Ever so slowly, he reached a hand out. For a moment, she thought he'd grasp her neck, open her mouth, and feed off her essence until she was too weak to stand on her own. Instead, his hand lowered down, and he ran a finger over her wet pussy.

"We're going to have fun with you." He brought the finger to his lips, licking it. Then he gestured to the erox who'd cut the restraints around her legs and stood off to her side. "Gag her."

"*No!*" she screamed. "Don't touch me!"

She'd run out of time, and she knew it. She floundered for her magic, but she couldn't focus past the haze of desire that muddied her mind.

This was it. Her body was going to be fucked and drained, and she'd never...

She'd never see *her* erox again or feel his touch.

And it was all her doing.

"*Elias!*"

She didn't know why—after everything—she called for him. It didn't matter. Nothing mattered. Her body would be used until there was nearly nothing left.

At least he's free, she thought. *He's alive, and Magnus hasn't found him.*

Something was pressed between her lips, stifling her remaining screams.

"Much better," the erox before her said. "We'll take that out later when you're more... compliant."

Even as he spoke, she felt her fisted hands opening above her head as her heartbeats slowed and blood flowed toward her core. Heat coursed through her, and she tilted her head back, leaving her neck bare for the male before her.

Why did she fight when these males could give her so much pleasure? All she had to do was open herself to them.

The eyes of the erox before her darkened until his pupils extended and blackened out his irises, and he reached for his pants. "That's a good girl." But before he could free his cock, she heard shuffling outside of the tent and stifled grunts.

The erox paused, gesturing to the males who held her feet. "Go see what that was."

With three of their gazes turned away, the haze of her mind cleared slightly, and she shook her head, teeth biting down on the gag before she swung forward with all her strength and kicked the male closest to her. She landed the strike to his gut, and he stumbled backward.

"You bitch!" he hissed.

She tried to land another kick, but she missed. Then he swung his fist, which connected with her cheek. The gag absorbed some of the momentum, preventing her teeth from clacking together. But his aim hit true, and her eye swelled as blood trickled down her cheek.

"You're going to regret that," the erox hissed.

Two of the males disappeared outside the tent, and there was a flash of blue light before two distinct thuds of bodies hitting the ground.

"What is that?" the male before her asked, fear evident in his voice. "No one can get through the ogres. And even if Breckett managed to, he can't wield essence." He gestured to the only other remaining erox in the tent. "Go out there and take care of it."

The male froze, glancing between the erox who'd given the order and the entrance of the tent.

Wield essence? What was he—

Realization dawned. Tears streamed down her cheeks as she knew at once who it was. There was only one erox who could weaponize the very energy that gave him life.

A blast of blue light tore through the tent, burning a hole through the entrance flaps. It struck down one of the erox, punching a hole through his chest—where his heart once was.

A dark silhouette stood in the tent's entryway, blue light glowing through fisted hands.

"Touch her," came the deep rumble of a masculine voice she knew as well as her own, "and I'll end you."

She made a sound somewhere between a relieved laugh and a sob, but it was muffled through the gag.

Elias' eyes settled on her, a brightened blue hue, and lingered on the blistering line down her chest and stomach and then to her swollen eye. "Are you okay?"

She nodded.

"Good." He lifted a hand and released a rope of essence, wrapping it around the erox in front of her and dragging the male, kicking and screaming, back toward him. Elias grabbed the male by his neck, holding him off the ground in front of him.

"Elias?" the male choked out, his voice disbelieving. "The Sorcerer will be so glad to hear you're back."

Elias' eyes widened for a moment before the look of unyielding fury returned. "He won't know I was here."

Without warning, he punched a fist through the chest of the erox and ripped it backward. He released the male's neck and dropped the body as though it were tomorrow's rubbish.

Arabella's eyes fixed on the object in his fist. A heart.

He dropped it to the ground alongside the body before striding to her. For a moment, he hesitated, his bloodied hands hovering in the air between them, but then he reached for the gag and untied it.

"You came."

"I always protect what's mine."

He untied her arms. As he did, her legs gave out, and she collapsed. Before she could fall to the ground, he caught her.

She blinked slowly, uncertain if she was about to pass out as a wave of dizziness crashed over her. If she could feel her arms, she would reach out and touch his blood-streaked face just to assure herself that he was real. That this wasn't all just some illusion her mind had made up in her last moments.

"I'm sorry."

He sniffed. "You missed."

She had. Even after everything, she didn't have the heart to kill him with the syphen when she'd had the chance. Some enchantress she was.

"Where's the syphen and amplifier?" he asked, glancing around the tent.

"I lost the syphen in the forest when the ogres took me."

She must have passed out because the next thing she knew, she was on the ground and Elias was removing his shirt and coat. He pulled his shirt over her head, slipping her arms through the sleeves before pulling his coat over her.

"Where's the amplifier?" he repeated.

"Magnus has it."

He cursed, which was followed by a string of words in a language she didn't recognize.

"I'm sorry," she said again, suddenly exhausted. "I had to… protect them."

Protect my family.

"Rest assured, we are going to have a long talk later. But now isn't the time."

His words surprised her, but she could only manage a bare nod. She started to close her eyes, but something tapped her cheek.

"Don't fall asleep just yet."

She tried to nod, but she found she didn't have the energy to. Instead, her body began to tremble.

"She's going into shock," he hissed before turning toward the back of the tent. "Breckett! Get us out of here."

Something sliced down the center of the fabric, but there was nothing there. Not a blade nor anyone holding it. She blinked repeatedly. Then Breckett appeared with a blade in his fist.

"Say my name louder, why don't you? It's not like this entire camp is looking for me."

"Your power is invisibility," she realized.

"Obviously." Breckett glanced behind him before beckoning

for them to come. "I don't know why I'm risking my neck for your sorry ass."

"Me either."

Elias scooped her up into his arms and strode forward, leaving the bodies of four erox behind.

"You should leave me here." The words were the faintest whisper as her eyelids became heavier. "Save yourselves."

She'd endangered both him and Breckett, and she hadn't even been able to protect her family.

A vein bulged in his jaw. "Don't make my effort in vain." Exiting the tent, he glanced around. "Now, be quiet. We have to get through the maze of enemies and hope none sense us if we have any hope of getting out of here alive—and that we can cover enough ground before they discover you're gone."

He nodded to Breckett, who reached out a hand to Elias. As his hand settled on Elias' shoulder, her ears popped and the world changed at once as though she viewed it through a glass pane. Summoning what strength remained to her, she looked around, mouth agape, before looking up to Elias as he held her. He nodded to her and then focused his gaze ahead as he and Breckett crept between tents, pausing in the shadows.

They were invisible.

Somehow, when Breckett touched them, he made them unseen as well.

Beyond the next tent that they crept behind, there were three males armed to the teeth with blades strapped across their backs. They also had smaller blades in more sheaths than she could count in the moment she spotted them before Breckett and Elias were dodging behind another tent.

The army's encampment extended as far as she could see in every direction, confirming what she'd suspected—Magnus' tent was at the center. He'd placed her where there wasn't hope of escape. At least... not without the help of two powerful erox. But like her, other magic wielders could sense their magic even if they were invisible to the eye. They had to move fast and couldn't remain in one place for long, and they'd have to hold on to hope that there were so many magic wielders and magical beings in the encampment that the presence of two more was of little significance.

There was a shout somewhere behind them, but Elias and Breckett never stopped, moving from tent to tent. They weaved from one to the next, trying to stay away from tent entrances. But as they strode toward one tent, creeping forward, a male appeared directly in front of them. Both Elias and Breckett froze, not daring to breathe. She held her breath as well, pulling her lips into her mouth and biting down.

She couldn't be the reason that these two erox—demons she'd too easily dismissed as dangerous and less deserving of protection and who'd helped her despite her actions—came to harm.

Like clockwork, desire thrummed throughout her whole body as the male glanced around, eyes studying the air before him —where they stood, unmoving.

Another. Fucking. Erox.

Just what was Magnus and this army up to? Why were there so many of this seemingly rare type of demon?

Behind them, footsteps sounded, and male voices called out, drawing near. Glancing back, she spotted two more males— presumably erox—coming up behind them and blocking them into the narrow pathway between tents. Both Elias and Breckett took a step back as all the males strode toward each other.

"The enchantress is missing, and Carlisle, William, and the others are dead. Sound the alarm—"

Elias leaped forward, out of Breckett's reach, a blade in his hand.

The world spun around her as he moved, slicing the blade left and right. Then everything stilled, and she realized Elias had cut their throats, all while holding her.

Their bodies dropped to the ground, the grass soaking up the pooling blood.

"Will that kill them?" she whispered.

"No." He shifted her weight under one arm, not even winded. "But it will give us time. Hopefully."

She bit her lip and nodded. Because of her, the very weapon he could have used to kill these erox was lost to them. The only way to kill them was to decapitate them or rip their hearts out, which took more time than they had.

"Why not jump through the shadows?" she said, voicing the question that had been lingering at the back of her mind.

"Using any magic will draw attention to us. Even Breckett using his magic is dangerous. But all erox know the feel of another erox leaping through shadows. They'd sense us instantly."

Adrenaline coursed through her, and her fatigue receded to the back of her thoughts. It would be back soon, crashing into her along with the shock of the day's events. But for now, her weariness had faded, and she wanted to help.

"I can walk."

"No."

That was all he said before they were moving again, weaving through tents, never stopping for more than a moment. Just as they neared the edge of the tents, the ground vibrated, and both Elias and Breckett stepped back—out of the way of a lumbering ogre as it strode past, a deer in its fist. The creature closed its massive jaw around the head of the doe, pulling. Its head popped off with a wet *crunch*.

Unable to help herself, she gagged and then covered her mouth. Thankfully, the sound was covered by the loud steps of the ogre as it strode past them. The creature must not possess any magical ability because it didn't even look their way, unlike the erox who'd turned their way immediately.

Silently, she prayed they'd make it through the rest of the army's encampment. The erox and other magic wielders were at its center while the ogres and other dark creatures formed the outer ring. As they moved, she spotted pockets of gray between the trees. There were forms... and they weren't entirely human.

Frowning, she squinted, trying to make out what they were, but Elias and Breckett were moving too fast.

Eventually, they neared the edge of the army's encampment. They'd gotten this far without alarms being raised. The ogres couldn't sense them, and the magic wielders were far behind. Hope swelled in her chest as they moved from tree to tree. They were going to make it. They—

A voice came from the darkness before them.

"At long last, my progeny has returned to me."

Chapter Twenty-Two
ARABELLA

Magnus appeared before them, his robes rippling in the still air. It was as though he was the center of a storm and the winds gusted around him, eager to be unleashed once more. His power rippling out hundreds of feet around him, laced with a stickiness that had her stomach turning.

Fear squeezed her chest even as hope was stripped from her. They'd been so close...

She wouldn't go back to his tent. She'd rather die fighting.

Questions swirled through her thoughts. Could Magnus detect the type of magic around him and not just the presence of magic? Did he have the amplifier? Was he using it?

Elias' hands trembled faintly as he placed her down on the ground, his hand in hers. Her legs wobbled, but she locked her knees. It still looked like she viewed the world through a glass pane, and she knew they were invisible to Magnus' eyes. Looking up at Elias, she could see fear in every rigid line of his features. She wanted to pull him close and comfort him, but she didn't. He wouldn't want reassurance from her anyway—not after everything.

"Show yourself," Magnus rumbled, demand laced in his words. He sounded like a male used to blind obedience.

Elias swallowed thickly, nodded to Breckett, and then squeezed her hand and released it. At once, the haze over the world receded with a pop. Beside her, Elias appeared, shirtless and chest glistening. Breckett remained invisible to her eye. His power grew more distant as though he walked in the opposite direction of them into the trees. Was he trying to escape without them?

As she returned her attention to the sorcerer, she resisted the urge to reach for Elias.

"I knew I'd find you one day," Magnus said, his scarlet eyes bright. "I just didn't expect you to evade me all this time."

The sorcerer's gaze raked over her, taking in the fact that she wore Elias' shirt and jacket before turning back to the erox.

"How long have you been working with Breckett?"

"If I'd known what he'd done," Elias said, "I would have offered my assistance far sooner."

Frowning, she looked between the two powerful males, not understanding. What had Breckett done? Why was Magnus hunting him down? What did he want with Elias?

"Come now, Elias. I'm certain you don't mean that. We were once so close, you and I, and we can be again. I'm doing this for us, all of us."

"I'd hardly call amassing an army selfless."

"Self-preservation, then."

While Elias' face remained carefully neutral, his hands trembled. But he held them at his sides, eyes fixed on the sorcerer. "You must pick, Magnus. Do you want Breckett and what he possesses? Or do you want me?"

Magnus' eyes narrowed. In a sweeping motion, he pushed his robes back, his hands held out before him.

"I'll have you both."

Power lashed out from Magnus' palms without warning. A brilliant red extended out to either side of him—toward them and toward where Breckett had gone. Where the sorcerer's power touched the forest, fire erupted, scarlet flames licking up trees. Ogres roared in fury and pain.

Did Magnus not care that he also injured some in his army?

But even as flames spread, she didn't see a male body drop to the ground.

He'd missed Breckett.

Elias stood in front of her, his hands moving in a complex swirling motion before a bright blue energy plumed out of his palms and blocked the red bolt of energy barreling toward them. As the two powers collided, shards broke off the main stream of energy and fell to the earth. Dry grass smoked, which trailed along the ground, alighting fallen leaves and other brush. Soon, the air was filled with smoke as neither sorcerer nor erox released their power.

"Why do you fight this, Elias?" Magnus called over the rushing of power and the sudden gusts of wind that swirled around them.

Her hair lifted from her shoulders from where she stood beside Elias.

"If I wanted to, I could end this little quarrel in an instant."

Little quarrel? Such a display of magic was like nothing she'd ever seen. The power amassing between the two of them was like the crashing of the seas. Elias' confrontation with the Alabaster, which she'd once looked upon with awe at the power they'd displayed, paled in comparison.

Suddenly, a thought struck her.

He's going to run out of essence.

He hadn't fed from her since the fae court, and she'd injured him before fleeing. It would have depleted whatever essence he had further.

They were on borrowed time, and the sorcerer knew it.

Elias was powerful, but his energy was finite compared to the sorcerer, who seemed to have an endless well of magic.

He also had the amplifier.

The sorcerer was toying with them, and the moment he tried in earnest, he would overpower them in an instant. Their only chance to escape would be to overpower him now, surprise him, and flee.

She turned to Elias. "Take my essence."

It wasn't a question, and she tried to hold as much confidence in her voice as she could. Weak as she was, she wasn't sure how much she could offer him. But it would have to be enough.

Palms up, a blue stream surging forward, he managed a sideward glance toward her. His gaze skated down her frame, taking in her swollen eye and the dried blood on her face.

"Take it, Elias. You need it."

"No." Sweat ran in rivulets down the sides of his face. "What I need will kill you."

Even as he spoke, the color of his eyes turned from the warm brown she loved to a burnt umber.

Beyond them, Magnus' brows rose. "Have you fallen for another human, my progeny?" He shook his head. "You should know better after what happened."

Magnus' left hand continued to release blasts of red energy toward the forest—where Breckett must be moving—while his right was directed at Elias. The sorcerer's eyes narrowed and a wicked smile spread across his lips. And then, he flicked his wrist.

Shards broke free of the red stream of magic and flew toward her.

Instinctively, she reached for her enchantress magic, preparing to form a shield with her weaves, but she struck that damned wall. The collar.

Screaming, she held her hands up, waiting for it to strike.

But no pain ever came.

Opening her eyes, she realized Elias stood between her and Magnus, blood dripping down his left shoulder and plopping onto the ground. He'd absorbed the magic for her, saving her life once again.

The essence coming from Elias' palms flickered, and Magnus' red plume of energy pushed forward, closing in.

Elias fell to a knee, his hands shaking. Sweat dripped off him as freely as the blood from his shoulder wound. His other knee dropped to the ground, and he strained to hold his arms up. A fainter, thinner stream of blue came from his palms, and the red energy crackled, drawing ever closer.

"Why do you resist, Elias? Join me, and we can be what we once were."

Elias shook his head.

"I can force your hand," Magnus continued. "But I'd rather have you willingly at my side."

"Never." The word was hardly more than a whisper, but she knew Magnus had heard it.

"I should kill you for your defiance." Magnus sent strike after strike into the forest where Arabella thought she sensed Breckett's magic. "Perhaps I will kill you... Or perhaps I'll let you turn into the creature you fear the most."

Beside her, Elias' eyes darkened to the deepest black, filling his entire eye. There was a glint coming from his lips, and she gasped at the sight of elongated fangs in place of canines.

Fear seized her chest, but she moved on instinct.

Once, she would have fled at the sight of a demon showing the deeper darkness within him. But she'd seen the heart of this male, and she wouldn't flee again.

She kneeled before him, hoping like hell he had enough strength to hold off Magnus' magic for a few more moments. Elias' eyes flickered between hers, and she could see regret and resignation in them in the way his brows drew together. She could also see fear and disgust as he pressed his lips together as though to cover his fangs, but they protruded between his lips.

Even with them, he was beautiful to her. And she knew it had nothing to do with his erox magic.

Leaning forward, she pressed her lips to his. This time, he couldn't resist her. Her chest squeezed, and an orgasm crashed through her as essence flew out of her in a powerful breeze. As he fed, she felt his fangs recede, replaced by the softness of his lips.

"Ah-ah," came Magnus' voice over the chaos. "Not so fast."

There was a flash of light and a rush of energy before she went flying. Pain exploded in her back, and she rolled across the forest floor before slamming against something hard. She blinked as the world spun.

Slowly, she realized she'd crashed into a tree. The leaves above her were aflame and branches were crashing down to the earth. She dove forward, narrowly avoiding them.

A few feet away, Elias lay on the ground, motionless.

Magnus stood across the small clearing with a smile on his face, eyes fixed on Elias. Then he directed both hands at the demon.

Her demon.

"No!" she screamed.

Reaching within her, she stretched toward the chasm deep within her chest, toward whatever the amplifier had broken free. There was a bridge now, as though this moment of desperation had formed a way across. Her mind flew down that bridge, and she found the darkness she'd never dared to acknowledge as fully hers and wrapped her fingers around it.

As a blast of crackling red energy soared through the air toward Elias, she released her shadows. It felt as natural as breathing, as though for the first time in her life all was right in the world.

She moved her hands in a motion she didn't understand and a wall formed before Elias. The sorcerer's magic crashed into it, sizzling as though the red crackling energy was flames doused in a bucket of water.

Magnus' eyes snapped toward her, his mouth uncharacteristically agape. But before he could send more magic crashing toward them, the sorcerer cried out, staggering forward and clutching a shoulder.

She blinked, not understanding, when suddenly Breckett appeared behind him, a blade in his fist. A blade that was plunged through Magnus' left shoulder. She prayed for all she was worth that it had pierced his heart.

"Looking for this?" Breckett hissed. "You can go to hell, you bastard."

This was it.

This was their distraction. If they were to get away, it was now.

Pulling the blade free, Breckett dashed across the clearing toward Elias. Somehow, Elias was on his feet, staggering toward her. She knew they had only a moment—a mere breath—to escape before the sorcerer recovered. Running forward, she reached for him, her fingers outstretched. Each heartbeat felt like an eternity, each breath like a lifetime. When they touched, hands grasping, Breckett fell onto them, and then the world was a swirl of shadows.

"No!" Magnus screamed somewhere outside of the darkness.

A darkness that wasn't hers.

She felt the two erox combining their energy as they moved across the forest's plentiful shadows, leaping from one to the next.

The smell of smoke and the growls of the ogres faded into the distance. Time passed, but for how long, she couldn't be sure. The surge of adrenaline slowly leaked from her, and she struggled to remain awake as Elias clutched her to his side.

There was a blinding light and then the feel of grass against her legs as she crashed onto the earth. Blinking, she noted the outline of Elias' castle and the faint sounds of small animals and the chirping of birds.

They were back.

Beside her, Elias clutched his shoulder. His shirt was soaked through. He'd lost too much blood. Once again, his eyes were pitch black, and she feared those fangs would soon return.

She crawled toward him, unable to rise to her feet.

"Take what you need," she said. "Take everything."

Before she could lean toward him, Breckett intercepted her, his lips crashing into hers. Essence leaked from her in streams, and he pulled it into his mouth greedily as she came. She hadn't fully realized that erox could rip orgasms from her. Knowing Elias had chosen to usher her toward the edge instead of kicking her over it made her heart twist even more for the male she'd once thought was nothing more than a demon.

Fangs nicked her lips, and she tasted blood. But Breckett never stopped pulling from her as he swallowed gulp after gulp. She grew dizzy and would have fallen to the ground if he hadn't held her face between his hands.

Suddenly, Breckett released her and crashed to the ground. Belatedly, she registered that Elias had pushed him. But then he had crashed into the ground face-first. Blood pooled in the grass.

She staggered to her knees, fear gripping her chest.

What happened if an erox didn't feed? It was clear they shifted into some kind of demon. Was that about to happen to Elias? Was he going to die?

Breckett had become overwhelmed by the demon, his need to feed, and had taken the last of her essence. She was so weak. One more pull, and she knew she'd die. But she had to save Elias. What could she do?

A thought struck her.

"Breckett," she rasped, her mouth dry. "Take this off." She pointed to the collar around her neck.

"As if I'd give you another chance to fuck us over," he hissed as he fisted the grass, struggling to get to his feet.

They were all spent.

"Please," she begged. "Let me make this right."

His nostrils flared. "You don't know the damage you've done. Magnus will never stop chasing us now." But even as he spoke, he crawled toward her. "It's your fault that he knows our location is nearby. It won't be long before his armies are upon us."

"I know," she whispered. "And I'm sorry." She pointed at Elias, who still hadn't moved. "But I *can* help him." When he didn't respond, she added, "If you don't let me help him, he'll die."

"I could help him feed on you."

"If this doesn't work, then I'll give myself to him willingly."

She meant every word.

With a final glare, Breckett reached over, his fingers wrapping around the collar before he yanked. The force had her staggering forward, coughing, and choking. Pieces of metal fell to the ground. Pain blossomed in her neck, but she paid it no mind as she moved toward where Elias lay motionless in the grass.

Reaching for the healing energy of the earth, she braided strands together, humming as she did to coax them to move through the air faster, *faster*. She didn't have the strength to force them into Elias' body, and the earth would resist him—would resist a demon. But she hummed, which turned to a melodic plea. Once the weaves were a criss-crossed pattern large enough to cover the wound in his shoulder, she lowered it onto his skin.

Electricity jolted through her limbs as the earth resisted, enraged that an enchantress, a magic wielder of the elements, would trick it.

"Please," she rasped, her strength failing her. "He's wounded..."

She didn't let go of the weaves, didn't move them from where they rested against his skin. Clinging to them, she prepared herself to hold on until the moment her strength failed her.

He couldn't die. He just couldn't.

He's kind and good and puts himself in harm's way to help others. And I... I can't live without him.

The unspoken words moved through the air like the scent of flowers on the wind, and she willed the earth to hear them. For a moment, she thought the earth wouldn't relent, but the piercing energy going up her arms stopped. The weave settled into his skin, closing the flesh until there was only unmarked skin.

Thank you, she thought before collapsing on the ground, utterly spent.

Her eyes fluttered closed, and she soon knew no more.

Chapter Twenty-Three
ARABELLA

Arabella dreamed of countless erox coming for her, and she was running as fast as her limbs would carry her but never able to outpace them. Her legs felt like they'd been submerged in mud or like she was trudging through water, taking only one step for the erox's five. They were on her heels, closing in, and she was a moth being pulled toward the flame. She saw the faces of the erox who'd come for her in the tent, who'd pulled her legs wide and prepared to fuck her.

Screaming, she bolted upright in bed, a sheen of sweat coating her skin. Pain lanced through her back and sides, and one of her eyes was nearly swollen shut. Glancing around with her good eye, she was surprised to find herself back in her room in Elias' castle. She'd been changed into a clean shirt and pants, and the smell of recently cleaned sheets wafted up to her. But even stronger than that was the smell of eggs, bacon, and toast as her door opened to reveal...

Fear gripped her chest.

A creature holding a tray of food stood in the doorway, rolling its eyes.

The creature was short, only three feet in height, with long eyebrows that extended out past the sides of its face. Wholly black eyes narrowed on her as it looked down its hooked nose at her, expression unyielding.

What—who—was this creature? She'd thought it was just Elias, Breckett, and her in the castle. Could this be one of Magnus' minions? How had it gotten through the ward? Had the ward fallen? Had it come here to kill her as retribution for attacking the sorcerer?

She struggled to her knees, trying to get out of bed.

"Yes, yes," it hissed in a gravelly voice that was entirely inhuman. In a high-pitched voice, it added, "'*Oh my goodness, there's a small scary beast in my room. Save me.*'" It rolled its eyes again. "This scary beast has also brought breakfast and medicine, you ungrateful human."

She had one leg off the bed and one knee still on the bed, hands fisted in the sheets. Gaping, she shook herself, searching for words. "You know, for a small, scary beast, you have a dark sense of humor."

The creature raised an eyebrow.

She eyed the food and the medicine on the tray and then the creature, noting that some bottles were the tinctures Elias had gotten for her.

Without her willing it, her shadows stretched out, creeping across the bed, across the plush carpet, and toward the creature in the doorway. The shadows swirled beneath it, and as they did, she realized suddenly that she'd felt this presence before.

All those times she'd felt like someone—or something—had been watching her, it had been this creature.

"You," she said. "You've been the one making food and cleaning up after us."

"Get that away from me, Shadow Whisperer. I'll have none of your dark magic in my presence." It harrumphed, striding across the room and placing the tray of food on the table. Turning to her, it said, "So, you aren't as stupid as you look. As if the castle took care of itself."

Pushing herself fully to her feet, she crossed her arms. "I'm going to choose to not be offended by that."

Again, it harrumphed, completely unbothered.

"What's your name?" she asked.

"My name isn't something you can utter on your human tongue. But you may call me Vorkle."

She nodded. "I've never seen your kind before. What are you?"

"You should be asking whether I intend to harm you, stupid human."

"I'm going to hope that the bearer of breakfast means well. Besides, you've had plenty of chances to kill me before. Instead, you've made my every meal, washed my clothes, and cleaned my room."

Vorkle sniffed. "I'm a goblin."

Her arms dropped to her sides as her mind swirled, and she had to sit down.

"You... your kind is extinct."

The goblin chuckled humorlessly. "It's true many of us have been killed for our abilities—at least those who refused to be used as pawns in the games of men, demons, fae, and all manner of other creatures. But some of us remain."

"How'd you get here?"

"That," he began, "is something you will have to ask Elias."

She opened and closed her mouth.

"Speaking of the master, you must eat. His strength wanes, and I don't know if he'll survive the day without your..." He paused, his eyes scanning her body. "Administrations."

Without my essence.

Her cheeks heated as she thought about the number of times Vorkle might have encountered them fucking. She'd sensed eyes upon them briefly in those moments, but she hadn't truly believed there were other beings here. Otherwise, she would have insisted they find somewhere more private...

"How long have I been asleep?" she dared ask.

"Two days."

She swallowed, nodding. "How is he?"

"Weak. Ravenous. Obviously." The goblin nodded to the tray of food on her table. "Eat. You must gather your strength if you're to lend it to the master."

When she tried to walk toward the table, her feet tangled, and she stumbled, grabbing onto the post of the bed. Vorkle rolled his eyes, grabbed the tray, and placed it on the bed.

"My kind cannot heal, but I've dressed your wounds with the ointments the master gathered from the human healer."

"Thank you," she said. "For everything you've done to help me."

Vorkle turned toward the door. "Thank me by helping the master regain his strength." Without a word of farewell, the goblin slammed the door shut behind him.

As she ate, she tried not to think of everything that had happened in the last few days. Everything had changed, and yet she was back to where she started.

Finishing her food, she quickly dressed into one of the small dresses before heading to Elias' room. At the door, she raised her fist to knock and hesitated. Vorkle had said he needed her essence, otherwise he may not survive the day. What she'd done with her enchantress magic must have kept him alive, but he was too weak for his body to fully heal itself. Or did he mean Elias was on the verge of turning into... whatever that had been with fangs?

Gathering her courage, she knocked on the door. No response. Again, she knocked, but there was no sound from within the room. Steeling herself, she opened the door.

Nothing had changed from the last time she'd been here—when she'd stabbed him, stolen the amplifier, and run away. And gotten them in a heap of trouble.

On the bed, a figure lay, unmoving.

Her chest squeezed, and she hurried over to him. Was she too late? When she neared him, she saw he was on his side, eyes closed, his chest moving up and down in ragged breaths.

"Elias," she whispered. "I'm here to help you."

Nothing.

He didn't stir or didn't open his eyes.

"Elias," she tried again, reaching toward him. Hand on his shoulder, she breathed a sigh of relief at the feel of his warmth.

Alive.

He'd never mentioned death was possible for erox because of a depletion of essence, but he'd been so weak... She found it unlikely that this weakened state couldn't kill him.

She shook him gently. "Wake up! You must feed."

His eyes snapped open, dark as pitch. Even the whites of his eyes were fully black. Lips peeling back in a snarl, revealing massive fangs, he reached for her. In a flash of movement, she was on the bed, her back against the blankets and Elias over her. He pinned her arms above her head, his legs on either side of her. She couldn't move, but she didn't try to.

"Take what you need," she said, her eyes flickering between his.

There was no hint of recognition in them.

He leaned forward, but instead of his lips connecting with hers, he closed in on her neck. There was a sharp pinch and then a sensation like a pull, and she gasped. She opened her mouth to scream, but a hand pressed over her mouth. His other hand held her wrists above her head.

Time passed. She couldn't tell how long, but he eventually pulled his head back, blood dripping from his lips. As dizziness crashed over her, she found her hips thrusting up into him. Desire blossomed in her as she took in his exquisite beauty. His dark, curly hair was ruffled, but his shoulders blocked out the faint light in the room. His beard was as thick as his hair, and veins bulged in his forearms. She'd never seen anyone like him with such primal, animalistic grace. As each day passed, the feeling of being drawn to him had only increased. She'd tried to fight it, but she could feel herself losing the battle. Even now, her weakened body couldn't fight the draw to his.

Lips and fangs pressed against hers, and she tasted blood as his tongue plunged into her mouth. He moved like a male who owned her, who knew every inch of her and was there to *take*. As he kissed her, his hips moved in time with hers until he was thrusting his hard cock against her. Her clit throbbed, and with the right friction, even with clothes between them, she'd come.

In a distant part of her mind, guilt swirled, and she knew that he'd never look at her the same as he had before she'd fled the castle. Any joining of their bodies would be for need only. But he'd said he'd never had sex with Scarlett when she'd been his offering. He could choose to feed off her essence for the rest of her life, never again having a joining of their bodies. The thought made her throat tighten.

But she didn't have long to think about it as he continued to move above her. Her dress hiked up her sides until she was bare before him from the waist down. His cock bulged in his pants, but he made no move to free it. Instead, he continued to ravish her mouth, his fangs nicking her as he moved. She tasted blood and felt him suck it into his mouth. Then something stirred in her chest as she felt his magic tugging on her. An orgasm crashed into her, and she moaned into his mouth as essence flowed into him in a powerful tide. He gulped, his tongue never stopping its exploration as he drank her in.

When her vision began to swim—black spots forming at the corners—her hips stopped moving and her muscles relaxed. He was going to take everything she had left. Let him. Dying so he could live was the least she could do after bringing Magnus' wrath and attention to them. She was no one—an enchantress with shadow parlor tricks. He was an erox with a rare ability to wield essence. He needed to survive if anyone had the hope of standing up to the sorcerer.

She thought of how Magnus was close—too close—to Shadowbank.

Save them, she thought. *Save my family and Shadowbank.*

Elias pulled back abruptly, and she noted distantly that the whites of his eyes had returned and his irises were no longer a deep black but his usual warm brown. Blood was smeared over his lips and chin, and she smiled.

She blinked slowly, her eyelids fluttering closed.

"You're okay," she said before the spots in her vision stretched out and consumed her.

DEATH WAS A DARK, endless abyss, stretching out in every direction. She was formless, floating within the depths. She was also tired. This surprised her, as she hadn't expected to feel anything at all once she passed from the realm of the living. But exhaustion seeped into her bodiless spirit, and she felt herself sinking deeper and deeper. Before she could succumb to it and become one with the deep, something grasped on to her. It wasn't a physical sensation, but it was as though someone's will had stretched out toward her, keeping her from floating into oblivion. Then there was a voice, distant and beckoning.

"*Arabella.*"

Yes. That was her name. But where was the voice coming from? She recognized it. It was warm and safe, and she found herself wanting to draw closer. She summoned strength from within her being, somehow floating upwards, away from the endless black and toward a lighter gray color. The gray faded to a lighter shade and then to a white as alluring as the moon.

She opened her eyes.

Hands gripped her shoulders, and she shook her head to clear the fogginess in her mind, but the motion made the room spin.

"I think I'm going to be sick."

Something hard pressed against her chest, and she heaved up her breakfast into a washbasin. A cloth pressed against her chin, wiping. Looking up, she saw Elias removing both the basin and the cloth.

"Elias."

Her voice was hoarse as though she'd been shouting for days.

"Stop trying to get yourself killed." His voice was as sharp as the edge of a blade, eyes cold.

There was no longer blood on his face, and his coloring was much improved. His curls were matted with blood and mud, and his face was streaked with dirt.

She'd never seen anything so beautiful in her life.

If what Vorkle had said was right, he must have been asleep for two days, just like her. The goblins likely didn't dare to clean him for fear he'd wake and try to feed on them—if erox could feed on goblins at all.

As she studied him, she watched the cuts on his face and shirtless chest close until there was nothing but smooth skin.

She tried to lean up in his bed, realizing she was beneath the blankets, head on his pillow. But her body failed her, and she slumped back down.

"I wouldn't let you... fade away," she said.

She still wasn't sure if he had been close to death or close to turning into the mindless creature with fangs.

"What happened? You were... different."

With a sigh, his head hung, and exhaustion was evident in the way his elbows locked, as though struggling to hold himself upright, and the slump of his broad shoulders.

"When the erox don't feed, we turn into the demon within. We lose our memories, and all we know is the desire to feed."

"You don't just consume essence. Do you?"

"I once saw an erox go too long without feeding. He turned into the demon, and there was no coming back for him. He'd lost his memories forever, roaming the earth in search of his next prey, consuming essence and blood recklessly. Feeding to kill, succumbing to gluttony." He hesitated. "It's been said that the origin of the erox is tied with the Undead—the vampires. But you're right. The erox feed on both essence and blood." With a sigh, he added, "I'm sorry for what I did to you... before."

273

"You don't have to apologize. I should be the one apologizing."

"Yes, you should." His words were hard and laced with such deep anger that she flinched.

"Why did you trick me and take the amplifier?" he demanded. "Just what did you hope to do?"

"Shadowbank's ward will fall if it hasn't already," she said. "You wouldn't listen..."

He shook his head, disbelieving. "So, you stole from me and stabbed me in the chest."

"I'm sorry. But *I* made the deal with Hadeon. The amplifier was mine by right," she snapped. "I wanted to share it with you, but there was no reasoning with you."

She still felt torn in her loyalties to both this male and her home. Somehow, the need to protect this male was as strong as her desire to protect her family.

"You've shown me that you can't be trusted. But as I've told you before, I protect what's mine. And you're mine until the ten years are through, as set out by our deal. Unlike you, I keep my promises."

So, he hadn't saved her because of his feelings for her. He'd done so out of obligation.

Something in her chest twisted, but she pushed it away. She didn't have a right to feel any sort of way after what she'd done. She must accept whatever he set forth.

I never promised anything about the amplifier, she nearly said. But it wasn't worth it. The amplifier was gone, and so was the hope of protecting either the castle or Shadowbank.

"You realize why I need the amplifier now, don't you?" Elias said. His voice was quiet, and his gaze was distant as he looked toward the open windows across the room.

Frowning, she shook her head but stopped.

The goblin that had been in her room that morning.

It was an impossibility she'd never considered. Goblins—beings who were rumored to be extinct and who'd been hunted down over the centuries for their ability to portal anywhere at any moment and without the need to have been to a location first— were alive. And hiding with Elias. Portalling was a rare and powerful magic, as they could not only carry messages over long distances, but they could also portal others with them.

"How many goblins are here?"

"Twelve."

"You rescued them and gave them sanctuary."

It wasn't a question.

This male she'd once considered a demon had remained in seclusion, in a castle in the forest that no one knew of, to protect one of the races of this land and keep them from being hunted by those who sought to use them.

"The amplifier you stole was my only hope to reinforce my failing wards. I'd also hoped to create an invisibility spell to keep people like Magnus away."

His voice faltered on the name of the sorcerer.

"You have a history with Magnus. So does Breckett. When he captured me, he'd said something had been taken," she said, slowly putting the pieces together. "Breckett stole something from him, didn't he?"

"Yes, I did."

She looked up, spotting a tall form filling the doorway. She hadn't even heard it open.

Breckett's straight black hair was clean, and he was dressed in trousers and a long-sleeved shirt. The thick boots and knives sheathed across his body implied that he was preparing for a journey—or a fight. He ran a hand over his face, his light brown skin a paler color than it had been at the ball.

"I can't believe I'm about to tell this to a disloyal mortal who nearly got us killed." He strode across the room. "Let it be known that the only reason you're alive is because he wished it." He pointed to Elias, his expression fierce. "I don't think you're worth the air you breathe."

Tell me how you really feel.

"But yes," Breckett continued. "I stole something from Magnus. Perhaps the most powerful weapon he has."

She waited, saying nothing.

"I stole his syphen."

Just what did a sorcerer need a syphen for? Only erox could make new erox. The blade would give him the ability to kill an erox, but surely his magical abilities could rip their hearts out or decapitate them.

Not to mention, with countless erox in his army, it was clear that he chose to surround himself with them rather than kill the demons.

"I don't understand..."

"I stopped him from controlling every single erox in that army," Breckett said.

Her brows drew together, and Breckett rolled his eyes as if this was the most obvious thing.

Elias said, "A magic wielder can control erox if they possess the syphen used to create them."

"It takes away their free will," Breckett added. "They become trapped in their bodies, seeing what they're doing and unable to do a damned thing about it."

"Breckett took away Magnus' ability to control the erox in his army," Elias finished.

She gaped. Then anger surged through her.

"You're saying you could have controlled the erox in that encampment with the syphen you stole, and you chose not to?" she demanded, her voice rising. If she had the strength, she would have been screaming. "We could have died! You could have wiped out half his army and had them kill each other. You could have had them attack the ogres and take down as many as they could—"

"No," Breckett said coldly, eyes filled with disgust. "I would never take someone's choice from them. It would make me no better than *him*."

It was true. But war was the time for hard decisions.

"Then why do the erox stay with him?" she asked. "They could leave at any time."

"They likely think he still has the syphen and could control them at any time," Breckett said. "He only uses the syphen when they disobey."

"What do they think you stole?" she asked.

"An amplifier or some other type of magical artifact, most likely," Breckett said. When her eyes narrowed on him, he continued, "Point that finger elsewhere. Magnus knows we're nearby after your little stunt. Now, he has the amplifier and another syphen—"

Elias shook his head. "Arabella dropped it in the forest. He may have it, but it may be lost."

Breckett's eyes widened. "We have to find it. Immediately."

"We wouldn't make it out alive," Elias said. "Magnus and his army will be on high alert and searching for us. It's too dangerous." He looked at Arabella. "We have only one hope now."

She frowned. "What?"

"Another amplifier," Elias said. "With it, there's a chance we can make the castle invisible to Magnus' eye. Maybe—just maybe—we can still shield the goblins from him."

"We should run." Breckett's voice was soft. "Get them somewhere safe. Maybe we could go back to the fae realm..."

"No. If the fae courts find out the goblins are alive, they'll be enslaved. There's no safe place for them," Elias said. "Or us. With the wards in their current shape, we have days at most before Magnus or his army find us."

To date, she hadn't been able to glean just what protections Elias' ward had. But it was time she found out.

"Can he sense us if we use our magic on the castle grounds?"

"Maybe," Elias said. "The wards make it harder for those outside to sense any magic wielders within it. But if they're close enough to the ward and those within are using strong enough magic, they'd be able to sense us. The ward, itself, is undetectable from far away. But if they draw near to it, they'd be able to see not only the ward but what's beyond it."

"That was before the ward started to weaken," Breckett said.

Her thoughts grew distant.

What could they do? They could return to the fae queen's court and beg her for the amplifier she had. But Elias had refused to turn her. He'd either have to do that which he vowed not to, or they'd have to find someone else with an amplifier they're willing to part with. She thought of the Circle's attempts to find an amplifier when the wards weakened at Shadowbank. Then she thought of her time with Lucinda in Shadowbank—and the power she had emanated.

Elias' voice was void of emotion as he said, "While I acknowledge that you made the bargain with Prince Hadeon to get the first amplifier, it's because of your actions, Arabella, that we lost the amplifier and we are all in danger. As such, it's your responsibility to find another one."

She sighed. "It's a good thing I have an idea, then."

Both males looked at her, gazes wary.

"I think I know where we can find another amplifier."

Chapter Twenty-Four

ARABELLA

After all this time, Arabella was returning to Shadowbank. But it would be as a shadow—moving unseen in and out of the village. Never glimpsing her friends and never saying goodbye.

She dressed in nondescript pants, boots, a long-sleeved shirt, and a plain cloak that a goblin must have laid out for her.

"You're not to speak to anyone you knew before. We can't be recognized." Elias had told her before bringing her back to her room. "That's an order. We get in, get what we need, and get out. Time is of the essence before Magnus finds us."

She couldn't allow herself to be recognized. And her enchantress garb would be like a beacon. Even with her nondescript clothing, she felt naked. But she did as Elias bid.

Within the hour, they had dressed, armed themselves, and gathered in the castle's entryway. Like her, Elias and Breckett wore plain garb, hoods of their long cloaks pulled up.

She frowned. "Aren't we going by horse?"

Elias nodded to Vorkle, who appeared in front of them. "With the safety of everyone in this castle on the line, I've asked the goblins to assist us."

Her eyes widened. They were going to *teleport*?

"Thank you for coming, friend," Elias said. "Arabella, describe where we must go."

"We are going to see a woman named Lucinda. She lives in the human village, Shadowbank, in the Wolford District. The entrance to her home is in an alleyway on the west side."

Vorkle stretched out his hands, and Elias and Breckett took them.

She hesitated. "How does this work?"

Elias stretched a hand to her. "You'll see."

Closing her fingers around his, the world twisted around them. In a blink, they were in the alley she'd been to not all that long ago. Only, this time, it was late morning, and the sun's rays lightened part of the narrow space. Looking around, she was struck with a sudden homesickness. She longed to return to her home with the enchantresses and missed Jessamine, Iris, Cora, Brynne, and the others with her whole being.

"Come get us within the hour," Elias said. "Don't come inside."

Vorkle nodded and disappeared.

Breckett gestured forward. "At your leisure."

The way he said her title was like poison on his tongue and held a mocking tone.

"The way we parted ways last time," she began, uncertain how to explain just what happened in the alley with Jessamine saving her ass as the witch's apprentice tried to rip out her suppressed memories. "Well, let's just say it wasn't amicable. Get ready."

Taking a breath, she strode forward, pounding a fist on the door.

"Madame Lucinda," she called. "It's..."

She hesitated. Could she say her name? Elias said they couldn't be recognized. But the witch's apprentice probably wouldn't allow her entry if she didn't.

"It's Arabella," she said at last. "My... friends and I need your help."

A minute went by and then two without a sound within the

building. The alley was windless, but the cool air seeped into her. She held her cloak tighter before pounding her fist again. "Madame Lucinda!"

Suddenly, the door creaked open of its own accord. The room was unlit, and Arabella strode inside. Elias and Breckett followed. As expected, the door slammed shut behind them, but the candles didn't flicker on. Instead, a voice whispered in the darkness.

"The bold enchantress has returned. And you've brought some very interesting guests." There was a sound like someone sniffing the air. "Erox. Two of them. You keep interesting company, child."

A flame erupted from the mantle, roaring as though personally offended by her presence.

The ageless woman stood before her, smelling of broken dreams and dark wishes.

"Lucinda," Arabella managed, pleased that her voice didn't shake. "We need your help."

"So soon after our last encounter?" She nodded to the erox. "I recall promising to remember just what occurred."

"You nearly killed me," Arabella said, narrowly avoiding gritting her teeth. "My friend was just trying to protect me." She gestured to the males beside her. "This is Elias and Breckett. We require an amplifier. I was hoping you or the witch might have one."

Lucinda's head tilted back as she bellowed a laugh, which turned into a deep, inhuman cackle. "I knew you were bold. You were the only of your order to seek me out. But this?" Again, the former witch's apprentice laughed as she strode over to the table in the corner of the room and sat. "Why would I help you?"

Licking her lips, Arabella said, "I wouldn't ask if it wasn't important."

"Oh, of course not." Lucinda's voice sounded patronizing.

Arabella clenched her fists. "Do you have an amplifier or not?"

"Careful, Enchantress," Lucinda said, eyes narrowing. "I may not be a full witch, but I know enough of the darker magics to turn you into a rat or curse you so that you can never see the sun again."

Magic wielders could train under a witch as an apprentice to see if they possessed the ability to use spirit, ghost, or blood magic —any of the darker arts. If they couldn't tap into the magic or weren't strong enough in them, they were dismissed. They could also turn people into animals and curse whoever displeased them.

Arabella hadn't been certain which magic Lucinda possessed, but it appeared she had manifested at least some of the darker magics.

Images of her facing Magnus glanced across her mind, and she recalled what it had felt like reaching into the chasm in her chest —and all the power she'd never been able to access before. For the first time, she thought she might be able to overpower Lucinda.

Reaching into the dark depths within her chest, she felt her shadows curling up her arms, twisting and flicking like agitated snakes. She allowed them to fill her, allowed the power to bloom within her chest. It was unlike anything she'd felt with her elemental powers. It was deeper, richer, and unyielding —temptation.

"I don't take kindly to threats," Arabella said, allowing her gaze to sweep over the shadows circling her arms.

When she glanced back up toward the former witch's apprentice, she was surprised to see a smile spread across her face. It was simultaneously beautiful and unsettling. It was like the eerie silence in the forest before demons descended.

"You've done it, then," Lucinda said. "You've reached your magic. Good."

Arabella's brows drew together as her thoughts swirled. "You... You knew this would happen. Is that why you reached for my memories? You were trying to tip me over the edge."

There was a dismissive wave of a hand as Lucinda said, "Some wielders must face darkness in order to be able to wield it. I thought perhaps unlocking your memories would unleash it."

Curiosity flickered in her gaze as sharp as an alley cat. "Just what have you been up to?"

Before Arabella could respond, Elias cut in, eyes a bright blue, clouds of essence swirling behind them. "Name your price."

Lucinda leaned back in her chair, flicking her wrist, and candles turned on across the room. Her eyes raked over Elias as though truly looking at him for the first time. No expression crossed her ageless face, and Arabella thought to wonder just how old she was. Perhaps she'd learned enough of the magic of the dead to delay such an *inconvenience.*

Then a smile spread across Lucinda's face. She had shockingly beautiful teeth—the color of untouched snow. But her smile was anything but warm. It was a mere showing of teeth, and Arabella had the distinct feeling that the witch's apprentice was toying with them.

"I don't possess such a powerful artifact," Lucinda said at last. "But the Witch of the Woods does."

Great, Arabella thought. She'd been hoping they wouldn't have to visit the powerful magic wielder. She was bound to be far, far worse than Lucinda—her student.

Elias bowed his head. "Thank you. What do you wish for as payment for this information?"

"Tell the witch I sent you. That's reward enough for me." The door to the alley flew open, and Lucinda's gaze darkened. "Now, get out."

WHEN VORKLE REAPPEARED in the alley, he took their hands, and they vanished in an instant. Once again, they stood in Elias' castle's entryway.

"Give me ten minutes," Elias said, heading for the stairs. "I'll find something the witch may find of value that we could trade." He looked at Arabella and nodded toward the kitchens. "Eat something. You look pale."

Breckett crossed his arms. "Where is your concern for me?"

Elias paused on the stairs, not turning back. "If Arabella consents, you may take some of her essence. You'll need your strength, too."

Arabella flinched.

Not long ago, Elias had threatened Breckett when he tried to touch her. Now, she was no longer something precious to him. The words stung.

She strode toward the kitchens, saying over her shoulder to Breckett, "Don't bother asking before I eat something, or the answer is no."

In the kitchen stood three goblins who looked up upon her entry. They said nothing to her and merely nodded before turning back to their work. Like Vorkle, they were short—only three feet in height. But they moved around in a way that implied good health and didn't seem unhappy. As they passed her a plate of cheeses, grapes, and freshly made biscuits, they whispered quiet words to each other in a language she didn't recognize.

Thanking them, she ate before returning to the entryway.

Breckett and Vorkle stood silently.

She sighed. Still weak and depleted from escaping from the sorcerer and being fed on by Elias, Breckett, and the erox in the camp, she didn't want to offer herself to Breckett. Not to mention, the idea of her body craving his left a sour taste in her mouth. But he needed to regain his strength as much as she did. She suspected they'd all need their strength for when they met the Witch of the Woods.

"You may feed on me, but only a little," she said, and Breckett turned to her. "I swear, if you make me weak enough that Elias has to carry me again, I will feed your boots to the fish."

To her surprise, one corner of Breckett's lips rose. "I'm terrified."

Breckett must have leaped between shadows because he was before her in a heartbeat, his hands wrapping around her neck as he pulled her into him. His body was warm, and he smelled of lavender and cinnamon.

Pressing his lips to hers, he coaxed an orgasm from her without touching her. She grunted as pleasure washed over her. He pulled essence from her chest, and she felt it flurry upward and into his mouth. As the essence flowed out of her, her knees wobbled, but she remained upright. As soon as it did, Breckett yanked himself backward.

"You reek," he hissed. Scrunching his nose, he wiped his mouth.

"Do I?" She ran her tongue over her lower lip and tasted the garlic from the clove she'd just eaten. "How strange."

"Disgusting mortals," Breckett muttered under his breath along with not a few obscenities.

It wasn't that she didn't like Breckett. He seemed like a decent male—wanting to free the erox under Magnus' control, or at least keep them from being controlled. But he was still a bastard and fed on her twice without her consent. A bastard who wanted her dead. She might regret her actions toward Elias, but she wasn't about to be a doormat. Her family needed protecting just as much as his.

Elias reappeared with a small bag tied to the belt at his waist. He nodded to Vorkle. "Take us to the Witch of the Woods."

"Fuck me," Breckett groaned and grabbed one of Vorkle's hands.

"No, thank you," she said as she took Elias' hand.

Breckett scoffed. "In your dreams."

With a sigh, Elias grabbed Vorkle's other hand, and they vanished into the space between.

Trees surrounded them, and she blinked, glancing around. The forest was dense wherever they were—far denser than the forest surrounding Elias' home. But through the trees, she spotted a gurgling stream weaving lazily before flowing down into a little valley. A cottage nestled by the stream. From the outset, it looked cozy with the vines growing up the walls of the cottage and the flowers and garden surrounding the entire house. The sun shone through breaks in the trees, reflecting off the water in the stream.

But a heaviness hung in the air, and the hairs on the back of her neck rose. It seemed like the sort of place that was welcoming to little children who'd strayed too far into the forest only to have a witch coax them inside and make their nightmares a reality.

A shiver ran up her spine, and she wondered if the others felt the same.

Elias released her hand, and she felt a pang in her chest as though she'd lost something.

"I will come for you at the setting of the sun," Vorkle said before disappearing.

Fear locked her knees, but she forced herself to take one step and then another. She couldn't let either of the erox know how she felt. Breckett would never let her hear the end of it. But the thought of meeting a powerful witch had her insides twisting and her legs turning to jelly.

"Today seems as good as any to die."

"This is not the day we die," Elias said, and she realized then she'd spoken aloud.

"If it's your life or mine, Enchantress, lots of hard feelings if I choose my safety over yours," Breckett said, sparing a glance toward her, eyebrow raised. "It's personal."

"I now understand the reason you left the fae ball so quickly," she said. "Even with your powers as an erox, all the females found you appalling. No one would let you feed off them."

Breckett's eyes narrowed, and his mouth drew into a thin line. She suppressed a smile and strode down the small hill toward the cottage.

Once before the door, she raised a hand to knock but hesitated as her body's shadows retreated to the base of her feet as though curling into itself. How strange. When she reached for her weaves, she sensed the magic of the earth and sky, but they, too, were different. Unlike the shadows, it didn't retreat, but it somehow held a darker hue that emanated from the deep, as though the ground beneath her felt like it had been corrupted.

Elias placed a hand on her shoulder, and she took a step back as he knocked.

Breckett raised an accusing eyebrow toward her.

"I didn't see you taking the lead," she snapped.

"Shh," Elias hissed. "If I'd have known I'd be overseeing two children today, I would have left you both at home."

Elias knocked three times on the door.

A tall woman in a long black gown opened the door with a smile. No power emanated from her—not a single drop. Could this be a human prisoner the witch kept? The welcome was starkly different from the magic the apprentice had used to usher them inside. Arabella had assumed after Lucinda's less-than-warm mannerisms that the witch would be similar.

The woman smiled at them, and it made warmth spread in Arabella's chest. She couldn't be over thirty-five years old. Her skin was free of freckles or blemishes, and she placed long, elegant fingers on the doorframe. Brown hair flowed to her shoulders in loose waves that felt as natural as the gurgling stream beyond the cottage.

"Can I help you?" the woman asked.

"We're here to see the Witch of the Woods," Elias said.

Never in her life had she thought she'd meet a witch in person. They weren't as rare as erox, but they were a reclusive people and hoarded their magic away.

The woman opened the door wider. "You've come to the right place. I am she. Please come in."

That was easy, Arabella thought. *Too easy.*

She wondered why she couldn't feel any magic from her if she was the witch. Could she be lying? All magic wielders could sense each other. So, why couldn't she sense the witch?

Turning, the witch strode into the house, leaving the door wide open. Unable to stop herself, she glanced at Breckett, who returned the look of hesitancy.

You first, they both seemed to say.

Elias walked inside without hesitation, and Arabella followed with Breckett at her heels.

The cottage was as cozy on the inside as it seemed on the outside. There were several lounging chairs and a round carpet before a hearth that boasted strong orange flames, above which was a bubbling cauldron. A kitchen of sorts was at the opposite end of the room with dried plants and herbs hanging from hooks on the wall and lines across the ceiling. There were also twice as many glass jars filled with what appeared to be parts of animals—eyes, fingers, bones...

"What brings you here?" the witch asked, striding to the cauldron and stirring it.

Desperation, she thought.

"We need a certain artifact," Arabella said, finding her voice. "Lucinda sent us."

"Is that so?" the witch said, pausing before stirring once more.

Arabella thought to wonder just what was in the cauldron. It smelled of sharp spices she couldn't identify.

"How is my former apprentice?"

"She lives amongst humans now," Arabella said carefully, uncertain if Lucinda would want the witch to know where she lived.

Placing the large spoon down, the witch grabbed a towel, wrapped it around the handle, and heaved the cauldron over to what must be its base a few feet away from the fireplace. Steam swirled into the air, and the smell of strange spices grew stronger.

The witch wiped her hands on the towel. "What is the artifact you seek?"

Arabella opened her mouth but hesitated. Did Elias want to take the lead? He'd said because she'd lost the amplifier, she was responsible for finding another one. But perhaps he wanted to be the one to bargain with the witch.

As she studied the woman across the room, she guessed the

witch was likely as old as Elias, if not much older. There was an air of ancient memory, as though she stood in a tomb, feeling the weight of ancestors around her. This woman had either found a way to freeze her body in time at a specific age, as Elias and Breckett, or she must have changed how she appeared to others.

At last, Arabella said, "An amplifier."

Elias' eyes flicked down to her before returning to the witch.

"Such a thing will come at a steep price," the witch said. She gazed at Arabella with a look of sympathy. "I'm afraid it's one you likely cannot afford."

"I have something that might be of interest." Elias reached for the pouch on his belt. "A scroll of one of the Ten. There are many spells in here, including some in the ancient tongue that I cannot translate. I imagine such an item would be of more use in your hands than mine."

The Ten were the original sorcerers—at least the first known to civilization—who lived a thousand years ago. They'd been the founders of many of the great cities and created many of the technologies used there.

The witch's gaze snapped up to him then, her pupils growing until her irises were completely engulfed. Unlike the erox whose eyes turned black when they needed to feed, pulling forth the sexual desire of their prey, this felt like a swell of darkness. It was as though the corruption from the earth beneath them seeped up the witch's body and leaked through her eyes.

"The Ten Sorcerers thought too highly of their abilities and prioritized the needs of males, thinking they were the stronger gender. They killed countless of my kind. I want nothing their hands have touched."

Arabella's eyes drew wide. It sounded as though the witch had known—or known of—the Ten. It sounded personal. Did that mean she had lived at least a millennium?

Elias opened and closed his mouth, clearly uncertain how to respond.

"What is it you want?" Arabella asked.

If they were to get the amplifier, they had to speak plainly. They needed to know the cost. It was either make a deal now or flee the castle and hope Magnus never caught up with them. If they didn't get the amplifier, they could be on the run for the rest of her days. And what would that mean for the goblins? They'd be hunted down once more as word of their existence spread.

From one day of teleporting with Vorkle, Arabella could already see how useful their abilities were. It could have taken days or weeks to get from the castle to Shadowbank to the witch's cottage, depending on where the cottage was located. She had no notion if this was even the same forest.

The witch placed her towel down on a nearby table, cocking her head to the side as she studied Arabella with inky eyes. Arabella's shadows receded further until they were entirely beneath her boots.

She tried to will her shadows to stay put, but no matter what she did, straining her mind toward them, they didn't listen. She could only hope the witch didn't glance down and notice that, unlike the erox beside her, she possessed no shadow... even with the streams of sunlight coming through the windows behind them.

Slowly, the witch took a step forward and then another. As she did, a shimmering haze the color of dreamless sleep hovered over her skin. For a moment, Arabella could sense the witch's magic, and it felt as though she stood in the center of a tornado, powerful winds surging around her.

"What are you?" the witch asked, sniffing the air just like Lucinda had. "I'd thought you were an enchantress at first. But there's something else, too."

The witch's eyes skirted down to the floor where Arabella's shadow was nowhere to be seen.

Come on, she thought. *You're going to fuck us both over.*

She tried to will it forth again. To make it act like a proper shadow. But it remained where it was beneath her feet.

The witch stepped toward her, claws appearing from the ends

of her fingertips. Arabella's heart pounded, and she started to take a step back. Before she could, Elias put himself between them.

"She's spoken for," he said. "She's bargained the next decade of her life to me."

A hiss came from the witch. The sound was entirely inhuman —deep and guttural as the space between realms. It wasn't like anything of this world.

Despite herself, Arabella reached for Elias, her fingers wrapping around his forearm. Even as she reached for him, his hand moved to the hilt of the sword at his hip. The gesture was clear— don't take another step forward.

Again, the witch sniffed the air, entirely unphased by Elias.

"Yours is a scent I haven't encountered in hundreds of years. But..." The witch inhaled deeply. "Do you even know what you are?"

Arabella's brows drew together. "An enchantress."

"I see."

The response was so noncommittal that for a moment Arabella felt tempted to defend herself, to insist that she was one of the Circle, but she bit her tongue. Such an argument did nothing to help her with retrieving an amplifier from this ancient magic wielder.

The witch's gaze skated between Elias and Arabella, her eyes lingering on where Arabella held his arm.

"An erox and an... enchantress. How very interesting," the witch said with an emphasis on "enchantress." "In all my years, I've never seen such a pairing."

"I'm just his... offering," Arabella said.

There was nothing between them now.

"That is not what I smell."

The witch strode to Elias, placing a hand on his chest, running it along to his shoulder and down his arm to where his hand rested atop the sword hilt. "It's rare that an erox falls in love. Most are too lost in their lust to think about the wellbeing of another." Her gaze lingered on Arabella before she strode to

Breckett, running a single clawed fingertip from the opening above his shirt, up his neck, to his chin. "Usually, erox in love cannot contain their lust, especially if mated. The lust becomes too much, and he kills off his lover. Then he must live the rest of the ages alone, knowing that he'd succumbed to his baser needs, and it cost him everything." The witch smiled. "But this isn't the first time you've fallen for an offering, is it?"

"Name your price," Elias spat.

The witch continued as though Elias had never spoken, fixing her eyes on Arabella. "It's also rare that true feelings are returned for an erox."

Elias turned, his brows drawn together as he looked down at Arabella. Disbelief and hope mingled in his eyes as he wordlessly pleaded for her to say something—anything. She took a breath, not understanding.

"I..."

Words failed her.

There had been a connection between her and Elias, certainly. She'd craved him, wanted all of him. But she'd dashed their connection to hell when she'd stolen the amplifier. But if that was the case, why was he looking at her like this?

"Don't try to deny it," the witch said with a chuckle. "I can scent mates."

Arabella finally found her voice. But when she spoke, there was an unmistakable tremble in it. "Only the fae can form that kind of bond."

Mated bonds were one of the most rare forces in this world. It happened by chance as far as she knew, and the bond could snap in place at any time—when couples met or after they'd known each other for a time. But it meant one thing: the two were matched in every way, complementing each other perfectly.

The witch smiled. "It's rare, true. But it's possible between any who possess magic." Turning, she strode over to her kitchen where there were countless shelves and cabinets filled to the brim with tinctures, bottles, and vials. "My price is simple: if you want the amplifier, I require *you*."

A weight settled on Arabella's shoulders as though she'd caught a boulder. Her hands shook, and she desperately tried to steady her breathing.

The witch pointed to Arabella and said, "As you've already bargained your time away, I require your memories."

"No!" Elias snapped, his fingers curling around Arabella's wrist as though preparing to flee with her at a moment's notice.

Breckett glanced between them, disbelief creasing his brows.

This was all too much.

Arabella's thoughts swirled. Just what did the witch mean? Was any of it possible?

Did it matter what she or Elias felt after how she'd betrayed him? Even if what the witch said was true and they were mates, there wasn't trust between them. And how could love exist without trust?

Eventually, one thought rose above the rest.

The goblins were in danger because of her. She had to right the wrongs from her actions.

"What kind of amplifier?" Arabella asked.

"I'll give you my shade amplifier," the witch said. "Its special ability is invisibility. And the winds told me you're in need of such a thing."

While any amplifier could strengthen a ward, it was nearly impossible to add an invisibility spell to a ward without a powerful magic wielder such as a sorcerer or without an artifact that had this ability. But with such an amplifier, not only could a ward be strengthened, but everything within would be invisible to those beyond it. Only the most powerful of magic wielders would be able to detect it.

"Stop this, Arabella," Elias said, his voice pleading.

It was still strange to hear her name on his tongue. The word was like velvet to her ears, and she savored it.

Elias' hands cupped her face, the touch achingly gentle. "We will find another way."

She looked past Elias to the witch. "How many of my memories? Weeks? Years?"

The witch's smile was wicked. "All of them."

Elias' hands pulled her gaze back to him. "No. Don't do this."

Raising a hand, she closed her fingers over his. "I'm sorry for what my actions cost you. I need to make this right." Closing her eyes, she breathed in his scent of citrus and pine, trying to memorize the feel of his hands on her skin.

"Deal."

Behind Elias, the witch's laughter filled the room.

Elias shouted something, but Arabella didn't register the words. Sounds grew distant as the room filled with a gray mist, curling around their bodies, filling the air. She looked up at Elias, running a finger down his cheek, a single tear trickling down his light brown skin as he shook his head.

Suddenly, the witch was between them, extending something toward her. Brows furrowing, she accepted it, realizing it was a pomegranate. The witch gestured to the fruit with an incline of her head, and Arabella nodded before taking a bite. As she did, a dark strand broke off the mist and struck her forehead.

Her life flashed before her eyes—from the moment she appeared from the forest and Iris found her to all the moments she'd spent with Jessamine, Scarlett, Cora, Brynne, and the other enchantresses in their youth, training and studying. She saw the wards that had led her to the forest where she'd seen Elias for the first time. Then her memories of Elias and their time together swirled before her, and it felt as though the witch plucked the moments from her mind one at a time, flipping through them as though they were pages in a book.

Arabella saw her first night in the castle, Elias nearly fucking her on the stairs, when he rescued her from the Alabaster, and his taking care of her and giving her food and chocolate. Their entangling in the waters, him fucking her against the rock, and their dancing at the fae court—each appeared before her. With longing, she watched their time behind the curtains at the fae court where he'd made her fantasy come true before her mind shifted to the moment he said he loved her, and she'd stolen the amplifier, stabbed him, and fled.

The final moment that lingered in her mind was when Elias wielded essence, protecting her with both his magic and his body from Magnus. She recalled the relief she'd felt when he'd taken her from that tent and all the guilt she'd felt since.

At that moment, she realized that, while she didn't understand the dynamic of mates, she understood one thing.

She was in love with Elias.

He was far more than just a demon to her. Slowly and without her realizing it, he had become her hope at the cresting dawn—hope for a future that was full of happiness. She didn't just enjoy his body, but she'd come to cherish her time spent with him. He was good and kind. He'd protected her at the risk of his life many times, and he held to his beliefs. Somehow, he'd become everything to her. And now, she'd give up everything to protect him and those he cared about.

Pain tore through her as the memories began to fade.

Her eyes locked with Elias'. She had to tell him before it was too late.

"Elias," she said past the pain clouding her thoughts. "I lo—"

Words failed her as pain split her head, bleeding into her senses. Something dark, like sludge, crept up her neck, filling her ears and penetrating her skull. She screamed as the substance spread through her mind, darkening every thought, every mental picture. Distantly, she was aware of arms catching her. But fissures formed within her, splitting her, fracturing her, rending her in two. She gasped, unable to draw a deep breath as the air thickened. Smoke filled her mouth, and it felt as though something tightened before the pressure in her head dissipated, and a sensation of something dripping out her ears followed.

Before the pressure left her head, there was a final swirl of images—ones of a small child held in the arms of a fae woman as she leaped through a gateway. The female stumbled onto the ground in her haste, clutching the child to her chest, protecting its head. A human male came through the gateway a moment behind her. He grabbed her by the elbow, hauling her to her feet. His lips moved, but she couldn't hear his words or the female's response. The fae woman turned and held a hand up, blasting shadow into the gateway. Not looking back, the two ran, the small child clutching the woman's chest.

The pain in her forehead receded along with the swirl of images. Then the pressure in her skull disappeared, and the room cleared.

Her mind was... empty.

A light hovered before her, illuminating the smoky room with a warm blue hue. With swift movements, a woman caught it in a bottle. Then her fully black eyes widened as they stared off into the distance. A laugh bellowed out from her, rumbling through the entire cabin like a thunderstorm had swept through.

"How very interesting," she hissed. "That's where you came from."

The woman pocketed the vial.

A male's face appeared above Arabella, his brown eyes flickering between hers. His features were creased with worry, though she couldn't understand why. For some reason, she wanted to stroke his cheek.

Glancing around, she realized she was on the ground and he held her in his arms. She lingered, enjoying the warmth of his touch.

Blinking, she said, "Who are you?"

Chapter Twenty-Five

ELIAS

f it wasn't for Breckett, Elias may have never made it back to the castle.

One minute, he was at the witch's cottage, clutching Arabella to him, and the next he was on the palace grounds—an amplifier in his hand and his mate at his side.

With no memory of him.

"Move, brother," Breckett said not unkindly.

Breckett ushered Elias toward the main entryway, and Elias realized then he'd been frozen in place, his eyes fixed on the grass beneath his boots.

Vorkle had brought them to the edge of the grounds, and perhaps this was a kindness from the goblin—allowing him a few moments to collect his thoughts before he had to speak to Arabella.

She hadn't spoken since her one damning question at the cottage.

Who are you?

"Elias," he'd said to her. "It's... nice to meet you."

After that, everything was a blur.

Now, he could feel the presence of his mate by his side as they strode quietly across the grassy lawn and through the main door into the entryway. He averted his gaze from the stairs, swallowing hard before turning to the woman he'd come to love.

He opened his mouth, but no words emerged. Beside him, Breckett's brows drew together, but he said nothing. The silence stretched on for so long that it felt like a tangible presence hovered between them—like a great weight had been dropped in a still pool.

After a moment, Elias said, "Welcome home."

There were several moments of silence.

Arabella's brown eyes held no hint of recognition. "Home?"

He nodded. "Your room is on the third floor."

"I don't remember this place." She glanced around the entryway, taking in the statues of dragons and demons, the large red carpet at the center of the floor, and the massive staircase that expanded to a single landing and then split into two separate staircases which led to different wings of the castle.

"The Witch of the Woods..." Elias began, but his throat grew tight and he had to choke out the final words. "She took your memories."

Arabella's brows drew together.

He had to get a hold of himself. This wasn't the time to succumb to sorrow or defeat. There was much work yet to be done. For one, there was a sorcerer just outside of his borders.

"You made a bargain to save others who are in danger," Elias said carefully.

For the first time, he thought to wonder what the witch would do with those memories—with the knowledge of the goblins and where Arabella's magic originated from. His only consolation was that Arabella still didn't know where the castle was located. Thus, neither would the witch. But there was nothing he could do about her origin. One day, perhaps years from now, they would learn, together, about Arabella's magic and how to harness it. He could give her that, at least.

"Good," was all she said.

His fingers itched to touch her, to cup her face and pull her against his body.

It amazed him to think that only hours ago, he'd been wrestling with his feelings for the enchantress and how they were at odds with just what to do with the amplifier—and who to protect. And how she'd betrayed him to protect her people. He'd wondered if he could learn to trust her again. For better or worse, he understood what she did. She'd wanted to protect her people. While she'd broken her word, she'd not done it out of hate or to spite him, which was something he'd once been certain was the case.

If the witch was to be believed, she hadn't hated him at all.

He shut that thought down. None of it mattered anymore. Her memories were gone and so were any feelings she might have had for him. Perhaps even the mating bond had been fractured irreparably with the loss of her memories.

Arabella bit her lower lip in the way he'd learned meant she was considering something. It made him want to lean in and run his teeth over it and pull it into his mouth...

"What do you remember?" he asked.

She shrugged, eyes skirting around the room. "Nothing."

Pausing, he waited for her to elaborate. When she didn't, he nodded. "If there's anything you wish to know, just ask. I will help where I can."

Which wasn't much outside of their time together. He knew nothing of her life before—where she came from, her friendships, family...

"Elias," Breckett said gently. "We must address the wards. Immediately."

He was right. If they didn't reinforce the wards, Magnus would find them. It wasn't a matter of if but *when*. Without a doubt, he was searching for them even now. It was why he'd asked Vorkle to teleport them during their search for another amplifier. There simply wasn't time for them to go on foot, especially not with the added risk of the sorcerer's sentries.

With a nod, Elias said to Vorkle, "Please take Arabella to her room and see that she has what she needs. Breckett and I will return soon."

Vorkle nodded before striding up the stairs. For a moment, Arabella hesitated, glancing back at him as though to say something. But she turned and followed the goblin without another word.

Goblins could teleport at any time, but they usually chose to walk around the palace to avoid the possibility of passersby sensing magic wielders within the woods. They didn't want to attract any more attention than necessary. Unlike the witch, they couldn't suppress the ability of others to sense their magic. Using magic increased the likelihood of others discovering them, as the presence of magic would grow stronger, billowing out wider. But all of that would be over soon.

Thanks to Arabella's sacrifice.

Elias and Breckett strode to a side staircase that led to one of the highest turrets of the castle.

No one had protected him from Magnus. He had been tortured and used in every way a male could be, and it was only by sheer luck that he'd escaped and remained hidden these recent decades. When he'd stumbled upon Vorkle in a human village, he'd seen the desperation in the goblin's eyes that he had once felt. Helping Vorkle and his kin hadn't been a question for him. He vowed to protect them—like he'd wished someone had protected him.

The abandoned castle in the forest had been the ideal location since it was far removed from civilization and the demons kept most away from the castle. Only Shadowbank and its occupants dared to linger close to the forest. The arrangement with the village had been a convenience. It was a way for him to sustain his life without having to venture into towns for feedings and risk revealing himself or his location to Magnus or one of his people.

For decades, Elias had kept a safe distance between himself and his offerings. Most had been like Scarlett—a companion of sorts that he never touched or lain with. Some, he'd fucked, but it was never outside of his need to feed. Distance was the best way to keep others safe from the demon he was beneath his skin—the monster he always feared he'd become. He hated what he was as much as the mortals did, though he hadn't dared voice that he'd never wanted any of this until Arabella. Even with her assumptions, she dared to challenge everything he'd ever believed about himself. The other offerings had been too scared.

One thing was certain—none of his offerings had he been drawn to like her.

His body had yearned for her since the moment she'd sought him out in the woods after he'd returned Scarlett. Desire ran through his mind so thick that he nearly revealed himself—his face—to her in that moment. He needed to have her, and he could scent that she returned the desire for him. But it was more than her body. She dared to challenge him, never backing down, and she was fiercely loyal. It was something he admired about her.

But now, all of that was gone. Everything that had built between them was no more.

"Dare I ask how you are?" Breckett asked as they walked up the winding staircase.

Elias kept his eyes ahead. "Best not."

"Don't be an emotionally constipated prick."

The words had Elias stopping, turning back to his friend.

"Now isn't the time for this."

Breckett made a sound that was somewhere between a scoff and a laugh. "Trust me, this isn't a conversation I'm keen to have. I don't like her after what she did to you. But being mates isn't something to just brush aside. This shit is serious. It's rare."

It's important, his eyes seemed to say.

Turning on a heel, Elias continued his ascension.

"Do you love her?" Breckett pressed, the sound of his footsteps close behind.

"Did you not hear as much from the witch?"

"I want to hear it from you."

A large wooden door with crisscrossing metal bars appeared before them at the top of the stairs, imbued with old magic that resisted dragon fire. It was from the days when there had been dragons and their flyers in this land. Like many other magical species, they had become a rarity. Elias had only heard of them through the older erox. He'd never seen them in his lifetime.

Heaving the door open, he strode to the edge of the turret, overlooking the small clearing in the massive forest that was the grounds. It wasn't much as far as space for the goblins to roam without fear, but it was all he could give them.

He tried to glance past his small haven to the forest beyond and see what lay beneath the trees, but the canopies were far too thick. It was impossible to spot ogres over or between the treetops, let alone the far smaller erox and other creatures under Magnus' control.

Fear clutched his chest, twisting until his breaths became shallow.

I can't go back. Never again.

The amplifier warmed in his palm. Unlike the amplifier Hadeon had given to them, there was no sticky magical residue, nothing beckoning him to filter his magic through it. It was a quiet warmth, waiting patiently. If it had sentience.

Guilt seeped into his bones as he looked up to the faintly shimmering dome that stretched above the castle to the edge of the grounds.

Arabella had sacrificed her memories for this, and protecting his home meant the humans would be left to their own devices.

Magnus' army was close to Shadowbank, only a few days' march. But the sorcerer likely turned his full attention on Elias and Breckett between Breckett's having the syphen that controlled the erox under his thumb—several hundred by his estimation—and by the simple fact of Elias' existence.

"He will come for me," Elias said, his voice a whisper.

Breckett nodded. "Yes. He's been obsessed with you for centuries."

Not denying it, Breckett knew as much as Elias did what the last several hundred years had been like. The sorcerer had wanted to control him, to have his ability to wield essence at his fingertips. It wasn't until Elias had found this castle one hundred fifty years ago that he'd found temporary respite from years on the run.

"He'll come for us both," Breckett continued, patting his jacket where the syphen was stashed.

"Thank you," Elias said, turning to him. "For coming with me to rescue Arabella. You put your life in jeopardy, and it's something I won't forget."

"Good. I intend to call in a favor one of these days." Breckett nodded to the dome above them. "Let's start with protecting our asses."

Hesitating, Elias' lips drew into a thin line.

Could he do it?

Some amplifiers only had so much power within them, and he would only know how much power this one possessed once he started using it. It could only be enough to power a single ward, or he may only have the power to reinforce a single ward but not create one. But there was one potential impact from using an amplifier that scared him the most.

Using an amplifier at its full capacity put some magic wielders into a dreamless sleep for centuries. It was the cost of using so much magic. It took so much out of a magic wielder that their body needed time to recover.

Would protecting the goblins and his home mean he'd never see Arabella again? Her life was far shorter than his. She could have aged and passed on by the time he awoke from the dreamless sleep. He and Breckett. But perhaps two magic wielders would mean that the toll it would take would be distributed amongst them both.

There was no simple decision.

Guilt filled him.

He'd been wrong to dismiss Arabella's request to help Shadowbank. She had been the one to make the deals with Hadeon and then with the Witch of the Woods. But he'd been unable to listen—to hear past his fear of Magnus and his need to protect the goblins. That inability to hear her had cost him everything.

Although he still needed to protect the goblins, he couldn't deny what Arabella would want. She'd have asked him to protect Shadowbank. By giving up her memories, she had put her faith in him to do so. Could he fix the ward of his home and completely ignore her wishes? What if someday she had her memories returned to her? She would hate him for not helping Shadowbank.

He'd seen the humans' wards and knew she was right—the ward would fall, and it would fall soon.

It was either protect the goblins or the humans. Protecting either could mean he'd never see his mate again. But not doing so would mean that Magnus would eventually find them here, and he'd never see Arabella again—not if he was under the sorcerer's control once more. Or it would mean life on the run. That was only if Magnus didn't find them as they moved from city to city, hiding amongst other magic wielders, never staying in one place for long.

Fear so overwhelming turned his stomach, and he nearly retched.

I won't go back.

Even with the fear gripping him, he somehow remained standing, overlooking the castle grounds and forest. The amplifier in his hand.

"You do love her," Breckett said. "Else, you wouldn't be hesitating."

Elias took a breath and then nodded. Recalling all the moments he'd shared with her, he said, "It happened so quickly. I've never experienced anything like it."

Had the energy drawing him to her from the very beginning been the strings of fate tying them together until their mating bond had snapped into place? Conflicting emotions warred in his chest. He simultaneously wanted to demand answers for why she'd stabbed him and bury his face between her legs. Fury filled him at the memory of the syphen in her hands as she straddled him in his bed. She'd dared to trick him when he was vulnerable and steal the amplifier. Somehow, she'd also figured out what the blade he'd given to her was.

But even though she could have killed him, she hadn't.

That knowledge warmed something inside of him and allowed him to hope for what could grow between them once more. Trust had been lost, but perhaps it could also be rebuilt.

Breckett nodded. "Do you want to say goodbye in case...?"

In case they fell into the dreamless sleep.

Shaking his head, he said, "No. I can't see her again. Not yet."

Not with the look in her eyes as though she stared at a stranger.

"What are you going to do?" Breckett nodded to the amplifier in his fist. "Use it? Run? I'll support you whatever you choose."

The blind trust of his friend had him turning from the forest. Sympathy showed in his eyes, and Elias reached out, clapping a hand on his shoulder.

"Thank you." Then Elias' thoughts faded, returning to the task at hand, and he dropped his arm. "How close were they?"

How close were Magnus' henchmen to catching you?

"Too much so," Breckett said. "I could have lasted another year or two, but... they were closing in."

It explained his presence in the Twilight Court. Breckett hated the fae more than most, but it was one of the few places that Magnus would hesitate to travel to.

If they ran now, they may only have a few years on the run before they were found.

"I can't risk Magnus getting his hands on the goblins or..."

"Or her," Breckett finished for him. "She's different. Her magic... It's unlike anything I've seen before."

Elias nodded, recalling the wall of shadow that had saved him when Magnus' beam of magic closed in and he'd been too exhausted to defend himself. The sorcerer likely wouldn't have killed him, but he would have brought him to the precipice—and then waited for Elias to be so broken, so desperate, that he begged the sorcerer to bring him back.

Arabella had saved him from a fate worse than death.

He'd seen shadow whisperers before but never anything like what she had done. There were none who could wield shadows like he could command essence, and none so powerful as Arabella. Could she be a rare type of witch?

There was no telling what Magnus would do with such a power under his control.

Elias looked back to the forest and then to the ward, coming to a decision and extending a hand to Breckett. "Do you trust me?"

Breckett raised a brow. "How far are we talking?"

But he clasped Elias' hand, opening his magic to him without objection. The erox's tongue was as sharp as Arabella's, and perhaps it had been one reason Elias had been taken by her initially. Unlike the other offerings from Shadowbank, she'd shown no fear. She reminded him of home until, one day, she became his home.

And then his home was ripped from him in a single instant.

Closing his eyes, Elias opened himself to the amplifier, reaching into the well of his magic, the bright essence that intermingled with a lurking corruption that threatened to take him under if he wasn't careful. It was the curse of the erox. To exist with their human memories was to be on a blade's edge with the constant threat of losing himself to the demon that only knew the desire to feed. Carefully, he avoided the inky corruption in his well, pulling the essence he'd taken from Arabella. It tasted of her, like lilacs and peppermint and a cool autumn breeze.

Pulling the essence forth, he guided it into a single stream. As he did, he pulled essence from Breckett, adding it to his. Some of it tasted of Arabella, but others tasted of other mortals and fae he'd fed off of, faint accents of wood smoke, sulfur, and sands of time. He held his hand out, fingers gripping the amplifier, and then released the torrent through it.

All at once, it was like his senses sharpened, and he could see everything in exquisite detail. The stones of the castle sharpened, every angle, every crack came into clear focus. He could see the veins of the leaves of the trees along with every individual blade of grass. It was like he'd been seeing the world in black and white until this very moment.

As he blasted his magic up toward the ward, exhaustion struck. He was already weak from the battle with Magnus, and there simply hadn't been time for him to recover. He also hadn't had the heart to feed on Arabella as much and in the way he truly needed. Fucking those he fed on increased their essence, multiplying it without the need to draw from their strength as much. But he hadn't been able to touch her after... after everything. Now, he wished he had.

But there was no changing the past, and he'd have to make do.

There were different paths within the amplifier. Different ways he could guide the torrents of his magic. He knew at once what to do.

Shifting, he released the torrent through a path as straight and sharp as ice above unmoving winter waters. The dome shimmered all around them in a warm blue hue. The color of his beloved's essence. He held on to the power as long as he could, his arm growing heavier with each passing moment. Beside him, Breckett fell to a knee. As a weight settled on his shoulders, he did as well.

But he needed more. He was nearly there. If he could just get a few more drops of power, it would be complete.

His head swam, and his eyelids grew heavy. At that moment, he knew he was on the cusp of falling into the dreamless sleep. He sunk the torrents of magic deep into the earth, saturating the ground hundreds of feet down until there was a sound like snapping and the new wards locked into place.

Gasping, Elias and Breckett collapsed onto the ground.

Elias clutched the amplifier in a sweaty palm, releasing his and

Breckett's magic, which filtered back out of it before releasing and separating.

"We did it," he gasped.

It's done.

"Risky bastard." Breckett gasped on the ground beside him. "Creating a cloak of invisibility."

Elias chuckled. "It might just work."

Power thrummed from his palm. From where he held on to the amplifier.

He'd reinforced the existing ward with invisibility. It made it so those on the outside not only couldn't see the castle, but they'd be turned away and prevented from entering the grounds without realizing it. It also cloaked the ability of any magic wielders from within. If, somehow, a magic wielder discovered where they were, they could break through the ward. He hadn't emptied the amplifier to strengthen the ward.

He'd saved what remained for Shadowbank

If Arabella somehow, some way, got her memories back, he wanted to be able to tell her that he'd done what he could to protect her people as well. The possibility of her memories returning was slim to none. Spells and curses by the Witch of the Woods were almost always too powerful to break. But he had to hold on to the hope that none of this was permanent. After all, she'd taken Arabella's memories and stored them away—she hadn't destroyed them. Which meant there was still hope to get them back.

Suddenly, an idea struck him.

He struggled to his feet, legs unsteady beneath him. Gripping the edge of the turret, he pushed off and staggered for the stairs.

"Where the fuck are you going?" Breckett said, barely managing to raise himself on an elbow.

"Shadowbank," Elias said as his heart held on to a single thread of hope. "I'm going to get her back."

Then he disappeared down the stairs.

Chapter Twenty-Six
ARABELLA

S mall chirping animals sang a sorrowful tune into the late autumn air, welcoming the morning and warning of the oncoming winter.

Arabella sat in the gardens outside the castle, wrapped in a blanket, staring at the flowers before her. They were a bright yellow and one of the few remaining this far into fall. The air smelled of falling leaves, though so many of the trees in the forest remained unchanged throughout the seasons. It was as though, in this oasis that was Elias' home, the seasons could make a show of dominance beside a forest that refused to submit to something so trivial as nature.

Someone appeared at her side. Vorkle, she thought. She wasn't sure what type of being he was, but he seemed kind enough, offering her a steaming cup of tea.

"Thank you," she said, taking it. "Where is everyone?"

The castle was empty except for Elias, Breckett, and Vorkle, and she hadn't seen either Elias or Breckett since the day before.

"We live in seclusion," Vorkle said, voice emotionless, long brows twitching. "And in secret."

Shadows rumbled beneath her feet, but she must have been seeing something. Such a thing wasn't possible.

She nodded. "Could I ask you something? Do you know why I'm here in this place?"

Even though Vorkle was only three feet in height, he looked down his hooked nose at her as he said, "You made a deal with the master."

"A fucking reckless deal," came a feminine voice from behind her.

Turning, Arabella's brows creased as her eyes settled on a woman garbed in black leather. She pushed her hood back, revealing long, thick blonde locks and a series of interwoven chains in her hair. A gemstone hung down from the chains at the center of her forehead.

Arabella stood, and as the woman approached, she noted that she came to her shoulder. But the woman didn't stop before her. Instead, she marched right up to her and wrapped her arms around Arabella. The hug had her taking a step back to catch herself.

"What in the actual fuck were you thinking?" the woman demanded into Arabella's blanket.

"Um," Arabella began. "Do I know you?"

The woman stepped back quickly, glancing up at her. "Right! I forgot. I'm Jessamine. We're... We were best friends when you lived in Shadowbank."

"Quit trying to piss on things," another woman's voice said, this one somewhat deeper in resonance. "Trying to lay claim to others is cliché."

Two other women dressed in similar black leather and silver headdresses appeared from around the shrubbery and strode toward them.

The taller woman who'd spoken was as muscled as Elias and Breckett and had a smile as bright as the sun. Beside her, a woman of medium build and darker blonde hair clasped her hands before her, a shy smile on her lips.

"It's good to see you, Arabella. We've been worried," said the shorter woman. "My name is Cora." She pointed to the woman whose muscles bulged as she crossed her arms. "This is Brynne. We're your friends."

Something tickled at the back of Arabella's mind upon seeing them, but as soon as she reached for it, the feeling slipped through her fingers like sand.

"How do I know you?" Arabella asked.

"We're enchantresses," Cora said. "We trained together since childhood."

Arabella's brows drew together. "Enchantresses...?"

Brynne sighed, pinching the bridge of her nose. "We've got a lot of ground to cover."

With a smack to Brynne's arm, Jessamine said, "It's an order of female magic wielders. We protect mortals from demons and creatures of the dark."

There was a pause as she glanced over her shoulder to where there was a flash of movement, but it was gone so quickly that she thought she might have imagined it. Vorkle was nowhere to be seen, and no one else was nearby.

"How did you get here?" Arabella asked. "I thought this place was a secret."

"It is," Jessamine said. "Elias brought us here."

"I don't know how the fuck to get back," Brynne said.

"Neither do I," Cora said.

Jessamine stretched a hand out, clasping Arabella's. The gesture was warm, and it had something stirring within her chest.

"Come on," Jessamine said. "Let's get you warmed up. Then we'll tell you everything."

HOURS LATER, Arabella was curled on a sofa in front of a fire, Jessamine sitting close beside her. Cora lounged on a sofa opposite them, legs stretched out, and Brynne sat on the floor, arm casually resting atop the sofa and fingers moving in circles on Cora's ankle.

They'd shared their history as enchantresses, their magic, Shadowbank, and so much about a world she couldn't remember. Arabella should be frustrated that details kept evading her; but with nothing to remember, she could only accept the gap in knowledge.

It was what it was.

"Then you were a reckless fuck and offered yourself without telling any of us," Jessamine said, firelight glimmering off tears in the corners of her eyes as she fixed her gaze on her entwined fingers. She looked up to Arabella then. "I knew you'd done it to protect us."

Arabella licked her lips. "If this place is a secret, and I bargained away ten years, why are you here? It doesn't seem like this is a place that frequents guests."

"Elias appeared to Iris, explained that the Witch of the Woods had taken your memories, and asked for her help," Cora said. "He also gave something to her—an amplifier. I don't know if she would have believed his sincerity without it. It's an unfathomable gesture." She tilted her head at Arabella. "I suspect we have you to thank for that."

Jessamine nodded. "Then Iris got us, and we offered to come as soon as we heard."

"We're here to help you remember, you self-righteous prick," Brynne added.

Cora smacked Brynne's shoulder. "That's not how you make friends, Brynne."

"What?" Brynne said. "It worked last time."

Warmth spread in Arabella's chest as she tried to grapple with this information. Her brain felt full after the hours they'd spent talking. None of it sparked recognition within her. All the same, she felt grateful for these women who'd risked their lives to come here. For all they knew, Elias could have never intended to bring them here and were luring them into the forest to feed on them. But they hadn't. Elias had asked them to come here for her. But why?

Reaching for more tea, Arabella refilled her cup with hot water and tea leaves.

"Brynne is a bitch," Jessamine said, leaning over and resting a head on Arabella's shoulder. "But she's our bitch."

The familiarity of the gesture had her starting.

"She's always like that." Brynne nodded with her chin to Jessamine. "Got a mouth a sailor would be embarrassed by but curls up against you like a house cat."

Jessamine's eyes narrowed. "You're one to talk. I heard from Cora that you—"

"Don't bring me into this." Cora's voice was like the tinkling of chimes in the spring wind. "The two of you are the reason for every one of the Head Enchantress' gray hairs."

Jessamine and Brynne spoke at once. The arguing didn't hold a note of animosity. Instead, there was a trace of familiarity, as if she'd seen this before but couldn't recall. She rested her tea down on her lap, her head leaning against the back of the sofa as her eyelids drooped.

Before she knew it, Arabella fell asleep to the pleasant sound of enchantresses uttering every variety of fucks and fuckeries—which, of all things, she felt like she could remember.

Chapter Twenty-Seven

ELIAS

The night whispered to him.

As it always did, it beckoned for Elias to give in to his darker instincts, to succumb to the thing he feared and hated—to truly become the demon. Instead, he pushed back the whispers, the tugging pull on his every sense, and strode ahead with arms full.

It was late into the night when he opened the door to the sitting room. No sounds came from inside, and he wasn't surprised when his eyes fell upon Arabella and her friends fast asleep. Cora had fallen asleep atop one sofa, her hand draping over the side where Brynne lay asleep atop a pile of pillows and cushions. Across from them, Arabella and Jessamine lay nestled together like long-lost sisters, as though time and memories could never separate them. One by one, he laid blankets over each of them. He grabbed the cup of tea from Arabella's lap and placed it on the coffee table between the sofas before draping a blanket over her last of all.

She was as beautiful in her sleep as she was during the day, the lines between her brows softening and her chest rising and falling in a steady rhythm. Lingering for a moment, his eyes traced down

KISSED BY A DEMON

the curve of her jaw to her wavy locks of dark hair, which fell over Jessamine's blonde curls.

Not long ago, he'd run his fingers through her long hair, pulling her into him for a kiss. He'd done much more than that to her. But he couldn't think of that now. He wasn't even sure if there was a future for them or if they were still mates.

For the first time in his one hundred fifty years at this castle, he'd brought in strangers—people who weren't goblins, close friends, or offerings—to this place. He'd done it for Arabella. He'd brought in Jessamine, Cora, and Brynne in hopes of somehow counteracting the Witch of the Woods' spell, to trigger some memory and have the others fall into place. As he'd glanced at their brief interaction in the gardens, the vacancy in Arabella's eyes lingered, but her shoulders seemed to lower, and her body held less tension. As though some part of her knew she was safe with these women. Perhaps that meant the Witch of the Woods' grip on Arabella's memories was weaker than he thought. Perhaps, with enough pressure, the spell would break, and her memories would soar free and come back to her.

As far as he was concerned, there was hope until the moment her memories were destroyed. He had to believe that.

For now, he had to put his focus on having something strike a chord for Arabella. And the enchantresses were just the ones to do it.

It had been a miracle that he'd found the Head Enchantress, and it'd been an even greater miracle that she'd agreed to help him even with the amplifier he'd given her. She'd said it would be up to the enchantresses whether they went with him. She would have to remain to protect Shadowbank and repair the ward. But she'd believed him.

Now, all he could do was wait. And he'd keep his distance, allowing the women to spend time amongst themselves. They didn't need him interfering, anyway.

After lingering for a final moment, he leaned down and pressed a kiss to Arabella's forehead, the touch no more than the caress of the wind, and then he was gone—moving between shadows.

Without realizing where he was going, he found his way to the top of a turret, studying the faint shimmering of the ward in the starry night sky. It moved faintly, as though a thin film of rippling water was between him and what lay beyond. The moon was full in the sky, casting light and shadows on everything it touched.

The shadows rippled, and then Breckett appeared. Dark smudges were beneath his eyes, and his features seemed haggard as though he'd just recovered from a month-long flu that had wracked him.

"You look like shit," Breckett said.

Elias snickered. "So do you."

He leaned against the side of the turret, looking down on the land.

Breckett moved to his side, resting his arms on the railing. "Think we stand a chance?"

"I don't know," Elias said honestly. "We've done what we can. All we can do now is wait."

"Or run," Breckett added.

"Or run," Elias agreed.

"I spoke with Cora and Brynne," Breckett said. "They agreed that we could feed on them to gather our strength. Assuming you're not comfortable consuming Arabella's essence."

Elias hesitated before making a brief nod.

Equal parts of him wanted to touch Arabella as wanted to remain on the opposite side of the ocean from her. Perhaps then this aching emptiness in his chest wouldn't seem so vast.

"Are you going to talk to her?" Breckett asked.

"She doesn't need my presence right now."

"Doesn't she?" There was a surprising sharpness in Breckett's voice.

Despite himself, Elias flinched.

"That little wench stole my friend's heart, and you've been

moping around the castle looking more lost than I've ever seen you."

Anger unfurled in Elias' chest, but he pressed it back.

"Is that concern I detect?" he said, turning from the landscape to face Breckett. "Or boredom?"

"She made a bad call," Breckett continued, ignoring him. "She fucked you over, and I'm struggling to forgive that. But I know you, and you can. You must. She's your mate." There was a pause. "There may not be much time left to us. What we did with the amplifier was nothing short of a miracle, and it's possible Magnus and his army won't find us. It's also possible they will be at our doorstep soon. If that happens, there's a good chance that you'll have to say goodbye to her and everything you've known."

If Elias took a stand and fought.

Such an idea was pointless. He'd lose to Magnus as he had every time. The only way out was to escape and hope he didn't find him.

But Breckett knew him, and he knew Elias would fight if it meant giving the others a chance to escape.

"It's not that I can't forgive what she's done," he began. "She had the syphen, Breckett. She could have killed me, but she didn't —she injured me to escape instead. I'm furious with her, and I'm torn between the desire to shake her and demand answers or throw her onto my bed and strap her down."

As an erox, Breckett was familiar with the many ways people could give each other pleasure. He also knew that Elias enjoyed withholding pleasure when he was mad. And he was furious. But it didn't take away from his desire to have Arabella, to possess her and consume every inch of her body and essence. He wanted her more than he wanted her essence, and never in his life had he felt this way.

A smile lifted the corner of Breckett's lips.

"It's that she made this decision that affects us both—gave up her memories—without talking to me," Elias continued. "She thought I'd choose to lose her over not having an amplifier."

He ran a hand through his hair, feeling his curls snag but didn't care. The pain was a welcome distraction.

"I tried to tell her how I felt before she stole the amplifier. But I was too late, and now I feel her absence like a physical pain..."

Words were failing him. How could he possibly describe just what this was like?

"When I saw her tied up in Magnus' tent with those erox, something primal came over me, and I thought I would ignite," Elias said. "I didn't hesitate to rip out their hearts. I lost control. I never..."

"You never lose control," Breckett finished for him. He paused, nodding, before adding, "I think this is what it means to be mates—to be emotionally and physically tied to each other."

"Every fiber of my being wants to throw her over my shoulder and run—run so far that Magnus can never find us," Elias said. "But I can't leave you or the goblins. I also can't bring myself to see her. To see that vacancy in her eyes and know I was too late in telling her my feelings and too late in the witch's cottage. This is all my fault."

"Cut that shit out right now," Breckett said, his hand clamping down on Elias' shoulder. "Arabella made her own decisions, and so did you. You made the decisions you could with the information you had. Hell, you were far more lenient with her than I could have been."

Slowly, Elias allowed their gazes to meet, seeing the conviction in his friend's eyes.

"And you risked bringing her friends here," Breckett said. "I've never seen you bring a single stranger here that wasn't one of your offerings."

Elias sighed, saying in a tone so low that it was barely a whisper, "I don't even know if we are still mates."

A thought had lingered in the back of his mind. Could the mating bond have dissipated since she lost her memories? Perhaps she was no longer mated to him.

"Then it's time you figure out whether the mating bond is

still there," Breckett said. "If it is, then you have a decision to make. Do you want to fight for this? If you do, I don't think it's only the enchantresses who can help Arabella get her memories back."

Breckett's gaze penetrated through him down to his core. "You're one of the bravest people I know. Find your courage."

Smiling, Elias reached out and pulled Breckett into an embrace.

"Thank you," Elias said. "I needed that."

"Needed someone to talk sense into you."

Elias nodded, knowing what he must do.

As they studied the shimmering dome between them and the night sky in companionable silence, he thought about how he could help Arabella get her memories back. Because Breckett was right—he needed to learn just what was between them.

ELIAS ALLOWED the enchantresses to enjoy their time together for several days before he crossed paths with them. As much as he wanted to spend time with Arabella, he also knew that their time together was good for her.

Stepping between the shadows, he appeared outside of the door to the banquet hall where they'd eaten a late lunch. Cora started at the sight of him, but Jessamine held her ground, eyes flickering between him and Arabella. Meanwhile, Brynne bore a look of indifference.

He only had eyes for Arabella. Her long brown hair was down rather than the braid he'd become accustomed to, and she didn't wear her headdress. His fingers itched to reach out and touch her wavy locks, but he resisted. As his gaze locked with hers, he was surprised to find heat in her eyes. The way she looked at him was as though he was the only one in the world. It made him think of how she'd looked at him before they'd gone to the witch—as though beholding liquid fire. And he wondered, if he couldn't get her memories back, would it be possible for their hearts to find each other once more?

A cleared throat reminded him that they were not, in fact, alone.

"I hoped I could steal Arabella away for a few hours," he said, eyes never leaving hers.

Arabella stared up at him, unspeaking.

"Of course," Cora said, eyes full of understanding. "We were just heading upstairs to rest." She took a step forward, squeezing Arabella's hand. "We'll catch you later, okay?"

Arabella nodded, shaking herself, before Cora strode down the hall with Brynne at her heels. Only Jessamine lingered, narrowed eyes fixed on him.

"You took her from me once," Jessamine said, pointing a finger at him. "If you try anything again, I will make besties with the Witch of Woods and come for you. Do you understand?"

Elias kept his face neutral as he turned from Arabella to study her shorter companion.

While Jessamine had more power than the average enchantress, his power far exceeded hers. Thus, an alliance with the witch would be the only way she could hope to overpower him. As his whole body tensed as if for a fight at the mention of the witch, he tried to remind himself that Jessamine was Arabella's friend and said this because she wanted what was best for her. Which was exactly what he wanted.

They were on the same side.

Taking a breath, he said, "I promise you I have no ill will toward Arabella."

"We'll see." Jessamine turned, stretching on tiptoes to press a kiss on Arabella's cheek. "I'm around if you need me. Come get me any time."

As Jessamine disappeared down the hallway, Elias spotted a flash of movement in the shadows before Breckett appeared, winking, and then was gone. He was likely as ravenous as Elias was, and the enchantresses had offered their essence—with no sexual dalliances.

But Elias couldn't take them up on it. Something inside of him couldn't stomach the idea of having anyone—tasting anyone —besides Arabella. As the darkness within him roared, demanding he feed, he did all he could to fight it back. Somehow, he had to control his hunger. He didn't want to feed on her, not yet. Not when he was still a stranger to her.

Extending a hand toward Arabella, he said, "I'd like to take you somewhere. A place I think you'll like."

She raised a brow. For a moment, as she beheld him with a challenge in her eyes, he saw flickers of the woman she once was. How she never backed down even in the small things.

Did memories make a person who they were? Could someone be themself without them? He wasn't sure. All he could do was hope that somehow he and the enchantresses could help her remember.

Without a word, she took his hand, and he immediately wanted to wipe the sweat from his palms. Was he getting nervous? Surely, after three hundred years of existence, he was past these kinds of nerves. Yet as he guided her down hallways and up stairwells, his heart beat quickly, and he found himself at a loss for words. He wasn't sure where to even start and held on to her hand, enjoying the feel of her calloused palm and fingers against his.

Too soon, they stood before two massive mahogany doors that bore crossing metal bars with curving embellishments. There were no windows, nothing that hinted at what lay inside.

"Dare I ask where you've taken me?" she said.

"Enchantresses value truth and knowledge as part of their order," he began, a small smile curving his lips. "I was also told that a certain enchantress once enjoyed becoming lost in other worlds."

Reaching for the doors, he wove some of the essence that

remained within him together, unlocking the magical wards protecting this place before swinging the doors wide.

Revealing a massive library.

A dozen bookshelves stretched three stories tall on either side. Stained-glass windows the height of the room filled the entire back wall, depicting the story of a beast of the forest who'd fallen in love with a fair maiden, offering her a single red rose. This place didn't boast the collection or quantity that libraries of other castles often had, but there were many rare volumes and forbidden texts he'd collected over the decades.

Arabella's eyes widened as hundreds of candles flickered on down rows of bookshelves with a snap of his fingers, releasing more of his essence. She was worth every drop of his waning strength if only to make her smile.

Darkness roiled within his gut. Swallowing it back, he took a step into the library.

"Welcome, little enchantress."

Smiling, her eyes rounded as she looked around.

"I hope I remember how to read."

As it turned out, she did. Hours later, they had explored every row of books and had settled in the back of the row filled with stories of dragons and the fae. They were mostly fables and tales of stories that had faded to legend. The history books were several aisles over. But she held a large tome of fairy tales from countless cultures that had large, detailed illustrations of dragons and riders in her lap, her head bowed. She'd been like that for the past thirty minutes, and he was content to sit back against a shelf, crossing his legs.

Closing his eyes, he breathed in her scent that reminded him of a cool autumn breeze—of old chapters and new beginnings. He'd never grow tired of it.

Suddenly, something in his chest tightened, and he gasped, eyes snapping open. Nothing had changed around him. The library was quiet, and he didn't feel the presence of a goblin nearby nor did he feel any other living creature. They were completely alone. But it was as though his hunger was a rabid beast, unfurling in his chest.

Sweat beaded on his brow, and he swallowed thickly.

Arabella glanced up to him then, eyebrows drawing together. "We were more than captor and captive, weren't we?"

Her words hung in the air between them.

The need of his inner demon interlaced with his primal desire to touch every curve, every inch of her body and to lose himself inside of her. He swallowed back the lust threatening to consume him.

"I feel..." She trailed off, a hand moving to her chest, grasping the long-sleeved shirt she wore.

She hadn't donned her enchantress garb, but it was clear she still preferred her tight trousers and shirts that didn't restrict movements.

"It's like my heart knows you. Something scratches at the back of my mind, but when I reach for it..." She placed her book on the ground beside her, leaning forward, studying his face. "There's nothing there."

His heart raced, and he kept his arms locked down at his sides, afraid if he moved, if he reached for her, his self-restraint would snap and his lips would claim hers.

Did that mean the mating bond was still there? He couldn't feel that strange sensation like a cord stretched between their hearts as he did in the witch's cottage.

"For what it's worth, I never saw you as my captive," he said, his voice breathy. "You never acted as one either."

Her lips quirked, and she tilted her head to the side. "Oh?"

"Yes. I demand obedience in many things. And you never caved without a fight. But with the right motivation... Well, let's say you saw reason to do as I say."

"I see."

Those two words were laced with such suggestion that his breath quickened, his heartbeat with it. Fuck, she didn't know what she did to him.

"And what did you demand of me?"

Just like that, his cock hardened, and he moved to cover himself. Clearing his throat, he said, "Let's discuss such things another time."

He couldn't lose it. He wouldn't touch her—not yet. But damn him, she leaned forward until she was on her hands and knees. The swell of her breasts was visible as her shirt hung down, and she crawled toward him.

"Why does my body crave yours, Elias?"

At the sound of his name on her lips, hearing that she wanted him, too, he nearly forgot all his inhibitions.

"I'm an erox," he said, not removing his hands where they covered his bulging cock. "My power amplifies sexual desire. If the other person is attracted to me, that attraction is amplified."

Slowly, she crawled toward him, pushing small stacks of books aside, and they tumbled softly to the floor. Leaning back, he held his breath as he felt the tingle of his pupils shifting, the demon ready to take over.

Before she could reach him, he leaped through the shadows, moving until he was a dozen feet away from her, pressing against the stacks of shelves along the back wall.

"Don't." Despite himself, his voice was breathless, pleading. "If you touch me, I won't be able to control myself."

She leaned back on her heels, confusion in her eyes. "You don't want me?"

"There's nothing I want more in the world than to touch every inch of you, little enchantress," he said, and the way her eyes lit up made hope swell in his chest. "But I won't. Not until you remember me."

Sadness crept into her gaze. "What if I never remember?"

Her voice was so small, the sound filled with defeat.

"You will," he said. "I won't stop until you do."

She looked up at him then.

"Why are your eyes dark?" she asked. "They weren't like that before."

"My eyes turn black when I need to feed or desire another person."

Or both, he didn't dare add.

After all, needing to feed and being attracted to his prey was the most dangerous combination. It was far too easy to lose control and become lost in the lust and feeding.

"Essence is a piece of you, part of your sexuality," he said. "I feed on your desire, and your essence will come back with rest and sustenance. But if I take too much, it can harm you. And when I hunger, it's far too easy to take more than is safe."

She nodded. "So, you need to feed?"

How is that what she came away with from all that?

"I'm fine."

Elias didn't dare lower his hands from where they were crossed over his crotch, or else she'd see his lie for what it was.

Slowly, she rose to her feet and took a step toward him and then another.

"You can feed off of me," she said, feet padding forward. She'd taken off her shoes long ago as they sat cross-legged on the floor combing through books. "That's why I was brought to the castle, isn't it? To be your source of energy when you need to feed."

"No." He shook his head. "I mean, yes, that's why you came here initially. But no, I'm fine."

Damn him, but he sounded like a bumbling idiot. He had to get it together.

When she stood before him, he watched the rise and fall of her chest, mesmerized at the mere existence of her and that her body still craved his.

"Do we need to have sex for you to take my essence?"

"No."

"Then take it."

He swallowed.

"If I feed on you, I don't know if I can stop."

She reached a hand toward where his arms had dropped to his

sides, interlacing her fingers through his. Slowly, she brought his hands up, placing them on either side of her neck.

"Take what you need," she said. "You may feel like we can't be with each other until my memories are back, but I know what I feel. And I want you to peel me out of these clothes and fuck me against these bookshelves."

Something carnal ripped through him, and a growl escaped his lips.

Pushing off the shelves, he grabbed her, spinning her around until her back pressed against the books lining the wall. He held her neck in a hand, the other pressed on a shelf behind her, pinning her in place.

She smiled. "Just like that."

He could have laughed. He may play at being in control, but this female had him wrapped around her fingers.

Leaning in, his lips hovered before hers, a breath apart.

Could he do this? He'd set out not to touch her until her memories had returned, and he was already near to going back on that. But she'd said she wanted him and that she was willing. Breathing in deeply, he scented her desire, heady and strong, and his eyes rolled back in his head.

"You were just like this when we first met," he growled. "Brazen and needy. You've always been a wanton little thing, haven't you? It's in your nature even now."

"I may not have my memories, but I don't think it's changed anything about my nature—or who I am and what I want."

As she spoke, one candle above them snuffed out, cloaking her in shadow. The surrounding shadows seemed twice as dark as they should, shifting as though swaying in a breeze.

When this was over and she had her memories once more, he intended to find out everything he could about this ability and what she could do. Ever since the moment she'd used her magic against Magnus, her scent had changed. There was still a lingering mortal smell, yes, but there was also something else. Even her abilities felt far stronger now.

Arching her back, she pressed herself into his aching cock. The friction of their clothed bodies felt sinful. He narrowly suppressed a groan.

"Why are you fighting this?" she said as she reached up, running her hands along his sides. "Let go."

He shook his head.

He was supposed to be learning whether the mating bond was still there. However, as time went on, he feared it had disappeared along with her memories.

"Just my essence, then," she said, chin tilted up to him. "You need to feed. Take it."

Just a taste.

She wasn't wrong. If he didn't feed, things would get dangerous quickly. Deprivation would increase his hunger and make it far harder to control when he did feed.

He came to a decision.

"You should know," he began, "that when erox haven't fed in a long time, we slowly succumb to the inner demon. Our fangs emerge, and we may also feed on blood. Essence is laced through blood, after all."

"I'm not scared," she said.

"There's one more thing," he said. "In order for me to access your essence, you must come."

"Take what you need from me." She blinked up at him through her dark lashes. "I want all you can give me."

Lacing his fingers through the hair at the base of her skull, he gripped it in a fist and pulled her to him. "Don't forget, little enchantress, I'm the one who gives commands."

Then his lips were on hers.

It was like the first sunrise in spring when the seasons shifted.

Her lips were warm against his, opening to him. Her tongue flicked against his, and it was like his final restraint snapped. The books on the shelves rattled as he pressed into her, their bodies flush against each other. His cock pressed into her abdomen, and she moaned into his mouth. Her desire was like a heady aroma, thick in the air, and he kissed her greedily. His tongue roamed her mouth, claiming her.

As her desire spiked, her essence swelled in her chest, multiplying. But he couldn't access it, not yet.

Over time, he'd learned that it wasn't just about fucking his prey. It was about coaxing their desire out of them. Have them wanting him so badly that they were overcome with desire. Their essence would multiply and taste even sweeter, its energy lasting longer than a quick feeding ever could.

"Please," she said between kisses.

Hunger surged within him, and his eyes burned as his whole body trembled. He normally had far better control over his need to feed, but it was like all the years of practicing restraint were utterly useless around this female. The desire was a hundredfold stronger than anything he'd ever felt as her essence crept up her being, waiting to be plucked. Another wave of hunger surged over him, sending a shiver down his spine, and he felt the prick of sharp canines.

Hands roamed beneath his shirt, touching him, fingernails scraping along his back. Her head tilted back, her neck bared for him.

He had his prey right where he wanted her.

Then he sunk his teeth into her neck, drawing out gulp after gulp of warm, delicious blood. Essence flowed within her blood, and it satisfied something dark within him even as his desire spiked hotter.

Soon, he was thrusting his hips against her, his cock desperate for a release.

But first, he needed to *feed*. Truly feed.

Blood might allow him to survive and consume essence without his prey climaxing, but it didn't slake his deepest need. It would never replace essence pulled from sexual desire.

Leaning in, he allowed her the pressure she needed to grind against him, and he felt her coming undone from that single touch. Then he was releasing her neck and sucking her essence into his mouth. It was pouring out, flooding his mouth, as eager for him as her body was. And *fuck,* it was the most delicious thing he had ever tasted. He'd tasted this prey before, but she'd never tasted like this.

His cock grew impossibly hard as he fed. He needed to be inside her.

Some distant part of his mind thought to wonder why this creature tasted so good to him. If he'd tasted her before, what had changed?

Awareness jolted through him, and the demon receded to the corners of his mind.

This wasn't his prey.

He wasn't on the hunt.

Pressed between him and the bookshelves was Arabella, his little enchantress.

All at once, he sobered.

His need to feed had been assuaged, and he could once more grasp on to reason, albeit not as tightly as he'd wish with his desire for her body as strong as ever. But he knew if he didn't stop, he would feed until there was nothing left of her.

Just as before.

Releasing her, he jerked backward, feeling as though he could take a deep breath for the first time in an age. Like when he used the amplifier, it was as though he saw the room in full color whereas before the world had been in gray scale. This female had changed absolutely everything, and there was no going back for him now.

She touched her neck, looking down at the faint traces of blood on her fingertips. Thank goodness he hadn't ravaged her throat. Her presence made his grip on his control tenuous at best, his hunger multiplying tenfold. Guilt swirled within him, but there was no disgust in her eyes as she looked up at him. Instead, there was a hint of challenge.

"Is that all you've got?"

A genuine smile had him grinning from ear to ear as he laughed so hard it echoed between the shelves.

"No, little enchantress," he said when he finally contained his laughter. "I have far more I can show you." He took a deep breath, centering himself. "But I meant what I said before. I won't go any further until you can remember me, and we both decide that this is what we want."

Slowly, reluctantly, she nodded.

Even while feeding on her, there hadn't been a single tug of the mating bond. It had disappeared with her memories. Even so, he couldn't deny the attraction he felt for her—or what his heart knew he wanted. After everything, he still loved her.

It was because he loved her he allowed himself to wonder about the final option available to them to regain her memories. But did he dare risk it? It could mean losing everything.

It was possible their hearts could find each other once more, but somehow, he knew that the mating bond wouldn't return without her memories.

"You'll have to excuse me," she said, walking past him to the stacks of books and re-shelving the ones in piles along the floor. "I have a date in my room with my fingers. Else, I won't sleep a wink tonight."

The air whooshed out of him, and he nearly choked.

Her bluntness had been one of the many things that had drawn him to her. But hearing her say she intended to touch herself until she unraveled around her fingertips did something deep within him. He wanted to watch. More than that, he wanted to be the one touching her. But he clung to the tatters of his self-restraint.

He'd need to take the edge off, too. And he needed a long, cold bath.

With a flick of his wrist, the rest of the books floated back to their places on the shelves.

"I'll see you to your rooms."

He offered her an arm, and she took it, a sad smile on her lips as she allowed him to lead her down the halls.

As they walked in the growing night, the shadows around her feet curled around his shadow as though nestling into him. As it did, he felt warmth swirl in his chest. He shouldn't be able to feel anything, but he sensed *something*.

When they arrived at her door, he said, "I'll leave you to it, then."

Turning, he strode down the hall, not daring to look back. If he did, he might succumb to the look of desire lingering in her eyes.

As he walked away, he heard her say, "Good night, Elias."

Chapter Twenty-Eight

ARABELLA

"Do I want to know?" Jessamine asked, lounging in one of the many sitting rooms, the morning sun brightening her blonde hair.

Arabella sipped on her tea, studying a book on aquatic fairy tales that Elias had left at her door with a note.

For your reading pleasure. Since I can't give you other pleasures just yet.

"I don't know what you're talking about," she said, ignoring the knowing look of her friend.

Somehow, Elias knew how to make her smile.

He'd shown her kindness by allowing her into his library after learning from her friends that reading was something she enjoyed. The idea of him learning about her and then doing something just for her did something to her heart that she couldn't quite understand.

What had they been to each other before she'd lost her memories? She'd asked him, but he hadn't answered—not truly. Not

KISSED BY A DEMON

when something was tugging at her heart that she couldn't understand.

She should have asked him more questions than she had. But she had been overcome by a need for his body. It was unlike anything she'd ever felt. Or, at least, from what she could remember.

Jessamine sighed dramatically, placing her tea down on the table between where their chairs nestled beneath a large window overlooking the lake.

"Did you fuck?" her friend asked.

"No."

Jessamine's eyes narrowed as she studied her. "I'm not sure I believe you."

Arabella laughed. "Think what you want, but nothing happened."

"But you wish it had."

Placing her tea down as well, Arabella said, "He said he wouldn't do anything until I got my memories back. He only fed on me."

Jessamine's brows inched up so high, she thought they'd connect with her hairline. "That's it?"

With a mischievous grin, Arabella added, "I humped his leg like an animal in heat, and we kissed. But yes, that's it."

"Huh," Jessamine said, leaning back in her chair. "The experience of letting Breckett feed off me was clinical. I felt no attraction to him, but Cora did. She said she would have fucked him senseless if he'd been interested. Brynne wasn't pleased, of course. Though I suspect she would have agreed to have him as a third if Cora insisted."

So, what Elias said had been true. Attraction impacted how a human reacted to an erox feeding on their essence.

"Are Cora and Brynne together?" Arabella asked.

Jessamine snorted. "I don't think they even know. Brynne would commit in a heartbeat. But I suspect Cora thinks they're just friends who hook up."

Arabella made a sound of acceptance, and Jessamine continued. "What do you think of him? Elias, I mean."

Lips feeling suddenly dry, Arabella licked them and cleared her throat. Did she dare tell the truth? Jessamine said they'd been friends before, and something in her heart said it was true. But the idea of divulging her heart to a stranger scared her. Not to mention, she wasn't entirely sure what she felt.

"I can't help but to be drawn to him," she began. "Last night, it felt like I was being drawn near to him, and only closeness could satisfy whatever this need was."

Before Jessamine could reply, a knock sounded at the door, and she went to open it. There was no one at the door. When she turned around, she was holding something long in decorative paper and placed it in Arabella's lap. There was a note attached to it.

"It's for you," Jessamine said.

Arabella recognized the handwriting at once. It was the same script she'd seen on the note left at her door that morning.

Elias.

Even before she pulled back the decorative paper, she knew at once what this was. Opening it, she ran a hand over the soft handle of the bow and the taut string. There was also a set of arrows in a leather quiver.

"I'll be damned," Jessamine said, and Arabella realized she'd returned to her seat beside the window. "I'd been skeptical the other day when he asked after some of your hobbies in Shadowbank, but I never told him about archery."

There was a tightness in her throat, and Arabella tried to swallow it back. Then she reached for the note, breaking the seal.

You once asked to practice archery. Don't go beyond the wards this time. Else, I may have to punish you for bad behavior.

Immediately, heat stirred in her core, and she crossed her legs. Folding the note, she tucked it into her pants pocket.

He said he wouldn't touch her until her memories returned. Yet, this note held so much wicked promise that she thought to wonder if he'd changed his mind.

Standing, she said, "Come on. Let's put this bow to use."

Jessamine smiled. "That's the Arabella I know."

Hours later, they were sweaty and spent. After collecting the arrows, they sat, leaning against a massive oak tree. The breeze lifted the hair from Arabella's shoulders, and she closed her eyes, taking a deep breath and enjoying the companionable silence.

"I've missed you," Jessamine said after a time.

Arabella turned to her, nodding, not sure what to say.

Part of her thought it was hard to miss something she couldn't remember she'd lost. Another part filled with despair and loneliness, longing to remember these people and the history they shared. But did she dare to hope? While everyone was clearly doing their best, it felt clear to her that little could be done to change anything. So, she tucked the feelings away.

"You don't have to say anything. I know you don't remember, and that's okay," Jessamine continued. "But you're one of the best people I know. You're hardworking and loyal beyond reason. And you helped keep me sane in Shadowbank. It wasn't the same when you left."

"I don't know why I left in the way I did," Arabella began. "But I'm sorry I hurt you."

"For a selfless reason," Jessamine said with a sigh. "I would've stopped your sorry ass, and I bet you knew it."

Arabella smiled. "I was pretty fabulous, wasn't I?"

A belting laugh had birds flying from the trees, and Jessamine wiped a tear from her eye. "We're going to get your memories back in no time."

But even as she spoke, something sunk in Arabella's chest like an anchor dragging her into the deep.

Her memories were lost. The others simply hadn't realized that yet.

RETURNING TO HER QUARTERS, Arabella bathed and redressed, heading for the dining hall. Before she'd gotten far, a figure appeared from the shadows.

"Elias," she breathed. "What are you doing here?"

He extended a hand toward her, which had the neckline of his shirt shifting, revealing the crest of muscles on his chest. The sight had her biting her lip. But even as desire pulsed inside her, so did a creeping sense of sorrow. If her memories never returned, then perhaps nothing would happen between her and the erox. That thought deepened the heaviness swelling inside her.

"There's something I'd like to show you," he said, and she took his hand.

"Another library?"

"No," he said. "This will be a more... serious conversation. Do you have space for that?"

Pausing, she did a mental inventory of her feelings. She felt overwhelmed and confused, but she also felt at peace here with Elias and her friends. If there was something he needed to show her, she wanted to see it.

She nodded.

They disappeared down the halls in a swirl of shadow. She knew he could have easily walked down the hallways, but she liked it when he held her close as they moved at such a fast pace. Her eyes couldn't fully register their surroundings beyond the veil of darkness, but the shadows hummed and sang to her.

Suddenly, they stopped, and she stood in front of a door. Glancing around, she realized they were in a hallway of the castle. It was one she didn't recognize. For some reason, she'd expected they'd be heading to the castle grounds somewhere. But the door in front of her was nondescript and appeared identical to all the ones she could see to either end of the long stretch of hallway.

Rays of the golden hour filtered in through nearby windows, covering the hallway in an amber light.

Elias turned to her. "When you first came to my home, you explored the castle and went into this room without my permission. And I..." He hesitated, seeming to consider his words. "I spoke harshly to you. For that, I apologize. I should have explained which areas of the castle were off-limits, and I didn't. No one before you dared to explore the castle, and I'd wrongly assumed you'd be the same."

Arabella blinked, uncertain of what to make of this. He knew she couldn't remember this... right?

"The reason I snapped was because this room once belonged to someone special to me."

Turning, he opened the door and entered the room. She followed.

The first thing her eyes registered was that the bedroom was covered in a layer of dust. The shutters were closed tight, and half-burnt logs littered the fireplace. At one end of the room, a four-poster bed lay unused, the quilt a motley maroon, which matched the canopy. Both were now a grayish-purple color.

"Who was she?"

Elias came to stand beside her, both of them staring at the enormous bed.

"Her name was Constance," he said. "She was my first offering."

"What happened to her?"

"I killed her," he said, his voice full of self-loathing.

He strode to the windowsill, not bothering to open the window. Even from where she stood, she could see his eyes were distant as he stared at the shutters.

She knew she should be afraid, but all she felt was pity for this male.

"Constance was from a remote village. She needed money for

her father, whose health was failing, and offered herself to me in exchange. I accepted." As he leaned forward on the windowsill, his back rounded as though there was a great weight on his shoulders. "Over time, we came to know one another. Like you, there was an immediate spark of attraction, and it drew us together."

The thought of another female having a connection with Elias had something twisting inside of her. Was that jealousy?

"But I... couldn't control myself. I was young and hadn't yet mastered restraint." Glancing over his shoulder at her, he added, "With you, I've lost my restraint once more. Only, this time it's far worse than anything I'd experienced with Constance."

Slowly, she walked over to him until she stood within arm's reach, but she didn't touch him.

"One night, I faced some monsters in the woods," he said. "I was weak and needed to feed. When I finally found her, I didn't think as my eyes turned dark and my fangs emerged. I just moved. As the lust receded, that's when I saw what I'd done. I'd snapped my lover's neck and fed on her until there was nothing left."

"Why are you telling me about this?" she asked. "About Constance?"

"This is part of the reason I made the deal with the founders of Shadowbank. If I don't feed, I could kill innocents. But I thought if I fed on someone I could keep myself distant from— someone who I wasn't physically or emotionally attracted to— that I could keep from repeating what I'd done to Constance. So, I made a deal. The founders feared for the safety of their people. I was one more demon of the forest, after all. They agreed to an offering every ten years. But I kept myself distant from each person I brought back here, only feeding when I must. I never let anyone get close to me. But now... With you... You've been different since the beginning. No matter what I tried, I couldn't stay away from you. And now, I'm more terrified than ever of losing you."

His voice became painfully soft.

"I've already lost you once."

KISSED BY A DEMON

Her memories.

She could feel a pull toward him and craved his nearness as much as his body, but she didn't love him—yet. Could they get there? She wasn't sure.

A knowing look filled his eyes.

"I don't expect you to say anything, and I know this is a lot for you. And I'm sorry for having to put this on you. But... one day soon, you'll have your memories back. When you do, I want you to know me. Why I've done what I've done. I thought I was protecting humans by taking offerings and keeping myself distant from them. They could return to their people, and I'd erase their memories. Then they could live out the rest of their lives in happiness without the burden of remembering. I wouldn't have to hurt anyone else."

Something clicked, and she gasped.

"Elias, you can erase memories... Can you return them, too?"

He shook his head. "If I could, I would have done so immediately. For reasons only the gods can give, the erox can only steal memories. They cannot return them."

The hope swelling in her chest deflated. As it did, her mind swirled as she tried to digest all this new information.

"What were we to each other?" she dared to ask. He'd evaded this question before, but she had to know. There was something else he wasn't saying. But what?

There was the press of a finger beneath her chin. Slowly, she allowed her eyes to connect with his.

"You made a sacrifice to protect my people and this place," he said. "For that, I release you from your bargain. You're free to leave. Be happy, little enchantress."

She shook her head, not understanding, as he broke away and strode toward the door.

"Elias," she began, but he'd disappeared into the shadows.

Something squeezed in her chest, though she didn't understand why.

Was he saying goodbye?

339

Chapter Twenty-Nine

ELIAS

Elias' heart thundered as he moved from shadow to shadow.

The entire forest floor was as black as the moonless night sky above them, and he moved faster than he ever had before. He didn't dare slow. If he did, he feared his knees would lock, and his chest would tighten so painfully that he'd be unable to take another step forward. And if he didn't, he wouldn't be able to accomplish what he'd set out to do.

The sound of ogres growling surrounded him, and he released his magic, appearing before them. The nearest creature turned to him, surprisingly fast for something of its size, narrowing its single eye on him. Raising a taloned hand toward him, it made a bellowing sound that he knew could only be a signal for one thing.

They'd found him.

Movements danced in the surrounding shadows, and he was soon surrounded by a dozen erox.

In the distance, he could hear the screams of females— humans for the erox to feed on, most likely. The sounds were somewhere between pleasure and pain.

"Look who's back," one of the erox hissed.

Elias didn't recognize the male. He had deep-set eyes and hair as long and fair as Jessamine's. His was plaited back in a series of intricate braids.

"I've come to see Magnus," Elias said.

He didn't fear these males. There was only one person in this world who could inspire fear down to his very core. The very male he'd come to see.

A fist connected with his gut and then another until he could no longer identify one hand from another as punch after punch connected with his stomach, his back, his arms, his face... Pain exploded in him as the erox surrounded him, pummeling him. But he didn't cry out. He clenched his teeth, bearing the pain, trying to breathe through it. Soon, his breaths came in ragged gasps, and it was all he could do to remain on his feet—his body not able to regenerate quickly enough.

"You cost us favor with the Sorcerer when you disappeared," one male hissed, which was followed by a fist to his side. A rib must have cracked because pain splintered through him, and he fell to a knee.

"That's enough," a voice called from somewhere nearby.

The fists stopped, and it was then he realized that one of his eyes had swollen shut, his lip had split, and he had several broken bones in his arms. But even as the erox stepped back, clearing the path in front of him, the essence flowing through him stitched his skin back together and pulled his bones into place. The darkness inside him spiked, and the need to feed grew sharper, but it was a distant roaring in his mind as a familiar figure appeared through the break in the circle of erox that surrounded him. Beyond them was a circle of ogres and other creatures of the dark.

Even if he wanted to, there was no escaping now.

"Elias."

As the male strode toward him, his extravagant floor-length robes moved around him, which were lined in fur. Blond hair flowed past his chest, straight and thick. He didn't hurry as he walked. Instead, each stride was purposeful, sure, as though he knew he'd won.

And he had.

"Magnus," Elias said, thankful there wasn't a tremble in his voice.

Power thrummed in Elias' veins, though not nearly as powerful as it had felt when he'd held the amplifier. He held on to his magic like a lifeline as though it alone would keep him from succumbing to the panic that threatened to overwhelm him.

Far exceeding his power was the sorcerer who now stood before him. It billowed out around him in perceptible waves. Unlike most magic wielders whose magic was a force around them, only visible to other magic wielders, Magnus' power appeared like a gray mist and hovered above the ground. Even the ogres and other creatures in his army would be able to see it.

The amplifier, he realized.

Magnus' power seemed so much stronger because he must currently have the amplifier somewhere in his possession.

Elias thought of the other amplifier. The one he'd given to Iris in Shadowbank. He allowed himself to think of the female who'd wanted so badly to protect her people, and he conjured an image of Arabella in his mind's eye.

After what they'd been through, after all the heartache the amplifiers had cost them, he'd given it freely. If only he'd been able to see the importance sooner. If they both had compromised, perhaps they could have shared the first amplifier. Instead, Magnus—one of the greatest sorcerers of their time—possessed it.

The sorcerer had been toying with them before they'd escaped. He could have blinked, and they'd be turned to ash. Yet, he'd allowed Elias, Breckett, and Arabella to fight until they were nearly too exhausted to continue. Had he wanted them broken, exhausted, desperate?

Which was exactly what Elias was now.

The sorcerer knelt in front of him, his robes pooling out

around him. A hand struck out, faster than his eyes could register, and fingers encircled his throat. The air whooshed out of Elias in an instant. Instinctively, his hand clutched Magnus' wrist, but there was no breaking his grip. His strength was that of a mountain, and all Elias could do was succumb to it until it crushed him.

"My prodigal son has returned once more," Magnus hissed. "We have much to discuss."

The gray mist encircled them both before there was a swirl of movement, and the erox and ogres disappeared.

When the world reshaped around him, he was inside of a massive tent, and the flaps were closed. At the center were two crossing beams of wood that formed a giant X and were staked into the ground. Metal handcuffs were at each end of the wooden beams.

Magnus released his neck, and Elias staggered forward, choking, his vision spotting.

"Go, my son. You have much to atone for."

Gathering his courage, Elias remained where he was and looked Magnus in the eyes.

"I've come to make a bargain," he said.

"You have nothing I want," Magnus said easily. "Now, get in before I make you."

Elias had to stop himself from glancing at the massive X in the center of the tent. It wouldn't be long before his screams echoed through the camp.

"For years, you've hunted me. You've wanted me to follow you willingly," Elias said. "And now, you can have me."

There was a hunger in Magnus' gaze, so faint that it was nearly imperceptible. But Elias knew he had the sorcerer.

"Give Arabella her memories back. They were stolen from the Witch of the Woods, and I'm yours."

Magnus' brows rose.

"You would cease fighting me and remain by my side for eternity for *her*?"

Elias swallowed. "Yes."

The corner of Magnus' lips flicked up in what could be called a smile, but it was a mere showing of teeth.

"I accept."

The sorcerer snapped his fingers, and a gust of dark mist swept out of the tent.

Elias sighed.

It was done.

Magnus was a male of his word, and Elias knew Arabella's memories would return to her soon. Now, he could give up and give in to what was to come.

Without another word, Elias strode to the center of the room. Turning to face Magnus, he grabbed the corners of his shirt and pulled it over his head before dropping it to the floor. The entire time, the sorcerer's gaze roamed over his body.

It was one of many reasons he'd kept away.

He didn't bother to reach for his trousers. Instead, he cuffed his ankles to the bottom corners of the X and held his arms up high. With a flick of Magnus' fingers, Elias' wrists were restrained.

The X was imbued with magic so that, once fully cuffed, an erox couldn't escape. Their strength and powers were suppressed.

He was utterly at the mercy of his captor.

Magnus' fingers tightened into fists. Then there was a gust of wind before a sharp pain surged in his groin as something gripped his balls in a vise grip, nearly tearing them off. For the first time, he screamed, unable to hold it back. But he didn't fight. He would keep his word, just as Magnus would.

It's what the sorcerer had taught him, after all—the value of one's word.

"Say it," Magnus purred, striding to the side of the tent, his tone sounding bored.

"I'm yours," Elias hissed through his teeth.

"And?"

"I will do as you say from this day forth," Elias managed through the pain. "I won't disobey you again."

There was a flash of movement, and Magnus was before him.

"No, you won't," Magnus said.

The pressure on Elias' balls had stars forming at the corners of his vision.

Despite himself, his cock grew hard, and desire coursed through his veins. He and Magnus were of a similar height, and he found his eyes flickering to the sorcerer's lips, craving his touch. The pressure on Elias' balls lessened, and a moan escaped his throat. It was the type of pressure he liked, and Magnus knew it.

"Repeat," Magnus said.

Elias knew what he was asking for.

"I'm yours," Elias said as desire billowed through him. It was all he could do to keep from thrusting his hips forward.

Magnus kissed him then, and Elias climaxed instantly—even without the sorcerer touching him.

He cried out as Magnus sucked essence—Arabella's essence—from him. The taste of her lingered on his lips for a moment before it disappeared, and Magnus' eyes glowed a brilliant blue.

"You are my creation," Magnus said as he fed. "Without me, you'd never have become an erox. You'd never have gained your powers. But all is well again now that you've returned. And I'll never let you go again."

Magnus had created erox. Elias had been his first of many experiments on humans.

Elias didn't want the sorcerer, had never wanted him. As the creator of the erox, only Magnus could feed on other erox. Like him, the sorcerer needed essence to survive, and feeding on his creations was a bit of a power move for him. To remind Elias and the other erox that they were only breathing because Magnus wished it.

He was the most powerful sorcerer Elias had ever met—and the only magic wielder powerful enough to release Arabella's memories from the Witch of the Woods.

Magnus sucked more essence from him. As he did, Elias' climax lengthened and his cock became painfully hard. As waves of oily pleasure rolled over him, there was a flash of movement and something glinted in the lantern light before pain tore through him—unlike anything he'd ever experienced.

He screamed in agony, knowing at once what this was.

The hilt of a knife stuck out from his gut.

"It was a fortunate happenstance that one of my men found this in the woods," Magnus said, scraping a nail over Elias' chest. "They'd thought it was my blade."

Tears streamed down Elias' cheeks as his body attempted to heal itself again and again but couldn't because of the blade.

The syphen.

The blade Magnus had used three hundred years ago to create him. The blade Arabella had dropped in her fight with the ogres.

Fear iced his veins.

"You'd somehow escaped with this," Magnus hissed, twisting the blade in Elias' gut, careful to avoid his heart.

He couldn't die from the blade, not unless it pierced his heart. But Magnus could rip him apart again and again, allowing his body to heal before peeling him apart once more.

"But now, you cannot fight me. Not ever again."

He knew the sorcerer was going to do all he could to break his spirit, but now he could control Elias' body, too. With that blade, his maker, the male he feared most in the world, could control him with a thought, and he couldn't object. Elias retreated to the corners of his mind and slammed the mental doors shut. He'd never come out ever again. Not with the syphen in Magnus' grip.

It's worth it if it means Arabella has her memories and is free.

Just then, something snapped in his chest and pulled taut over his heart. He cried out, but this time it had nothing to do with the pain. Desire and a sweet fulfillment unlike anything he'd felt before blossomed in his chest, but it also tugged at him, demanding that he be near her again.

Her memories were back. The mating bond was back.

Magnus turned on a heel and strode for the edge of the tent. Then he paused and spoke over his shoulder. "One more thing. That little enchantress of yours is more powerful than you know.

You don't know what she is though, do you? Or else, you wouldn't have left her so vulnerable. So unprotected."

Fear so thick overwhelmed his senses, making it hard to think.

"That shadow magic she has is rare—so rare in fact that I haven't seen it in an age," Magnus continued. He turned back to Elias fully then. "Tell me. Do you recall where syphens come from?"

Elias' eyes flicked down to the syphen in his gut, slowly eating away at his magic. Pain rippled through him as his fangs sunk into his lower lip, and he tasted blood. "Syphens are imbued with the magic of earth and shadow. Only shadow fae can create them. But the shadow court was wiped out during the fae wars. That's why you've been hunting Breckett and I down. We have two of the few syphens in existence."

"It's true there are only a few syphens remaining in this world," Magnus said. "Like you, I'd thought the shadow fae had passed from existence. But not anymore." His gaze settled on Elias like a physical weight. "That girl isn't just any shadow whisperer. She wielded shadows just like one of the lost fae court. Only they can move shadows."

Elias thought of the shield she'd used to protect him from Magnus' powers.

He shook his head. It wasn't possible...

"And if she's the last shadow fae alive, she will be mine," Magnus said, his eyes becoming fully black. "So, thank you, Elias, for finding this little gem and bringing her to my attention. She will be a marvelous addition to my army. With her, I'll be able to make many, many more syphens to create new erox until my army is large enough to rival all others."

Horror laced with the pain coursed through him, and he jerked against the chains.

"I shall check on you throughout the night," Magnus said over his shoulder as he turned back toward the exit. "Don't worry, I won't let you succumb to the demon. Perhaps I'll let you feed on a few humans, let you wring them dry until that conscience is long gone."

This male would break him, fracturing every facet of what made him who he was until he was an empty, obedient shell. And now that Magnus had Elias' syphen, he could make Elias do anything he wanted—even to Arabella.

And there was nothing he could do to protect her.

Run, he thought toward his mate. *Get away from here before he has you, too.*

Then Magnus was gone, and Elias succumbed to the panic he'd narrowly held at bay, screaming until he knew no more and blackness took him.

Thanks for reading Kissed by a Demon*!*

Want to see what happens when Arabella gets her memories back? I wrote an exclusive bonus scene just for you! **Click here to download** *(e-book only) or go to* **bit.ly/KBAD-bonus-chapter**.

Click here **to preorder the second book in the Wild Shadows Series,** **Devoured by the Shadows,** **or go to bit.ly/ DBSamazon.**

If you'd like to be considered for an advanced review copy (ARC) of Devoured by the Shadows, *please fill out this form (e-book) or go to:* **bit.ly/readDBS**.

Acknowledgments

Publishing a book takes a village.

First of all, I want to thank you, the reader, for taking a chance on me. I know reading a book by a debut author is a bit of a wild card, and I appreciate you sharing your time with me and sharing in Arabella and Elias' story!

This book wouldn't be in your hands without the help of so many. I'd like to thank my family and friends for all their love and support in launching my debut novel. Of course, I'd also like to give a shout-out to my critique partners, beta readers, editors, and cover designer. My book wouldn't be what it is without all of you. Thank you endlessly.

Stay tuned for *Devoured by Shadows*!

About the Author

Rosalyn Stirling is an author of steamy fantasy romance. In her free time, she enjoys reading and watching stories where love wins against all odds and the lovers find their happily ever after. She can be found at your nearest bookstore, tea in hand, dreaming of other worlds.

Want to stay up to date with everything Rosalyn is doing? Join her newsletter! You'll get first access to cover reveals, teasers, and giveaways.

www.RosalynStirling.com/Join-Newsletter

Connect with her on social media:
Instagram (@rosalynstirling)
TikTok (@rosalynstirling)
Facebook (Author Rosalyn Stirling)